March 2012

Dear Friends,

Life is often filled with the unexpected. The other day my daughter, who had just reread these two romances I'd written in the 1980s, surprised me by saying, "Gee, Mom, you were a good writer even then." An unexpected compliment is a blessing—but an unexpected husband? Well, that's something else entirely.

I hope the title intrigued you enough to want to read this two-book collection. As I said, my daughter went through these books and so did I. We changed some details (mostly to do with technology and cultural references) to bring the stories into the twenty-first century. After nearly thirty years it's gratifying to read my earlier work; like Jenny Adele, I find I still enjoy the stories. My hope is that you will, too.

My readers have always been the guiding force in my career. I appreciate your feedback and personally read every message you send, either through my website at DebbieMacomber.com, my Facebook page, or by regular mail at P.O. Box 1458, Port Orchard, WA 98366. However you choose to communicate with me, you can be assured I will read and take to heart what you have to say.

Thank you again and I hope you discover an unexpected pleasure in reading these pages.

Warmest regards,

Debbie Macomber

Praise for the novels of

DEBBIE MACOMBER

"Popular romance writer Macomber
has a gift for evoking the emotions that are
at the heart of the genre's popularity."
—*Publishers Weekly*

"Debbie Macomber writes characters who are
as warm and funny as your best friends."
—*New York Times* bestselling author Susan Wiggs

"Macomber's assured storytelling and affirming
narrative are as welcoming as your favorite easy chair."
—*Publishers Weekly* on *Twenty Wishes*

"Whether [Debbie Macomber] is writing lighthearted
romps or more serious relationship books,
her novels are always engaging stories
that accurately capture the foibles of real-life men
and women with warmth and humor."
—*Milwaukee Journal Sentinel*

"Macomber...is no stranger to the *New York Times*
bestseller list. She knows how to please her audience."
—*Oregon Statesman Journal*

"Bestselling Macomber...
sure has a way of pleasing readers."
—*Booklist*

DEBBIE MACOMBER

The Unexpected
HUSBAND

MIRA®

Recycling programs for this product may not exist in your area.

ISBN-13: 978-0-7783-1341-0

THE UNEXPECTED HUSBAND

Copyright © 2012 by MIRA Books

The publisher acknowledges the copyright holder of the individual works as follows:

JURY OF HIS PEERS
Copyright © 1986 by Debbie Macomber

ANY SUNDAY
Copyright © 1988 by Debbie Macomber

For questions and comments about the quality of this book please contact us at Customer_eCare@Harlequin.ca.

www.Harlequin.com

Printed in U.S.A.

Also by Debbie Macomber

CONTENTS

JURY OF HIS PEERS

To
Ted Macomber, our son, the wonderful negotiator.

One

There was something vaguely familiar about him. Caroline Lomax's gaze was repeatedly drawn across the crowded room where the prospective jury members had been told to wait. He sat reading, oblivious to the people surrounding him. Some were playing cards, others chatting. A few were reading just as he was. It couldn't be Theodore Thomasson, Caroline mused, shaking her head so that the soft auburn curls bounced. Not "Tedious Ted," the childhood name she had ruthlessly given him because of his apparent perfection. The last time she'd seen him had been the summer he was fifteen and she was fourteen, just before her father's job had taken them to San Francisco. It wasn't him; it couldn't be. First off, Theodore Thomasson wouldn't be living on the West Coast and, second, she would have broken out in a prickly rash if he were. Never in her entire life had she disliked anyone more.

Determined to ignore the man completely, Caroline picked up a magazine and idly flipped through the dog-eared pages. If that was Theodore, which it obviously couldn't be, then he'd changed. She would never openly admit that he was handsome back then. Attractive, maybe, in an eclectic way. But this man... If it was Theodore, then his eyes were the same intense blue of his youth, but his ears no longer had the tendency to stick out. The neatly trimmed dark hair was more stylish than prudent, and if Tedious Ted was anything, he was sensible, levelheaded and circumspect. And rational. Rational to the point of making her crazy. Admittedly, her own father was known to be rational, practical, discriminating and at times even parsimonious. As the president of Lomax, Inc., the fastest growing computer company in the world, he had to be.

The thought of her stern-faced father produced an involuntary smile. What a thin veneer his rationality was, at least where she and her mother were concerned. He loved his daughter enough to allow her to be herself. Caroline realized that it was difficult for him to accept her offbeat lifestyle and her choice to go to culinary school with the intent of becoming a chef, not to mention that she'd opted for a lower standard of living than what she was accustomed to. She knew he would rather see her in law school. Regardless, he supported her and loved her, and she adored him for it.

A glance at the round clock on the drab beige wall confirmed that within another fifteen minutes the prospective jurors would be free to go. Her first day of jury duty had been a complete waste of time. This certainly wasn't turning out as she'd expected. Her mind had conjured up an exciting murder trial or at least a dramatic drug bust. Instead she'd spent the day sitting in a room full of strangers, looking for a way to occupy herself until her name was called for a panel.

Fifteen minutes later, as they stood to file out of the room, Caroline toyed with the idea of saying something to the man who resembled Theodore, but rejected the idea. If it was him, she decided, she didn't want to know. In addition, she needed to hurry to the Four Seasons Hotel. Her dad had a business meeting in Seattle with an export agency, and her mother had come along to visit Caroline, a plan that was derailed when fate decreed that Caroline would spend the day in a crowded, stuffy room being bored out of her mind. Tonight the three of them were going out to dinner. From the restaurant they would take a cab, and she would see her parents off on a return flight to San Francisco.

At precisely five, she walked down the steps of the King County Courthouse and glanced quickly at the street for the bus. She swung her backpack over her shoulder and hurriedly stepped onto the sidewalk. Thick, leaden-gray clouds obliterated the March sun, and she shook off a sensation of gloom and oppression. This feeling had been with her from the moment she'd walked into the jury room, and she suspected that it didn't have anything to do with the early spring weather.

A few minutes later she smiled at the doorman in the long red coat who held open the heavy glass doors of the posh hotel. Moments later she stepped off the elevator, knocked, and was let into her parents' suite.

Ruth Lomax glanced up from the knitting she was carrying, and her eyes brightened. Her bifocals were perched on the tip of her nose, so low that it was a wonder they didn't slip completely free. "How'd it go?" she asked as she sat back down.

"Boring," Caroline answered, taking the seat opposite her mother. "I sat around all day, waiting for someone to call my name."

A smile softened her mother's look of concentration. There was only a faint resemblance between mother and daughter, which could be attributed mostly to their identical hair color. Although Ruth's was the deep combination of brown and red that was sometimes classified as chestnut, Caroline's was a luxuriant shade of brilliant auburn. Other similarities were difficult to find. A thousand times in her twenty-four years, Caroline had prayed that God would see fit to grant her Ruth's gentle smile and generous personality. Instead, she had been pegged a rebel, a nonconformist, bad-mannered and unladylike—all by her first grade teacher. From there matters had grown worse. In her junior year she was expelled from boarding school for impersonating a nun. Her father had thrown up his hands at her shenanigans, while Ruth had smiled sweetly and staunchly defended her. Ruth seemed to believe that Caroline could have a vocation for the religious life and the family shouldn't discount her interest in this area. Caroline was wise enough to smother her giggles.

"You know who I thought I saw today?"

"Who, dear?" Folding her glasses, Ruth set them aside and gave her full attention to her daughter.

"Theodore Thomasson."

"Really? He was such a nice boy."

"Mom!" Caroline exclaimed. "He was boring."

"Boring?" Ruth Lomax looked absolutely shocked

and smiled gently. "Caroline, I don't know what it is you have against that boy. You two never could seem to get along."

"Being with him was like standing in a room and listening to someone scrape their nails down a blackboard." Irritated, Caroline yanked the backpack off and tossed it carelessly aside. "I suppose you're going to want me to wear a dress tonight." Her usual jeans and T-shirt had been a constant source of aggravation to her father. However, tonight Caroline wanted to keep the peace and do her best to please him.

Ruth ignored the question, her look thoughtful as she set aside her knitting. "He was always so well-mannered. So polite."

"'Stuffy' is the word," Caroline interjected. "It's the only way to describe a fifteen-year-old boy who takes dancing lessons."

"Lots of people take dance lessons, dear."

Caroline opened her mouth to object, then closed it again, not wishing to argue. As a boy, Theodore had been so courteous, charming and full of decorum that she'd thought she would throw up.

"He was thoughtful and introspective. As I recall, you were dreadful to him that last summer."

Caroline shrugged. Her mother didn't know the half of it.

"Sending him all those mail-order acne medications was outrageous." She wasn't able to completely disguise a smile. "C.O.D. at that. How could you, Caroline?"

"I wanted him to know what it was like not to be perfect in every way."

"But his skin was flawless."

"That's just it. The guy didn't have the common decency to have so much as a pimple."

Slowly, her mother shook her head. "And you had pimples and freckles."

"Don't forget the braces."

"And he teased you?"

Caroline tossed her jacket over a chair without looking at her mother. "No, he wouldn't even do that. I'd have liked him better if he had."

"It sounds to me as if you were jealous."

"Oh, really, Mother, don't get philosophical on me. What's there to like about a kid whose favorite television program is *Meet the Press?* Believe me, there's nothing to envy."

Although her mother didn't comment, Caroline felt her frowning gaze as she busied herself, pulling out a skirt and sweater from the backpack. "What ever became of him, Mom, do you know?"

"The last I heard, he was working for the government."

"Probably the Internal Revenue Service," Caroline said with a mocking arch of her brow.

"You may be right."

That secret smile was back again, and Caroline wondered exactly what her mother was up to. "He's the type of guy who would relish auditing people's tax returns," Caroline mumbled under her breath, running a brush through her thick hair until it curled obediently at her shoulders.

"By the way, Caroline, your father and I are definitely getting you a bed for your birthday."

"Mom, I don't have room for one."

"It's ridiculous to pull that…thing down from the wall every night. Good grief, what would you do if it snapped back into place in the middle of the night?"

Caroline smiled. "Cry for help?" It wasn't that she didn't appreciate the offer, but her apartment was small enough as it was. Having a fold-up bed was the most economical use of the limited space. The apartment was cozy—all right, snug—but its location offered several advantages. It was close to the Pike Place Market and the heart of downtown Seattle. In addition, her school was within walking distance. As far as she was concerned, she couldn't ask for more.

"You need a decent bed," her mother argued. "How do you expect to find a job if you don't get a good night's rest?"

"I sleep like a baby," Caroline returned, hiding a smile. "Now, about dinner tonight. Would you prefer to take a taxi to meet Dad, or are you brave enough to try the backseat of my scooter?" She only suggested this for shock value. The scooter was safely tucked away in the basement of her apartment building.

"Your scooter?" Ruth's voice rose half an octave as she turned startled eyes toward her daughter.

"Don't worry, I can see you'd prefer the taxi."

Since Charles Lomax was tied up later than expected in a meeting, Caroline and her mother took a taxi directly to La Mer, an elegant Seattle restaurant that overlooked the ship canal connecting Lake Union with Puget Sound. A large stone fireplace with a crackling fire greeted them. As they checked their coats, Caroline glanced around the expansive room, seeking her father's burly figure. When she caught sight of two men rising from a table in the middle of the room, her heart dropped. Next to her father was the same man she'd seen in the jury room, and something told her it really was Theodore Thomasson. So this was the reason for her mother's strange little smiles. Everything fit into place now. This business deal with the export outfit was somehow linked to Theodore.

"Ted, how nice to see you again." Ruth Lomax embraced him and stepped back to study him. "You've grown so tall and good looking."

"The years have only enhanced your beauty." He looked beyond Ruth to Caroline. "I wondered if that was you today."

So he had noticed her. Caroline's throat felt scratchy and dry. On closer inspection, she was forced to admit that Theodore had indeed changed. The boyish good looks of fifteen had matured into strikingly handsome sculpted features that were the picture of both strength and character. Theodore Thomasson was attractive enough to cause more than a few heads to turn. And Caroline was no exception. Her bemused thoughts were interrupted by his deep male voice, which was as intriguing as his looks.

"Hello, Caroline." His eyes moved with warm appraisal from her mother to rest solidly on her. Then the friendliness drained from the brilliant blue gaze as they sought and met hers. "It's good to see you again, Hot Stuff."

Caroline fumed at the reference to that last summer and the incident she sincerely hoped her parents never connected with her. With an effort, she managed to shrug lightly and smile. "Touché, Tedious Ted."

With a hearty laugh, Charles Lomax pulled out a chair and seated his wife. Before Ted could offer her the same courtesy, Caroline seated herself.

"I see you're not intimidated by my daughter," her father told Ted with a smile.

Silently, Caroline gritted her teeth. Theodore Thomasson wasn't getting the best of her that easily. Her chance would come later.

Her gaze was drawn to the huge windows that provided an unobstructed view of the ship canal. Sailboats, their sails lowered, glided past, with the brilliant golden sun setting in the background.

Inside the restaurant, the tables, covered in dark red linen, were each graced with a single long-stemmed rose. La Mer was rated among the best restaurants in Seattle. She had never eaten here before, but the elegance of the room assured her that no matter what the food was like, this was going to be a special treat.

"I understand you work for the government. The Internal Revenue Service, is it?" Caroline asked Ted with mock-sweetness, then turned away to study the elaborate menu. She hoped the dig hit its mark.

"And exactly what is it that *you* do?" From beneath dark brows he observed her with frank interest. She noted that he hadn't answered her question. Although his eyes didn't spark with challenge, there was an uncompromising authority in the set of his jaw that wasn't the least bit to Caroline's liking.

Her mother spoke up quickly. "Caroline graduated cum laude from—"

"I'm training at the Natalie Dupont School," Caroline interrupted. Unsure that he would recognize the name of the nationally famous culinary school, she added, "I'm a chef—or I will be shortly. I've just completed a year's apprenticeship." Her father had had a difficult time accepting the fact that she'd chosen a career as menial as cooking. Ambition and hard work had driven Charles Lomax to the top of his profession. Caroline didn't doubt that she would have to work just as hard making a name for herself, but though he rarely argued the point with her, she knew her father didn't agree.

The aggressive vitality in Ted's eyes demanded that she look at him. "So you didn't grow up to be a fireman," he said with a smile.

Caroline felt a cold sweat break out across her upper lip. Her family knew nothing of the fireworks display she had rigged outside his bedroom the night of July third.

"No." She forced her voice to sound as innocent as possible, as if her memory had blotted out that unfortunate chain of events that had set the balcony on fire.

"Shame," he responded casually. "You displayed such a talent for pyrotechnics."

"What's this?" her father asked, his gaze swinging from Caroline to Ted.

"Nothing, Dad." She gave him her most engaging smile. "Something from when we were kids."

Ted's mouth quirked in a half smile.

Caroline tilted her chin and haughtily returned his gaze. "You were such an easy target," she whispered.

"Not anymore, I'm not."

Smoothing the starched linen napkin over her lap, Caroline gave him a cool look. "I never have been able to turn down a challenge."

"Am I missing something here?" her father demanded.

"Nothing, Dad," Caroline answered. "Tell me, Theodore, what brought you to Seattle? I always thought you'd think of Boston as home."

"Most people call me Ted."

"All right...Ted."

"Seattle's a beautiful city. It seemed a nice place to live."

"Are you always so vague?" Caroline's voice was sharp enough to cause her mother to eye her above the top of the menu. Unbelievable! She actually found Theodore—Ted—as irritating now as she had when they were teenagers. Worse, even.

"Only when I have to be," he taunted lightly, doing a poor job of disguising a smile.

Caroline itched to find a way to put him in his place and was surprised at the intensity of her feelings.

The meal was an uncomfortable experience. Countless times Caroline found her gaze drawn to Ted. In astonishment, she noticed the way his eyes would warm when they rested on her mother and immediately turn icy cool when they skimmed over her. He didn't like her, that much was obvious. But then, he had little reason to do anything but hate the sight of her.

Through the course of the conversation, Caroline learned that though Ted might have worked for the federal government at one time, but he didn't now. From the sound of things, her guess had been right and he was employed by the export company that had brought her father to Seattle. She didn't want to ask for fear of sounding interested.

The meal was as delicious as she'd been led to believe it would be, so she focused on that and made only a few comments, spoke only when questioned and smiled demurely at all the appropriate times.

"So you two are both serving jury duty this week," her father said after an uncomfortable pause in the conversation. "What a coincidence."

Caroline's and Ted's eyes met from across the table.

"I call it bad luck," Caroline answered. She toyed with the last bit of baked potato as she dropped her gaze.

"And neither of you was aware that the other lived here?"

"No." Again it was Caroline who answered, then mumbled under her breath that moving to California was looking more appealing by the minute. If she expected a reaction from Ted, he didn't give her one. He'd heard her, though, and one corner of his mouth jerked upward briefly. Somehow she doubted that the movement was in any way related to a smile.

"Never served on a jury myself," her father continued. "Don't know that I ever will."

"It must have been twenty years ago when I was called. You remember the time, don't you, Charles?" Ruth chimed in, and detailed the account of the robbery trial on which she'd sat.

When Caroline did chance a casual look Ted's way, she was rewarded with a slightly narrowed gaze. Outwardly, he looked as if he hadn't a care in the world and was thoroughly enjoying himself. She couldn't imagine how. He couldn't help but feel her obvious dislike. Occasionally she would catch him studying her and flush angrily. His pleasant, amused expression never varied, which only served to aggravate her more. He should be the uncomfortable one. Instead, he exchanged pleasantries with her parents, then spoke affectionately of his own family. When the bill was presented, Ted insisted on paying, and in the same breath offered to drive her parents to the airport.

"But I thought I was taking you," Caroline objected.

"Your father and I can hardly ride on the back of your scooter," her mother said with a teasing glint in her eye.

"Scooter?" Ted repeated with a curious tilt of his head.

Caroline bristled, waiting for a cutting remark that didn't come.

"It's the most economical way of getting around," she supplied and granted him a saccharine smile.

"It's a shame my daughter has to be economical about anything," her father said with a rumbling chuckle. "She's taking this cooking business seriously. Living within her means. I give her credit for that."

Caroline had to bite her tongue to keep from reminding him that she was training to be a chef, not a short-order cook. A year of schooling, plus another year's apprenticeship, proved that this was serious business. In four years of college she hadn't worked as hard as she had in the last two years.

"It will work out fine to have you drop us off at the airport," her father continued.

"I'll take a taxi from here," Caroline said. The thought of getting stuck alone with Ted Thomasson on the return ride from the airport was more than she could tolerate.

"Nonsense. I'll see you home," Ted said smoothly, one dark brow rising arrogantly, daring her to refuse.

"Theodore, you were always so polite," Ruth said, smiling at her daughter as if to point out that Caroline had indeed misjudged him all these years.

Personally, Caroline doubted that. He might have matured into a devilishly handsome man, but looks weren't everything.

From the restaurant, the foursome returned to the Four Seasons Hotel so the Lomaxes could collect their luggage. The ride to the airport took an additional uneasy twenty minutes. Caroline buried her hands deep inside her pockets as she walked down the concourse at Sea-Tac International. She dreaded the time when she would have to face Ted without her parents present to buffer the conversation.

Her father and mother hugged her goodbye and Caroline promised to email more often. In addition, they promised to pass on her love to her older brother, Darryl, who lived in Sacramento with his wife and two young sons. All the while they were saying their farewells, Caroline could feel Ted's eyes studying her.

He didn't say anything until her parents had disappeared into the security line.

"The cafeteria's open."

She cast him a curious glance. "We just ate a fantastic meal. You couldn't possibly want another."

One brow arched briefly. "I'm suggesting coffee."

"No thanks."

"Fine." His long stride forced her to half walk, half run in order to keep up with him. By the time they were in the parking garage, she was straining to breathe evenly. Not for anything would she let him know she was winded.

The ride back into the city was completed in grating silence. It wasn't until they were near the downtown area that she relayed her address. Even then, she said it in a mechanical monotone. Ted glanced at her briefly and his fingers tightened around the steering wheel. This was even worse than she'd imagined.

When he pulled into a parking lot across from her apartment, turned off the engine and opened the car door, butterflies filled her stomach. "I didn't invite you inside," she said indignantly.

"No," he agreed. "But I'm coming in anyway." A thread of steel in his voice dared her to challenge him. In disbelief, she watched as his slow, satisfied smile deepened the laugh lines at his eyes. Too bad. Whatever he had in mind, she wasn't interested.

"Listen," she said, striving for a cool, objective tone. "If you want an apology for what happened that summer, then I'll give you one."

Ted acted as if she hadn't spoken. Agilely, he stepped out of the car and slammed the door closed. Caroline climbed out on her own before he could walk around to her side. Opening a lady's car door was something he would obviously do, given the kind of man he was.

She stopped and looked both ways before stepping off the curb. A hand at her elbow jerked her back onto the sidewalk. "What are you doing?" he demanded.

Caroline stared at him speechlessly. "Crossing the street," she managed after a long moment.

"The light's this way."

Ted hadn't changed, not a bit. Good grief, he didn't

even jaywalk. She clenched her jaw, hating the thought of him invading her home.

"Did you hear what I said earlier?" she asked. "I owe you an apology. You've got one. What more do you want?"

His hand cupped her elbow as they stopped at the traffic light. She pulled her arm free, angrier with her body's warm response to his touch than the fact that he'd taken her arm.

The light changed, and they crossed the street. The brick apartment building was four stories high. Caroline's tiny apartment was on the third floor. All the way up the stairs, she tried to think of a way of getting rid of Ted. She realized that arguing with him wasn't going to do any good. She might as well listen to what he had to say and be done with it.

The key felt cool against her fingers as she inserted it into the lock. A flip of the light switch bathed the room in a gentle glow.

Standing just inside the apartment, Ted made a sweeping appraisal of the small room. Caroline couldn't read the look in his eyes. Hooking her backpack over the doorknob, she turned to him, hands on her hips. "All right," she said in a slow breath. "What is it you want?"

"Coffee."

Seething, she marched across the room to the compact kitchen. With anyone else she would have ground fresh-roasted beans. As it was, she brought down one earthenware mug, dumped a teaspoon of instant coffee inside and heated the water in the microwave.

"Satisfied?" she asked sarcastically as she handed him the steaming mug.

"Relatively so." His half smile was maddening.

Pulling out a chair, he sat and looked up at her standing stiffly on the other side of the narrow room. "Have a seat."

"No thanks. I prefer to stand."

He shrugged as if it made no difference to him and blew on the coffee before taking a tentative sip.

Stubbornly, Caroline crossed her arms in front of her and waited.

"I want to know why," he said at last.

"Why what?" she snapped.

"Why do you dislike me so much?"

"Have you got a year?"

"I have as much time as necessary."

"Where would you like me to begin?" Her voice was deceptively soft, but her feelings were clear. By the time she was finished, his ears would burn for a week.

"That last summer will do." He still refused to react to the antagonism in her voice.

"All right," she said evenly. "You were perfect in every way. Honest, sincere, forthright. What kind of kid is that? Darryl and I had stashed away fireworks for weeks, and you acted as if we'd robbed a bank."

"They were illegal. You're lucky you didn't blow your fool head off. As it was—"

"See." She pointed an accusing finger at him. "If you didn't want any part of it, that was your prerogative, but tattling to my dad was a spiteful thing to do. It's that goody-goody attitude I couldn't tolerate," she continued, warming to the subject.

Ted looked genuinely taken back. "What? I didn't say a word to your family."

Caroline's lungs expanded slowly. Ted Thomasson probably hadn't stretched the truth in his life. She couldn't do anything but believe him. "Then how did Dad find out I had them?"

"How am I supposed to know?" His eyes nearly sparked visible blue flame.

"At least he never found out how I got rid of them."

"What were my other crimes?"

Uneasy now, Caroline shrugged weakly.

"Well?" he demanded.

"You wouldn't go swimming with me." The one afternoon she'd made an effort to be nice, Ted had flatly rejected her offer of friendship.

A brief smile touched his eyes. "True, but did you ever ask yourself why?"

"I don't care to know. What was the matter? I was trying to be nice. Were you afraid I was going to drown you?"

"Knowing your past history, that was a distinct possibility."

"It wasn't my fault the brakes on that golf cart failed."

"Don't lie to me, Caroline. You never hid what you thought of me before."

Guilt colored her face a hot shade of red. "Okay, I'll admit it. I never liked you. And I never will." She crossed her arms again to indicate that the conversation was closed.

"Why didn't you like me?" he asked softly, setting his coffee aside. The chair slid back as he suddenly stood.

Caroline pinched her mouth tightly closed. When he moved so that he loomed over her, she clenched her jaw.

"Why?" he repeated.

"I...just didn't...that's all." She detested the way her voice shook.

"There's got to be a logical reason." His eyes cut through her.

"Your hair was always perfectly trimmed." Her gaze locked with his in a fierce battle of wills. "It still is," she added accusingly.

"Yours is still the same fiery red." As if he couldn't resist, he reached out and wove a thick strand around his index finger. "I remember the first time I saw it and wondered if your hair color was the reason you were so hot-tempered."

"A lot you know." Her voice gained strength and volume. "My hair is auburn."

He laughed softly, as if he found her protestations amusing.

"You've probably never done anything daring in your life," she went on. "You were always afraid of one thing or another. You're the most boring person I ever met."

"And you're a hellion."

"But I've never bored anyone in my life," she snapped defensively.

"Neither have I. You simply didn't give me the chance to prove it to you." He released her hair to slide his fingers around her nape in a slow, easy caress.

Caroline drew in a sharp breath and tried to shrug his hand free. A crazy whirl of sensations caused her stomach muscles to tense.

"Take your hand off me." She grabbed his arm in an effort to free herself.

He ignored her protests. "Was there anything else?"

"You...took dancing lessons."

Nodding, he laughed softly. "That I did. Only I hated them more than you'll ever realize."

"You—never wanted to do anything fun." Desperately her mind sought valid reasons for her intense dislike of him and came up blank.

"I want to do things now," he drawled in a voice that was barely perceptible. Ever so slowly, he lowered his mouth to hers.

Mesmerized, her heart pounding like the crashing waves upon a sandy shore in a storm, Caroline was powerless to stop him. When he fitted his mouth over hers, she made a weak effort by pushing against his chest. No kiss had ever been so sweet, so perfect, so wonderful. Soon her hands slid around his neck as she pressed her soft figure to his long length, clinging to him for support.

When they broke apart, she dropped her arms and took a staggering step backward. The staccato beat of her heart dropped to a sluggish drum roll at the wicked look twinkling in Ted's eyes. He'd wanted to humiliate her as she'd done to him all those years ago. And he'd succeeded.

"I bet you didn't think kissing 'Tedious Ted' could be so good, did you, Caroline?"

Two

Caroline woke with the first light of dawn that splashed through her beveled-glass window. The sky was cloudless, clear and languid. Her first thought was of Ted and her overwhelming response to his kiss. Silently, she seethed, detesting the very thought of him. To use sensory attraction against her was the lowest form of deceit. He'd wanted to humiliate her and had purposely kissed her as a means of punishment for the innocent crimes of her youth. And what really irritated her was that it had been the most sensual kiss of her life. Her cheeks burned with mortification, and she pressed cool palms to her face to blot out the embarrassment. Ted Thomasson was vile, completely without scruples, and that was only the tip of the iceberg as far as she was concerned.

The morning was chilly, but Caroline had her anger to keep her warm. If she'd disliked Ted Thomasson at fourteen, those feelings paled in comparison to the intensity of her feelings now. Yet she had to paint on a plastic smile and sit in the same room with him today, pretending she hadn't been the least bit affected by what had happened. If she were lucky, she would be called out early for a trial, but at the rate her luck was running, she would end up stuck sitting next to him for the next four days.

The brisk walk to the King County Courthouse helped cool her indignation. She bought a cup of coffee from a machine and carried it with her into the jury room. The bailiff checked off her name and gave her a smiling nod. Caroline didn't pause to look around, afraid Ted would see her and think that she was seeking him out. As far as she was concerned, if she saw him in another eighty years it would be a hundred years too soon.

The coffee was scalding, and she set it on a table to cool while she reached for a magazine—an outdated copy of *Time*. Flipping through the pages, she noted that the stories that had captured the headlines six months ago were still in the news today. Little had changed in the world. Except Ted—he'd changed. His aggressive virility had captured her attention from the minute they'd stepped into the restaurant. Forcibly, she shook her head to reject the thought of him. She detested the way he'd invaded her mind from the minute she'd climbed out of bed.

She caught a movement out of the corner of her eye and turned to see. Ted stood framed in the doorway of the large, open room. He wore an impeccable three-piece gray suit with leather shoes. Italian, no doubt. After spending a restless day lounging in the jury room, almost everyone else had dressed more casually today. She herself had slipped on dark cords and an olive-green pullover sweater. But not Mr. Propriety. Oh, no, his long legs had probably never known the feel of denim. Angrily she banished the image of Ted in a pair of tight-fitting jeans.

"Morning." He claimed the empty chair beside her. "I trust you slept well. I know I did."

Wordlessly, she took her cup of coffee and moved to a vacant seat three chairs down.

Without hesitating, Ted stood and followed her. "Is something wrong?"

Despite her anger, she managed to make her voice sound calm and reasonable. "If you insist on pestering me, then you leave me no option but to report you to the bailiff."

"Did I pester you last night, Caroline?" he asked in a seductive drawl that sent shivers racing down her spine.

"Yes." She felt like shouting but made an effort and kept her voice low.

"Funny, that wasn't the impression I got."

"You're so obtuse you wouldn't recognize a—"

"Your response to me was so hot it could have set off a forest fire."

She drew a rasping breath. She tried and failed to think of a comeback that would wipe that mocking grin off his face.

"From the time we were children, I've disliked you," she murmured, her gaze fixed on her coffee. "And nothing's changed."

His soft chuckle caught her off guard. She'd expected something scathing in retaliation, but certainly not laughter. In hindsight, she realized that Ted had probably never raised his voice to a woman.

"That's not the impression you gave me last night," he taunted.

Seething, Caroline closed her eyes. Her mind groped for a logical explanation of what had happened. She'd only had one glass of wine with the meal, so she couldn't blame her response on the influence of alcohol. Telling him that her biorhythms were out of sync would make her sound like an idiot. "Knowing that you've always been perfect in every way, I don't expect you to understand a momentary lapse of discretion on my part," she finally said.

"I don't believe that any more than you do," he said with cool calm.

Crossing her arms in front of her, she refused to look at him. "Fine. Believe what you want. I couldn't care less."

"You care very much," he returned flatly.

Pinching her mouth tightly closed, she refused to be drawn further into the conversation.

"You intrigue me, Caroline. You always have. I've never known anyone who could match your spirit. You were magnificent at fourteen. With that bright red hair and freckles dancing across your nose, I found you absolutely enchanting."

Slowly, she appraised him, searching each strongly defined feature for signs of sarcasm or derision. She was so taken aback by the gentle caress of his voice that any response died in her throat. "How can you say that?" she managed at last. "I was horrible to you."

"Yes," he chuckled, "I know."

"You should hate me," she said.

"I discovered I never could."

The bailiff began reading the names on the first panel of jurors, and Ted paused to listen, along with the hundred and fifty other people seated in the room. Periodically during the day, the court sent requests down to the jury room and names were drawn in a lottery system, and this same hush fell over the crowd every time.

Caroline's name was one of the first to be called. At last, she thought, she was going to see some of the action. A few seconds later she heard Ted's name. They were being called along with several others for the same trial.

They were led as a group into an upstairs courtroom and seated outside the jury box. Caroline sat down on the polished mahogany pew, uncomfortably distracted by the knowledge that Ted was behind her. Their conversation lingered in her mind, and she wanted to free her thoughts for the task that lay before her. She looked up and noticed that several people were studying the potential jurors. The judge, in his long black robe, sat in the front of the courtroom, his look somber. The attorneys were at their respective tables, as was the defendant. She found her gaze drawn to the young man who stared at the group with a belligerent sneer.

Everything about him spoke of aggressive antagonism—his looks, his clothes, the way his eyes refused to meet anyone else's. His slouched posture, with arms folded defiantly across his chest, revealed a lack of respect for the court and the legal proceedings. The defense attorney leaned over to say something to him, but the defendant merely shrugged his shoulders, apparently indicating that he didn't care one way or the other. What an unpleasant man, Caroline thought, holding back her instant feelings of dislike. Above all, she wanted to be impartial and, if she were chosen for the jury, base her decision on the evidence, not the look of the defendant.

The judge spoke, announcing that the defendant, Nelson Bergstrom, was being tried for robbery and assault. Twelve of the panel members were led to the jurors' box. Caroline was the last to be seated in the first row. A series of general questions was addressed to the prospective jurors. No one answered out loud, instead raising their hands if their response was positive. No one on the jury knew the defendant personally. Several had heard of this case through the media, since there had been a string of similar late-night assaults against female clerks. No one had an arrest record of their own. Three members had been the victims of crime. After the general questions, each juror was interviewed individually.

The attorney who approached the box smiled at Caroline, who thought that Ted was dressed more like a lawyer than this lanky guy with an easy grace and charming grin. One by one, he asked the prospective jurors specific questions regarding friends, attitudes and feelings. When he was finished, his opposite number stepped up and had his own questions for them. Neither attorney challenged Caroline for cause, but she was surprised at the number of available jurors who were dismissed for a variety of reasons, none of which seemed important to her. The two lawyers went through the first twelve-member panel and called for another. In the end, she, Ted and eleven others were chosen. The thirteenth member was an alternate who would listen to all the testimony. However, he would be called into the deliberation only if one of the jurors couldn't continue for some reason, a procedure intended to prevent the need for a retrial.

The trial began immediately, and the opening statements made by each attorney filled in the basic details of the case. A twenty-three-year-old clerk, a woman, had been robbed at gunpoint at a minimarket late one night shortly before Thanksgiving. Terrified, the woman handed over the money from the till, as requested. The thief then proceeded to pistol whip her until her jaw was broken in two places. Although the details of the crime were relayed unemotionally, Caroline felt her throat grow dry. The defendant revealed none of his feelings while the statements were being made. His face was an unyielding mask of indifference and hostility, a combination she had never thought was possible. Again and again she found her gaze drawn to him. In her heart she realized that she fully believed Nelson Bergstrom was capable of such a hideous crime. As soon as she realized that she was already forming an opinion, she fought to cast it from her mind.

By the end of the first day, Caroline's thoughts were troubled as the jurors filed from the courtroom. Serving on a jury wasn't anything like what she'd anticipated. When she'd been contacted by mail with her dates of service, her emotions had been mixed. This was her first free week after completing her apprenticeship, and she'd hated the thought of spending it tied up in court. Now that she was sitting on a case, the reality of the crime genuinely distressed her. The victim was no doubt sitting in the courtroom. Caroline hadn't picked her out of the small crowd, but she knew she had to be there. Absently she wondered how the poor woman could endure the horror of that night.

"Are you all right?" Ted asked her once they hit the steps outside the courthouse.

"Of course," she said, struggling to sound offhand. It had been another stroke of bad luck to have Ted on the same trial. She hadn't seen him in ten years, and now, in a mere two days, he had become an irritating shadow she couldn't shake.

The jury had been warned against discussing any of the details of the case with each other. Caroline yearned to ask Ted what his impression of the proceedings had been but bit back the words. She felt strangely, unaccountably melancholy. Bemused, she frowned at the brooding sense of responsibility that weighed her down. This was only the beginning of the trial, and already she felt intimately involved with the victim *and* the defendant.

"Let's go have a drink," Ted said, taking her elbow. "We both need to relax."

She felt as if she'd been anesthetized and didn't argue—another clear sign of her confusion.

It wasn't until they entered the bar that Caroline realized she was acting as docile as a lamb being led to the slaughter.

"The Tropical Tradewinds?" She raised questioning eyes to Ted.

"You look like you're in the mood for something exotic."

She shook her head and released a slow sigh. Honestly, it was just like Ted to bring her somewhere like this. Oh, the Tropical Tradewinds had a wonderful reputation, but it certainly wasn't her style. She doubted that a place like this even carried something that didn't call for at least six ingredients. "What I'm in the mood for is a good ol' fashion beer."

"Fine, I'll order you one," he returned, pressing a hand to the small of her back as he directed her toward a vacant table. Politely, he held out a chair for her, and, struggling to hold her tongue, she took a seat. She never could understand why men found it necessary to seat women. They seemed to assume that the weaker sex was incapable of something as simple as sitting without assistance. Obviously Ted felt she needed his help, and this once she would let it pass; she simply wasn't in the mood to get into a fight with him.

The waitress arrived, and before Caroline could open her mouth, Ted placed their order. Unable to restrain her reaction, her blue eyes clashed with his as the waitress headed to the bar.

"What did I do wrong now?" he asked quietly, his gaze studying her.

"Does it look as if I've lost control of my tongue?"

"No, but I was hoping." His devilish grin served only to aggravate her further.

"Incidents like these irritate the hell out of me," she said, crossing her legs.

"Incidents like what?"

"Pulling out my chair, ordering my drink, opening a car door. Do I honestly look so helpless?"

"A gentleman always—"

"Can it, Thomasson. I'm not up to hearing a dissertation on the proper behavior of the refined adult male."

"Caroline," Ted replied curtly, "in this day and age a man is often placed in an unpleasant position. Half the time I don't know which a lady prefers. If I don't hold out her chair, I'm considered a creep, and if I do, I'm a chauvinist. It's a no-win situation."

"I suppose you'll pay for this with a gold-plated credit card, too."

"What's that got to do with anything?" His mouth hardened with displeasure, then softened into a faint smile as their waitress approached. She placed two thick paper coasters on the round tabletop, and set down Caroline's beer and Ted's scotch.

One look at his drink and Caroline rolled her eyes.

"Now what?" The acid in his voice was scathing.

"You're drinking scotch?"

"I would have thought that much was obvious when I ordered." He started to say more, then stopped, as if he couldn't trust himself to speak.

Remorse brought a flush of guilt to Caroline's cheeks. Ted was only trying to be nice, and her behavior was inexcusable. "Listen, Ted, I apologize for… I don't mean to be so rude. It's just that we're so different. We'll never be able to agree on anything."

Her casual apology didn't seem to please him either.

"If it's any consolation, you turned out about a thousand times better than I ever imagined," she continued. More than his good looks prompted the statement. He really wasn't the bore she would have expected. He was a little too concerned with propriety, but some women would appreciate that quality. Not her, but someone else.

His blue gaze frosted into an icy glare as he stared at her.

"See," she murmured triumphantly, catching his look. "You and I grate against each other. I prefer a beer out of a can."

"And I enjoy the finest scotch."

"Exactly." She supposed she should be pleased that he agreed with her so readily. "I'm a morning person." She looked at him questioningly.

"I do my best work at night."

"Baseball is my favorite sport." She leaned back in the chair and took a drink of the cold beer. It helped ease the dryness in her throat. "I suppose you enjoy polo."

"No." He shook his head and lowered his gaze to his glass. "Curling."

"Of course." She did her best to disguise a smile.

"I'm certain that if we looked hard enough we'd discover several common interests."

"Such as?" Her look was skeptical.

The beginning of a smile added attractive brackets to the corners of his mouth. "You're a chef, and I definitely enjoy eating."

"Well, you didn't deny working for the Internal Revenue Service at one time, but I don't enjoy paying taxes."

"Caroline," he muttered with obvious control, "I was employed for a brief time by the federal government, but that was years ago. I'm in exports now."

He regarded her steadily with sky-blue eyes. He really had wonderfully expressive eyes. The thick lashes were the same dark color as his hair. If she allowed it, she realized, she could watch him forever. She lowered her own eyes, fearing what he might read in them.

"We should concentrate on the interests we share."

"Good idea." She scooted closer to the table. "Do you play cards?"

"I'm a regular shark."

"Great." Perhaps the real problem between them was something as simple as her own attitude. They were bound to find several things to enjoy about each other if they looked hard enough.

"How about bridge?" he asked.

"Bridge?" Caroline spat out the word. "I hate it. It's the most boring game in the world. I like poker."

Ted stared at her in amazed disbelief. "Okay, we'll forget cards."

"What about music?" At the cynical arch of his brow, she added, "My tastes may surprise you."

"Everything about you surprises me."

"Ha!" She was beginning to enjoy this. "I already know your tastes. You appreciate Michael Buble, I bet."

"Talented guy," Ted agreed.

"And," she paused to give some thought to his tastes, "I imagine you enjoy some of the early rock and roll stars like Buddy Holly. I'll throw in the Kingston Trio just to be on the safe side. In addition, I'm sure you're crazy about classical."

"Very good." His smile was devastating. "I'm impressed."

"All right." Gesturing with her hand, she offered him the opportunity to add his own speculations regarding *her* musical tastes. "Do your worst—or best, as the case may be."

He chuckled, and amusement flickered across his features. "I couldn't begin to venture a guess. You are a complete enigma to me and always have been. That's what makes you such an enchantress."

Caroline's smile was filled with confident amusement, sure she was about to surprise him. "I adore Mozart, Gene Autry and Billy Joel."

"Not Kermit the Frog?"

"Don't tease," she replied cheerfully. "I'm serious."

"So was I."

For the first time that evening, she felt completely at ease. She lounged back in the chair and tucked one foot under her. "Shall we dare venture into television?"

"Speaking of which, did you see the recent PBS special on fungus?"

For a moment she assumed he was teasing, but one look assured her that he was completely serious. All her energy was expended in an effort not to laugh outright. "No, I must have missed that. I was watching old reruns of *I Love Lucy.*"

"From the sounds of this, perhaps it would be best to move on to something else."

"What was the last book you read?"

He shifted uncomfortably and took a sip of his drink. "I think we should skip this one, too."

"Ted," she whispered saucily, "don't tell me you're into erotica."

"What? *No,*" he responded emphatically, obviously uneasy. "If you must pursue this, I recently finished Homer's *Iliad.*"

Caroline pushed the errant curls from her forehead. "In the original Greek?"

He nodded.

"I should have known," she muttered under her

breath. Absolutely nothing about this man would surprise her anymore. He was brilliant. She wanted to resent that fact, but instead she found a grudging respect taking root.

"What about you?"

"I enjoy romances and science fiction and Dick Francis."

"Dick who?"

"He writes horse-racing mysteries. You have to read him to believe how good he is. I'll lend you some of his books if you'd like."

"I would."

Caroline offered him a bright, vivacious smile as she polished off her beer. "You realize we haven't found a single interest we share."

"Does it matter?" Just the way he said it sent a chord of sensual awareness singing through her, igniting an answering reprise within her heart. She couldn't believe that she was looking at Theodore Thomasson and hearing music. That was something reserved for novels. Romances. No, science fiction.

"Caroline…"

She shook her head to clear her thoughts. "Sorry, what were you saying? I wasn't listening."

"I was asking you to have dinner with me."

"Here?"

His look was one of tolerant amusement. "No, you choose."

"Great." Mentally she discarded her favorite Egyptian restaurant and asked, "Is Italian okay?"

"Anything's fine."

She sincerely doubted that but managed to hide her

knowing grin. "There's a seafood place within walking distance if you'd rather."

"The choice is yours," he said.

"Don't be so accommodating," she said, raising her voice. "There's only so much of that I can take."

With a wide grin, Ted stood. She noted that he didn't offer her his hand as she got out of her chair, a small courtesy for which she was disproportionately grateful.

Dusk had settled over the city as they moved onto the sidewalk. Streetlights were beginning to flicker around them.

"Your dad said you went to college. What's your degree in?"

"Biochemistry." She watched the surprise work its way over his features and marveled at the control he exhibited.

"Biochemistry," he repeated in bewilderment. "And now you're in culinary school?"

"Yup. I felt that of all the majors I could have chosen, biochem would be the most value to me."

Confusion shone from his expressive eyes. "I don't think I care to follow your line of reasoning."

"It's not that difficult," she answered brightly. "You see, Dad never was thrilled with my ambitions in the kitchen. I am, after all, his daughter, and he didn't feel I was aiming high enough, if you catch my drift."

"I understand."

"So instead of constantly arguing, we made an agreement. I'd go to college and get my degree, and in exchange he'd continue to support me while I went to culinary school afterwards."

"That sounds like a fair compromise. Did you come up with it?"

"Who, me?" She pressed her palm to her breast. "Hardly. I was too involved in defending my individual rights as a human being to see any solution. Mom was the one who suggested that course of action."

"But why did you choose biochemistry?"

"Why not?" she tossed back. "I'd like to think of myself as a food scientist. There's a whole world out there that has only been touched on."

"I'm surprised your father didn't insist on sending you to Paris, if you were so sure that cooking was what you wanted to do."

"He offered." The frustration remained vivid in her memory. "Only the best for his little girl and all that rot. But I didn't want to go overseas. The Natalie Dupont School here in Seattle is one of the best, and it offers a focus on baking. I'd like to focus my efforts in the area of breads. The average person looks at a loaf and thinks of sandwiches or toast. I see lipids, leaveners, proteins and biological structures. Yeast absolutely fascinates me."

"Obviously I'm a less complicated soul. What fascinates me most is you."

The tender look in his eyes nearly stopped her heart. "Me?" She stared at him, hardly believing the pride and wonder in his gaze. His blue eyes were full of warmth, and he was smiling at her with gentle understanding in a way she never would have suspected.

"Have you noticed your sense of timing is several years off?"

"My what?" Caroline's look was bewildered. "How do you mean?"

"At a time when most women are happy to get out of the kitchen, you're battling your way in."

Smiling, she nodded and placed her hand in the crook of his arm. Within the span of one day, she felt as if Ted and she had always been the closest of friends. True, they didn't share a lot of common interests, but there was a bond between them that was beyond explanation. The knowledge stunned her, and she paused, wanting to speak, but not knowing what to say or how to say it.

Caroline knew when he lowered his head that he intended to kiss her, and her eyelids slowly fluttered closed with eager anticipation. When nothing happened, her eyes shot open to discover him staring down at her. Reluctantly, it seemed, he kissed the top of her head and took her hand as they continued to stroll down the street.

Mortified, she felt the embarrassment extend all the way to her hairline. Seconds earlier they'd experienced a spiritual communication that left her breathless with wonder, and now... The traffic light changed, and a long series of cars whizzed past. In a flash, Caroline understood that as much as he might want to, Ted wouldn't kiss her on a busy Seattle street. Not with the possibility of them being seen.

Their meal was wonderful. It could have been the wine, but she doubted it. In spite of their many differences, they found several subjects on which they shared similar opinions. They both enjoyed chess and Scrabble and, most surprisingly, shared the same political affiliation, though Ted's sense of humor was more subtle than her own. By the time they left the Italian restaurant, Caroline couldn't remember an evening she'd enjoyed more. She'd laughed until her stomach ached.

Ted's hand at the back of her neck warmed her spine as they lazily strolled toward her apartment.

"I had a good time," she said casually, reaching over and entwining her fingers with his.

"Don't sound so surprised." His chin nuzzled the crown of her head.

"I can't help it. Darryl would keel over if I told him I'd spent an enjoyable evening with you."

She basked in the warmth of his slow, easy smile.

"I never did understand how your parents could possibly have two such completely different children. Darryl's exactly like his father, and you...well, it's just hard to believe you're his sister."

Caroline pulled her hand free. Disappointment and anger burned through her. "I've already apologized for my childhood bad behavior. You're right, I treated you terribly. I tricked you. I lied about you. I nearly burned the house down in an effort to undermine you. But that was twelve years ago." Whirling, she marched away.

"Caroline?" Hurried footsteps sounded behind her. "What did I say?"

"You know exactly what you said." She tried to walk faster, her pace just short of an outright jog.

"I *don't* know," he countered. His hand on her shoulder stopped her. Turning her around, he held her shoulders while his bewildered gaze roamed her face. A frown drew his thick brows together. "I've hurt you."

"What you said about not knowing how...how I could

possibly be Darryl's sister, when you know good and well that I'm not."

A stunned look drained the color from his face. "Are you saying you're adopted?"

Her narrowed, fiery glare answered the question for him.

"That's impossible," he whispered.

Three

"Just what exactly do you mean by that remark?" Hands on her hips, Caroline stared into his face.

"You look—"

"Like my mom? No I don't."

"The hair—"

"That's the only thing, but otherwise we're nothing alike. Mom's gentle, patient, forgiving. Every day of my life I've wanted to be exactly like her. I've honestly tried, but I'm—"

"Stubborn, quick-tempered and often impertinent," Ted supplied for her.

She opened her mouth to argue, then thought better of it. "Yes," she admitted, then rammed her hands inside the pockets of her cords and began shuffling backwards. "Thank you for tonight, I'm sorry it has to end this way."

"Come on, Caroline. I can't be blamed for an innocent mistake. I didn't know."

"You do now."

"What difference does it make?"

"Think about it," she snapped. "You're a smart man. You'll figure it out."

"Since we're tallying your faults, you can add unreasonableness to your growing list. I've never met a more frustrating woman."

Turning, Caroline made her escape, running up the three flights of stairs that led to her apartment. She knew she was behaving badly, but she couldn't help it. From childhood, Ted had been Mr. Prim-and-Proper and she had ridiculed him for it. But that wasn't the real reason she'd disliked him so intensely. The truth was, he was everything she wanted so badly to be.

If she were even half as refined as Theodore Thomasson, her mother would have been so proud. If only she could have maintained high grades and managed to stay out of trouble, everything would have been so grand. But no matter how hard she tried or how many promises she made, she simply couldn't be something she wasn't. Her temper flared with the least provocation, her poise was as fragile as fine china, and her self-confidence was shattered by every grade school teacher who was unfortunate enough to have her in class. Perhaps she could have accepted herself more readily if her mother hadn't been so tolerant and forgiving. She'd wanted to cry and beg her mother's forgiveness for every minor blunder, but her mother would never allow that. She loved her daughter exactly the way she was. Often when Caroline was sent to her room without dinner by her father— the ultimate punishment—her mother would smuggle in fruit and cookies. More times than Caroline could count, her mother had calmly intervened between her and her father. Amazing as it was, she shared a strong relationship with her mother. There wasn't anything Caroline felt she couldn't share with her. No mother could have been more wonderful.

Each year, on Caroline's birthday, her mother told the story of how she'd longed for a daughter. Darryl was her son and she loved him dearly, but she wanted a daughter and had prayed nightly that God would smile upon her a second time and grant her another child—a girl. After five years it became apparent that she wouldn't have more children, and they'd decided to adopt. On their first visit to the caseworker, Ruth had seen a picture of a fiery-haired, two-year-old toddler and known instantly that this was just the little girl she wanted. At that point in the tale her father always interrupted to add that the caseworker had discouraged them from adopting the tiny hellion. But Ruth had persisted until the case-worker relented and brought the four of them together for the first time. Usually at this point her brother, Dar-ryl, would insert that the first time he'd seen Caroline, she'd bitten him on the leg. He claimed she'd marked him for life and had the scar to prove it. So she had been adopted into this family who loved her in spite of her rambunctious behavior. For their love, Caroline would be forever grateful, but in her heart she would never really feel a part of them. Theodore Thomasson was a constant reminder of exactly how different she was. Next to him, her imperfections were magnified a hundred times.

An air of expectancy hung over the proceedings early the following morning. The jury was seated in a closed room adjacent to the courtroom, but Caroline arrived in time to see the defendant being brought into the court and seated. Again she noted his apparent lack of concern. It was almost as if he didn't care what the jury or anyone else thought. He was purposely making himself unlikable, and she couldn't understand that.

She stepped into the room reserved for the jury and sat beside a grandmotherly woman who paused in her knitting and said hello.

"I want to talk to you," Ted whispered.

Caroline smiled apologetically to the older woman, who had already gone back to her knitting. "I don't know that man. Would you kindly tell him that if he continues to pester me, I'll be forced to report him to the bailiff?"

"I can't understand what's the matter with these young men today." The metal needles clicked as they wove the fine strands of yarn in and out. She had been knitting through the entire proceedings the day before, and Caroline had dubbed her Madame La Farge.

Now Madame La Farge turned and gifted Ted with what Caroline was sure was a scathing look. "Kindly leave this young lady alone."

"Caroline…" Ted ground out her name, his voice ringing with frustration.

Ignoring him, she scanned the faces of her fellow jurors, thinking that they resembled a fair cross section of society. All the men were dressed casually, except Ted, who wore a pin-striped suit. There were an electrician, a real estate broker, an engineer and others whose occupations Caroline couldn't recall. The other four women on the jury were all middle-aged.

"All rise, this court is now in session," the bailiff

announced, and a rustling sounded in the jury room as those in the courtroom rose to their feet.

Within minutes the door opened and the jury was led in and seated. The prosecutor stood to present his case, calling several witnesses. The defendant, Nelson Bergstrom, had been tried and found guilty of assault and robbery five years before, and had been on parole only six weeks at the time of the minimarket robbery. His parole officer testified that Nelson had been living within ten blocks of the market. Another witness testified that he had seen Nelson at the store the day before the robbery.

The arresting officer followed with his report.

The next witness, Joan MacIntosh, was called. Caroline saw a young woman slowly enter the courtroom. Obviously nervous and shaky, Joan cast a pleading glance to the large man who had walked in with her. He gave her an encouraging smile and squeezed her hand, then took a seat. From the fear in the woman's eyes, Caroline realized that Joan MacIntosh must be the woman who had been assaulted. She was petite, barely five feet, with a fragile, delicate look. If she weighed over a hundred pounds, it would have been a surprise. The woman was terrified, that much was obvious. She hesitated once and glanced back. The man who'd come in with her nodded reassuringly several times, and Joan squared her shoulders before continuing forward.

The scene was poignant. Whatever physical harm had been done her had apparently healed, but it was obvious that the psychological damage had been far greater. Caroline looked at Joan and was overcome with sympathy. They were close in age, and from the address,

Caroline knew they didn't live more than three miles apart. It could have been her instead of Joan who had been treated so brutally.

After being sworn in, Joan took the witness stand. Following a series of perfunctory questions, the prosecutor leaned against the polished banister. "Joan, to the best of your ability, I'd like you to tell the court the events of the night of November twenty-third."

Joan's voice had been weak and wobbly, but as she began speaking, she gained confidence and volume. "I was working as a clerk for the market for only two weeks. There—really isn't much to tell. I was alone, but that didn't bother me, because there had been a steady stream of customers in and out most of the night."

The prosecutor gave her an encouraging smile. "Go on."

"Well…it must have been close to eleven, and things had slowed down. I noticed someone hanging around outside, but I didn't think much of it. A lot of kids hang around the store."

Caroline noticed that Joan's hands were tightly clenched, and that a tissue she was holding was shredded.

"Anyway—he…the man who had been outside, came into the store. He went to the back by the refrigerator unit. I assumed he was going to buy beer or something. But when he approached the register I noticed that he had a ski mask over his face. And he had a gun pointed at my heart." Joan's voice grew weak as she remembered the terror. Briefly, she closed her eyes.

"Go on, Joan."

"He…he didn't say anything to me, but he pointed

the gun at the cash register. I wanted to tell him he could have everything, but I couldn't talk. I was…so scared." She blinked, and Caroline could see tears working their way down her face. "I would have done anything just so he wouldn't hurt me."

"What happened next?"

"I opened the till to give him the money." She hesitated and bit her trembling bottom lip. "He told me to put all the money in a sack. I did that—I even gave him the change. I was so frightened that I dropped the bag on the counter. All the time I was praying that someone would come. Anyone. I didn't want to die…. I told him that over and over again. I begged him not to hurt me." Her voice cracked, and she placed a hand over her mouth until she'd regained her composure. "Then he looked inside the sack and told me it wasn't enough."

"What did you tell him?"

"I said I'd given him all the money there was and that he could take anything else he wanted."

"How did he react to that?"

"He told me to give him my purse, which I did. But I only had a few dollars, and that made him even angrier. He started waving the gun at me. I begged him not to shoot me. He told me to get more money. He shouted at me over and over that he needed more money. Then he started hitting me with the gun. Again and again he hit my face, until I was sure I'd never live through it. The pain was so bad that I wanted to die just so it would stop hurting."

Caroline could barely make out the words, because Joan was sobbing now. The man who'd accompanied her stood and clenched his fists angrily at his sides.

The bailiff pointed to him, indicating that he should sit down again. The man did, but Joan's testimony was obviously upsetting him.

Caroline doubted that anyone could remain unaffected by the details. Joan MacIntosh was a delicate young woman who had been brutally attacked and beaten for less than twenty dollars. Caroline felt that any man who could beat someone so much smaller and virtually defenseless—or anyone, for that matter—should rot in prison.

After a few more questions, the prosecutor stepped back and sat down, and the defense attorney came forward. Joan sat up and eyed him suspiciously.

"Can you describe to the court what the man who attacked and robbed you looked like?" he asked in a calm, cool voice.

"He…he was average height, about a hundred and sixty pounds, dark hair, dark eyes…."

"Did you ever get a clear view of his face?" the defense attorney pressed. "I noted in your testimony that you claim that the man who beat you had been hanging around outside the store."

"Well, I…"

"It seems to me that you would have had ample opportunity to clearly see his face," he pressed.

"Not entirely. He wore a ski mask."

"What about before, when he was outside the store? When he first came in?"

"He…he averted his… I only saw his profile."

"Before you answer the following question, Ms. MacIntosh, I want you to think very carefully about your answer. Is the man who attacked you in this court-room today?"

Caroline's eyes flew from Joan to the defendant. Nelson Bergstrom was sneering at the young woman in the witness box, all but challenging her to name him.

"Is that man in the courtroom today?" the defender repeated.

"I...think so."

The attorney placed the palms of his hands on the bannister and leaned forward. "A man's entire future is at stake here, Ms. MacIntosh. We need something more definite than 'I think so.'"

"Objection." The prosecutor vaulted to his feet.

Caroline listened as the two men argued over a fine point of law that she didn't entirely understand, and then the defense attorney went back to questioning Joan. When the cross-examination was complete, the judge dismissed the court for a one-hour lunch break.

After the defendant was led away, the courtroom emptied into the hall. Ted was standing outside the large double doors waiting for Caroline. She paused, and their eyes met and held. Listening to the morning testimony had drained her emotionally and physically. She waited for the rising tide of resentment she'd so often experienced in his presence, but none came. After last night she realized that it would be best to keep their relationship strictly impersonal.

His look was long and penetrating, as if he were reading her thoughts. A full minute passed before he spoke. "Are you going to talk to me, or am I going to be forced to send you notes through your bodyguard with the knitting needles?" The quiet tenderness in his deep voice softened her struggling resolve to remain detached. He hadn't done anything to provoke her, not really. She could hardly blame *him* for the circumstances of her birth.

"We can talk," she said, and looped the long strap of her purse over her shoulder. "Really, I should be the one who does the talking."

Ted touched her elbow, guiding her in the direction of the elevator. As if forgetting himself, he quickly lowered his hand. Caroline managed to hide a secret smile. He was trying so hard to please her. She simply couldn't understand why he would want to go to that much trouble.

"Once again, I find myself in the position of having to apologize to you," she began as they paused on the outside steps. "I realize now that you didn't know I was adopted. In fact, I find it a compliment that you hadn't guessed years ago."

"Apology accepted," he said, smiling down at her. Together they walked down the long flight of stairs that led to the busy sidewalk. "I don't know what made you so angry, but then, I've given up trying to understand what makes you tick."

In spite of herself, Caroline laughed. "Dad said the same thing to me when I as ten."

"I'm a slow learner," Ted admitted and slipped an arm around her shoulder. "It took me until late last night to realize that I'll probably never understand you. With that same thought came the realization that you mattered enough to me to keep trying."

"Why would you even want to?" His reasoning was beyond Caroline. And he thought *she* was difficult to comprehend!

His expression softened, and he looked at her with an unbearable gentleness. He traced a finger along the delicate curve of her jaw and down her chin to linger at the pulse that hammered wildly at the base of her neck. The muscles of her throat constricted, and she swayed involuntarily toward him.

"I'm not exactly sure why," he admitted, slowly shaking his head. "Maybe it's as simple as the magnetic attraction between opposites."

"No one is more opposite than you and I."

"That is something we can definitely agree on," he said, and led her across the street.

"Where are we going?"

"There's an excellent French restaurant a couple of blocks from here." There was a guarded edge to his voice as he studied her. "You don't like French food." It was more statement than question.

"It's fine. It's just I'm not very hungry. I was thinking of walking down to the waterfront and ordering clam chowder from Ivar's."

"Listening to the testimony this morning bothered you, didn't it?"

They had been strictly warned against discussing any of the details of the trial. Fearing that once she answered she would blurt out the opinions she was already forming, Caroline simply nodded. "I could feel that poor woman's terror."

"I don't think there was a person in the room who wasn't affected by it," he agreed.

She dragged her eyes from his, wanting to say more and knowing she didn't dare. "Jury duty is so different from what I thought it would be. Monday morning I was hoping I'd get on an exciting murder trial. Today I'm having difficulty dealing with the emotional impact of an assault and robbery. Can you imagine what it's like for the jury on something as horrible as a murder case?"

"I don't think I want to know," Ted murmured with feeling.

They strolled down to Seattle's busy waterfront. The smell of salt water and seaweed drifted toward them. A sea gull squawked as it soared in the cloudless blue sky and agilely landed on the long pier beside the take-out seafood stand.

Caroline insisted on paying for her own lunch, which consisted of a cup of thick clam chowder, a Diet Pepsi and an order of deep-fried mushrooms. Ted ordered the standard fish and chips.

They sat opposite each other at a picnic table. As much as she tried to direct her thoughts into other channels, her mind continued to replay the impassioned testimony she'd heard that morning.

"Are you seeing anyone?" Ted's question cut into her introspection.

"Pardon?"

"Are you involved with someone?"

Caroline stared at him and noted that his dark brows had lifted over inscrutable blue eyes. That he didn't like asking this question was obvious.

But even if he didn't like asking it, ask it he had, and she wasn't all that pleased to be answering it. "Not this month," she said flippantly.

"Caroline," he said with a sigh. "I'm serious."

"So am I. Romance is a low priority right now. I'm more interested in finding a job."

He didn't even make a pretense of believing her. "Who was he?" he asked softly.

"Who?"

"The man who hurt you."

She laughed lightly. "And people say *I* have a wild imagination."

"I'm not imagining things. The minute I asked you about a man, a funny, hurt look came over you."

Still? Caroline expelled her breath in a slow, even sigh. Clay had broken up with her over two months ago, but the memory of him was still as painful as it had been the night they'd finally split. She opened her mouth to deny everything, then realized she couldn't. The only person who knew the whole story was her mother. Caroline had enjoyed being with Ted the last couple of days, but that didn't mean she was up to sharing the most devastating experience of her life with him. And yet she couldn't stop herself from speaking.

"His name was Clay," she began awkwardly, repeatedly running her index finger along the rim of her cup. "There's not much to say, really. We dated for a while, decided we weren't suited and went our separate ways."

Ted's smile was sympathetic but firm. "You're not telling me the half of it."

"You're right, I'm not," she confirmed hotly. "Who said you had the right to butt into my personal life? What makes you think I'd share a painful part of my past with you? Good grief, I'm not even sure I like you. At any minute you're likely to turn back into 'Tedious Ted.'" Tension and regret were building within her at a rapid rate. She regarded him with cool disdain. How dare he put her in this position? "What would you know about love? In your orderly existence, I doubt that you've…" She stopped before she said something she would regret. "I didn't mean that," she finished, feeling wretched.

He took her hand, his fingers folding around hers. "I'm sorry I asked."

She refused to lower her gaze, although it demanded every ounce of her willpower. "It was over several weeks ago.… I don't know why I reacted like that."

"Are you still in love with him?" he asked meaningfully.

Caroline pasted a smile on her mouth and glanced his way with a false look of certainty. "No, of course not." Not if she could respond to Ted's kiss the way she had. Her overwhelming reaction to him had been a complete shock. His mouth had claimed hers and it was as if Clay had never existed. However, that night, that kiss, had been a fluke. It had been so long since a man had kissed her with such passion that it was little wonder that she'd responded.

An uneasy silence stretched between them, until Ted slid off the bench and stood. "We should think about getting back."

"Yes, I suppose we should," she replied stiffly. She rose. Pausing, she turned her eyes toward the long row of high-rise structures, her gaze seeking the courthouse. A sinking sensation landed in the pit of her stomach. "I have the funniest feeling about this case," she murmured, and stopped, surprised that she'd spoken out loud.

Ted was giving her a look that said he was experiencing the same mixed feelings. "Come on, let's get this afternoon over with." He reached for her hand, and Caroline had no objection.

The jury entered the courtroom using the same procedure as they had that morning and sat down to hear testimony.

The defending attorney presented his defense by recalling two of the morning's witnesses for an additional series of questions.

Caroline kept expecting Nelson Bergstrom to take the stand in his own defense, but it soon became obvious that he wasn't going to be called. It didn't take much to understand why. With his attitude, he would only hurt his own chances.

The closing arguments were completed by three o'clock, and the jury entered into deliberation at three-fifteen. By the time they were seated at the long jury table, Caroline's thoughts were muddled. She didn't know what to think.

The first order of business was electing a foreman. The first choice was Ted, which surprised her. She decided to attribute it to his crisp business suit, which made him look the part. He declined, and the engineer was elected.

A short discussion followed, in which points of law were discussed, and then they went on to the evidence. This was the first time any of the jury members had been given the opportunity to discuss the trial and voice their opinion.

"If looks count for anything, that young man is as guilty as sin," Madame La Farge said, her knitting needles clicking as her fingers moved with an amazing dexterity.

"They don't," Ted said in a flat, hard voice.

"Everything that was said today, every piece of evidence, was circumstantial." Caroline felt obliged to state her feelings early. From the looks of those around her, everyone else had already made up their minds.

"As far as I see it," the real estate agent inserted, "it's an open-and-shut case. That man repeatedly hit that poor girl, and nobody's going to convince me otherwise."

"None of the money was recovered."

"Of course not," Madame La Farge inserted, planting her needlework on the tabletop. "That boy was desperate. Obviously he spent it as fast as he could on drugs. Crack, no doubt. One look at that man and anyone can tell he's an addict. No one in his right mind would act the way he did otherwise."

"He was wearing the same jacket as the assailant. What more evidence do we need?" someone else piped in.

"He was wearing a Levi's jacket, which is probably the most popular men's jacket in America. We can't convict a man because of a jacket," Caroline added heatedly.

"He lived in the neighborhood, and he had been seen there the day before."

"I know," Caroline agreed, backing down. She looked at the faces studying her and realized that she could well be standing alone on this. "I am as appalled by what happened to Joan MacIntosh as anyone here. I would like to see the man who did this to her rot behind bars. But even stronger than my sense of righteousness is the fact I want to be certain we don't punish the wrong man."

"That's everyone's concern," the foreman told her.

"The evidence is overwhelming."

"What evidence do we really have?" Ted asked.

"She identified him," Madame La Farge commented as if she were discussing the weather, pausing to cover her mouth when she yawned. "I really would like to be home before five today. Do you think we could have a vote?" She directed her question to the foreman.

"I'm not ready," Caroline insisted. "And she *didn't* identify him," she added, contradicting the older woman's statement. "Joan MacIntosh said that she *thought* it was him. In her mind there was a reasonable doubt. There's one in mine, too."

Half the room eyed her balefully. An hour later Caroline was convinced they would never reach a unanimous decision. Caroline felt taxed to the limit of her endurance. The only other person in the room who had voiced the same doubts as she was Ted.

"I have misgivings, as well," he said now.

"Maybe these two are right," one woman said softly. Groans went up around the room.

"Are we going to let that…that beast walk out of here after what he did?" The real estate agent rolled his pencil across the table in disgust. "Come on, folks. The sooner we agree, the sooner we can go home."

"Listen, everyone," Ted said, squaring his shoulders as he sat straighter. "I'm as anxious to get home as the next person, but we can't rush these proceedings."

A half hour later the judge sent in a note, asking if they were anywhere close to reaching a verdict.

"See?" the real estate agent fumed. "Even the judge is shocked at how long this is taking. We should have been out of here an hour ago."

The foreman wrote out a reply and sent it back to the judge. Within fifteen minutes they were dismissed and told to return in the morning.

This time it was Caroline who was waiting in the hallway for Ted. Her hands were clenched at her sides as waves of intense anger washed over her. He paused and grinned at her, but she waited until they were alone to speak, then struggled to make her voice sound normal. "Just what do you think you're doing?"

"Doing?" he asked in confusion.

"Listen, I don't need anyone to defend me, so step off your shining white horse and form your own opinions. I don't appreciate what you're doing." She caught his startled look and ignored it.

"What are you talking about?"

"This case. Don't you think I know what you're doing? It's that chauvinistic attitude of yours. The fanatical gentleman in you who refuses to let me stand alone against the others."

A look of sorely tried patience crossed his face. "Believe what you will, but I happen to share your sentiments regarding the case."

"Ha!" she snapped.

The controlled fury in his eyes was enough to knock the breath from her lungs. She noted the red tinge that was working its way up his neck and the tight, pinched look of his mouth. "I can assure you, Miss Lomax, that I consider it a miracle that we share any opinion. I would appreciate it, however, if you'd afford me the intelligence to decide for myself how I feel about this case without making unwarranted assumptions."

Suddenly drowning in resentful embarrassment, she murmured, "If I've misjudged your actions, then I apologize."

"From the time you were a girl your mouth has continued to outrun your brain," he said with deadly calm. "I have endured your anger, your lack of manners, even your temper. But I have no intention of being further subjected to your stupidity."

Hot color invaded her cheeks, and Caroline experienced an unwanted pang of misgiving. "Maybe I spoke out of turn."

The look he gave her would have frozen rainwater. Without a word, he pivoted sharply and left her standing alone in the wide hall. She pushed the curls from her face and forcefully expelled her breath. Tendrils of guilt wrapped themselves around her heart. She'd done it again. And this time she'd messed it up good. Ted wouldn't have anything to do with her now. She should be glad, but instead she discovered a sense of regret dominating her thoughts. Maybe they could settle things after the trial. Maybe, but from his look, she doubted it.

Four

"Has the jury reached a verdict?" the stern-faced judge asked the foreman. The engineer rose awkwardly to his feet. The courtroom was filled with tense silence. Every face in the crowded room turned to stare expectantly at the twelve men and women sitting in the jury box.

The foreman shifted uneasily, casting his gaze to his nervously clenched hands. "No, we haven't, Your Honor."

Low hissing whispers filled the room. Caroline lifted her gaze to the young victim and watched angry defeat dull her eyes as she cupped her trembling chin. Joan MacIntosh gave a small cry before burying her face in the shoulder of the man Caroline suspected was her husband.

After long, tedious hours of holding her ground, repeating the same arguments over and over until she longed to weep with frustration, Caroline was unsure about the evidence and how she should vote. As much as anyone, she wanted the man who had so brutally attacked Joan MacIntosh punished. But as much as she yearned for justice, she also needed to feel sure that she was sending the right man to prison.

Holding her ground hadn't been easy. Neither she nor Ted had wavered from their earlier stand, although others had made some persuasive—and heated—arguments. Still, Caroline couldn't change what she believed simply because someone else saw things differently. A mistrial was the worst possible outcome, as far as the courts were concerned. The jury members had been warned earlier that if it were possible to make a decision, one should be made. But since they couldn't agree unanimously, there had been no choice but to return to the courtroom and the judge.

"What was the vote?" The deepening frown in the judge's weathered face revealed his displeasure.

"Ten to two," the foreman returned, pausing to clear his throat. "Ten of us felt the defendant was guilty, the other two," he hesitated and swallowed, "didn't."

The judge studied the twelve jury members, then called for a jury poll.

When her turn came, Caroline slowly, reluctantly, said, "Not guilty." Unable to meet the judge's penetrating glare, she lowered her eyes. Unexpectedly her gaze clashed with the surly defendant's. A ghost of a grin hovered around his mouth, as if he were silently laughing at everything that was going on around him. Caroline was reminded again that Nelson Bergstrom had already been proven capable of such a hideous crime.

"You leave me with no option but to declare a mistrial." The judge spoke in a solemn voice, and it seemed to Caroline that his tone was sharp and angry. "The defendant is free on ten thousand dollars bond. A new court date will be set at the end of the week. The jurors will return tomorrow to fulfill the rest of their obligation to serve."

Joan MacIntosh burst into tears, her sobs reverberating against the hallowed walls. A dark shroud of uncertainty wrapped around Caroline's tender heart. She felt tears prickle the corners of her eyes, and she pinched her lips tightly together as the gavel banged down and the jurors were dismissed.

It seemed as if everyone in the room was accusing her with their eyes. She wanted to stand by Ted, lean on him for support, but since their last argument, he had barely spoken to her. Even her greetings had been met with clipped, disinterested replies. Ted wasn't the sort to get angry easily, and to his credit, he'd put up with a lot from her over the years. But when she'd questioned his integrity, she had committed the unforgivable. A hundred times since, she'd wished she could have pulled back the thoughtless words, but the truth was, defending her decision was just the kind of thing Ted would think chivalrous. If anything, she was pleased they shared the same opinion. If ever she needed a friend, it had been today, standing against her the fellow members of the jury. Yet even when their decisions concurred, they were treating each other as enemies.

The line of accusing faces didn't fade when Caroline and Ted entered the wide hallway outside the courtroom. The man who had sat with Joan MacIntosh was waiting for them, as were photographers from the local newspapers.

The moment Caroline appeared, the presumed Mr. MacIntosh started spewing a long list of obscenities at her with the venom of a man driven past his endurance. At first she was stunned, too shocked to react, and then she couldn't believe anyone would talk to her that way. She had been called some rotten things in her life, but nothing even close to this.

"I didn't mean to upset you," she pleaded, yearning desperately to explain. "I'm so sorry," she went on, "but if you only understood why I voted the way I did—"

She wasn't allowed to finish, as another tirade of harsh, angry words broke across her explanation. Bright lights flashed as the press took in the bitter scene.

"Caroline," Ted said sharply, coming to her side. "It won't do any good to reason with him. Let's get out of here."

"But he needs to understand. Everyone does," she insisted, turning toward the reporters. "Ted and I agonized over the decision."

"Ted?" one reporter tossed back at her.

"Ted Thomasson," she clarified.

"And you are?" the reporter pressed.

"Caroline Lomax."

"Caroline," Ted snapped angrily, "don't give them our names."

"Oh." She swallowed quickly. "I didn't mean… Oh dear." She felt utterly and completely confused.

Without allowing her to speak further, Ted took her hand and led her away. Even as they briskly walked down the wide corridor, they were followed by the reporters, who hounded them with a series of rapid-fire questions.

To every one, Ted responded in a crisp voice, "No comment."

"What about you, Miss?"

Still reeling from the shock of the encounter outside the courtroom, she opened and closed her mouth, unsure what to say. A fiery glare from Ted convinced her to follow his lead. "No comment."

Because his stride was so much longer than her own, she was forced to trot to keep even with him. "Where are we going?" she asked breathlessly as they raced down the steps and sped toward the parking lot.

"I'm taking you home."

"Home," she echoed, disappointed. Tonight she would have enjoyed a leisurely drink or a peaceful dinner out.

He stopped in front of his car, took out his key and pressed the button to unlock the doors. Before he had a chance to open the passenger door for her, Caroline climbed inside. Ted stared at her for a long moment, then opened his own door and slid in. He braced his hands against the steering wheel and exhaled sharply. She understood his feelings. She had never been so glad to be out of a place in her life. Not even when she'd been caught raising prissy Jenny Wilson's gym shorts up the flagpole had she felt more glad to escape a situation. The leather-upholstered seat felt wonderful, almost comforting. The tension eased from her stiff limbs, and she slowly expelled a long sigh of relief as she leaned her head back. It felt like heaven to close her eyes.

Wordlessly, Ted started the engine and pulled out of the narrow space.

The silence was already grating on her as they pulled onto the busy Seattle street, which was snarled with rush-hour traffic. She searched her mind for something casual to say and came up blank. When she couldn't stand it any longer, she gave in and asked the question that had been paramount in her mind.

"Are you still angry with me?" she asked tentatively, surprised by how much the answer mattered to her.

"No."

"Good." For the life of her, she couldn't come up with something more clever to say. She was too drained emotionally to be original and come up with some witty remark that would restore the balance to their relationship. The funny part was that though she wasn't entirely sure they were capable of being friends, a whole day of hostility had left her decidedly upset. Previously, she'd delighted in tormenting him, had taken pride in coming up with ways to needle "Tedious Ted." Lately, though, she'd been hard-pressed to know who was tormenting whom.

Instead of pulling into the parking lot across the street from her apartment building, Ted eased to a stop at her curb.

"You aren't coming in?"

"No."

"Why not?" He made no move to turn and look at her, which only served to upset her further.

"It's been a long day."

"It's barely four-thirty," she countered. In her mind she'd pictured spending a quiet evening together. She'd even thought of cooking a meal for him, so she could impress him with her considerable culinary skills. After a day like theirs, they needed to talk and unwind.

"Another time, maybe."

Just the nonchalant way he said it grated on

Caroline's nerves. She knew a brush-off when she heard one. What did she care if he came inside or not? She wasn't desperate for a man's companionship. She didn't even like Theodore Thomasson, so it wasn't any skin off her nose if he preferred his own company. At least that was what she told herself as she swallowed back the unpleasant taste of disappointment.

"All right. I'll see you tomorrow, then," she said, tightening her hand around the door handle. Still she hesitated, not wanting to part. "Thanks for the ride."

"You're welcome."

If he didn't stop being so polite, she was going to scream. Finally she got out, and when she was safely on the sidewalk and had closed the car door, he pulled away. He didn't even have the common decency to speed. She would have liked him better if he had. For a long moment she didn't move. He might claim that he'd forgiven her, but she knew he hadn't. His sleek Chevrolet was long out of sight when she finally sighed with defeat and entered her apartment building.

As it turned out, she didn't even bother cooking a meal. After years of schooling to be a cordon bleu chef and countless arguments with her father over her chosen vocation, she ate a bowl of corn flakes in front of the television. The mistrial was barely given a mention on the local news, leaving her relieved. She felt as if she were wearing a scarlet letter as it was.

Tucking her bare feet beneath her, she leaned her head back and closed her eyes as a talk show came on after the national news. The next thing she knew, the sound of shrill ringing assaulted her ears, jolting her into full awareness. Straightening, she searched around her for the source. The phone pealed again, and she reached for it.

"Hello."

Hollow silence was followed by an irritating click.

Angrily, she stared at the receiver, silently accusing it of rousing her from a sound nap. A deep yawn shuddered through her, and she wrapped her sweater more tightly around her. She supposed she was glad Ted hadn't come inside after all. As sleepy as she was, she wouldn't have been much of a hostess. She told herself he had probably recognized how much the day had drained her, that he was only being thoughtful when he refused her invitation. She told herself that, but deep down she knew it wasn't true.

Although she'd had a long nap, she slept well that night and woke refreshed early the next morning. She dreaded another day at the courthouse. There was a possibility she could be called to sit on another trial. The thought filled her with apprehension.

As she was grabbing her raincoat, the phone rang. She answered it on the second ring, and once again the caller immediately disconnected. Slowly Caroline replaced the receiver, perplexed.

Ted was already seated in the jury room when she arrived. She felt a sense of relief at seeing him and took the vacant chair next to him. He glanced up from his crossword puzzle but didn't greet her.

"Did you try to phone me last night?" she asked, sipping coffee from the steaming cup she'd picked up on her way in. It burned her mouth, and she grimaced.

"No." He gave her a look of condescension, as if to

say she ought to know enough to let her coffee cool before trying to drink it. But that was the sensible thing to do, and she had never been sensible.

"What about this morning?" she asked.

"I didn't phone you this morning, either."

He didn't need to sound so pleased with himself. So he hadn't phoned. Deep down, she'd hoped it had been him.

"The reason I asked," she hurried to explain, "is that twice now someone has phoned and hung up when I answered. Caller ID just said private caller."

"Surely you don't think I—"

"No," she interrupted. "Listen, I'm sorry I asked. It was a mistake. Okay?" Irritated, she crossed her legs and studied his crossword puzzle, amazed that it was nearly complete. She hated the ones that gave the average solution time. It took her twenty minutes just to sharpen her pencil, find a comfortable position and figure out one-across. Since she was lousy at them, it naturally meant that Ted was a whiz at crossword puzzles. If the one he set aside now was any indication, he could win competitions.

The morning passed slowly. Several panels were called out for jury selection, but her name was not among them. That was more than fine with her.

At lunchtime Ted left the building without suggesting they eat together. She'd expected that, although she couldn't help feeling a twinge of regret. Without meaning to follow him, she discovered that they'd chosen the same place along the waterfront where they'd eaten a few days earlier. As usual, the outdoor restaurant was crowded, and once her order had been filled, there wasn't a place to sit. She could ask some strangers if they would mind sharing a table with her, but no one looked that interesting.

"Do you mind if I sit down?" she finally asked, standing directly in front of Ted.

"Go ahead." He didn't sound welcoming, but at least he didn't sound unwelcoming, either.

"I didn't follow you here," she announced, pulling out the bench opposite him. Vigorously she stirred her thick clam chowder.

"I didn't think for a minute that you had." He avoided her eyes and sat looking out over the greenish waters of Puget Sound.

"Are you always like this?"

"How do you mean?" He turned his gaze to her for an instant, then looked back to the choppy waters, seeming to prefer the view of the busy waterway to her.

"Are you always sullen and uncommunicative when you're angry with someone?" She considered it her greatest weakness that she really was miserable when someone was upset with her. In the past, this personality quirk had only applied to people she cared about, which meant that her current uneasiness over Ted was troubling her more every minute.

"Usually," he agreed.

"How long does it last?"

"That depends," he said, nibbling on a French fry.

"On what?"

"On how offended I am."

"How much have I offended you?"

"On a scale of one to ten," he stated casually, "I'd say a solid nine."

A thick lump worked its way down Caroline's dry throat. She had done some regrettable things in her life, and pulled enough shenanigans to cause her father a headful of gray hair. But there hadn't been a time when she regretted any words more than she regretted the ones she'd spoken to Ted. She'd felt recently that they had been on the brink of something special. She didn't know how to explain it. She wasn't even sure she liked him, but she felt a strange and powerful attraction to him. "I can't do anything more than apologize."

"I know." A sad smile touched the edges of his mouth. He didn't say anything when she slid off the bench and stood. She wanted to ask him how long he planned to be this way but didn't. They only had one more day of jury duty, and from the looks of things it would take far more time than that.

If the morning was dull, the afternoon was doubly so. Caroline intentionally sat as far away from Ted as possible, doing her best to ignore him. Yet again and again, as if by a force more potent than her own will, her gaze was drawn to him. He was by far the most attractive man in the room. There was a quiet authority about him that commanded the respect of others. The masterful thread in his voice hadn't gone unnoticed, either. From her experience being on the jury with him, she knew that he was quick, sure and decisive. If it hadn't been for his strength against the others, she sincerely doubted that she would have been able to withstand the concerted pressure to change her vote.

Later that afternoon she returned to her apartment, which didn't feel as welcoming as it usually did. Sluggishly she removed her backpack and looped it over the closest doorknob. She was physically drained and mentally exhausted, and thoroughly disgusted with life. Once again her sense of timing had been off-kilter. She didn't know how to explain her life in better terms. It was as if everyone else was marching "left, right, left, right," and she was loping along her merry way—"right, left, right, left." Another woman would have looked at Ted Thomasson and immediately recognized what a devastatingly attractive man he was. She saw it, didn't trust it and chose to insult him. Only when it was too late did she recognize his appeal. At least after tomorrow their forced proximity would be over and she could go about her life, forgetting that she'd ever had anything to do with Tedious Ted Thomasson.

The phone started ringing at six that evening. The first time she was scrambling eggs for dinner and reached for it automatically. The pattern was the same. She picked up the phone, heard some distant breathing and then the caller disconnected. Obviously some weirdo had gotten her number and was determined to play games with her. Fifteen minutes later it happened again. After the third time, she unplugged her phone.

Refusing to give in to fear, she told herself that calls like these were normally harmless. What she needed to stir her blood was a little exercise. She changed into her jogging outfit and ran in place. She stopped only when the tenants below her began pounding on their ceiling. Panting, she turned off the record and slumped onto the sofa, panting.

Feeling invigorated and secure, she plugged her phone back in. It rang immediately. She practically jerked the receiver up to her ear. "If you don't stop both-ering me, I'm calling the cops." That should frighten the jerk who was playing these games.

A moment of stunned silence followed. "Caroline, is that you?"

It was her mother.

"Oh, hi, Mom." She laughed in relief and briefly explained what had happened as she slumped against the thick sofa cushions. "I thought you were my prank caller."

"I'm so relieved," her mother said, and laughed softly. "You know how I live in fear of the police." Then she said, excitement brimming in her voice, "I have news. Your father and I are taking off for a little while." She paused, then added, "To China."

"China!"

"We leave tomorrow, and we're both very pleased. You know this is just the market he's been wanting to reach."

"How long will you be gone?"

"Two weeks. It's going to be a wonderful trip."

"It sounds like it." Caroline would miss her mother. Although they lived several hundred miles apart, they talked at least twice a week.

"Have you seen Theodore again?" The question had been asked casually, but she knew her mother well enough to sense the interest she was struggling to dis-guise.

"I see him every day in the jury room."

"He's grown up into someone pretty impressive, don't you think?"

"Yes, Mom, I do."

"You do?" Her mother was clearly having trouble disguising her surprise, and the line went silent for a moment. "You like him, don't you?"

"I insulted him. I didn't mean to, but it just slipped out, and now I doubt that we're capable of anything more than a polite greeting."

"He'll get over it," her mother said knowingly.

"Sure, just as soon as the moon turns blue."

"Caroline, I saw the way he looked at you. He'll come around, don't worry."

Caroline wished she had as much confidence as her mother, but she didn't.

The next morning it was Caroline who arrived at the federal courthouse first. She'd brought along a book to occupy her time—a best-seller that was said to be irresistibly absorbing. She certainly hoped so.

When Ted entered the room, she pretended to be immersed in the thrilling plot of the book, though she couldn't even remember its title, let alone the characters or the story.

He took the seat beside her. "Morning." The greeting was clipped.

"Hello." She continued reading, proud that she'd resisted the urge to turn and smile at him, then cursed her heart for pounding because she was so glad he'd chosen to sit beside her.

"Did you try to phone me last night?" he questioned dryly.

So that was it. "No."

He leaned back in his chair and rubbed a hand over

his face. "Someone was playing tricks on me half the night. Phoning, then hanging up."

"Surely you don't think I would do something like that?" She snapped her book closed and stiffened. "I'll have you know—"

"Caroline," he said, and gently placed a hand over hers to stop her. "Weren't you telling me the same thing was happening to you?"

"Yes," she said, still angry that he would think she'd done something so childish and trying not to remember that she'd all but accused him of the same thing just yesterday.

"Did it happen again last night?"

"Yes." She turned frightened eyes to him as she felt her facial muscles tense. "I thought it was a prankster… a joker, but now it's happening to you, too?"

"I don't think it's anything to worry about."

"Probably not," she agreed, but in truth she was frightened out of her wits. "But I think there has to be some connection between the phone calls and the trial."

"Still…a friend of mine is a detective. It might be a good idea if we have a chat with him."

"Do you think it's necessary?"

"I don't know, but I'd feel better if we knew where we stood."

"We're not standing anywhere. We're sitting ducks."

"Caroline, we're not. Whoever is doing this is angry because of the mistrial, but it will blow over in a day or two." His face revealed none of his thoughts.

"Right," she said, crossing her legs and starting to nibble on her bottom lip. She wished he hadn't said anything about the calls he'd gotten. Ignorance really was bliss.

"Listen," he announced a minute later. "I'm sure I'm just overreacting. We've both gotten a few harmless phone calls, but there's no need to contact the police."

She wasn't nearly as convinced, but she let the subject drop.

They sat together for the rest of the day, though they barely spoke. At lunchtime they bought sandwiches and ate in the cafeteria.

"I'll drive you home," Ted announced at the end of the day.

Caroline didn't argue. Silently they walked toward the parking lot. Her hands were tucked deep within the pockets of her light jacket. She had a sinking feeling that something was about to happen, which caused chills to run up and down her spine. She would never lay claim to possessing any supernatural insight, not in the least, but her imagination had flipped into overdrive.

Ted stopped abruptly and released a mumbled curse.

"What's wrong?"

He pointed to his car, which had been smeared with raw eggs.

Caroline's earlier chill became so intense that she feared frostbite. "The person who did this has to be the same one who's making the phone calls," she murmured, struggling to disguise her alarm. If he was doing this to Ted, then something was bound to happen to her, as well.

"We don't have any proof of that."

He sounded so calm and reasonable that she wanted to shake him. "What are we going to do?"

"For starters, we'll head for a car wash."

"And then?"

"And then my friend's office."

"Okay." She was more than ready to agree.

Detective Charles Randolph was a brown-haired, clean-shaven man whose mouth widened with a ready smile when Ted walked into his office. Caroline followed closely on his heels and nodded politely when introduced. She resisted shaking hands, since hers were clammy with fear.

Ted briefly explained the reason for their visit. Detective Randolph sympathized, but he told them that chances were good their tormentor would stop his games in a day or so, and then he added that there was little he could do. He did offer some helpful suggestions, and assured them that the minute they could pinpoint a suspect or prove anything, he would do everything within the limits of the law to put an end to the problem.

Afterward Ted escorted Caroline to her apartment, and this time he accepted her invitation to go up for a cup of coffee. This time she ground the beans and went through elaborate steps to prolong the process to keep him with her as long as possible.

"You're not frightened, are you, Caroline?" he asked, his eyes dark and serious as he studied her.

"Who, me?" She laughed bravely and claimed the overstuffed chair across from him, her hands cupping her steaming mug.

"I agree with Randolph. Whoever is doing this is unlikely to hurt either one of us."

"Right." *Wrong*, her mind countered.

Ted didn't take more than a few sips of his coffee before he stood. Caroline sent him a pleading glance, but she wasn't about to ask him to stay if he was intent on leaving. She might be frightened half to death, but she still had her pride.

"Don't let any strangers into your apartment," he cautioned.

Was he kidding? Her own brother would have to break down the door.

"Call me if anything happens. Okay?" he went on.

Wonderful. She had to wait until her life was in danger before contacting him. "Define 'happens.'" Her eyes were begging him to stay, to move in if necessary, at least until this craziness passed.

Ted appeared to be weighing her question. "You'll know."

"That's what I'm afraid of."

He hesitated in the open doorway. "You're sure you'll be all right?"

"I'll be fine." She was shocked that she could lie with such ease, but if he was determined to leave her to an unknown fate, then she would let him. No wonder she'd disliked him so much all these years. Maybe this was how he'd chosen to take his revenge.

He waited on the other side of the apartment door until she turned the lock and it clicked into place.

After he left, she managed to push the crank caller to the back of her mind by keeping busy. She baked bran muffins and ate one with a slice of bologna and cheese for dinner. Everything on television bored her, so she picked up the book she'd tried to read earlier that day with no success. By ten-thirty her eyelids were drooping. Chastising herself for being afraid to go to sleep, she slipped into her nightgown and started humming the national anthem. Her duty as a patriotic citizen had gotten her into this mess.

She crossed the room to pull the drapes closed when she noticed a burly figure of a man standing on the sidewalk below. He looked like the same man who had accompanied Joan MacIntosh. The resemblance was enough to cause her heart to flutter wildly and panic to fill her.

Ted had told her to wait until something happened. But she wasn't waiting until the commando below decided to break into her apartment.

Her fingers were shaking so badly that she could barely punch out Ted's telephone number.

He answered on the first ring.

"Ted." She heard the nervous tremor in her voice and tried unsuccessfully to calm herself.

"What is it?" He was instantly alert.

"A man... The man from the trial...he's here."

"In your apartment?"

"Not yet. He's standing outside my building. I...went to close the drapes, and I saw him staring up at my window."

"Did he see you?"

"I don't know," she said sarcastically. "Do you want me to stick my head out the window and ask him?"

"Are you sure it's him? Nelson Bergstrom?"

"Not Nelson, Joan MacIntosh's husband. At least I think it's him. He was standing in the shadows, but it looked like it was him, and..."

"Caroline," he said her name so gently that she

wanted to cry. "You're worrying too much. It's probably nothing."

"Nothing?" she echoed, hurt and angry. "I'm locked in an apartment with a man seeking revenge outside my door. In the meantime you're probably sitting there in front of a cozy fireplace, smoking your pipe and...and you have the nerve to tell me I'm overreacting."

"Caroline—"

A loud knock sounded against her door and echoed like a taunt around the room.

"What was that?" Ted asked.

"He's here," she whispered, so frightened she thought she was going to faint.

Five

"Caroline!" Her name was followed by frantic pounding on her front door. "Caroline! Are you all right?"

"Ted?" His name was wrenched from the stranglehold of shock and fear that gripped her throat. Her hands were trembling so hard that she could barely unlatch the door and open it. A shock wave shuddered through her bones at the sight of him. His eyes were narrowed and hard, and flickered possessively over her like tongues of fire, checking to see that she was unharmed. She had never seen a more intense expression. At that moment, she didn't doubt that he would have seriously hurt anyone who'd hurt her.

"Thank God." He closed the door and swept her into his arms, crushing her slender frame to his with such force that the oxygen was knocked from her lungs. She didn't care how hard he held her. He was here, and she was safe. She wanted to tell him everything that had happened, but the only sounds that escaped her fear-tightened throat were gibberish.

The unexpected strength of his kiss forced her head

back so that she was pressed against the apartment wall. He moved his hands to cup her face, and his mouth pillaged hers with such hunger that her knees gave way. Her grip on his shoulders was the only thing that kept her upright. Consuming fear gave way to delicious excitement as she opened her mouth to him and met his lips with burning eagerness. His touch chased away the freezing cold of stark fear, and she nestled closer to his warmth, trembling violently. When his mouth trailed down her throat to explore her neck, Caroline fought her way through the haze of engulfing sensations. For days she'd wanted Ted to kiss her. She'd planned to treat him as he'd done her and make fun of him with some cutting remark. But one kiss and she'd melted into his arms. Her resistance amounted to little more than wafer-thin walls. Of course, the circumstances undoubtedly had something to do with the strength of her response. And now, instead of rejecting him, she held him as if she wasn't sure she could survive if he let her go.

"He didn't hurt you?"

"No." Her voice wavered, betraying the havoc he was causing to her self-control.

"When I saw the blood, I think I went a little crazy."

"Blood?" He wasn't making any sense. She hadn't answered the knock, and whoever wanted in had been content to make a few strange noises outside her door before leaving.

"The door," Ted muttered. His hands roved gently up and down her spine, molding her closer to him, as though he couldn't let her go.

"I didn't let him in." She still wasn't sure what he

was talking about, but it didn't seem to matter when he was touching her with such tenderness.

"Caroline." He lifted his head long enough for the intimate look in his sapphire eyes to hold her captive.

"Yes?"

He shook his head from side to side, as if he couldn't bring himself to speak. Ever so slowly he lowered his mouth to hers again. She breathed deeply to control the excitement that tightened her stomach. If his first kiss had shocked her into melting bonelessly, this kiss completely and utterly devastated her.

Her hands strained against his shirt, clenching and bunching the material, but she didn't know if she meant to push him away or pull him closer. After a moment she didn't care.

"I would have hurt him—a lot—if he'd touched you," Ted growled against her lips.

Remembering the feral light in his eyes earlier, she didn't doubt his words.

His breath filled her lungs. It felt warm and drugging, muddling her already-confused thoughts. "But he didn't, and I'm fine." Or she would be once her blood pressure dropped, but she didn't know who to blame for that—the lunatic or Ted.

Relaxing his hold, Ted slid his arm around her waist and securely locked the front door. "All right, my heart's back where it belongs. Tell me what happened."

His heart might have been fine, but hers wasn't. She felt as if she was standing on a dangerous precipice where the view was heavenly and heady, and stepping off looked like a distinct possibility. But she had only to look down the deep abyss below to realize what dangerous ground she was standing on. Mentally she took a step in retreat.

"Caroline," he coaxed, tenderly guiding her to the cushioned chair and sitting her down. He knelt in front of her, his hands clasping hers. "Tell me what happened. Tell me everything."

"Nothing happened, really. He—or whoever it was—knocked a few times. I...I didn't answer, and after a little while and a few weird noises, he went away." She didn't add that she'd stood stock-still, deathly afraid that whoever was doing this would come back. Not knowing if she should run from the apartment or stay put, she had waited, praying that Ted would arrive before her tormentor decided to return.

Ted expelled his breath. "I think I broke the land speed record getting here. If anything had happened to you, I never would have forgiven myself."

"I wouldn't have forgiven you, either," she said, rallying slightly, remembering how he'd abandoned her to an unknown fate earlier. "Why didn't you stay with me before? I was frightened and you knew it, yet you chose to leave."

"I couldn't stay." He raised his head, but he refused to meet her gaze. "I had another commitment."

"Another commitment." She spoke the words with all the venom of a woman scorned. So Theodore Thomasson had some hot date that was more important to him than her welfare. How incredibly stupid she'd been not to have guessed it sooner. No wonder he hadn't been able to get out of her apartment fast enough.

Raging to her feet, she stalked to the other side of the room as two bright spots of color blossomed in her cheeks. He'd left the arms of another woman to rescue her, then had the nerve to kiss her like that. She felt as if she was going to be sick. The worst part was that she'd kissed him back, encouraged him, and, yes, wanted him. Her throat ached as she battled back stinging tears.

"Well, as you can see, I'm unscathed." She did her best to sound normal. "Now that you've assured yourself of that, you'll want to go back to the ready arms of your calendar girl. I apologize if I inconvenienced your plans in any way."

"My calendar girl? What are you talking about?" he asked in confusion. "Have you taken leave of your senses?"

"Yes," she said. She had indeed abandoned sanity the minute he'd pulled her into his arms. "And don't you ever…ever—" She whirled on him, pointing her index finger at him like a weapon. "Don't you ever touch me again."

A weary glitter shone in his eyes, as if he were attempting to make sense of her words. "From the impression you gave me, I'd say you were enjoying my kiss."

"I was in shock," she countered, her expression schooled and brittle. "I didn't know what I was doing."

He ran his fingers through his hair, mussing it all the more. "All right, all right, we both didn't know what we were doing. Chalk it up to the unpleasant events of the last week. I'll admit kissing you was a mistake."

"I don't want it to happen again."

His frown deepened into a dark scowl. "It won't. Does that soothe your outrage?"

She swallowed past the lump that was choking her throat. Her answer was little more than a curt nod. "You can go now," she finally managed. She shivered, then wrapped her arms around herself to ward off the sudden chill. Ted opened her closet and took out a bulky-knit cardigan. It cost her more pride than he knew to let him drape it around her shoulders.

"Where's a bucket?" he asked, taking off his coat and rolling up his shirt sleeves.

"A bucket?"

"A couple of rags, too, if you have them?"

"Why?"

"Why?" he repeated, glancing at her as though she'd lost her mind. "Because of the blood."

Her face went sickly pale as she suddenly remembered what he'd said earlier. "What blood?"

"You didn't see your door?"

"No. What's wrong with it?" She marched across the room, but Ted stopped her before she made it halfway to the door. Their eyes locked in a battle of wills. "Ted?"

"There are a few unsavory words painted on it. I'm sure you've read them before."

"He—he wrote something on my door...in blood?"

"It's probably spray paint, but I thought...never mind what I was thinking."

"But..."

"Just get me a bucket, Caroline."

Numbly, she complied, leading the way into her kitchen and taking out a yellow plastic pail from beneath her sink. "Why would he knock if all he wanted to do was write some ugly words on my door? That doesn't make any sense."

"After spending this week in your company, there's little left in this world that does. How do I know what he was thinking? Maybe he wanted to know if you were home before he defaced your property," he said, and his mouth thinned with irritation. He took the plastic pail from her hands and filled it with soapy water. "And for that matter, who knows what he would have done if you *had* opened the door."

"There was no chance of my doing that. Maybe he would have gotten scared if I answered and gone away."

"There's no way of knowing that." Preoccupied, he pulled open a kitchen drawer and withdrew a couple of clean dishrags.

"There's no need for you to clean up. I'm perfectly capable of washing my own front door. Besides, you probably want to get back to your hot date."

"My hot date?"

"Would you stop repeating everything I say?"

His gaze seized hers in a hold that felt as physical and punishing as if he'd grabbed her arm. Pride demanded that she meet his eyes, but it wasn't easy. Never had Caroline seen anyone look so angry. His dark blue eyes were snapping with fire. "You certainly have a low opinion of me."

"I— You were the one who said you had an earlier commitment."

"And you assumed it was with a woman."

"Well…yes." She wished her voice would stop wavering. "You mean it wasn't?" Each word dropped in volume until they emerged in little more than a low whisper.

He didn't answer her. "Why don't you change your clothes while I wipe down your door?"

"Change my clothes?" For the first time she realized that she was wearing a five-year-old flannel night-gown that had faded from a bright purple to a sick blue from years of washing. As if that wasn't bad enough, the hem had ripped out and was dragging against the floor. Complementing her outfit was a pair of glorious, scarlet knee-high socks.

"For once in your life, don't argue with me," he said in a voice that told her his patience was gone.

"I wasn't going to."

Ted's expression revealed surprise, but he said nothing more as he carried the yellow pail full of soapy water out her front door.

While he was about his task, Caroline changed into deep burgundy-colored cords and a fisherman's knit sweater. She knew that with her hair she shouldn't wear colors like burgundy, but such taboos had always been mere challenges to her. How she wished she didn't have this penchant for being so contrary.

Her hair was combed and tied at the base of her neck with a pale blue nylon scarf by the time Ted returned. She followed him into the tiny kitchen and watched as he emptied the bucket, rinsed it out and placed it back under the sink. When he turned, he looked surprised to find her close.

"You might want to pack a few things."

"Pack a few things?"

"Now who's sounding like a parrot?"

In other circumstances she would have laughed, but there wasn't any humor in the look Ted was giving her.

"Why should I pack?"

"I'm taking you home with me."

"Why?" He made her sound like a puppy dog that needed a place to stay.

"Because I refuse to spend the rest of the night worrying about you." Each word was dripping with exasperation.

"It didn't seem to bother you earlier."

"It does now." Apparently that explanation was supposed to satisfy her. "Don't argue with me, Caroline. It won't do you any good."

From the scathing look he gave her, she could see that he was right. She could put up a valiant argument, but she was tired and afraid, and the truth was that she wanted to be with Ted so much it actually hurt. The lunatic on her doorstep was only an excuse for enjoying his company. She'd been bitterly disappointed when Ted had left her earlier that evening. She'd longed to spend a quiet evening alone with him. There was a peacefulness about him that attracted her, an inner strength that drew her to him naturally. Yet all she'd managed to do was offend him. She reminded herself that he wasn't taking her to his apartment to enjoy her tantalizing company but out of a sense of duty. She swallowed her pride and followed him. She was going for more reasons than she cared to analyze.

Ted's apartment wasn't anything like what she'd imagined, though she *had* been right about the fireplace, which dominated the living room, with tan leather furniture positioned in front of it. Brass light fixtures were accentuated by the cream-colored carpet. Several paintings adorned the walls. Compared to her tiny apartment, Ted lived in the lap of luxury.

"I'll take your coat."

With a wan smile, she gave it to him. He'd barely spoken to her on the way over, and she once again sought for a way to tear down the concrete walls she'd erected between them with her thoughtless accusations. "Your apartment is very nice."

He looked as if he were about to answer her when the phone rang.

Her eyes widened with apprehension as he crossed the room. His back was to her, and although she couldn't hear much of the conversation, she saw Ted's shoulders sag in defeat. She had felt as if she'd been slowly crumpling under the oppressive weight of the pressure they'd been under these last few days, but Ted hadn't once revealed in any way that the trial and its outcome had affected him, so whatever was being said now must be far worse than anything they'd experienced so far.

Replacing the receiver, he turned to her. His eyes showed both anger and defeat.

"What is it?"

He rubbed his eyes and pinched the bridge of his nose. "That was Randolph."

"And…?"

"He just wanted me to know that there's been another assault against a woman in a mini-mart."

"Nelson?"

"They don't know, but the MO's the same. Assuming our problems are tied to the trial, that can only inflame whoever's been harassing us, so he thinks it might be a good idea if we got out of town for a few days until the heat blows over."

Six

"Leave town? Whatever for?" Caroline watched with concern as Ted rubbed a hand across the back of his neck, looking as if the weight of the world were pressing against his shoulders.

"Don't you understand what I'm saying?" he barked. "Another young woman—a mini-mart clerk just like Joan MacIntosh—has been brutally assaulted. Pistol whipped in the same way as Joan, and from what Charles said, the cops are betting the same man who attacked Joan struck again tonight. And once again it was within walking distance of Nelson Bergstrom's address."

Caroline felt the strength leave her legs, and she slowly sank into a leather chair. Her voice wobbled as the tears that had hovered near the surface broke free. "And...and we set him free." Sniffling, she pressed her fingers to her eyes, but that did little good and the moisture ran unheeded down her ashen cheeks.

"We did what we thought was right," Ted countered.

"We still don't know if Nelson Bergstrom is guilty or not. No one does."

"But it must've been him."

"Apparently the newspapers have gotten hold of this, and according to Randolph, the morning paper is doing a story about the mistrial in connection with this latest assault." He gave her his handkerchief and lowered himself into the chair beside hers. "Listen carefully, Caroline. The press have our names, and our addresses aren't exactly top-secret. They're going to have a field day with this, and we could be stuck in the middle of it."

"So we have to leave?"

"We don't *have* to, but Randolph advises it. I've been meaning to visit your parents anyway, and this seems like the perfect opportunity."

"We can't go see them. They've gone to China."

Ted nodded. "What about your brother?"

"No." She was just beginning to formulate her thoughts. She had a key to her parents' home. There wasn't any reason why she couldn't steal away there for a few days. "It shouldn't matter if Mom and Dad are gone. I'll take a couple of days and drive home, lounge around for a day or two, and head back. By then this thing will have been settled."

"You?" He gave her a disgruntled look. "We're in this together. Wherever *you* go, *I* go."

"You?" Caroline would have thought from the way he had been acting that the last person in the world he wanted to spend time with was her.

"Don't look so pleased," he murmured sarcastically, propelling himself out of the chair. "Believe me, I'm not all that thrilled to waste my time in *your* company, either."

"Then why do it?" she asked, feeling hurt and unreasonable. "I don't need you to escort me to San Francisco. I'm perfectly capable of taking care of myself."

"Listen, Miss High and Mighty, I had enough of you when I was fifteen to last any man a lifetime." He paused and pointed out the window. "But some loon is out there, seeking revenge because our actions set a guilty man free. You can bet that once this latest development hits the papers it's going to be more phone calls and messages smeared on doors—and maybe worse." His look cut right through her. "Now get this through that thick, stubborn skull of yours. I'm not sending you any place where I can't keep an eye on you. We're in this thing together, whether you like it or not."

Caroline had never seen Ted's eyes so flinty. Each word forced her deeper into the chair, until she felt as though she were physically embedded in the leather cushion. She crossed her arms in front of her in an attempt to ward off the hurt his words were inflicting, instead hugging the warm memory of his kiss to her heart. The burning heat from her cheeks dried her tears.

"Well?" he challenged, standing over her, apparently expecting an argument.

"When do you want to leave?"

Some of the diamond hardness left his eyes. "First thing in the morning."

"My clothes…"

"We'll pack tonight, catch what sleep we can, and leave first thing in the morning." He spoke impersonally, and Caroline had the impression that his thoughts were elsewhere. She could be a slab of marble for all the notice he gave her.

It took what felt like half the night to make the necessary preparations for the trip. Once she was packed and her apartment securely locked, they returned to his place. She offered to help and was refused without so much as a backward glance. When he went to get his things together, she sat on the sofa. She only meant to close her eyes and give them a rest, but the next thing she knew Ted was gently shaking her awake.

She sat up with a start. "What time is it?"

"Five-thirty. It might be a good idea if we left now."

"Okay." A headache was pounding at her temple, and she pressed her fingertips to it and inhaled deeply.

"There's coffee, if you'd like a cup."

She nodded, since conversation felt as if it would require a monumental effort. He stepped into the kitchen, then returned a moment later with a steaming mug. Her smile of appreciation drained her of strength, and she sagged back against the sofa cushions. He gazed at her, and she lowered her eyes, unwilling to let him see how miserable she felt. She could hear him moving around the apartment, and she took another sip of coffee, feeling the need for caffeine to inspire her to get moving.

"Here." Ted pried off the safety cap from a bottle of aspirin and shook two tablets into her palm.

"Thank you," she mumbled, accepting the glass of water he offered next. The tablets slid down the back of her throat easily. He had ranted at her earlier with an anger that had shocked her. Now he was tenderly seeing to her aches and pains. "Did you get any sleep at all?" she asked.

"No."

He didn't elaborate, but Caroline realized that, like her, he was feeling the heavy burden of responsibility for this latest assault case. Rationally, she recognized that they'd done what they felt was right by sticking to their convictions. But the fact they had felt the shadow of a doubt over Nelson Bergstrom's guilt didn't matter now. Every piece of evidence against the man had been circumstantial; they hadn't felt confident enough to hand over a guilty verdict. But this latest assault had jerked the rug out from under Caroline's feet. In her heart, she was sure that she had set a guilty man free.

"Did—did your friend at the police station mention how badly the latest victim was hurt? I mean…" She let the rest of the words fade, not wanting to know, yet realizing she must.

"She's in the hospital. Randolph said she's in pretty bad shape."

Caroline felt like weeping again, but she managed to hold back the tears with a suppressed shudder.

Twenty minutes later they were heading south on Interstate 5. Neither spoke and the air between them hung ominously heavy and still.

"How's the headache?" Ted asked as they approached the outskirts of the state capital in Olympia.

"Better." Her hand tightened on the armrest of the car door. She doubted that the headache would go away until Nelson Bergstrom was in jail where he belonged—where she should have put him.

When Ted exited the freeway onto a secondary highway, she gave him a surprised glance. He answered her question before she voiced it.

"We're both drained. I thought we'd spend the day in Ocean Shores. I have a cabin there."

"That sounds like a good idea." She shifted to a more comfortable position in the seat, and his dark blue eyes slid briefly to her.

"When we get to the cabin we can catch up on some sleep, then leave again when it's dark and we won't be seen."

"Leave tonight? Why?" The idea of spending a relaxing day on the beach was appealing to her. She needed the peace and solitude of a windswept shore to exorcize the events of the past week from her heart.

"I thought we should probably do our traveling by night," Ted explained. "It will be to our advantage to attract the least amount of attention possible."

Staring out the window at the lush green terrain, Caroline swallowed down a ready argument. The world outside the car window looked serene and peaceful, with its pastoral farms and grazing animals. The day was glorious, especially now in the light of early morning, as they raced down the highway with the rising sun that stood boldly out to greet them in hues of brilliant orange. She didn't want to argue with Ted, not now when she felt so tired and miserable. Telling him that he'd been watching too many cop shows wouldn't be conducive to an amicable journey.

More silence followed, but it wasn't harsh or grating; it was almost pleasant. Without being obvious, Caroline studied Ted. The image of him sitting in an office all day seemed strangely out of sync. His shoulders were too broad and muscular for a man who was tied to a desk. His jawline was solid, and there was a faint bend to his nose, as if it had been broken at one time. She couldn't picture him fighting, though she was sure he would if necessary. The last few days had taught her that. Another thing that amazed her was that he had never married. Fleetingly, she wondered why. He was more than attractive, compellingly male, and he stirred her blood as no one else ever had.

"You're looking thoughtful," Ted commented, his gaze momentarily turning toward her.

Caroline continued to study his handsome profile for a thoughtful second. "I was just wondering why you'd never married."

"No reason in particular." Amusement gleamed briefly in his eyes. "I've been too busy to settle down. To be honest, I've wondered the same thing about you."

"Me?" She half expected him to add a comment that she would be fortunate if any man wanted to put up with her. He had never seen the softly feminine part of her that yearned for a family of her own. No, he had only been witness to the shrewish part of her nature. "I've been too busy to think about a husband and home." The lie was only a small one.

"Your career is more important?"

Proving to her father that she could be the best cook in America had been more important. Her pride demanded it, but she couldn't tell Ted that. He would scoff and call her stubborn, and add a hundred other unsavory adjectives. And he would be right.

"Yes, I guess it is," she answered finally.

They didn't speak again until the road signs indicated that they were entering the community of Ocean Shores. Although she had heard a great deal about the resort town, with its rolling golf courses and luxurious summer homes, she had never been there. For herself, she would have chosen a less populated area, one with wide open spaces and room to breathe. She wouldn't want to worry about nosy neighbors or invading another's privacy. But her tastes weren't Ted's, and every minute together proved how little they shared in common.

When he turned off the main street and took a winding, narrow road that led down a secluded strip of windswept shore, then turned down his drive, Caroline was pleasantly surprised. His log cabin was far enough off the road so that it couldn't readily be seen.

He parked on the far side of the house, so that his car wouldn't be easily visible from the road, either, and turned off the engine. He rested his hands on the steering wheel for a long moment as he closed his eyes.

"You must be exhausted."

They were less than three hours out of Seattle, but it felt as if they'd traveled nonstop to California.

"A little," was all he would admit.

The fireplace was the only source of heat inside the cabin, and Ted immediately started a fire. The place was small and homey, with only a few pieces of furniture.

Caroline looked around and came up with enough odds and ends from the kitchen cupboards to fix them something to eat. They were both hungry, and ate the soup and canned fruit as if it were ambrosia. While she washed and put away the few dishes they'd used, he sat on the sofa, staring into the fire, and promptly fell into a deep slumber. For a time she was content to watch him sleep. A pleasant warmth invaded her limbs, and she yearned to brush the hair from his brow and trace her hands over his strongly defined masculine features. Finding a spare blanket, she spread it over him, lingering at his side far longer than necessary.

A walk along the deserted beach lifted her heart from the doldrums and freed her eager spirit. Even when the sky darkened with a threatening squall, she continued her trek along the windy beach, picking up odds and ends of sea shells and bits of rock. The surf pounded relentlessly against the smooth beach. Crashing waves pummeled the sand until the undertow swept it away into the swirling depths. Caroline felt her own heart being lured into the abyss that only a few hours before had seemed so frightening. She was half a breath from falling in love with Ted Thomasson, and it frightened her to death.

Ted found her an hour later, building a sand castle with an elaborate moat and a bridge made from tiny sticks.

"I wondered where you'd gone," he said, and sat on a dried-out driftwood log. "You shouldn't have let me sleep so long."

"I figured you needed the rest." She glanced up into his warm gaze. Quickly she averted her eyes.

"We should be leaving soon."

"No." She shook her head for emphasis, her cloud of auburn curls twisted with the strength of her conviction.

"What do you mean—no?"

"I refuse to run away." She leaned back, sitting on her heels. Her hands rested on her knees as she met his puzzled gaze with unwavering resolve. "I realize that I've probably had a lot more experience in deal-

ing with guilt than you have, and the first thing I've
learned is—"

"Caroline—"

"No, please listen to me. We—*I*—did what I felt
was right even when the decision wasn't easy. I refuse
to punish myself now because I may have made the
wrong choice. If there's someone out there who wants
me to suffer because of that, then I'd prefer to meet him
head-on rather than sneak around in the dark of night
like a common thief. I simply won't do it."

The expression that crossed his face was so like her
father's when she'd utterly exasperated him that Caroline suppressed the urge to laugh.

"You know I won't leave you," Ted admitted slowly.

"I'm hoping you won't, but I wouldn't stop you," she
said, feeling brave. She hadn't planned on him driving
off without her—she hadn't seen the necessity. He was
much too much of a gentleman.

"It would be a simple thing for anyone looking for
us to learn about this cabin. Our coming here makes
sense."

"Don't worry, I've got that all figured out. We'll sleep
on the beach tonight."

"We'll do *what?*" he exploded. "It's cold out here."

Caroline did an admirable job of holding back her
laugh of pure delight. In the last twenty hours Ted had
taken great pains not to touch her. Of course, she'd
asked him not to, but that shouldn't matter. If they
pitched a makeshift tent here on the sandy beach, he
would be forced to seek her body's warmth. Although
he would have every intention of avoiding it, he would
wake up holding her in his arms. The mental image

was one of such delight that she experienced a tingling warmth up and down her arms.

"I'll keep you warm," she promised under her breath, smiling.

He wasn't pleased with the rest of her ideas, either, so she was astonished that he did as she asked. For dinner they roasted hot dogs on sticks and melted chocolate bars over graham crackers. By the time they'd eaten their fill, the first stars were twinkling in the purpling sky.

"I thought it might rain earlier this afternoon," she mentioned conversationally.

"If it did, maybe you'd listen to reason."

"Maybe," she said with a gleeful smile. "But I doubt it. I've always loved the ocean."

"It's cold and windy, and it's only a matter of time before everything smells like mold," Ted grumbled, tossing another dried piece of wood on the fire.

"Yet you bought a place by the beach, so you must not dislike it half as much as you claim."

His answer was a soft snort as he wrapped a blanket more securely around his shoulders. "I don't need to worry about anyone hunting me down. One night with you and I'll be dead from pneumonia."

"Stop complaining and look at how beautiful the sky is."

"Bah humbug!" He rubbed his hands together and stuck them out in front of the sputtering fire.

The pitch-black night darkened the ocean, while the silvery beams of a full moon created a dancing light on the surface of the water.

"When I was a little girl I ran away to the sea. I was

utterly astonished when they told me I couldn't board the ship."

Ted chuckled. "I remember my parents telling me about that. How old were you? Ten?"

"About that. I'd pulled one of my usual shenanigans—I can't even remember what it was anymore—but I knew that once again I'd embarrassed my mom and dad, so I decided to go to sea. I'll never forget when they came down to the docks to pick me up. My mother burst into tears and hugged me close. For the first time in my life, I realized how much she loved me."

"Had you doubted it before?"

"No, I'd simply never thought about it. No matter how I tried, I could never do things right. There would always be one reason or another why my marvelous schemes failed and I ended up with egg on my face. When I ran away I thought it was for the best, so I wouldn't embarrass Mom again. That night I learned that it didn't matter how many escapades I got myself into, she would always love me. I was her daughter."

"Did you ever try running away again?"

"Never. There wasn't any need. My home was with her and Dad." She centered her concentration on the bark she was peeling from an old stick. She didn't often speak of her youth, chagrined by her behavior.

"You were marvelous, Caroline Lomax. Full of imagination and sass. Your parents had every reason to be proud of you." He spoke with such insight that she raised her head, and their gazes met over the flickering fire. The mesmerizing quality in his eyes stole her breath. Her heart pounded so loud and strong that she was convinced he could hear it over the crashing of the ocean waves. When his attention slid to her softly parted lips, she was certain he was going to reach for her and kiss her. She held her breath in helpless anticipation, yearning for his touch.

Abruptly, he stood and tossed the blanket to the sandy ground. "I've had enough of this wienie roast. You can sleep out here if you want, but I'm going inside."

She tried to hide her disappointment behind a taunting laugh. "You always were a quitter."

He ignored her derision and shook his head. "I don't have your sense of adventure. I never did."

"That's all right," she mumbled, standing. She brushed the sand from the back of her legs. "Few men do."

"You're coming with me?" He looked stunned that she'd conceded so easily.

"I might as well," she grumbled, mostly to herself. Ted helped her put out the fire, and haul the blankets and leftover food back to the cabin.

If she was disgruntled with his lack of adventure, the sleeping arrangements irritated her even more. "You go ahead and take the bed." He pointed to the bedroom, and the lone double bed with the thick down comforter and two huge pillows.

She had to admit it looked inviting. "What about you?"

"Me?" His Adam's apple worked as he swallowed convulsively. "I'll sleep out here, of course."

"But why?"

"Why? Caroline, for heaven's sake think about it."

"You can sleep on top of the covers if it will soothe

your sense of propriety. I read once that if we each keep one foot on the ground, it's perfectly fine for two unmarried people to sleep in the same bed."

Clearly flustered, he waved his hand toward the bedroom. "You go on. I slept most of the day. I'm not tired."

A smile curved Caroline's full lips. She was enjoying riling him and, true to form, Ted was easy to rile. "I trust you."

"Maybe you shouldn't," he barked, and rubbed the back of his neck in a nervous gesture. "I can't believe you'd even suggest such a thing."

"Why? It only makes sense to share, since there's only one bed."

"Good night, Caroline." He crossed his arms, indicating that the discussion was closed, and turned his back to her, standing stiffly in front of the fireplace.

"Good night," she echoed, battling to disguise her amusement.

She had no trouble falling asleep. The bed was warm and comfortable, and after only a few hours' sleep the night before, she slipped easily into an untroubled slumber.

Ted woke her at dawn and brought her in a cup of coffee. "Morning, bright eyes."

"Is it morning already?" she grumbled, yawning. Propping herself up on an elbow, she brushed the hair off her forehead. "How'd you sleep?"

"Great. You were right. Spending the night on the sofa was silly when there was a comfortable bed and a warm body eager for my presence."

She bolted upright. "You slept in this bed?"

"You're the one who suggested it."

"Here? In this bed?" she said again, too amazed to come up with anything else.

"Is there another one I don't know about?"

"You didn't really!"

"Of course I did. Honestly, Caroline, have you ever known me to tease?"

She hadn't. Her mouth dropped open, but a shocked silence followed. For the first time in recent history, she was stunned into speechlessness.

"I'd like to leave in twenty minutes," he said, and set the steaming coffee mug on the dresser top. "Will that be a problem?"

She answered with a shake of her head, still not quite believing his claim about sleeping with her. Mystified, she watched him leave the room and gently close the door, offering her privacy.

Biting her bottom lip, she cocked her head as an incredulous smile touched her eyes. Faint dimples formed at the corners of her mouth. Maybe this trip wouldn't be such a disaster. It could turn out to be the most glorious adventure of her life. Even now, she had trouble believing that she found Ted Thomasson so appealing. Would wonders ever cease? She certainly hoped not.

Oregon's coastal Highway 101 stretched along four hundred miles of spectacular open coastline. With her love of the ocean, Caroline had made several weekend jaunts to the area. She never tired of walking the miles of smooth beaches, clam digging, beachcombing and doing nothing but admiring the breathtaking beauty of the unspoiled scenery.

"We'll need to stop in Seaside," she informed him once they crossed the Columbia River at Astoria.

"Why Seaside?"

"Historians agree that the Lewis and Clark trail ended on the beaches there."

"I don't need a history lesson. Unless it's important, I think we should press on."

From the minute they'd left the beach house that morning, he had seemed intent on making this trip a marathon undertaking. He didn't want to travel the freeway, and, to be honest, she was pleased. The coastline made for far more fascinating travel, and she had several favorite spots along the way.

"It's not an earth-shattering reason," she concluded, disappointment coating her tongue. "But Seaside has wonderful saltwater taffy, and I'd like to get a box for my mother. Taffy's her favorite, and she likes Seaside's the best, so—"

"All right. We'll make a quick stop," he agreed.

"Thanks." Sighing, she smoothed her palms down the front of her dark raspberry shorts. She couldn't understand Ted. His moods kept swinging back and forth. Last night he'd been good-natured and patient. This morning he was behaving as if they were fleeing a Mafia gang hot on their tail.

When they reached Seaside, he parked along the beachside promenade and cut the engine. "I'll wait here."

"In the car?" she asked disbelievingly. "But it's a gorgeous day. I thought you'd like to get something to eat and walk along the beach."

"I'm not hungry."

Glaring at him, she climbed out of the car and closed the door with unnecessary force. Maybe *he* wasn't hun-

gry, but *she* was. They'd stopped for coffee and dough-
nuts at a gas station hours earlier, and that hadn't been
enough to keep her happy. Fine! He could sit in the car
if he liked, but she wasn't going to let his foul mood ruin
her day. Every stride filled with purpose, she walked to
the end of the street near the turnaround and bought a
large box of candy for her mother. A vendor was selling
popcorn, and she purchased a bag and carried it down
the cement stairs to the sandy beach below.

Ted found her fifteen minutes later, sitting on a log
and munching on her unconventional meal. "I've been
looking all over for you," he said accusingly.

"Sorry." She offered some popcorn in appeasement,
but she had no real regrets. "I got carried away. It really
is lovely here, isn't it?"

"Yes." But he sounded preoccupied and impatient.
"Are you ready to leave now?"

"I suppose."

Back on the highway, he turned and gave her a disgruntled look. "Is there any other place you'd like to
stop?"

"Yes—two. Cannon Beach and Tillamook."

"Caroline, this isn't a stroll down memory lane. You
must have seen these sights a hundred times. We're in
a hurry. There's—"

"Correction," she interrupted briskly. "*You* appear to
be in a rush here, not me. I explained once before that I
refuse to run away. You can let me off at the next town
if you insist on acting like this."

His hands tightened around the wheel until she was
surprised he didn't bend it. "All right, we can stop in

Cannon Beach and Tillamook, but what's there that's so all fired important?"

"You just wait and see," she said, feeling much better.

Less than a half hour later he pulled into a public parking area near Cannon Beach. While he grumbled and complained under his breath, she found a vendor and bought a huge box kite. Tight-lipped, he helped her assemble it, but then he only sat on the bulkhead while she raced up and down the shore, flying the oblong contraption. The wind caught her laughter, and she was breathless and giddy by the time she returned.

Ted gave her a sullen look and carted the kite to the car, setting it in the backseat next to the box of salt-water taffy.

Caroline wiped the wet sand from her bare feet before joining him in the front seat. Snapping the seat belt into place, she closed her eyes and made a gallant effort to control her tongue but lost. "You know, you're about as much fun as a bad case of chicken pox."

"I could say the same thing about you."

"Me?" she gasped, outraged. She was shocked at how much those words hurt. She swallowed back the pain, crossed her arms and stared straight ahead.

He started the engine and backed out of the parking space. The tension was so thick in the close confines of the car that it resembled a heavy London fog.

Thirty-five minutes later Ted announced that they were in Tillamook. She had been so caught up in her hurt and anger that she hadn't realized they were even close to Oregon's leading dairy land.

She pointed out the huge building to the left of the road. "I want to stop at the cheese factory," she said, doing her best to keep her voice monotone. She didn't bother to explain that her father loved Tillamook's mild cheddar cheese and she was planning on bringing him a five-pound block.

Ted sat in the car while she made a quick stop in the factory's visitor shop. He climbed out of the front seat when he saw her approach. She made only a pretense of meeting his cool gaze.

"Would you open the trunk, please?" she asked with a saccharine smile.

When he did, she lifted her heavy suitcase from inside and set it on the ground.

"What are you doing?" he demanded.

"What I should have done in the beginning." She opened the car door and took out the box of saltwater taffy and the kite, and sat them on the ground beside her suitcase. "This isn't working," she replied miserably. "It was a mistake to think the two of us could get along for more than a few hours, let alone a week."

He raked his hand through his hair. "Just what do you intend to do?"

She lifted one shoulder in a delicate shrug, hoping to give the impression of utter nonchalance. "The Greyhound bus comes through town. I'll catch that."

"Don't be ridiculous."

"I thought you'd be pleased to be rid of me," she countered smoothly. "From the minute we left Ocean Shores this morning, you've been treating me like I was a troublesome pest. Here's your chance to be free. I'd take it if I were you."

"Caroline, listen...."

"Believe me, I know when I'm not wanted." She'd

suffered enough rejection when she was young to know the feeling intimately.

"I should have told you earlier," he said with gruff insistence, "but I didn't want to frighten you."

"I told you before, I don't scare easily."

"Do you remember when I gassed up the car this morning?"

She nodded.

"I phoned Randolph, and…" He paused, his look dark and serious. "There's no easy way to say this. Apparently there's been a death threat made against us."

Seven

"A death threat." The ugly words hung in the air between them for tortuous seconds. "Who?"

"They don't know."

"So the threat wasn't phoned into the police station? Because they could have traced it then, right? So... how—how did Randolph hear about it?" In spite of her calm voice, her heart was pounding so hard she thought it might burst right out of her chest.

"Apparently someone wrote on the walls outside my apartment, as well. This time the message was more than a few distasteful names. The neighbors phoned the police after an article came out in the morning paper."

"Your name was in the paper?" Caroline breathed in sharply and briefly closed her eyes.

"It turns out this is the seventh robbery of a minimart in which the cashier was pistol whipped. The MO's are identical in each case. The paper interviewed Nelson Bergstrom's arresting officer, and followed his case through the trial and what's happened since. The two of us aren't exactly going to be asked to run for the Seattle city council, if you get the picture."

Caroline did, in living color. "I see," she murmured, and swallowed at the lump thickening in her throat. An unexpected chill raced up her spine. "But surely whoever did this wouldn't follow us…."

"No one knows what they're capable of doing." Ted rubbed his face, as if to erase the tension lines etched so prominently around his eyes and nose. "Randolph suggested that we stay clear of your parents' place in San Francisco, as well."

She agreed with a quick nod. "Then where do you think we'll be safe?"

"Brookings. Randolph has some connections there. He's making arrangements for us to rent a secluded cottage. That way he'll know where he can reach us."

No wonder Ted had been so disagreeable all morning. Numbly, she responded, refusing to allow fear to get the best of her, "That sounds reasonable."

His rugged features hardened into glacier ice. "I'm not letting you out of my sight anymore, Caroline, not for a minute. Do you understand?" His cutting gaze fell to her suitcase.

"I wish you'd said something before now. I thought you were sick of my company."

"Never that, sweetheart, never that." He used the affectionate nickname as if it had slid off his tongue a thousand times. Then, with deliberate, controlled movements, he lifted her suitcase and placed it back inside the trunk.

"Ted?"

He turned toward her, the hard mask of his face discouraging argument. "Yes?"

"Would you…mind holding me for a minute?" For all her brave talk about refusing to run away, she was scared. Her blood was cold, and she felt weak with fright. People had disliked her over the years, but never enough to want to kill her.

Ted wrapped his arms around her and gathered her close. The warmth from his hard body warded off the icy chill that had invaded her limbs. She relaxed against him, letting her soft curves mold to the masculine contour of his body. She felt his rough kiss against her hair, the even rhythm of his pulse, and a soothing peace permeated her heart.

"Nothing's going to happen to you." His whispered promise felt warm and velvety, like a security blanket being draped around her. "Whoever comes after you will have to get through me first."

Scalding tears burned the backs of her eyes. For years she'd treated Ted Thomasson abominably. When they were younger, she'd teased him unmercifully, to the point of being cruel. Even as an adult and with the best of intentions, she'd managed to outrage him. Yet he was willing to protect her to the point of risking his own safety. She had never felt more humbled or more grateful. Frantically, she searched for the words to express her feelings, but nothing she could think of seemed appropriate.

"Would you like some cheese?"

"Pardon?" He relaxed his hold and lifted her chin so their gazes met.

"Mild cheddar," she said, and sniffled, though she

managed to hold all but a few emotional tears at bay. "I...I thought you might like some cheese."

"Another time. Okay?"

"Sure." She wiped the dampness from her cheek with the back of her hand and quickly redeposited her accumulated items inside the car.

Silence reigned as they took up their journey. Finally he reached for her hand and squeezed it reassuringly. "I should have told you sooner."

"I shouldn't have been so self-centered. Something was clearly troubling you. I was the one at fault for being so oblivious."

"Don't be ridiculous."

"Oh, Ted, how can you say that? I bought the kite just to spite you. I don't deserve anyone as good as you in my life and you certainly rate someone better than a troublemaker like me."

"Maybe, but I doubt it," he answered cryptically.

Before this latest stop she had felt his urgency and resented it. Now the need for haste was in her blood, as well. They barely spoke after that, both of them wrapped up in the troubles of the moment. Brookings represented safety; there were people there who would help them, people who were in contact with Detective Randolph in Seattle.

"Are you hungry?" Ted asked as they approached the outskirts of Lincoln City.

Caroline was convinced he'd asked because her stomach had been rumbling, but the pangs weren't from hunger. She glanced at him consideringly. Although she'd eaten the bag of popcorn, he hadn't had anything today except coffee and a sugar-coated doughnut. A look at her watch confirmed that it was after noon.

"Maybe we should stop."

"Anyplace special?"

"No," she said, "you choose." Lincoln City was a seven-mile-long community, the consolidation of five former small cities, with a wide assortment of restaurants and hotels. Caroline had visited there often on her way to San Francisco and enjoyed the many attractions.

Ted parked in the center of the town. Eager to stretch her legs, she stepped out of the car and lifted her arms high above her head as she gave a wide yawn.

"Tired?" he inquired, and smiled lazily.

"No," she assured him. "I'm just a little stiff from sitting so long." As she spoke, a German Shepherd approached her, his tail wagging eagerly. "Hello, big guy," she greeted him, stooping to pet his thick fur, which was matted and unkempt. "What's the matter, boy, are you lost?" The dog regarded her with doleful dark eyes. "He's starving," she announced with concern to Ted, who had walked around the car to join her.

"He probably smelled the cheese." Absently, he patted the friendly dog on the top of the head. "There's a good restaurant around the corner from here, as I recall."

"What about the dog?" she asked, slightly piqued by his indifference to the plight of the lost animal.

"What about him?"

"He's hungry."

"So am I. If he's lost, the authorities will pick him up sooner or later." A hand at her elbow led her toward the restaurant.

She resisted, shrugging her arm free. "You're honestly going to leave him here?" She twisted around to discover the dog seeking a handout from another passerby.

"I don't see much choice. A stray dog is not our responsibility."

From his crisp tone, Caroline could tell the discussion was closed. Her mind crowded with arguments. But he was right, and she knew it. Nonetheless, there had been something so sad in those dark eyes that it had touched her, and she couldn't put the pitiful dog out of her mind.

Even after they'd eaten and were lingering over their coffee, she continued to think about the lost dog. Neither of them spoke much, but the silence was companionable. When Ted stood to pay the cashier, she placed a hand on his arm and murmured, "I'll be right out front."

As she'd suspected, the German Shepherd was outside the restaurant, glancing hopefully at each face that walked out the door.

"I bet the smells from here are driving you crazy, aren't they, fellow?" She took a few scraps she'd managed to smuggle into a napkin without Ted noticing and gave them to the dog. He gobbled them down immediately and looked at her for more.

"How long has it been since you ate?" The poor dog was so thin his ribs showed. Glancing around her, she spied a food vendor down the street. "Come on, boy, we'll get you something more."

The dog trotted at her side as she hurried down the block, past Ted's parked car and toward the beach. She bought four hot dogs and found a sandy spot off the side street to feed the starving dog.

After he'd eaten his fill, she regarded the sad condition of his fur. "You're a mess, you know that? What you need is a decent bath. Someone needs to comb your fur."

A flicker from those dark eyes seemed to say that he agreed with her.

"Caroline."

Her name was spoken with such anger that she whirled around.

In her concern for the dog, she'd forgotten about Ted, and he was clearly furious. She forced herself to smile, but her heart sank to the pit of her stomach at the angry twist of his features. She hadn't meant to wander off, but she'd been so busy trying to take care of the dog that she had forgotten he didn't know where she'd gone.

"Just what do you think you're doing? You said you'd be right outside."

Responding to Ted's anger, the dog moved to Caroline's side and took up a protective stance, emitting a low growl.

"It's all right, boy. That's Ted." Caroline gave the dog a reassuring pat on the head.

"I should have known that animal was somehow involved in this," Ted snarled. "Right out front, you said. Can you imagine what I thought when you weren't there? I swear, Caroline, my heart can't take much more of this. What do I have to do? Handcuff you to my side?"

"I'm sorry…honestly, I didn't mean to take off, but I couldn't stop thinking about the dog and—"

"Just get in the car. I'll feel a whole lot better once we're in Brookings."

"But..."

"Are we going to argue about that as well?"

She didn't want any more dissension between them. "No."

"Thank you for that." He turned and headed toward the car with a step that was as crisp as a drill sergeant's.

Gently patting the side of her leg to urge the dog to follow her, Caroline followed in Ted's wake. The German Shepherd didn't need any urging and trotted along happily at her side as if he'd been doing so all his life.

When she started to open the rear door, Ted cast her a scathing look. "Now what are you doing?"

"I—I was thinking that it might not be a bad idea to take the dog with us. He's hungry and needs a home. And I bet he'd offer us a lot of protection. I'm going to name him Stranger because—"

"We're not taking that filthy dog!" Ted exploded.

"But—"

"You've already managed to accumulate a box of candy, a slab of cheese and a sackful of worthless sea shells, in addition to a man-size kite. I absolutely refuse to take that dog. The answer is no. N. O. No."

Caroline turned away. "I get the picture," she replied tightly. She crouched down on one knee. "Goodbye, Stranger," she whispered to the dog. "I did the best I could for you. You take care of yourself. Someone else will come along soon—I hope."

The car's engine roared to life, and she swallowed down the huge lump in her throat before climbing in beside Ted, who sat still and unyielding, arms outstretched, gripping the steering wheel. She closed her eyes, biting back the words to ask him to reconsider. It wouldn't do any good; his mind was made up.

"Next stop is Brookings," he said as he checked the rearview mirror and pulled out of the parking space.

"Right," she agreed weakly.

Turning the corner, they merged with the highway traffic as it sped through town. Not wanting Ted to see the emotion that was choking her, Caroline turned and stared out the side window. A flash of brown and black captured her attention from the side mirror. Stranger was running for all his worth, following them down the highway. Cars were weaving around him, and horns were blaring.

"Stranger!" she cried, twisting around despite the seatbelt, so she was kneeling in the front seat and staring out the rear window. She cupped one hand over her mouth in horror as she watched the dog, his tongue lolling from the side of his mouth, persistently running, unaware of the danger.

"All right. All right." With a mumbled curse, Ted pulled over to the side of the road. "You win. We can take that stupid dog. Heaven only knows what else you're going to pick up along the way. Maybe I should rent a trailer."

The sarcasm was lost on Caroline, who threw open the car door and leaped out with an agility she hasn't known she possessed.

As if he'd been born to it, Stranger leaped into the open backseat of the car, curled into a compact ball and rested his chin on his paws. Still panting from exertion, he looked up at her with grateful eyes. She sniffled, and ruffled his ears before closing the back door and slipping in beside Ted.

"Thank you," she whispered brokenly to him. "You won't regret it, I promise."

"That is something I sincerely doubt."

The tires spun as he pulled the car pulled back onto the highway. Having gotten her way when she'd least expected it, she tried her best to be pleasant company, chatting easily as they continued south.

He made a few comments now and again, but his lack of attention irritated her. The least he could do was pretend that he was interested.

"Am I boring you?" she asked an hour later.

"What makes you think that? I'm thrilled to know the secret ingredient in bran muffins isn't the bran." His well-defined mouth edged up at one corner in a mirthless grin that bordered on sarcasm.

Fuming, she crossed her arms over her breasts and focused her gaze straight ahead. Ted wasn't pleased about the dog, but he didn't need to pout to tell her that. For that matter, she wasn't exactly sure what *she* was going to do with Stranger, either. But leaving him behind to face an uncertain fate was an intolerable thought. She simply couldn't do it. To be truthful, she had been shocked that he had been so heartlessly willing to leave the dog behind, though he'd redeemed himself by pulling over and letting Stranger in the car. In her own way, she'd been trying to tell him that by being chatty, witty and pleasant. She was tired of arguing with him. She wanted them to be friends. Good friends. "I won't bother you anymore," she grumbled, swallowing her considerable pride.

Ted's gaze didn't deviate from the road, and his quiet low-pitched voice could barely be heard over the hum of the engine. "Not bother me? You've been nothing but trouble from the time we met."

She forced herself to relax against the seat, refusing to trade insults with him, though the words burned on her lips to tell him that he'd been easy to terrorize. That gentlemanly streak of his was so wide it looked like a racing stripe down the middle of his back.

"Has anyone ever commented on how your eyes snap when you're angry?" he inquired smoothly ten minutes later.

"Never."

"They do—and very prettily, I might add."

"You should be in a position to know."

He chuckled and turned on the radio. Apparently listening to the farm report was more interesting than her attempts at conversation had been.

They stopped for gas in Florence, outside of Dunes City. Had things been more amiable between them, she might have suggested that they stop and explore the white sand aboard rented camels. It had always been her intention to hire a dune buggy and venture into the forty-two-mile stretch of sand, but she never had. The camels were a new addition, and she would have loved to ride one. Knowing Ted's preferences, he would have chosen to stand at the lookout point, utterly content to snap pictures.

Thinking the situation over, it shocked her once again to realize how different she was from this man. Even more jarring was the knowledge that it would be so easy to fall in love with him.

"I might have been tempted to stop here and take a few pictures," he confessed, echoing her thoughts, "but I don't think the car is big enough to hold both a camel and a dog." Amusement gleamed in his eyes, and she chuckled, appeased by his wit. He was full of surprises. Until recently, she had thought the highlight of his week was breaking in a new pair of socks. Now she was learning that he had wit and charm, and she had to admit, she enjoyed being with him when he was like this.

They drove for what seemed an eternity. She couldn't recall ever being so comfortable with silence. He was content to listen to the radio. Stranger, who had slept for most of the journey, now seemed eager to arrive at their destination. He sat up in the backseat and rested his paw beside her headrest.

The car's headlights sliced through the semidarkness of twilight, silhouetting the large offshore monoliths against the setting sun. The beauty of the scene was powerful enough to steal Caroline's breath.

"It's lovely, isn't it?" she murmured, forgetting the reason for this exile.

"Yes, it is," he agreed softly. "Very beautiful."

Briefly, their eyes met, and he offered her a warm smile that erased a lifetime of uncomplimentary thoughts.

"We'll be there soon."

She responded with a short nod. The quiet felt gentle. She could think of no other word to describe it. A tenderness was growing between them. They'd both fought it, neither wanting it, yet now they seemed equally unwilling to destroy the moment.

"Caroline," he finally murmured, then paused to clear his throat.

"Hmm?"

"There's something I should tell you now that we're near Brookings."

"Yes?"

Whatever he had to say was clearly making him uneasy. He studied the road as if they were in imminent danger of slipping over the edge and crashing to the rocks below.

"This morning, when I talked with Randolph…" He hesitated for a second time. "I want you to know that he was the one who suggested this."

"Suggested what?" She studied him with renewed interest. The pinched lines around his mouth and nose didn't speak of anger as much as uneasiness.

He ran a hand along the back of his neck and expelled his breath in a low groan. "What I'm about to tell you."

"For crying out loud, would you spit it out?"

"All right," he snapped.

Stranger, apparently sensing the tension, barked loudly.

"Tell that stupid dog to shut up."

"Stranger is not stupid." Twisting around, Caroline scratched the German Shepherd behind the ears in an effort to minimize the insult. "He didn't mean that, boy," she whispered soothingly.

"Caroline, listen, what I'm about to tell you is none of my doing. Randolph seemed to feel it was necessary."

"You've said that twice. Would you kindly quit hedging and tell me what's going on?"

"We're going to have to pose as a newlywed couple."

"What?" she exploded, stunned.

"Apparently the people who own the cottage are old fashioned about this sort of thing, but it's safest if we stay together, so Randolph suggested the newlywed thing. I don't like it any better than you do."

A bemused smile blossomed on her lips. "Does this mean I'm going to have to bat my eyelashes at you and fawn over your every word?" She couldn't help giggling. "Will I need to pretend to be madly in love with you?" She was afraid that wouldn't call for much acting on her part.

"No," he returned sharply. "It just means we're scheduled to share a cottage."

"Oh, good grief. Is that all?"

Ted glanced at her sharply. "Well, doesn't that bother you?"

"Should it?"

"You're behaving as though you do this sort of thing often."

She decided to ignore the censure in his voice. 'I don't see much difference between sharing a honeymoon cottage and spending the night in your one-bed cabin."

"Well, you needn't worry, I'll sleep on the couch."

"Now that's ridiculous. I'm a good six inches shorter than you. If anyone sleeps on the couch, it'll be me."

"Can we argue about that later?"

Caroline released an exaggerated sigh. "I suppose."

Ten miles later she couldn't stay quiet a moment longer. "You know what's really bothering you, don't you?" There was no holding back her lazy smile.

"I have the feeling you're going to tell me." The sarcasm was back, although he tried to give an impression of indifference.

Reading him had always been so easy for her. She wondered if others could decipher him as well as she could, then doubted it. "The fact that we'll be sharing the same cottage isn't the problem here." His grip on the steering wheel was so tight that she marveled that it hadn't collapsed under the intense pressure. "What's troubling you is that we'd be living a lie. Pretense just isn't part of your nature."

"And it *is* yours?"

"Unfortunately, yes," she admitted with typical aplomb.

Her answer didn't appear to please him. "Then you should take to this charade quite well."

"Probably. For a time I toyed with the idea of being an actress."

"Why didn't you?" He tipped his head to one side inquisitively.

"For obvious reasons." Her fingers fanned the auburn curls falling across her smooth brow. "With this red hair and my temperament, I'd be typecast so easily that I'd hate it after a while."

"That's not the real reason."

His insight shocked her. "No," she admitted slowly with a half smile. "Mom didn't like the idea." It had been the only time in her life that her mother had asked anything of her. She'd been a college freshman when she'd caught the acting bug. A drama class and a small part in the spring production had convinced her that she was meant for the silver screen. As usual, her timing was off. Her mother had taken the announcement with a gentle smile, then nodded calmly at Caroline's decision to enroll in additional drama classes. But when it looked like it was more than a passing fancy, Ruth had taken Caroline out to lunch and asked her to abandon the idea of changing her major to drama. She'd given a long list of reasons, all good ones, but none were necessary. Caroline knew this was important to her mother and had forsaken the idea simply because she'd asked.

The road sign indicating that they were entering the city limits of Brookings came into view, and Ted pulled over to the side of the highway and pulled out his phone, calling up the GPS app.

"What are you doing?"

"Getting the directions."

While he punched buttons, Caroline crossed her arms and asked, "Is there anything else that was said in this morning's conversation that I don't know?"

Glancing up from the screen, Ted regarded her with unseeing eyes. "No, why?"

"You keep dropping more and more tidbits of information. Just how long were you on the phone?"

"Five minutes."

She hated being kept in the dark this way. Circumstances being what they were, she would have preferred knowing what they faced instead of bumping into it bit by bit.

After pulling back onto the road again, Ted took a right-hand turn and followed an obscure side street that led downhill as they approached the beach.

Checking the name printed on the mailbox, Ted stopped in front of a white house with a meticulously kept yard. Azaleas lined the walkway, which was illuminated by the porch light.

Eyeing Stranger, Ted murmured, "Maybe you'd better stay here."

"Of course…darling," Caroline whispered seductively and batted her eyelashes.

'Don't forget, your name's Thomasson now."

"Naturally." She couldn't resist a languid sigh.

He rubbed his hand over his eyes. "This situation has all the makings of a nightmare."

"Tell me about it," she grumbled under her breath.

She waited with Stranger beside the car, while Ted knocked on the front door of the white house. He was greeted by a short, dark-haired woman with a motherly look. She cast Caroline a sympathetic smile, and when her husband appeared and began talking to Ted, she hurried over to Caroline.

"I'm Anne Bryant. Charles phoned and told us of the unfortunate circumstances of your visit. Now, don't you worry about a thing. You'll be safe here." She smiled curiously at Stranger, no doubt taken aback by his unkempt condition. "And of course your dog is welcome, too."

"Thank you. I'm sure we'll enjoy it here." Caroline liked Anne immediately and wondered if it was because the loving concern in the older woman's eyes reminded her of her mother.

Ted and Mr. Bryant strolled toward the car, still talking. Ted introduced the other man as Oliver. Together the four of them headed down the steep bluff to the cottage, hauling the suitcases, with Stranger traipsing behind on the narrow pathway and the steep stairs that led the last thirty feet.

"We don't have many visitors this time of year," Anne explained. "And none now, so if you see anyone along the beach it might be best to get back inside. No one knows you're here except Oliver and me."

"Unfortunately there's no cell service around here, but if you need a phone, we've still got a land line," the white-haired Oliver explained.

"What a terrible thing to happen to you on your wedding day."

Ted and Caroline's stricken gazes clashed. She had thought pretending to be a loving wife was going to be so easy, but it wasn't. She hated having to lie to these nice people. Seeming to sense her unease, Ted slipped an arm around her waist and pulled her close to his side. She made the effort to smile up at him, but his mouth curved in an expression that was devoid of enjoyment.

The feel of his arm around her brought with it a welter of emotions. His touch felt warm and gentle, and caused her pulse to trip over itself. When his gaze slid to her lips, she was shocked at the desire that shot through her. She yearned for him to turn her in his arms and kiss her there and then. Mentally shaking herself, she pulled her eyes from his.

"The missus and I feel sorry that things are working out so badly for you two lovebirds."

"Yes," Ted murmured. "We're quite upset ourselves."

"Oliver and I wanted to do something special for you to make your wedding night something to remember," Anne continued. "So we spruced up this cottage and turned it into a honeymoon suite."

"Oh, please," Caroline gasped. "That wasn't necessary."

"We thought it was," Oliver said with a delighted chuckle as he swung open the door to the small cottage.

A fire burned in the fireplace, casting a romantic light across the room. A bottle of champagne rested in a bucket of ice on the coffee table, flanked by two wineglasses.

"Now," Oliver said, stepping aside, "you kiss your bride and carry her over the threshold, and we'll get out of your way."

Eight

Anne's look was as tender as a dewy rose petal when Ted slid his arm around Caroline's waist and effortlessly lifted her into his arms. His lips nuzzled her ear.

"If you ever wanted to be an actress, the time is now," he whispered.

Looping her arms around his neck, she tossed a grateful glance over her shoulder and laughed gaily. "Thank you both for making everything so special."

"The pleasure was ours," Oliver said as he pulled his wife close to his side.

"We'll never forget this, will we, darling?" Caroline batted her thick lashes at Ted.

"Never," he grumbled, then stepped inside the cottage as she waved farewell to their hosts. He closed the door with his foot. Almost immediately her legs were abruptly released. Her shoes hit the floor with a loud clump. "Good grief, how much do you weigh?"

She decided to ignore the question. "This is a fine mess you've gotten us into."

"Me?" he snapped. "I told you, I didn't have anything to do with this wedding day business."

"Whatever." As she stomped into the tiny kitchen, she was met with the most delicious aroma. She paused, closed her eyes and took in the fascinating smells before peeking inside the oven. A small rib roast was warming, along with large baked potatoes wrapped in aluminum foil. An inspection of the refrigerator revealed a fresh tossed green salad and two thin slices of cheesecake.

Silence filled the room, and the sound of the refrigerator closing seemed to reverberate against the painted walls.

A scratch on the front door reminded her that Stranger was impatiently waiting outside with their luggage. By the time she returned to the living room, Ted had let the dog inside and was lifting their luggage.

"I'll put your suitcase in the bedroom," he announced.

She was too tired to argue. As her fingers made an unconscious inspection of her blouse buttons, she said, "Dinner is in the oven."

Being ill at ease with each other was easy to understand, given the circumstances. The intimate atmosphere created by the low lights, the flickering fire and the chilling champagne did little to help.

Ted returned from the bedroom and lifted the champagne from its icy bed. A look at the label prompted his brows to arch. "An excellent choice," he murmured, but she had the feeling he wasn't speaking to her. "I'll see about opening this."

The kitchen was infinitely better lighted than the living room, and she opted to remain where she was. With the honeymoon atmosphere slapping them in the face, it would be too easy to pretend this night was something it wasn't. "Okay," she agreed reluctantly.

After turning off the oven, she set the roast out to sit a few minutes before being carved. A quick check of the living room showed Ted working the thin wire wrapping from around the top of the champagne bottle and Stranger sleeping in front of the fireplace. The dog raised his head as the cork shot out of the bottle, but he seemed to realize that he wasn't needed for anything and promptly closed his eyes.

Looking for something to occupy her time and keep her in the kitchen, Caroline turned her attention to the table. She noted that it was already set for two. She busied herself tossing the already-tossed salad and then set it in the center of the table.

Not knowing what else she should do, she stood in the arched doorway and skittishly rubbed the palms of her hands together. "Stranger needs a bath."

"Now?" Ted looked up, holding two filled wine-glasses in his hands.

"Yes...well, as you may have noticed, he's dirty."

"But the champagne is ready, and from the smell of things, I'd say dinner is, too."

"I believe you also said something about me needing to lose weight. I'll skip dinner tonight," she said stiffly, her voice weakly tinged with sarcasm.

"I didn't say a word to suggest that you're over-weight."

"You implied it."

"In that case, I beg your pardon because—" he paused, appraising her intimately "—you're perfect."

Her feet dragging, Caroline stepped into the living room. The fire had died down to glowing red embers, and music was playing softly in the background. She could feel the romantic mood envelop her and had no desire to fight it any longer. What puzzled her most was that Ted had fallen into the mood so easily.

"We've been through a lot together," he commented, handing her a wineglass. "Let's put our differences aside for tonight and enjoy this excellent meal."

She stood nervously to one side. The warm, cozy atmosphere was beginning to work all too well. "It *has* been a crazy day, hasn't it?" She took her first sip and savored the bubbly taste. "This is wonderful."

"I agree," he murmured, sitting on the sofa beside the fireplace.

Reluctantly, Caroline joined him, pausing to pet Stranger.

Ted's gaze fell to the dog, and his startling blue eyes softened. "To be honest, I'm glad he's with us."

"You are?"

"Yes." He stood and added a couple of logs to the fire, then knelt in front of it, poking the embers into flames. Flickering tongues of fire crackled and popped over the bark of the new logs. He stood and turned, but made no effort to rejoin her on the sofa. "Are you enjoying the champagne?"

"Oh, yes." She hugged her arms across her stomach, attempting to ward off her awareness of how close he was to her. She was overly conscious of everything about him. He seemed taller, standing there beside her, and more compelling than she remembered. She could feel the warmth of his body more than the heat of the fire, even though he wasn't touching her.

"I don't think I've ever noticed how beautiful you are," he whispered in a voice so low it was as though he hadn't meant to speak the words aloud.

"Ted, don't," she pleaded, closing her eyes. "I'm not beautiful. Not at all, and I know it." Her hair was much too bright, and those horrible freckles across the bridge of her nose were a humiliation to someone her age. Not to mention her dull brown-green eyes.

"I can't help what I see," he murmured softly, sitting beside her at last. Gently he brushed a stray curl from her face, and then his finger grazed her cheek. Her sensitive nerve endings vibrated with the action, and an overwhelming sensation shot all the way to her stomach with such force that she placed her hand over her abdomen in an effort to calm her reaction. "I've thought so since I first met you."

"Oh?"

"You must have known." His voice remained a husky whisper, creating the impression that this was a moment out of time.

Whatever was happening between them sure beat the constant bickering. They'd done enough of that to last a lifetime. "How could I have known?" she whispered, having difficulty finding her voice. "Sometimes things have to hit me over the head before I notice them."

"I know." He bent his head toward hers, his jaw and chin brushing near her ear.

Caroline's stomach started churning again as his warm breath stirred her silken auburn curls. She gripped the stem of her wineglass so tightly it was in danger of snapping.

Ted pried the glass from her fingers and set it aside. "Relax," his soothing voice instructed. "I'm here to protect you."

She closed her eyes as if to still the quaking sensation, but the darkness only served to heighten her reactions. "Ted," she murmured, not knowing why she'd spoken. His mouth explored the side of her neck, renewing the delicious shivers over her sensitized skin.

"Hmm?"

"Nothing." She slipped her arms around him and rolled her head back to grant him access to any part of her neck he desired. He seemed to want all of it.

A soft moan slipped from her throat when his strong teeth gently nipped her earlobe. The action released a torrent of longing, and she melted against him, repeating his name over and over. If he didn't kiss her soon, she would die.

Somehow he shifted their positions so that she was sitting in his lap. "Here's your champagne," he murmured.

She looked up, surprised. She wanted his kiss, not the champagne, but when he raised the glass to her lips, she sipped rather than protesting. When she'd finished, his eyes continued to hold hers as he took a drink from the same glass. As he set the champagne aside, his smoky blue eyes paused to take in the look of longing she was convinced must be written on her face for him to see. He cupped her cheek, his fingers sliding down the delicate line of her jaw to rest on the rounded curve of her neck. Then he dipped his head and kissed the corner of her mouth. She yearned to intercept the movement and meet his lips, but she felt like a rag doll, trapped by her strange emotions.

At last his mouth claimed hers in a study of patience. Her breath faltered; she was choked up inside. The kiss was a long, slow process, as he worked his way from one side of her lips to the other, nibbling, tasting, exploring, until Caroline wanted to cry out with longing. When she attempted to deepen the contact and slant her mouth over his, he wouldn't let her. "There's no hurry," he whispered.

"So...dinner?" she mumbled, not knowing why. The only appetite she had was for him.

"More of this later," he promised, and leisurely kissed her again.

His mouth, she decided, was far headier than the champagne and twice as potent.

"You're so very beautiful," he whispered.

"Thank you," she mumbled.

He kissed her again, his mouth lingering on her lips as though he couldn't get enough of the taste of her. She didn't mind. She loved it when he kissed her. He was so gentle and caring that the emotions swelled up in her until she wanted to cry with wanting him. When he raised his head, she noted that his eyes were a darker blue when they met the troubled light in hers. He inhaled, attempting to control his desire. With unhurried ease he carefully lifted her off his lap and set her back on the couch.

"Did you say something about dinner being ready?"

Reluctantly, she glanced toward the kitchen. "It can wait a few more minutes."

"Maybe," he agreed. "But I can't. If we don't stop this soon, I'm going to carry you into that bedroom, and it won't be for sleep."

"Oh," she muttered, and twin blossoms of color invaded her cheeks. She practically leaped off the couch in her eagerness to escape. Hurrying into the kitchen, she went about the dinner preparations without thought. Thinking would have reminded her how much she wanted Ted to touch her, to kiss her. If he hadn't stopped when he did, she would have gone with him into that bedroom. Love did crazy things to people, made them weak—and strong. During all the years of repeatedly saying no to every boyfriend, she had never come so close to surrendering to a man. Heaven knew Clay had tried to get her into bed with him, and although she'd cared for him, she had never been tempted to give him what he wanted most. If he had been more subtle about his desire, she might have succumbed. In the end, when he'd broken off their relationship, he'd used the fact that she hadn't given in to him physically as an excuse, claiming she was a cold fish, not a real woman at all. Challenging her femininity had been the worst possible tack to take if he'd still hoped to get what he wanted. If Ted had lifted her in his arms and carried her into the bedroom, she knew in her heart that she wouldn't have resisted. She'd wanted him and would have willingly given him what so many others had sought.

Ted joined her a few minutes later, standing awkwardly behind her in the close confines of the kitchen. "Is there anything I can do to help?"

For one insane moment she was tempted to ask him

to hold her again, kiss her—and make passionate love to her. Thankfully, she suppressed the urge.

The atmosphere at the dinner table was strained. They ate in silence, and although the meal was wonderful, she didn't have much of an appetite.

"Caroline?" Ted said at last, avoiding her eyes as he sank his knife into the roast beef as if he wasn't sure if he should kill it before taking a bite.

"Yes?"

"You mentioned this man you were seeing recently. Did the two of you...I mean..."

"Are you asking if I'm a virgin?" She would rather swallow fire than admit that to him.

He glared at her, and she nearly laughed. "Are you?"

"That's a pretty personal thing to ask a man."

"But it's all right for a man to ask a woman?"

"In this case, yes."

Caroline sliced her meat so hard it nearly slid off the plate, but a smile hovered just below the surface. "Why do you want to know?"

"Because we nearly..."

"Did it," she finished for him. "You needn't worry, I was in complete control the entire time."

"That's not the impression I got."

She ignored that and said, "We make a good team."

"Yes, we do," he agreed, and the amusement in his vivid eyes threw her further off balance then she was already. "And you've already given me the answer to my question."

"I sincerely doubt you know what you're talking about." She swallowed and boldly met his gaze, not giving an inch.

Looking pleased with himself, he pushed his plate aside and leaned back, crossing his arms over his chest. "No woman blushes the way you do if she's accustomed to having a man appreciate her beauty, and you are definitely beautiful."

"You sound awfully sure of yourself."

"Because I am," he said with maddening calm.

Caroline took twice the time necessary to clean the kitchen after dinner. Giving Stranger a bath and cleaning the bathroom afterward took up even more time. By the time she'd finished three hours later, she was exhausted. Avoiding Ted could become a full-time occupation, she realized. But she couldn't trust her reaction to him, and being alone with him in the small cottage made the situation all the more intolerable.

He was watching television when she reappeared with a thick towel draped over her arm. Stranger traipsed along damply behind her and eyed Ted dolefully. The dog seemed to be asking him what he'd been up to while they were gone. The dog paused in the middle of the room and shook his body with such force that water droplets splattered across the room.

"Hey, what's going on?" Ted asked, brushing at the wet spots on his shirt.

"Sorry," Caroline murmured, hiding a smile.

"Things must be bad when you apologize for a dog," he teased. His eyes grew warm and gentle, and she glanced away rather than risk drowning in their deep blue depths. "You look beat."

"I am." She sat on the floor in front of the fireplace,

leaned the back of her neck against the couch and studied the ceiling.

Ted didn't continue with the conversation. She supposed that he was caught up in his television program. She opened one eye, noted what was on and groaned inwardly. He was watching televised fishing—and liking it.

"Ted, since we're asking each other personal questions…"

"We are?"

"You know, like the one you asked me at dinner."

"Oh. That."

"Yes, that. Now I have a question for you."

"All right."

He was too agreeable, but she didn't want to turn around and read his expression. "Do you remember the night you dropped me off at the apartment and left because of an appointment?"

"I remember." Reluctance coated his voice.

"Were you telling the truth when you said you weren't seeing a woman?"

It took him so long to answer that she grew concerned.

Finally he said, "No, to be honest, I lied that night. I didn't have an appointment."

Caroline straightened, giving up all pretense of resting. "You lied?" She would have sworn that he was the most honest man in the world. To have him admit to lying was so out of character that it left her feeling shocked. "But why?"

A muscle close to his eye twitched as he tightly clasped his hands. "We were both feeling a bit unsure that night, and the truth is, I was afraid if I stuck around much longer, drinking coffee and sharing a meal, I wouldn't be going home until morning."

Abruptly Caroline closed her eyes and resumed her earlier position. The way she'd been feeling that night lent credence to his observation. She'd wanted him to stay so badly. "I see."

"At the time I was sure you didn't."

"I thought you preferred not to be with me."

He draped his hand over her shoulder, and she raised hers so that they could lace their fingers together. "Rarely have I wanted anything more than I wanted to be with you that night," he whispered, and bent forward to kiss the crown of her head.

Caroline's heart beat wildly against her rib cage as her brain sang a joyous song. She dared not move, fearing a repeat of what had happened earlier. The realization that Ted found her physically attractive pleased her, but he'd given no indication that his heart was involved.

"I'm going to bed," she announced on the tail end of a long and exquisitely fake yawn. She needed an excuse to leave and think things through.

"Stay," he prompted gently. "The best part of the program is coming up. In a minute they're going to show how to tie flies."

She grimaced. "Isn't that inhumane?"

"Not those kinds of flies," he chided, squeezing her fingers. He urged her up on the sofa so that she ended up sitting beside him. His smiling eyes met hers as he looped an arm around her shoulders.

To her amazement, the fly-tying part of the program was interesting. Bits of feather and fishing line were wrapped around a hook, disguising it so cleverly that she actually had difficulty seeing the hook. But finally, after a series of very real yawns, she couldn't keep her eyes open a minute longer.

"Go to bed," he urged with such tenderness that she had to fight the urge to ask him to come with her. Struggling to her feet, she paused midway across the room. "Where do you want to sleep?"

Without so much as glancing away from the television, he replied, "The better question would be where *will* I sleep?"

"All right," she whispered, embarrassed. She was infuriated with herself for the telltale color that roared into her cheeks. "Where will you sleep?"

"Here."

He was several inches too long for the sofa, but the choice was his, and she was much too fatigued to argue. Tomorrow night she would insist that he take the bed, and she would sleep on the sofa.

A moment later, sitting on the end of the mattress, she yawned again. She really was exhausted. The day had begun early, and it had been long and tiring. It didn't seem possible that so much had happened since they'd left Seattle.

After gathering blankets and a pillow, she contained a deep sigh as she walked back into the living room and wordlessly set them on the far end of the sofa where Ted was still sitting. He was so engrossed in his program that he didn't even seem to notice.

Back in the bedroom a few minutes later, after quickly washing up, she didn't waste time before putting on her nightgown and climbing between the clean, crisp sheets. Almost immediately after she rested her head on the pillow, the living room lights went out.

"Good night, Ted," she called.

"Night."

A minute later she was wandering in the nether land between sleep and reality. Then the bedroom door creaked open, and her heartbeat went berserk. Had Ted changed his mind and decided to join her? She wanted him. Oh, dear heaven, she wanted him with her. Every night for the remainder of her life she wanted him.

Her courage failed her, and she dared not open her eyes. She would play it cool, she decided, and wait until he was beside her before turning into his arms and telling him all the words that were stored in her heart. But nothing happened. Silence reigned until she couldn't tolerate it a minute longer. As she eased herself up on one elbow, her eyes searched the darkened room. Perplexed, she wondered at the tricks her mind was playing on her. She'd heard the door open. She was sure of it.

A soft whimper came from the floor and, shocked, she tugged the blanket up to her nose as Stranger laid his snout on top of the mattress, seeming to seek an invitation to join her.

"No, boy," she whispered. "You'll have to stay on the floor. This place beside me is reserved for someone else." Then she rested her head back on the thick feather pillow and promptly fell asleep.

Sunlight splashed through the window, and Caroline stirred, feeling warm and content. Long after she was awake, she lay in the soft comfort of the bed and let the events of last evening run through her mind. Ted had held her and kissed her. He'd desired her the other night when he left her, inventing an excuse because he feared he would end up spending the night with her. He'd desired her then, and he wanted her now. Knowing that was better than any dreamy fantasy.

Stranger scratched at the door, wanting out, and she tossed aside the blanket and quickly dressed. A happy smile lit up her face as she pulled jeans up over her hips and snapped them at her waist. She felt rejuvenated after a good night's sleep and was eager to spend the day with Ted. For the first time she looked forward to their time together, almost hoping that days would stretch into weeks. This picturesque cottage by the sea would become their own private world, where they would learn to overcome their differences. "Opposites attract" was an old saying, one she had heard most of her life. The strong attraction she felt for Ted was living proof. They were powerfully and overwhelmingly fascinated with each other. This time together would teach them the give and take of maintaining a solid relationship.

As she entered the living room, the happiness drained from her eyes. The cottage was empty. The blankets were neatly folded at the end of the sofa, and for an instant she wondered if they'd even been used. Then she realized that Ted wouldn't have abandoned her; she knew him well enough to realize that. His sense of chivalry wouldn't allow him to leave her alone and unprotected.

Stranger had gone to sit patiently by the front door, wanting out. Feeling hurt and a little piqued at finding Ted gone, she opened the front door. Surprise caused her eyes to widen when she realized that it had been left unlocked. Anyone could have walked in. So this was the protection Ted offered her!

In the kitchen, she discovered that the coffee was made and had been sitting there long enough to have a slightly burned taste. A note propped against the salt shaker on the table informed her that Ted had gone grocery shopping. She knew it was ridiculous to feel so offended, but she was the one who'd gone through two years of training to become a chef. If anyone should do the grocery shopping, it was her. Or they could have had fun doing it together.

Her appetite gone, she went to try her cell and discovered that the Bryants hadn't been kidding. No bars. She pulled a sweater over her head and hiked the trail up to the Bryants' house.

Anne was outside, on her knees, pulling weeds from the flower beds. "Morning," she said cheerfully, awkwardly rising to her feet. She gave Caroline a wry smile. "These old bones of mine are complaining again, but I do so love my flowers."

"They're beautiful." One looked at the meticulously kept yard revealed the love and care each blade of grass and plant was given.

"Can I help you with something? Your husband was by earlier."

For a wild second Caroline had to stop and think of who Anne was talking about. "I'd like to use the phone, if that's all right." In the rush to leave Seattle, she had neglected to make arrangements to have her mail picked up. Mrs. Murphy lived down the hall and would willingly collect it for her. They had each other's mail key for just such instances as this. Normally there wasn't much to worry about, but Caroline had filled out applications for jobs at several restaurants and was hoping employment was in the offing. The sooner she became self-sufficient, the sooner she could prove to her father that she had made the right choice. If she couldn't be reached by phone, then an employer would probably contact her by mail. At least she sincerely hoped so.

"Go right in and help yourself to the phone. It's there on the kitchen wall."

"Thanks."

Stranger followed her to the back door and stayed outside while she made the quick call. Just before she hung up, she asked Mrs. Murphy to mail a smoked salmon from the Pike Place Market to the Bryants as a thank-you for all they'd done. Mrs. Murphy said she would be pleased to do it and didn't mind waiting until Caroline was home to be reimbursed.

On her way back to the cottage, Caroline stopped to chat. Anne explained that Brookings was famous for its azaleas. The flowers were in full bloom in May, and Anne spoke with pride of their beauty. Native azalea bushes covered more than thirty acres of a state park north of town, and Caroline hoped that she would have the opportunity to see them in bloom someday.

The cottage felt empty without Ted. To kill time, she took Stranger for a long walk, trying to teach him to fetch by throwing a stick she found along the way. Anyone observing her would have found her efforts hilarious, she mused sometime later as she sat on a driftwood log, watching the waves come crashing in to shore. No matter how long she stayed, the sight would never bore her. Stranger lay at her feet, panting. Despite that, he was eager for more, as he demonstrated by offering her his stick.

When she heard her name carried by the wind, she turned and waved. Ted jogged to her side, then sank to the sand at her feet. "You weren't at the cabin."

"Brilliant observation," she said with a hint of a smile.

"I thought I told you that I didn't want you running off?"

So they were about to start their day with an argument. She didn't want that. Their time together should be spent building a relationship.

"I didn't run off." The denial was quick, although she strove to appear indifferent.

"I couldn't find you," he returned. The words were sharp enough to sound like an accusation.

"If you were afraid the boogie man was going to get me, then you might have locked the door."

"Caroline…" He turned to her in a burst of impatience and rubbed the back of his neck. "Listen to me. I had to get out of the house this morning."

"Why? We would have had a good time doing the shopping together. I like to cook, remember? I *am* a chef, you know."

"I know." He leaped to his feet and began pacing back and forth in front of her. His steps were quick and sharp, kicking up sand. "Listen, Caroline, we're going to have to help one another. I can't be around you without wanting you. If I'm going to resist, then you'll have to help."

A warm glow of happiness seeped into her blood. "But, Ted," she whispered seductively. "Who says I wanted you to resist?"

Nine

"I wish you hadn't said that," Ted said. He stood looking toward the rolling waves that crashed against the beach. "Being together like this creates enough temptations without you adding to them."

He sounded so stiff and resolute that Caroline wanted to shake him. "So what do you want me to do?" she asked, trying not to sound too defensive. "Sleep in the car or camp out on the beach?"

"Don't be silly."

"Me be silly? I thought you knew me better than that." She picked up a handful of the sand and slowly let it slip through her fingers. The grains felt gritty and damp. She'd awakened with such high expectations for this day, and already things were beginning to fall apart.

Lowering himself onto the log beside her, he claimed her hand with his. "The problem isn't you," he admitted with a wry twist of his mouth. "I'm the one having difficulties. It's nothing you've done—or not intentionally, anyway. You can't help it if I find your smile irresistible." He bent his head toward her and tucked a strand of hair behind her ear. "And you have the most incredible eyes."

She could feel the color working its way up to her face but was powerless to resist when he lowered his head and tenderly explored the side of her neck, sending delicious shivers skittering down her spine. Her stomach was tightening as waves of longing lapped through her. Her fingers clawed against the wood as she resisted the urge to slide her arms around him and lose herself in his embrace.

"See what I mean?" he groaned. "I can't even be close to you without wanting to kiss you."

"But I want you to touch me," she whispered candidly.

"I know."

"Is that so bad?" she asked in a prompting voice, leaning her head on his shoulder. "You make me feel beautiful."

"You *are* beautiful."

"Only to you."

"Is the world so blind?"

"No," she returned softly. "You are."

His hand found her hair. Braiding his fingers through the thick length of it, he pressed her closer to him. "That's my greatest fear."

"What is?"

"That what's happening between us isn't real. I'm afraid that circumstances have put us under unnatural stress. It's only logical that our feelings would become involved."

"Are you saying that I'm not feeling what I think I'm

feeling?" She cocked her head a bit and grinned. "That doesn't make sense, does it?"

"The problem is that, as a couple, *we* don't make sense."

"Oh." She swallowed down the hurt. "I thought we balanced one another out rather well."

"Maybe, but that's something we won't know until this ordeal is over. As it is, we're playing with dynamite."

"What do you suggest, then?" She was sure she wasn't going to like anything he proposed.

"No touching. No kissing. No flirting."

"Oh." She straightened, lifting her head from his shoulder as a chill that had nothing to do with the weather ran through her. "Nothing?"

"Nothing," he confirmed.

She ran her fingers through her hair, not caring about the tangles. She needed something to do with her hands.

"Do you agree?"

There was little else she could do. "All right, but I don't like it."

"Constantly being together isn't going to make this easy." He clenched his jaw and shook his head. "But that can't be helped."

Ted had made her feel lovely and desirable. When he'd held her, it hadn't mattered that her eyes were dull and her nose had freckles. To him, in those brief moments, she had been Miss Universe. Now she felt as if she had a bad case of the measles.

"I—I think I'll put away the groceries," she said, rising to her feet and pausing to wipe the sand from the back of her jeans. "Is there anything special you'd like for lunch?" She couldn't look at him for fear he would read the misery in her eyes.

"No," he answered on a solemn note. "Anything is fine."

Caroline spent the remainder of the morning in the kitchen, baking a fresh lemon meringue pie and a loaf of braided holiday bread. Heavenly smells drifted through the cottage. She loved to bake. From the time she was a child, she'd enjoyed mixing up a batch of cookies or surprising her mother with a special cake. Kneading bread dough was therapeutic for her restless mind. She thought about her relationship with Clay and was surprised to realize that the pain of their breakup was completely gone now. She was grateful for the good times they'd shared, but he'd been right—she simply hadn't loved him enough. He'd asked her to prove her love—admittedly, in all the wrong ways—and she'd balked. Her hesitation had caused the split, and for a time it had hurt so much that she had wondered if she'd done the right thing. But she had. She knew that because now she was in love, really in love, with no doubts or insecurities. But Ted doubted. Ted was filled with uncertainties. Ted wanted them to wait and be sure. How like him to be cautious, and how typical of her to be impulsive and impatient.

By evening a plan had formed. Bit by bit, day by day she would prove to him that they weren't really so different. They shared plenty of things in common, and she simply needed to accentuate those. Within a few days he would realize that she would make him the perfect wife. She would cook fantastic meals, be enthralled by what he had to say, and laugh at his corny jokes. Within a week he would be on bended knee with stars in his eyes. In fact, she was shocked that he didn't see how perfect they were together. They'd been meant for each other from the time they were teenagers. Unfortunately, circumstances had led them apart, but no longer.

Dusk had settled when Ted returned to the cottage, hauling in an armload of wood for the fireplace. She had wondered what he'd done with himself all afternoon. He'd eaten lunch with her, then left almost immediately afterward. She hadn't seen him since, but Stranger had gone with him and returned at his side now.

"Something smells good," Ted commented, setting the uniformly cut logs on the hearth.

Wiping her hands on the terry-cloth apron she'd found in a drawer, she joined him in the living room. "I hope you like pot roast in burgundy wine with mushrooms."

His brows arched appreciatively. "I don't know, but it sounds good."

"I would have attempted something more elaborate, but..."

"No, no, that sounds fantastic."

"There's homemade bread, and fresh lemon meringue pie for dessert." After days of traveling and living together, she suddenly felt awkward and a little shy. She hadn't been bashful a day in her life, so this reaction was completely out of character for her.

He didn't look any more confident about their arrangement than she felt. They stood with only a few feet separating them, both looking miserable and unsure. "I'll wash my hands if everything's ready," he murmured after an awkward moment.

"It is."

At the dinner table they sat across from each other, but neither one of them spoke. Caroline literally didn't know what to say. The silence was thick enough to taste. Again and again her gaze was drawn to him, and every cell in her body was aware of him sitting so close, and yet they were separated by something more powerful than distance. Once she glanced up to discover him studying her, and her breath caught. He looked away sharply, as though he were angry at being caught. But if he was looking at her with half the interest with which she was viewing him, then they were indeed in for trouble.

The next morning Caroline woke to find that once again Ted had already left the cottage. The pattern repeated itself in the days that followed. She could sometimes see him working in the distance, chopping wood. What else he did to occupy his time, she didn't know, and she had no idea what the Bryants thought of a honeymoon couple who barely spent time together. Evenings proved to be both their worst and their best times. Since she did all the cooking, he insisted on cleaning the kitchen. At times she was convinced he only volunteered because it limited the time they spent in close proximity to each other.

To their credit, they both did their best to put aside their almost magnetic attraction. And despite everything, there were times when she could almost believe things were natural and right between them. Ted taught her how to play backgammon and chided her about beginner's luck when she proceeded to win every game. Later they switched to chess. Oddly enough, they discovered that although their strategies were dissimilar, their skills were evenly matched. When their interest turned to cards, she insisted that he play poker with her. He agreed, as long as she was willing to learn the finer techniques of bridge. One evening of poker and bridge was enough for her to realize that cards was one area they would do better to ignore.

Some nights they read. Ted's tastes were so opposite to her own that she found it astonishing that she could love such a man. And love him she did, until she wanted to burst. Doing as he'd asked and avoiding any physical contact had proven to her how much she did care for him. He seemed so staid and in control. Only an occasional glance told her that his desire for her hadn't lessened. When he looked at her, all the warmth he had stored in his heart was there for her to see. Some nights she wanted to cry with frustration, but she'd agreed to this craziness, and in time her plan would work. It was taking far longer than she'd expected, though.

Late nights, when the cottage was dark and she lay in bed alone, proved to be the most trying times. They were separated by only a thin door that was often left ajar so Stranger could wander in and out at will. Some nights, when she lay perfectly still, she could hear the rhythmic sound of Ted's even breathing. She wanted to be with him so much that sleep seemed impossible and she lay awake for hours.

Seven days after they'd arrived in Brookings, Caroline had experienced enough frustration to last her ten lifetimes. True to his word, Ted hadn't touched her. Not even so much as an accidental brushing of their hands. He seemed to take pains to avoid being near her. If she was in the kitchen, he stayed in the living room. After dinner, he lingered in the other room so long she had to call him into the living room for their nightly games. It was almost as if he dreaded spending any time with her and each minute together tried his resolve. Yet in her heart she knew that he desired her, wanted to be with her, and hated this self-imposed discipline with as much intensity as she did.

On the afternoon of the eighth day, she was finished baking a cake and had set it out to cool before frosting it. Surely by now he could see what fantastic wife material she was, she thought. If he didn't, then she would be forced to take matters into her own hands. But she would much prefer it if he recognized his love for her without forcing her to resort to more…forceful methods.

The sun was bathing the earth in golden light when Caroline pulled on a thin sweater. In moments she was on the beach, where Stranger came racing to her side, kicking up sand in his eagerness to join her.

"Hiya, boy." She sank to her knees and ruffled his ears as he demonstrated his affection. From the way he was behaving, an observer would have assumed they'd been separated for weeks.

More by accident than design, Stranger had become Ted's dog. In the beginning she hadn't even been sure he wanted the dog tagging along after him. He neither encouraged nor discouraged the dog. Stranger simply went.

What Ted did during the days was a thorn in

Caroline's side. Not once had he mentioned where he went, although she had phrased the question in ten different ways and with as much diplomacy as possible. He would smile and look right through her, then direct the conversation in another direction. Her curiosity was piqued. There was nothing to do but wait impatiently for him to explain himself in his own time, which he would—or she would torture it out of him.

Petting Stranger, she noticed that he was wearing a collar. She did know that Ted had taken the dog to a veterinarian in town one afternoon and she'd been pleased to learn he was suffering no ill effects from his days as a stray. Later she'd discovered a doggie toy that Ted had obviously bought.

"Stranger," she whispered, elated, "I love him. I really do. I think it's as much of a surprise to me as anyone," she said, and ran her hand through the dog's thick fur. "You love him, too, don't you, boy?"

The dog cocked his head at her inquisitively and she thought how strange it was that she could talk so freely to him.

"Come on, let's go for a walk." Agilely, she rose to her feet. Maybe she would stumble on Ted and discover his deep, dark secret. Surely he spent his days doing more than chopping wood. By now he'd chopped enough to supply the cottage for two long winters. After an hour's jaunt up and down the sandy shore, Caroline was convinced he wasn't anywhere around.

As she started back to the cottage, Anne waved to her from the top of the bluff. The two often shared a cup of coffee in the afternoon, and Caroline waved in return and started up the creaky walkway.

"The salmon arrived this afternoon. I can't thank you enough."

"Ted and I wanted you to know how much we appreciate everything you've done."

"You're such a sweet couple. It's obvious that you two were meant to be together."

Obvious to everyone but Ted. "What a nice thing to say," Caroline murmured, glancing at the green grass between her feet.

"At first I was concerned, I don't mind telling you. It didn't seem right that a honeymoon couple spent so much time apart. Your husband painting, and you down there in that cottage cooking your heart out."

So Ted was painting. Probably helping Oliver out every day just so he could avoid being with her.

"He's so talented. When I saw the beach scene he did of you and the dog, I was utterly amazed. Oliver offered to buy it, he liked it so much. But Ted refused—said it wasn't for sale."

Caroline's head shot up. Ted was an artist! He'd never said a word to her, not a word. So that was what he did with his time. And he'd shown Anne his work, but not her. An unbearable weight pressed against her heart, and she swallowed back the bitter taste of discouragement. "He's wonderful," she agreed weakly.

"Do you have time for coffee?"

"Not today, Anne. Sorry."

"Thanks again for the salmon."

With her hands buried deep inside her pockets, Caroline started walking along the top of the bluff. If Ted was painting, he was probably doing it from this vantage point.

"Caroline!" Anne called, pointing in the opposite direction. "Ted's over that way."

"Of course, thanks," she returned, and gave a brief salute.

Stranger raced on ahead. She rounded a curve in the windswept landscape and hesitated when she saw Ted. He was so caught up in what he was doing that he didn't notice her until she was only a few feet away. When he did see her, he glanced up and a look of incredible guilt masked his features.

"Is anything wrong?" he asked.

"No." She laced her fingers in front of her and looked out over the beach below. The cottage was in clear sight, and there was a long stretch of beach on either side, so that no matter where she walked, he could see her. "It's lovely from up here, isn't it?"

"Yes," he said and swallowed. "It is."

"I hope I'm not interrupting you," she lied.

"No, not at all." He set his easel aside and stood so that he was blocking her view of the canvas.

Caroline got the message louder than if he'd shouted it. He didn't want her looking at his painting any more than he wanted her to be there. "I just came up to say hello, and—and now that I've done that I'll be on my way."

"You can stay if you want."

She didn't believe a word of his insincere invitation. "No thanks. I've…I've got things to do at the cottage." Like count dust particles and watch the faucet drip.

"I'll be down in time for dinner."

Her answer was a hurried nod as she turned sharply and retreated with quick-paced steps that led her away from him with such haste that she nearly slipped on the path leading down the bluff to the cottage.

Stranger elected to stay with Ted, seeming to sense her troubled mood and her desire to be alone. The pain of Ted's simple deception hurt so much she could hardly bear it.

All this time that they'd been together, she'd been open and honest with him. She trusted him implicitly. While waiting for him to make his moves in chess, she'd shared her dreams and all the things that were important to her. One night in particular, when neither of them had been sleepy, they'd sat in front of the fireplace, drinking spiced apple cider. They'd ended up talking away half the night. She had never felt closer to anyone. That night had convinced her that what she felt for Ted was a woman's love, a love that was meant to last a lifetime. Unwittingly she'd given him her heart that night, handed it to him on a silver platter. Not until now did she realize that she'd been the one doing all the talking. He had shared a little about his life; he'd spoken of his job and a few other unimportant items but revealed little about himself. He certainly hadn't mentioned the fact that he painted or even that he appreciated art. She'd admired the canvases on his apartment walls and realized with a flash of renewed pain that he'd probably done those, as well. Anne was right. Ted was a talented artist.

He found her about four-thirty, sitting on the beach, looking out over the pounding surf. He lowered himself beside her, but she didn't acknowledge his presence.

"You're looking thoughtful."

"I'm bored," she murmured. "I want to go home."

He forcefully expelled his breath. "Caroline, I'm sorry, but we can't."

He'd probably been talking to Randolph again and not telling her about it. Ted liked keeping secrets.

"Not we—me! I'm the one who's going."

"What brought this on?"

Staring straight ahead, yet blind to the beauty that lay before her, Caroline shook her head. "Eight days stuck in a cottage with no contact with the outside world is enough for anyone to endure."

"I thought you liked it here," he countered sharply. "I had the impression you were having a good time."

She leaned back, pressing her weight onto the palms of her hands, and raised her face to the sky. "I told you before I was a good actress."

"So this whole time together was all an act." A thread of steel ran through his words.

"What else?" She could feel the hard flint of his eyes drilling into her.

"I don't believe that, Caroline, not for a minute."

She gave an indifferent shrug. "Think what you want, but I'm leaving."

"No you aren't."

Clenching her jaw so hard that her teeth hurt, she refused to argue. She would leave. Finding someplace else, any place away from Ted, was essential. He had discovered a place within her where only he could cause her pain. If he'd wanted to punish her for the sins of her youth, he'd succeeded. She'd never felt so cold and alone, so emotionally drained or unloved. She had given him a part of herself that she had never before shared, only to learn that he didn't trust her enough to trust her with that same part of himself.

When she chanced a look at Ted, his expression of mixed anger and bewilderment tugged at her heart. The best thing for them both would be for her to leave as quickly as possible before they continued to hurt each other.

"I'll go wash up for dinner," he announced, rolling to his feet with subtle ease.

She refused to look up at him. "I didn't cook anything."

"I'll do it, then."

"Do whatever you want, but only cook for one."

He ignored the gibe. "Come on."

"Where?"

"You're coming to the house with me."

"I thought you said you were going to fix your own dinner?"

"I am, but I don't want you out here alone."

"Why not? You leave me alone every day."

His hand under her arm roughly pulled her up from the sand. "I'm not going to argue with you. You're coming with me."

Jerking her arm aside to free herself from his touch, she took a step backward. Stranger gave the two of them an odd look, tilting his head, unaccustomed to their raised voices.

"You're confusing the dog," she said.

"The dog?" Ted shot back. "You're confusing *me*."

"Good." Maybe he would feel some of the turmoil that was troubling her. Trying to give an impression of apathy, she rubbed the sandy grit from her hands, feeling more wretched every second.

"Good?" Ted exploded. "Why do you want to do this to me? Just what kind of game are you playing?"

"I'm not playing a game. I just want out." To her horror, her voice cracked and tears welled up, brightening her eyes. She shoved her hands in her pockets and started toward the cottage.

"Caroline."

She quickened her pace.

"Caroline, stop! You're going to listen to me for once."

"I'm through listening!" she shouted, wiping away a tear and fighting to hold back the others. When she heard his footsteps behind her, she started to run. She didn't have any destination in mind, she only knew she had to escape.

His hand on her shoulder whirled her around, throwing her off balance. A cry of alarm slid from her throat as she went tumbling toward the sand. Ted wrapped his arms around her and twisted so that he accepted the brunt of the fall. Quickly he changed positions so that she was half-pinned beneath him.

"Are you all right?"

A scalding tear rolled from the corner of her eye, and she averted her face. "Yes." Her voice was the weakest of whispers.

Gently, with infinite patience, he wiped the maverick tear from her cheek. His hands were trembling slightly as he cupped her face. "Caroline," he whispered with such tenderness that fresh tears misted her eyes. "Why are you crying?"

Unable to answer him, she slowly shook her head, wanting to escape and in the same heartbeat wanting him to hold her forever.

"I don't think I've ever seen you upset like this." He smoothed the hair from her face. "You've got to be the bravest, gutsiest woman I've ever known. It's not like you to cry."

"What do you care if I cry?" she sniffled, shocked at how unnatural her voice sounded.

"Trust me, I care."

Not believing him, she closed her eyes and turned her face away from his penetrating gaze. Her hands found his shoulders and she tried to push him away, but he wouldn't let her.

"Caroline," he groaned in frustration. "I care. I've always cared about you. I want you so much it's tying me up in knots so tight I think…" He didn't finish as his mouth crushed down on hers, kissing her with a searing hunger that left her breathless and light-headed.

"Ted," she groaned, "Don't, please don't." Having him touch and kiss her made leaving all the more impossible, and she had to go. For her sanity, she had to get away from him before he claimed any more of her. She'd already given him her heart.

"I've wanted to do that every minute of every day." Again his mouth claimed hers, tasting, moving, licking, until she feared she would go mad with wanting him.

"Ted, no…you said…" But her protest grew weaker with every word.

He cut off her protest by pressing his lips against hers, tasting them as though they were flavored with the sweetest honey. The urgency was gone, replaced with a gentleness that melted her bones. She felt soft and loved, and he was male and hard. Opposites. Mismatched. Different.

And yet perfect for each other.

But not perfect enough for him to share a part of himself, she remembered. No, he didn't need her—not nearly enough. With a strength she didn't know she possessed, she pushed against his shoulder, breaking the contact.

Stunned, he sat up, while she remained on the sandy beach, lying perfectly still. Every part of her throbbed with longing until holding back the tears was impossible. She covered her face with her hands.

"I thought you said you wanted me?"

"No," she whispered, sitting up beside him. She looped her arms around her knees and took deep, even breaths to calm her heart.

The muscles in his jaw knotted. "That wasn't the impression you gave me the other night when you invited me to your bed."

"That was the other night." Another lifetime, when she'd felt they'd had a chance.

"And this is now?" he asked with heavy sarcasm.

"Right."

"You don't know what you want, do you? Everything is a game. It doesn't matter who's caught up in your—"

Caroline had heard enough. She put out a hand to stop him from talking, and then, with a burst of energy she struggled to her feet and rushed inside the cottage. Stranger was lying beside the fireplace, waiting for her.

"You stay here with Ted," she told the dog as she hurried into the lone bedroom and dragged out her empty suitcase.

"I told you I wouldn't let you go," Ted said, his large frame blocking the doorway between the bedroom and the living room.

"You don't have any choice. Please, Ted," she pleaded. "I don't want to argue with you over this. I'm leaving."

"But why now?" he asked firmly. "What makes today any different from yesterday?"

She could hardly tell him the truth, that her heart was breaking a little bit more every day as it became clear that he would never feel about her as she felt about him. "Because I'm bored, and if I spend one more minute cooped up in this place I'll go crazy," she lied.

Ted ran his fingers through his hair in agitation and then curled his hand around the back of his neck. "I'm sorry. I guess I haven't been very good company."

"That's not it. For Tedious Ted, I'd say you did a fine job, but I want out. Now." Delaying the inevitable would only prolong the pain. She opened the suitcase and began dumping her clothes inside.

"I'm sorry, Caroline, but I can't let you go."

"You don't have any choice." She would have thought he knew her better than to lay such a challenge at her feet.

"If I need to, I'll tie you up."

"You'll have to."

"I won't have any qualms about doing it."

Her eyes sparked with determination. "You'll have to catch me first."

Ted's gaze hardened. "I can't believe you're doing this."

"Believe it," she said, then slammed the suitcase shut and swung it off the bed.

A loud knock at the front door diverted their attention.

"Stay here," Ted commanded. He checked the window before swinging open the door. "Hello, Oliver, what can I do for you?"

"There's a call for you. Detective Randolph."

Tossing a look over his shoulder at Caroline, Ted nodded. "I'll be right there." He closed the door and turned to face her.

"Go answer your important call."

"I want your promise you won't try to sneak out of here while I'm on the phone."

Her mouth thinned to a brittle line. "My promise?" He had no right to bring up promises. He'd said he wouldn't touch her, and then he'd kissed her until she'd thought she would die from wanting him. Childishly she crossed her fingers behind her back in an effort to negate her words.

"Caroline, promise me you won't try to leave. Either do that or I'm dragging you up that path with me."

"All right, I won't leave." Her heart ached with the lie.

His facial muscles relaxed. "Thank you. I'll be down to let you know what's happening as fast as I can."

It didn't matter, because the minute he was safely out of sight she was leaving. She didn't like breaking her word, but he had forced her into it.

Emotion clouded her eyes. Checking her purse for

cash and credit cards, she decided the best thing to do was to take her chances walking along the beach. For the first few hours she would need to avoid the highway. Eventually she could find a town and rent a car.

She paused only long enough to say goodbye to Stranger and assure the dog that Ted would be good to him.

Her heart tightened as she took one last look around the cottage. She would always remember these days with Ted as a special time in her life.

She wasn't more than a few feet out of the door when a shadowy figure moved from behind a large rock.

Her heart rose to her throat, and fear coated the inside of her mouth, as the brawny, angry man she'd seen in the courtroom with Joan MacIntosh stepped directly in front of her.

Ten

Caroline felt her panic rise. She was alone and defense-less. She'd intentionally left Stranger inside, afraid that the dog would follow her down the beach. Ted and Oli-ver wouldn't hear her cries, and, from the size of this man, she doubted that she could outrun him. Her hands felt weak, and she dropped her suitcase to the sand.

He seemed to sense her fear and took a step toward her.

Raising her hands defensively, she met his glare head-on. "I would advise you to leave now. I've taken karate lessons," she said with as much bravado as her thumping heart would allow. She didn't mention that she'd quit after three classes. Her breathing was shal-low as she edged backward with small steps, praying he wouldn't notice that she was working her way toward the bluff. If he raced after her, she would have more of an opportunity to escape. At least if she got above him, she would be able to kick at him. In addition, there was a chance Ted would hear what was happening. Some-how, some way, she had to warn him. Otherwise he would come down the bluff to tell her what was going on and walk into a trap.

The man shifted slightly, and his dark shape was outlined by the sun, making it impossible for her to see his face clearly. He looked around, but she couldn't tell what he was thinking. Why had she left Stranger in the cottage? She wanted to reason with her attacker, plead for him to understand, but alarm clogged her throat, and the words tangled helplessly on the end of her tongue.

"Where's Ted Thomasson?"

The heel of her tennis shoe hit the edge of the bottom step, and with a frenzy born of fear and determination she turned, grabbed a handful of sand and threw it in his face. Taking the creaky wooden stairs two at a time, she ran from him, screaming for Ted at the top of her voice.

"Ted! Ted!"

She heard Stranger begin barking wildly and scratching at the front door to get out.

"Caroline!" Miraculously, Ted appeared at the top of the bluff.

"He's here!" she cried. "He found us!" She was trapped between the two men, positioned halfway up the stairs. She turned toward Joan MacIntosh's companion. From this height, she could better see the bulky man. He looked surprised, almost stunned.

Ted raced down the bluff to Caroline's side. "If you've touched a hair on her head," he called to the other man, who hadn't moved, "you'll pay." He put his arm around her, his fingers biting into her side. "Are you all right?" he whispered near her ear.

"Fine, I think," she whispered back.

He attempted to step in front of her, but she wouldn't let him.

"Caroline," Ted groaned with frustration as they juggled for position. "Let me by."

"No," she argued, stepping one way and then another on the narrow stair, blocking him.

"If you two would stop being so willing to die for each other, maybe you could listen to what I've come to say."

"You listen!" Ted shouted, placing his hands on Caroline's shoulders and holding her still. "I just finished talking to Detective Charles Randolph from the Seattle police department. They've caught the man who's responsible for the attacks."

"Was it Nelson Bergstrom?" She twisted around, needing to know.

Ted didn't seem to hear her; his gaze was focused on the man below. She returned her attention to him as well.

"I know!" he shouted up at them. "I've come to try to make amends to you for everything I've done."

"You mean you don't want to kill us?" she asked, her tensed muscles relaxing in relief.

"Don't act so disappointed," Ted said in a low murmur as he smoothly altered their positions so that he stood directly in front of her.

"So you're the one who kept calling us?" Ted asked.

"Yes." The stranger laced his fingers together in front of him and looked almost boyish as his eyes shone with regret. "And I was the one who spray-painted the outside of your apartment and made those threats." He swallowed and lowered his chin. "I want you to know that I'll pay for any damage."

"We can discuss that later," Ted replied. "For now, it would be best if you returned to Seattle. I'll contact you once we return."

"I *am* sorry."

Caroline felt compassion swelling in her. "I can understand how you felt," she told him, and was rewarded with a feeble smile.

"It's the most helpless feeling in the world to have something like that happen to the person you love most in the world. However, that doesn't make up for the things I did to the two of you. Venting my anger and frustration on you was wrong."

"I understand, and I accept your apology," she said.

"Thank you for that. But I'm ready to pay for what I did, even if that means going to jail. I deserve it for having put you two through so much. If it's any consolation now, I want you to know I didn't mean any of those threats. That's all they were—empty threats."

"It took courage to come here and face us."

"I had to do something," the man continued. "You can imagine how I felt when the police contacted Joan. The attacker made a full confession. If it had been up to me, I would have condemned an innocent man."

"We did the right thing to let Nelson Bergstrom off," Ted informed her—needlessly, since she'd already figured that out.

"Oh, thank God." Relief washed through her until it overflowed. The guilt she'd experienced when another woman was attacked had been overwhelming. She'd tried to convince herself that following her conscience was the important thing. But that knowledge hadn't relieved the weight of the albatross that had hung around her neck—until now.

"I'll be leaving now. When you want to contact me back in Seattle, the name's John MacIntosh." He turned away and started walking down the beach.

"John!" Ted called, stopping him. "How did you know where to find us?"

Caroline had been wondering the same thing herself.

"Miss Lomax's neighbor told me the address."

"I see," Ted said slowly.

His look narrowed, cutting into Caroline as she searched for the words to exonerate herself. "I gave it to her so she could mail the salmon to—"

"What salmon?"

"—Anne and Oliver as a thank-you for all they'd done."

"You told someone where we were?"

"Just Mrs. Murphy, but I assumed that—"

"I can't believe you'd do something so incredibly stupid. So...insane."

"Stupid?" she sputtered almost incoherently, her temper rising. "The dumbest, most insane thing I've ever done is take this crazy trip with you."

"I couldn't agree with you more." Ted stalked down the stairs, leaving her standing there, feeling both humiliated and ashamed. All right, she would concede that giving Mrs. Murphy their address wasn't the smartest thing she'd done in her life, but it was far saner than falling in love with Ted.

He stopped outside the cottage doorway when

he found her suitcase in the sand. He hesitated, as if stunned, and a renewed sense of guilt filled her.

He turned and gave her a look of such utter contempt that she knew she would remember it the rest of her life. "So you were planning to leave anyway." He stopped to study her flushed, guilt-ridden face. "Even after you'd given me your word."

"Yes," she admitted, and her chin rose a notch. "Not that it matters anymore. Now that everything's been settled, there's no reason for me to stay." Her lips trembled as she struggled to regain her composure. Without knowing why, she followed Ted inside the cottage and watched as he took out his own suitcase and began to pack. His movements were short and jerky, as if he couldn't finish the task fast enough. He was normally so organized and neat, but now he merely stuffed the clothes inside, then slammed the lid closed.

"I'll tell the Bryants we're leaving."

"Not together we're not," she corrected him briskly. "I'm not going back to Seattle."

"Just where do you plan to go?"

"San Francisco." The name came from the top of her head. Her parents' house would be empty and cold, but she couldn't remain with Ted. She had too much pride for that, and too little self-control. He had to know she loved him. She'd done everything she could to prove she wanted to be his—everything except propose marriage. From the things she'd realized lately, she recognized that he simply didn't want her. The knowledge seared a hole into her heart. She would recover, she told herself repeatedly as she picked up her suitcase and followed him up the creaky old stairs. But her heart refused to listen.

Caroline had assumed that familiar surroundings would lessen the void in her soul. She was wrong. A three-day stint alone in San Francisco had taught her that she couldn't return home like a little girl anymore. She was a woman now, with a woman's hurts. She'd wandered aimlessly around the empty house, and all she could think about was Ted.

He had dropped her off at the airstrip in Brookings and left almost immediately afterward, with Stranger looking forlornly at her from the backseat of the car. She hadn't heard from him since, not that she'd really expected to.

Her return to Seattle a couple of weeks ago had been uneventful. She found part-time employment the first week. Having a job lent purpose to her days and proved to be her salvation.

Her mother telephoned, full of enthusiasm after they returned from China, but for the first time in her adult life, Caroline couldn't bare her soul to her mother.

"For a minute when I walked in the door, I thought you might have come for a visit."

"I *was* in San Francisco, Mom."

"When? Why?"

"It's a long story."

Her mother seemed to sense that Caroline wasn't eager to share the events of her latest escapade. "You don't sound like yourself, honey. Is something wrong?"

"What could possibly be wrong? I've got the very

thing I've always wanted. I'm working as a chef and loving it."

"But you don't sound happy."

"I'm...just tired, that's all."

"Have you seen any more of Ted Thomasson?"

The pain was so intense that Caroline hesitated before speaking. "No, not for a couple of weeks now." Two weeks, four days and twenty-one hours, she mentally calculated, glancing at her watch.

An awkward silence followed. "Well, I just wanted you to know that your father and I arrived back home safely, and that China was wonderful."

"I'm pleased you're home, Mom. Thanks for calling. I'll give you a ring later in the week."

"Caroline, don't you want to tell your father about your job?"

"You can go ahead and tell him, if you want to."

It wasn't until she hung up that she realized her mistake. At any other time in her life, she would have been puffed up like a bull frog at having achieved her goal of working in a restaurant kitchen. Now her profession was nothing more than a means to fill the empty days.

She'd barely finished the conversation with her mother when a hard knock sounded against her front door. She glanced at it, inexplicably knowing in her heart that Ted stood on the other side. The entire time she'd been back, she had subconsciously been waiting to hear from him. Now, like a coward, she waited until the hard knock was repeated. Forcing a brittle smile to her lips, she finally turned the lock and opened the door.

"Hello, Caroline." His eyes caressed her like a warm, golden flame.

"Hello, Ted. How are you?" Pride demanded that she not reveal any of the emotional pain these weeks apart had cost her. He looked wonderful. Everything she'd remembered about him seemed even more pronounced now. His features were even more rugged and compelling. His eyes were an even deeper shade of blue, if that were possible. The strong, well-shaped mouth that had shown her such pleasure slanted into a half smile.

"I brought your kite and your other things."

The instant she'd seen what he was carrying, she had realized with a sinking heart that the reason for his visit wasn't personal. "How's Stranger?"

"Fine. My apartment doesn't allow pets, so I had to find a home for him."

"You gave Stranger away?" She breathed in sharply, unbelievably hurt that he would so callously give up their dog.

"Could you take him?"

Her apartment building had the same restriction. "No," she admitted, subdued. "You...did the right thing. Is he happy in his new home?"

"Very."

Her smile wavered, and she murmured with a breathless catch in her voice, "Then that's what counts." Realizing that she had left him standing in the doorway, she hurriedly stepped aside. "Come in, please."

"Where do you want me to put all this?"

"The kitchen counter will be fine. Thanks." She threaded her fingers together so tightly that they ached. She knew her features were strained with the burden of maintaining an expression of poise. She tried unsuccessfully to relax.

"Do you still make that fancy coffee?" he asked softly.

"Yes…would you like a cup?"

"If you have the time."

Time was something she had plenty of these days. Time to remember how his mouth tasted on hers. Time to recall the velvet smoothness of his touch and how well their bodies fit together. Time to compile a list of regrets that was longer than a rich kid's Christmas list.

Their gazes held for several seconds. "Yes, I have the time," she murmured at last, breaking eye contact.

He followed her into the kitchen. "How have you been?"

"Wonderful," she lied with practiced ease. "I have a job. It's only afternoons for now, but I'm hoping that it'll work into full time later this summer." Actually, she'd taken the first job that was offered, even though she would have preferred a regular forty-hour work schedule. But anything was better than moping around the house day after day.

"I'm pleased things are working out for you."

"What about you?" She couldn't look at him, knowing it would be too painful.

"I've been fine," he supplied, leaning against the kitchen counter.

She put as much space between them as possible in the cozy kitchen. Her gaze centered on the glass pot, praying the water would boil quickly.

"We need to talk," he said quietly. "You know that, don't you, Caroline?"

She gripped the counter so hard it threatened to break

her neatly trimmed nails. "About what?" Wildly she looked away as her heart jammed in her throat.

"About us."

"Us?" She forced a laugh that sounded amazingly like a restrained sob. "Within two hours we were at each other's throats. How can you even suggest there's an 'us'?"

"That's not the way I remember it."

The minute the coffee finished brewing, she filled two cups and handed him one. He immediately set it on the counter. "Coffee was only an excuse, and you know it."

She took a quick step away from him. "I wish you'd said something before I went through the trouble of making it."

"No you don't."

Without her noticing, he had moved closer to her, trapping her in a corner. Mere inches separated them. Her breathing had become so shallow it was nearly nonexistent.

"I thought I'd give myself time to sort out my feelings." He lifted the luxurious silky auburn curls away from the side of her neck. Her pulse hammered wildly as his thumb stroked her skin. "Every time I was close to you, I had to fight to keep myself from kissing you."

Magnetically, Caroline's gaze was drawn to his eyes. "It's only natural that under the circumstances we—we feel these—these strong physical attractions."

"Problem is," Ted said softly, his breath caressing her face, "I'm experiencing the same things now, only even more powerfully, more intensely, than ever."

"That can't be true," she insisted, too afraid to believe him and seeking an escape. Abruptly she turned and reached for her coffee, nearly scalding her lips as she took a sip. She clenched the mug with both hands. "What we had on the beach wasn't real," she said in a falsely cheerful voice. "You warned me that things would look different once we returned to Seattle, and now I'm forced to admit that they do."

"Caroline," he said her name with a wealth of frustration. "Don't lie to me again."

"Who's lying?" Her voice cracked, and she struggled to hold back stinging tears as she chewed on the corner of her bottom lip.

"Is your pride worth so much to you?"

Unable to answer him, she stared into the black depth of the coffee mug.

"Maybe we should experiment."

"Experiment?"

"Let me kiss you a couple of times and see how you feel." He took the mug from her hands and set it on the counter.

"There isn't any need. I know what I feel," she argued, knowing that if he touched her, she would be lost. With her hands behind her, guiding her, she edged her way along the kitchen wall.

"It may be the only way," he continued, undaunted. "It seems that we've come to different conclusions here. There's too much at stake for me to let you pass judgment so lightly."

"I know how I feel."

"I'm sure you do." He cupped her shoulders with his hands, halting her progress. "I just don't think you're being honest with yourself—or me—about your feelings."

"Ted, please don't."

"I have to," he breathed, bending toward her.

She averted her mouth, so that his lips brushed her cheek. "Please," she whispered. "It won't do any good."

His hands slid from her shoulders up her neck to her chin, tilting her face to receive his kiss. The pressure of his mouth was as light as the morning sun touching the earth. Soon the magnetic desire that was ever-present between them urged their mouths together in a kiss that left Caroline clinging to the counter to stay upright.

"Well?" he asked hoarsely, spreading kisses around her face, pausing at her temple.

She kept her eyes pinched shut. "That was...very... nice."

"Nice?" His hands slid around her waist, bringing her to him until she was pressed hard against his chest. "It was more than nice."

"No," she offered weakly, pushing against him.

He kissed her again, only this time his lips stayed and moved and urged and tested. Caroline was lost. Her arms rose from his chest to link around his neck, so that she was arched against him. Softly, she moaned, unable to hold back any longer, clinging to him, weak with longing and desire. Again and again his mouth met hers, until she saw a glimpse of heaven and far, far beyond.

When he broke the contact, she buried her face in the curve of his neck. The irregular pounding of his heart echoed hers.

"Does that convince you?"

"It tells me that we have a strong physical attraction," she answered, breathless and weak.

"More than that. What we share is spiritual."

"No." She tried to deny him, but her feeble protest was broken off when he raised his mouth to hers and kissed her again. The kiss was tempestuous, earth-shattering.

"Don't argue," he said with a guttural moan. "I love you, Caroline. I want us to marry and give Stranger a home."

"I thought you said you gave him away." It was far easier to discuss the dog than to think about the first part of his statement.

"No, I didn't." Tenderly he kissed the bridge of her nose, as if he couldn't get enough of the feel of her. "I said I found him a home. And I have. Ours."

"Oh." She pressed her forehead to the center of his chest as she took in everything he was saying. She loved him. Dear Lord, she loved him until she thought she would die without him. But sometimes love wasn't enough. "I—I don't think anyone should base something as important as marriage on anything as flimsy as making a home for a stray dog."

"I love you," he whispered against her hair. "I think I've loved you from the time I first saw you."

Slowly she raised her eyes so that she could see the tenderness in his expression and believe what he was saying. Her fingertips traced the angular line of his jaw.

"Why didn't you tell me?"

"That I loved you? Honey, surely you can understand why, given the—"

Her fingers across his lips stopped him. "You're an artist, aren't you?"

He blinked and captured her hand, then kissed it. "So that's it." He forced the air from his lungs. "I should have told you, but to be honest, I was wary. I was afraid that if you saw my work, you'd think it was another one of my interests, like dancing lessons, that always made you think less of me."

"You thought that of me?" she asked, forcibly trying to break free. It hurt to believe that he saw her as so insensitive.

"Listen to me." His hold tightened, not allowing her out of his embrace. "That was only in the beginning, before I realized how much you'd changed. Later, I thought I'd surprise you with the painting and make it a wedding gift."

"That's why you didn't want me to see it that day on the bluff?"

He wove his hand into her hair, running her fingers through her curls. "The only reason."

"Oh, Ted." She pressed her head over his heart, hugging him hard. "I was so hurt... I'd talked for days and days, sharing the most personal parts of my life with you. And when...when I saw that there was a part of yourself that you hid from me, I felt terrible. I lied about being bored. I loved being with you every minute that we were together. It nearly killed me to leave you."

"I knew you were lying all along. What I couldn't figure out was why."

"I lied because I thought you didn't care. But... how did you know?" She had thought she'd given an Academy Award–winning performance.

"No one could shine with as much happiness as you did and be faking it," he replied, smiling tenderly.

She closed her eyes, holding on to the rapture his words spread through her soul. "You're sure you want to marry me? I'm stubborn as a mule, contrary, proud—"

"Headstrong, reckless and overbearing," he interrupted with a chuckle. "But you're also warm, loving, creative and so many other wonderful things that it will take me a lifetime to discover them all."

"I'll marry you, Ted Thomasson, whenever you want."

His gaze took in her happiness. "We're going to have some fantastic children, Caroline Lomax."

They kissed lightly, and Caroline grinned. "I think you may be right," she whispered, bringing his mouth down to hers.

* * * * *

ANY SUNDAY

In memory of Darlene Layman
My treasured friend through the years.

One

Marjorie Majors's deep brown eyes widened as a flash of burning pain shot through her side. Feeling hot and flushed again, she guessed she was running a fever. Her smile was decidedly forced as she walked across the showroom floor, weaving her way around the shiny new Mercedes while lightly pressing her hand against her hipbone. She'd thought that if she ignored the throbbing ache, this unexplained malady would vanish on its own. So far her reasoning hadn't worked, though, and the mysterious discomfort had persisted for days.

"Is your side hurting you again?" Lydia Mason, the title and license clerk for Dixon Motors, called from behind the front counter.

"A little." Now that had to be the understatement of the week, Marjorie mused. The shooting pain had been coming and going all day with no real rhyme or reason. She should have known she wasn't going to be able to fool Lydia. Her friend had a nose for news. Little transpired at Dixon Motors without Lydia knowing about it.

"Honestly, Marjorie, why don't you just see a doctor?"

"I'm fine," she protested. "Besides, I don't have a doctor."

Lydia, who stood barely five feet tall and wore heels that increased her height an additional two inches, moved around the counter. Her mouth was pinched into a tight line of determination. "But you haven't been feeling good all week."

"Has it been that long?"

"Longer, I suspect," Lydia murmured, shaking her head. "Listen, no one is going to think less of you for needing a doctor, for heaven's sake. Just because you're one of only three female salespeople here, that doesn't mean you have to behave like Joan of Arc."

"But it's just a little stomachache."

"What did you have for lunch?"

Marjorie shrugged noncommittally, preferring not to lie. A wry smile lifted the corners of her full mouth as she pretended to survey the parking lot, hoping a prospective buyer would magically appear so she would have an excuse to drop the conversation. She didn't want to admit that with her stomach acting up, she hadn't bothered to eat lunch. And now that she thought about it, breakfast hadn't appealed to her, either.

"You didn't have any lunch, did you?" Lydia challenged.

"I didn't have time since…"

"That's it, Marjorie—that's the final straw. I'm making you an appointment with my gynecologist."

"You're what?"

"You heard me." Lydia didn't wait for an argument.

With her manicured fingernails, she flipped the hair that had fallen across her cheek to the back of her shoulder and marched around the counter with the authority of a marine drill sergeant.

"Don't call a gynecologist! That's crazy. I don't need a woman's doctor—an internist maybe…"

Ignoring Marjorie's protest, Lydia pressed the telephone receiver to her ear and turned her back to her friend. "What's crazy," she said, twisting her head around, her eyes sparking with impatience, "is suffering for days because you're afraid to see a doctor."

"I am not afraid! And a gynecologist is the last person I want to see." Marjorie couldn't seem to get it through her friend's thick skull that a queasy stomach was unworthy of all this fuss. From the way Lydia was behaving, Marjorie fully expected her friend to dial 911 to report a minor pain that came and went without warning. She'd lived with it for the last few days—a little longer wasn't going to matter. More than likely it would disappear as quickly and unexpectedly as it had come. Or so she continued to hope.

"Today, if possible." Lydia spoke firmly into the telephone. She placed her hand over the receiver and turned to Marjorie. "Listen, I had a friend once with similar symptoms, and it ended up being female problems and—" She broke off abruptly. "Five o'clock would be fine. Thanks, Mary."

Although Marjorie knew it wouldn't do any good, she tried again. "Lydia…"

The telephone was replaced in its cradle before Lydia turned around. "And something else. Dr. Sam isn't your run-of-the-mill doctor. He's wonderful! If you need to see someone else, he'll refer you, so stop looking so worried."

"But I'm sure this pain is nothing."

"Then checking it out won't be any big deal. Right?" Marjorie shrugged.

"He has an opening this afternoon at five."

"His name is Dr. Sam?" Now Marjorie had heard everything. "Will Nurse Jane be there, too?"

"He's really terrific," Lydia announced with a loud sigh, obviously choosing to ignore Marjorie's sarcasm. "I think I fell in love with him in the delivery room just before Jimmy was born. He was so gentle and understanding when I was in labor. He made me feel like I was the most noble, heroic woman in the world for enduring the pain of childbirth."

"Hey, I've got a stomachache. I'm not looking to find Prince Charming."

"But he's handsome, too."

"Does Dr. Sam have a last name?" She wasn't bothered by the thought of seeing a physician, exactly, but the simple truth was that Marjorie hated relying on anyone else. She could take care of herself very well, and relying on another person went against her fiercely independent nature.

"His name is really Sam Bretton, but everyone calls him Dr. Sam."

Marjorie rolled her eyes toward the ceiling. "I don't know if I can trust a man who sounds like he keeps an office on Sesame Street."

"Wait and see," Lydia claimed, writing out directions to the medical center on a piece of paper and ripping it free of the tablet before handing it over to Marjorie. "He's marvelous—trust me."

Marjorie folded the paper in half and stuck it inside her purse. If nothing else, it would be interesting to meet the guy. Lydia wasn't generally free with her praise, yet she hadn't been able to say enough good things about this guy.

"You'll like him, I promise," Lydia added.

Marjorie made a barely perceptible movement of her head, as if to say it made no difference to her how she felt about him. She didn't care what he looked like as long as he could give her something for this blasted pain.

At precisely ten minutes to five, Marjorie pulled into the parking lot of the large medical complex north of Tacoma General Hospital. The ache that had troubled her most of the day had vanished, just as she'd known it would, and she felt better generally. If she'd had a fever earlier, she was convinced it was gone now. Briefly she toyed with the idea of heading back to her apartment and forgetting the whole thing, but that would be irresponsible, and if Marjorie knew anything, it was the meaning of responsibility. Besides, her friend would be furious with her for canceling at the last moment.

Two other women were seated in the waiting room. Both were in the advanced stages of pregnancy. One sat with her hands resting on her protruding belly, looking content, while the other was knitting. The thick needles, encased in a pastel shade of yarn, moved furiously. Their smiles were friendly as Marjorie stepped up to the reception desk to announce her arrival. An older, gray-haired woman asked Marjorie to fill out several forms and handed her a clipboard.

Marjorie took it and located a seat in the corner beside a dying houseplant. The yellowish leaves did little to boost her confidence in this unknown physician.

"Is this the first time you've seen Dr. Sam?" one of the soon-to-be-mothers asked.

Marjorie nodded. "My friend recommended him."

"He's absolutely wonderful."

"And good-looking to boot," the knitter added.

"Real good-looking!"

The two pregnant women eyed each other and shared a smile.

"I suppose all women fall in love with their doctors," the woman with the knitting needles commented, "but I've never known a man who's as caring as Dr. Sam is."

"I'm not pregnant." Marjorie didn't know why she felt it was necessary to tell them that. This physician might do wonders with mothers-to-be, but all Marjorie cared about was his expertise with sharp, persistent pains.

"You don't have to be pregnant," the two were quick to assure her.

"Good." Marjorie completed the information sheets and returned them to the receptionist, then subtly glanced at her watch. She hadn't experienced any real discomfort in hours and was beginning to feel like a phony. Again, the thought of skipping out of the appointment sprang to mind. Sheer stupidity, of course. If nothing else, it would be interesting to stick around and meet this doctor who seemed to be a paragon of virtue. From what Lydia and the two patients in the waiting room had said, Dr. Sam Bretton was a cross between Brad Pitt and Mother Teresa.

"It'll only be a few minutes," the receptionist told her.

"No problem," Marjorie answered softly, wondering if the woman had read her mind.

A few minutes turned out to be fifteen. Marjorie was escorted into a small cubicle by a nurse who was dressed as though she were shooting a scene from a daytime soap opera. Her gray hair was perfectly styled in a bouffant, and even after a full day in the office, not a single strand was out of place.

Marjorie stopped just inside the room, her mind whirling. She'd been in her teens when she'd last seen a physician. Over the years there'd been minor bouts with the flu and a bad cold now and again, but overall she'd been incredibly healthy. There might have been times when she should have seen a physician and hadn't, mainly because she wasn't particularly fond of anyone poking around her body, but usually she could take care of herself just fine.

"Go ahead and have a seat," the nurse instructed, gesturing toward the upholstered examination table.

Reluctantly Marjorie walked into the room and pressed her backside against the oblong examining table, her elbows resting on top of the padded cover. She crossed her ankles as though she posed this way regularly, hoping to give the picture of utter nonchalance. Chagrined, she realized she'd failed miserably.

Thankfully the nurse didn't seem to notice. "What seems to be the problem?"

Marjorie shrugged. "A little pain in my side. I'm sure it's nothing."

"We'll let Dr. Sam decide that." The woman pulled out a digital thermometer and, before Marjorie could protest, stuck it under her tongue. Motioning with her hand, the nurse told Marjorie to sit on the end of the table and skillfully took her blood pressure.

"Go ahead and get undressed," the nurse said afterward. She leaned over and pulled a paper gown from a cupboard. "When you've finished, put this on. The doctor will be with you in a couple of minutes." She left, quietly closing the door.

Marjorie mumbled grumpily to herself as she pulled the paper gown over her head and sighed with disgust when the opening for her arm hung far wider than necessary. Keeping her arms tucked close to her side for fear the gown would reveal the sides of her breasts, she wrapped the tissue sheet around her waist and sat on the end of the paper-lined examination table. The whole idea of introducing herself to a man when she was nude felt ridiculous. All right, so he was a physician, but all that stood between her body and this stranger was a piece of tissue that felt as though a big sneeze would destroy it.

Her bare feet dangled, and she kicked at the air aimlessly. Her brilliant red toenails looked funny, and she absently decided to change the color. Next time she would use a more subdued shade.

Just when she had convinced herself she was wasting her time, a polite knock sounded at the door. The knob twisted, and Marjorie painted a welcoming smile on her lips, doing her best to swallow the panic that un-expectedly gripped her.

Dr. Sam Bretton entered the examination room, reading Marjorie's chart, his wide brow furrowed as he took in the information.

The first thing Marjorie noticed was his stature. Five foot seven in her stocking feet, she'd never considered herself short, but this man dwarfed her. His shoulders were broad and fit his height. His chest was deep. He wore his hair short, and his sideburns were clipped neatly around his ears. A few strands of gray at his temple provided a distinguished, sophisticated touch. He was good-looking-not strikingly handsome, but attractive enough to give credence to Lydia and the other women's claims. His eyes were a deep, dark shade of brown and the gentlest Marjorie had ever seen in a man. For an instant they mesmerized her into speech-lessness. A stethoscope hung from his neck and rested against his broad, muscled chest.

"Ms. Majors." Sam smiled at his newest patient. Mary, his receptionist, had come to him earlier and asked about fitting this young woman into his already-tight schedule. A friend of Lydia Mason's, Mary had said, and Sam had agreed because he was fond of Lydia. Later he'd regretted the impulse. His day had started early, and he was tired, but with one look at the wide, frightened eyes of the woman sitting on the examination table he realized he'd made the right decision. Rarely had he seen a more expressive pair of brown eyes. Marjorie Majors was as nervous as a young mother and struggling valiantly to disguise it. Her chin trembled slightly, yet she met his gaze with pride and more mettle than he'd seen in years. She resembled a lost kitten he'd once found in a rainstorm; her wide eyes were round and appealing, and she looked as though she might turn and bolt at any moment.

"Doctor." The return of her voice brought with it the reappearance of her poise and aplomb. Her chin came up with the forced determination not to let him know how nervous she was. She handed him her business card.

"I realized I forgot to put my work number on the form," she said by way of explanation.

He removed the card from her stiff fingers, read it casually and nodded before sticking it inside the folder. "Your chart states that the last time you saw a physician was at age fourteen." He grimaced; whatever was bothering her now must be traumatic for her to seek medical help. In the last ten years he'd seen everything, and now a list of possibilities ran through his mind, most of them unpleasant.

"I had an ear infection." Marjorie pointed to her right ear while her heart beat at double time. She was literally shaking. She couldn't understand why she was reacting this way. Certainly this doctor didn't frighten her. His demeanor inspired confidence, not fear.

"You're experiencing pain in your right side?"

"That's correct," Marjorie said, and her voice wobbled as she jabbered on witlessly. "I don't think it's anything to be concerned about...probably one of those common female problems. No doubt it will go away in a couple of days."

"How long has it been bothering you?"

"A few days...maybe longer," she admitted reluctantly.

His thick brows contracted into a single, dark line. "Fever?"

Marjorie nodded. "But not high. It seems to be worse at night."

"Nausea? Dizziness?"

Again Marjorie answered with a nod.

"How has your back felt?"

"Sore." She wondered how he knew that. "Is that bad?" she asked hurriedly. "I mean, I can suffer with the best of them… In fact, I have a high tolerance for pain, and if you tell me it'll simply go away, I'm sure I can get through it."

"There's no need for you to do any suffering. Go ahead and lie back." He gave her his hand to guide her into a reclining position.

His hand curved around her fingers, and Marjorie's grip was surprisingly tight. What the others had said was true: Dr. Sam did inspire faith. She only wished he would stop looking at her as though she were a pathetic, scared doe caught in a hunter's sights.

"There's no need to be nervous," he said softly. "I promise not to bite."

"It's not your teeth that bother me."

He smiled again and stepped closer to the table to stand at her side. "Are you always such a wit?"

"Only when I'm forced to introduce myself to a strange man when I'm in the nude."

"Does this happen often?" Sam couldn't believe he'd asked her that. He clamped his jaw tightly. As a physician, he had taken an oath to treat all patients equally, but this one struck a chord, and the danger of looking upon her as a warm, desirable woman was strong.

"Meet men when I'm nude? No!"

He laughed outright at that, relieved. "I guessed as much." Carefully he lifted up the tissue sheet at her waist and placed his fingers on her abdomen, suspecting he would find rigidity and tenderness at McBurney's point, halfway between the navel and the crest of the hipbone.

"Actually, I've been feeling better the last couple of hours," Marjorie said hurriedly, hoping to suggest that whatever was wrong was curing itself. His hand felt cool and soothing against her heated flesh, and she closed her eyes. However, the instant he glided his fingers to her side and pressed down, her eyes shot open at the excruciating pain searing through her like red-hot needles.

She swore loudly and jumped from the examination table. "What do you think you're doing?" she shouted, her hands crossed protectively over her stomach. The agony lingered, and she nearly doubled over with the force of it.

"Miss Majors…"

"And what were all those platitudes about not needing to suffer?"

"Miss Majors, if you'd kindly return to the table…"

"Are you crazy? So you can do that again? Forget it, buddy."

"I may be able to forget it," he said solemnly, with a hint of chastisement, "but you won't. The pain isn't going to go away. In fact, it will get worse. Much worse. You should have seen a doctor days ago."

"It's already worse, thanks to you."

"Miss Majors…"

"For heaven's sake, call me Marjorie."

"Marjorie, then. Running out of here like a terrified rabbit isn't going to make everything all right."

So he'd noticed the way she was eyeing the neat pile of her folded clothes. She wouldn't run, because that would be silly and stupid, but she couldn't keep from looking at the door longingly.

"You have an inflamed appendix."

She swallowed past the tightness in her throat. The shooting pain hadn't ebbed; if anything, it had gotten steadily worse from the moment he had touched her tender abdomen. Oh, dear heaven, her appendix. She didn't need a fortune-teller to explain what would happen next. Surgery. The sound of the word was as ominous as that of a trumpet in a funeral march.

"Your temperature is rising, and my guess is that your white cell count is sky-high," he continued. "A blood test will confirm that easily enough."

A weak smile wobbled at the corners of her mouth. "My appendix," she repeated.

Sam nodded. "Go ahead and get dressed. When you've finished, I'll have my nurse draw some blood and escort you into my office. That'll give me a few minutes to make the necessary arrangements. We'll talk, and I'll explain where we go from here."

"Okay." Her voice sounded scratchy and thin, like an ailing frog's.

He eyed her again, his gaze tender and concerned. He regretted having hurt her. The look of suppressed pain in her eyes bothered him more than he'd expected, and he tried to lend her some of his own confidence. "Don't look so worried—everything's going to be fine."

"Everything's going to be fine?" Marjorie echoed, unable to disguise her sarcasm. "Sure it is." The minute he left the room, she snapped her teeth over her bottom lip and bit down unmercifully. Her hand trembled as she brushed a thick strand of hair away from her face, and the room appeared to sway slightly. The last time she'd felt this shaky had been at her parents' funeral.

As if on cue, the nurse reappeared the minute Marjorie had completed dressing and led her into another room, where she drew blood from her arm.

While he waited for Marjorie, Sam contacted Cal Johnson, a surgeon and good friend. His instincts told him the sooner they had her in the hospital, the better. When he explained her symptoms to Cal, his friend concurred and agreed to take the case. His second telephone conversation was with a member of the staff at Tacoma General.

When Marjorie appeared in the doorway of his office, Sam saw her from the corner of his eye. She hesitated, and he motioned for her to come inside and take a seat.

"I don't think we should wait any longer," he said into the receiver. "Good. Good. Yes, I can have her over there in a half hour. I'll assist."

In an effort to keep from looking as though she were listening in on his conversation, Marjorie scanned the walls. Certificates, diplomas and service awards decorated every available spot. His desk was neat and orderly. The sure sign of a twisted mind, she mused darkly. She glanced his way again and sighed. Heavens, she hoped he wasn't discussing her! He must have been. If he felt surgery was necessary, then she would at least like a couple of days to mentally prepare herself. A week would be even better.

Marjorie's soft, expressive eyes pleaded with him, but Sam's gaze just missed meeting hers, and she realized that, although he hadn't mentioned her name, he wasn't likely to be talking about another patient.

"Sorry to keep you waiting," he said, when he'd hung up.

"No problem." She smiled, and her fingers curved around her purse in her lap.

"I was just talking to Tacoma General."

Marjorie pointed her finger over her shoulder. "Did you know that you have a dying houseplant in your waiting room?" she asked in an effort to delay the bad news she knew was coming.

"I wasn't aware of that."

"You want to operate on me, don't you?"

"We don't have a lot of options here, Marjorie. I've contacted a friend of mine. He'll be doing the actual surgery, but I'll be there, as well. Your appendix is at a dangerous stage and could burst at any time."

He said her name in a soft, caressing way that she knew would have made another woman's knees turn to tapioca pudding. Not Marjorie's. Not now. Panic was overwhelming her, dominating her thoughts and actions.

"Where's your family?" he asked in a low, reassuring voice.

"I don't have one."

The memory of the orphaned kitten returned to Sam's mind. Cold. Lost. Frightened. And vulnerable.

At his look of surprise, Marjorie hurried to explain. "No parents, that is... One sister, but she doesn't live in Washington State. Jody's attending the University of Portland."

"What about a boyfriend?"

With effort she held her head high, her chin jutting out proudly. "I've only been in Washington a few months." She was about to add that she didn't have time to date much, not when she had to earn enough money to support herself and keep her sister in school. She managed to stop in the nick of time. This man was almost a complete stranger, yet she had been about to spill her guts to him. He had a strange effect on her, and Marjorie found that oddly intimidating.

"Is there anyone you can call?"

"No." No one she felt she could trouble. She'd made it on her own this far; she could get through the operation and a lot more if necessary. "When do you want to do the surgery?"

"Soon. Cal Johnson will make that decision."

A lump worked its way up her throat. The battle to hold back the fear was nearly overwhelming. Even breathing normally had become a difficult task as she labored to appear unaffected and calm.

"So *you* won't be doing the surgery?" This was a man she could trust. Like the others, she had known that instinctively. Now he was pawning her off on another physician, and the thought was almost as terrifying as the actual operation.

"Do you think you should trust a doctor with a dying houseplant?"

"I...don't know." Marjorie realized he was attempting to help her relax, and she appreciated the effort. He really was a nice man. Lydia and the others were right about that. She envisioned him with other women, offering security and assurance. He'd chosen his profession well.

"The truth is, I may not have a green thumb, but when it comes to surgery you don't have any worries."

"Then why won't you operate on me?"

"The appendix isn't my area of expertise. Dr. Johnson has done countless appendectomies, whereas I've only done a few. I'll assist."

"But I know you." As soon as the words ran over her tongue, Marjorie realized how ridiculous they sounded. They'd met less than a half hour earlier.

"You'll do fine with Dr. Johnson."

"I suppose I will," she said without much confidence.

"I can honestly say that you're the first woman who's jumped off the examination table, ready to swing at me." His smiling eyes studied her.

"Hey, that poke hurt."

"I know, and I apologize," he answered sincerely. "I don't want you to worry about this surgery. I'll be there with you. Cal Johnson's an excellent surgeon, and there shouldn't be any problems, since we've caught this in time."

Marjorie nodded.

"I'm not going to let you down."

"You say that to all your patients, don't you?"

His eyes widened briefly. "No." He opened the top drawer and took out a single sheet of paper. "Here. Let me show you what we're going to do."

Marjorie wasn't sure she wanted to know. He must

have read the doubt in her eyes, because he added, "I learned long ago that my patients aren't nearly as nervous if they have an idea of what's going to happen."

She nodded and cocked her head so that she could see the picture he had started drawing.

"As you're probably aware, the appendix is a small pocket, from one to six inches in size." He illustrated it, dexterously moving his pencil across the sheet of paper.

Marjorie understood only a little about what he was telling her, but she nodded as though she had recently graduated from medical school and knew it all.

He talked for several minutes more, explaining where Dr. Johnson would be making the incision and what he would be doing. "Once you're admitted to the hospital, you'll undergo a series of tests, including several X rays."

"X rays? Why?"

"We want to be sure that your lungs aren't congested. No need to borrow trouble."

"I see," Marjorie commented, although she didn't really. Whatever he and the other doctors thought was fine with her.

"You'll only be in the hospital a couple of days, depending on how you feel, and you'll be back to work within three weeks."

"Three weeks," Marjorie echoed. "I can't take off that much time!"

"You don't have any choice."

"Wanna bet?" Defiantly, she slapped the challenge at him. "In case you don't realize it, a car salesperson works solely on commission. If I don't sell cars, I don't eat."

His mouth tightened momentarily. "Let's play that part by ear. No doubt you'll surprise me."

"No doubt," she echoed.

Sam rubbed the pencil between his palms. "How'd you get into car sales?"

Marjorie shrugged. "The usual way, I suppose. I started out working in a computer store four or five years back. We worked on commission, and I did well."

"That figures. So where did you go from there?"

"Boats."

"Do you know a lot about them?"

She crossed her knees, winced in an effort to hide the pain, then grinned sheepishly. Naturally he noticed, but he was kind enough not to comment. "At the time I didn't know a thing, but before long I learned everything there was to know."

"And from there it was a natural progression to cars?"

"More or less. I like selling a top-of-the-line product, so selling Mercedes sedans and sports cars was a natural next step."

He continued working the pencil back and forth across his palms. He didn't normally spend this much time with a patient, but he wanted her to feel comfortable with him. She was alone and scared to death, and it was his job to do what he could to reassure her. Success in health care had a lot to do with attitude, and he wanted Marjorie Majors to feel confident and secure about whatever lay ahead.

"I've always wanted a Mercedes," he said.

Marjorie realized he was doing everything he could to ease her fears and help her relax. It was working; the tense terror that had gripped her only moments before was slipping away.

He placed his hands against the edge of the desk and rolled back his chair. "I'll see you at Tacoma General," he said, his gaze holding hers.

"I wasn't planning to run away."

"I didn't honestly think you were."

The smile that curved his mouth did funny things to her heart rate, but Marjorie quickly dismissed the effect as having anything to do with attraction. She was grateful, that was all. Grateful—nothing less, nothing more.

Two

Marjorie felt strange. She lay on her back, staring above her as the dotted white tile loomed closer and closer, then gradually faded back into place. Her eyes narrowed, and she tried to tell herself that the ceiling wasn't actually closing in on her. This phenomenon was the result of the shot the nurse had given her a few minutes earlier to help her relax before they came to roll her into the operating room.

"How are you feeling?" Sam Bretton moved beside her gurney and placed his hand over hers.

Again Marjorie was struck by how gentle his dark eyes were. A man shouldn't possess sensitive eyes like that. In her drugged condition her imagination was running away with her, suggesting thoughts she had no right to think. She stared back at him, then blinked twice, because it seemed as though she could see straight into his heart. It was large and full, and his capacity to care and love seemed boundless.

"Marjorie?"

She pulled her gaze past the I.V. drip to Sam and

lightly shook her head in a futile effort to clear her befuddled mind. "You wouldn't believe the treatment I
got," she said, trying to disregard the strange effect of
the medication.

"You met Cal Johnson?"

She nodded. He wasn't another Sam Bretton, but he
would do, especially if Sam felt he was the right man
for the job.

"So they put you through the mill?"

His smile dazzled Marjorie, and she reminded herself
anew that at the moment her senses couldn't be trusted.
"Your call must have done the trick, because there was
a whole crew just waiting to get their hands on me the
minute I walked in the door."

"You can thank Cal for that."

"Oh sure! If you think I believe that, then there's
some swampland in Nevada that might interest me,
right?"

"Are you saying you don't trust me?" Sam's eyes
widened with feigned outrage. He liked Marjorie. Even
now, when she was dopey from the effects of medication, he found her sense of humor stimulating. Her ready
smile had wrapped itself around him the moment he'd
walked into the room. She was fresh and alive; her mind
was active, her wit lively, and her courage in difficult
circumstances was admirable.

"I'll have you know that in the last hour I've been
poked, pinched, prodded and a bunch of other disgusting things I don't even want to discuss."

His lips trembled with suppressed mirth, and he
squeezed her fingers reassuringly. "Is there anything
I can get you?"

Marjorie tried to smile, but her mouth refused to co-operate. "That sounds suspiciously like a last request."

The dark eyes that studied her crinkled at the corners as he revealed his amusement. "It wasn't."

"You mean I don't need to ask for a priest?"

"Not this time around. Anything else?"

The inside of her mouth felt thick and dry. "Something to drink. Please."

He reached behind him and took a chip of ice from a water jug. Again the urge to reassure her, to stay with her, was strong. Her hair spilled out across the pillow, and the red highlights suggested that her temper would be as quick as her smile. "This will have to do for now. Suck on it and make it last."

Obediently she opened her mouth, and he slipped the ice chip inside, then paused to wipe a drop of moisture from her chin. It wasn't until then that Marjorie noticed he was dressed entirely in green. A cap covered his head, and a surgical mask hung free around his neck.

"Green surgical gowns?" she asked, holding the ice chip against the back side of her mouth so she could speak clearly. "Is that because red stains are so difficult to remove from white fabric?" She sucked in her breath and closed her eyes. "Don't answer that—I don't want to know."

"Don't let your courage fail you now, Marjorie, you're doing fine."

Her eyes shot open. "It's not you who's going under the knife. I'll be scared if I want, and I don't mind telling you, I'd rather be anyplace else in the world but right here." Shot or no shot, sedative or no sedative, she'd never been more unsure about anything. More than that, she was astonished that she had admitted how afraid she was to Sam. It wasn't like her. That shot must have contained a truth serum.

"Everything's going to work out," he said in that calm, confident voice of his.

Without much effort Marjorie could envision him talking someone out of jumping off the Tacoma Narrows Bridge. He had the kind of voice a salesman would kill for—low-pitched, confident, effortless, sincere.

"Don't worry," she said with feigned composure, seeing herself standing on the edge of the steel precipice, looking into the swirling waters far below. "I'm not going to jump."

He gave her a funny look but made no comment.

"That didn't make any sense, did it?" She tossed her head from side to side in an effort to clear her thoughts. It didn't work. Everything scrambled together until she wasn't sure of anything.

He patted her hand. "Don't worry about it. The medication has that effect."

Marjorie wondered if it actually was the shot. No, she was convinced his silk-edged voice and kind eyes were the cause of all this, mesmerizing her. Her eyes drifted closed, and she moistened her lips as she imagined Sam Bretton leaning over her and whispering words of love in her ear, then taking her in his arms and kissing her with such tenderness, such passion, that her thoughts forcefully collided inside her head. A fireworks display that rivaled a Fourth-of-July celebration exploded, and she forced her eyes open and felt the blood rush through her veins.

"Go ahead and sleep," he said softly. "I'll be here when you wake up."

"Please don't leave me." Her eyes rounded, and her mouth filled with the bitter taste of panic. She needed this man she barely knew more than she'd ever needed anyone. The terror that gripped her as she stared ahead at the wide double doors that led to the operating room was intense and nearly overwhelming.

"I'm not going anywhere," Sam assured her, continuing to hold her hand, his fingers firmly entwined with hers.

Somehow it seemed vitally important that he be there every minute. Still, she hated needing anyone. People had always let her down. She was a stronger person than this, and Dr. Sam Bretton was little more than a stranger. Yet she trusted him enough to place her life in his capable hands.

"Don't worry, I'll be fine," she said, and realized her voice was barely audible. "You...you don't need to stay with me. I'm a big girl. I'll get through this...really... Don't tell Jody, she'll only worry... Must call Lydia."

"That's all taken care of," he said, and his voice seemed to come from a great distance.

"Thank you, Sam," Marjorie mumbled, and started slipping into a light sleep.

A female voice made its way through to her fading consciousness. "Dr. Johnson is ready, doctor."

An invisible force pushed the gurney forward, and Marjorie struggled to open her eyes. Someone lifted her head and placed her hair inside a confining cap.

She managed to open one eye and was greeted by blinding lights. Sam was at her side, and Cal Johnson,

who she'd briefly met earlier, stood on the opposite side
of the room, examining her X rays. Sam leaned over
her and explained that the anesthesiologist would be
there any minute. Marjorie nodded, even managed a
weak smile, then decided that it was better not to look
around. She settled back down and tightly shut her eyes.

Soon other voices met over her head, some deep, others crisp, and a few soft. In her drug-induced drowsiness
Marjorie sorted through them and tried to assimilate
only Sam's words. The nurses joked and flirted with
him like a longtime friend. She sighed with the realization that if his patients fell in love with him, then the
women on the hospital staff must be equally vulnerable to his charms. Maybe he was already married. Of
course, that was it! Sam Bretton had a wife. Her disappointment was keen. He was married. He had to be.
Rats! All the good ones were already taken.

Finally it got too difficult to concentrate, and she
gave up trying. When she woke, this troublesome episode would all be over, and she could get on with her
life and forget that any of this had ever happened.

Impatiently, Marjorie waded through huge billows
of thick, black fog. She shivered with cold and sighed
when Sam's familiar voice asked for a heated blanket.
She felt the weight of a quilt on top of her, and she
sighed contentedly. The fog parted as warmth seeped
into her bones, and for the first time she could decipher
a path that led through the haze. She tried to speak, but
her lips seemed glued together, and no amount of trying could pry them apart.

"Marjorie?"

Getting her eyes to open required an equal amount of effort, but when she managed that task, she was blinded by a flash of high-intensity light. She groaned and lowered her lashes.

"Am I in the morgue?" she mumbled, having difficulty getting the words over her uncooperative tongue.

"Not yet," Sam answered.

"That's reassuring."

"You're in the recovery room. Everything went without a hitch. We're lucky we got the appendix when we did. From the look of things, it was ready to burst, and then there could have been some unpleasant complications."

"Close, but no cigar, huh?"

"In this case you don't want a cigar."

"So I'll live and love again?"

Sam brushed the hair from her temple. "You're good for at least another fifty years."

For some inexplicable reason it seemed easier to concentrate with her eyes closed. Her lids fluttered shut even though she strained to keep them open.

"Go ahead and sleep," Sam told her softly. "I'm here, like I promised."

Marjorie wanted to thank him; she searched for some way to let him know how grateful she was that she hadn't woken up alone. The hospital might seem a warm, congenial place to him, but he was there every day. To her, it was a disinfected torture chamber, and she was scared witless. It seemed so important to tell him that his presence comforted her that she wrestled to keep awake even as she felt herself slipping back into the thick, dark fog.

Pain woke Marjorie up the second time—a dull, throbbing ache in her side, quite different from what she'd experienced before meeting Sam. She raised her hand, rubbed her eyes and yawned. The room wasn't as brilliant as before. The light appeared muted, and she was grateful. She rolled her head and realized she was in a small room. The drapes were closed, but a ribbon of light entered between them. A noise distracted her, and she turned her head in the opposite direction and discovered Sam Bretton sitting at her bedside, reading the latest Scandinavian thriller.

"Sam?"

He closed the book, turned to face her and smiled. "Hello again."

"What time is it?"

He rotated his wrist. "Almost six."

"In the morning?"

He nodded and stood, setting his novel aside. He took her wrist and pressed his fingers over her pulse while he stared at the face of his watch.

"Have you been here all night?" It seemed incredible that he would have stayed with her ever since her surgery. She noticed then that the blood-pressure cuff was wrapped around her upper arm, and fear renewed itself within her. There had been problems! Big problems! She swallowed around the tightness in her throat. All night she'd teetered on the brink of death, and Sam had stayed with her and fought for her very life. For hours her fate had hung by a delicate thread, and this man had valiantly battled to save her.

"What happened?" Her question was hoarse, revealing a hundred doubts.

"Nothing," he answered crisply. "All surgeries should be such a breeze."

"Nothing went wrong?"

He frowned, puzzled. "Nothing."

"But...the blood-pressure cuff... And you stayed with me all night. Why?"

His frown deepened, marring his smooth brow with three nearly straight lines. "Because I said I would. You needed someone."

Guilt fell heavily upon her shoulders. She certainly hadn't meant for him to do this. He must have gone without sleep the entire night, and all because of a few silly words she'd uttered in the throes of panic. "But, I didn't—"

"Hey, don't worry about me," he interrupted quickly. "I've got the day off."

"I suppose you golf on Wednesdays?" she asked.

"I don't play golf."

Marjorie feigned shock. "You don't golf? Just what kind of doctor are you? No one told me that before I made my first appointment with you."

"Count your blessings, Majors."

"Oh?"

"I could charge by the hour."

The effort to smile was painful, but holding back her amusement would have been impossible. "Hey, don't make me laugh—it hurts." She groaned and placed her hand over her abdomen. "How soon will the pain go away."

"In a few days."

"A whole lot of good that's doing me now."

"Stop being so impatient."

He spoke with just enough of a challenge for her to quit arguing. She would grin and bear it.

"I'll get the nurse," Sam informed her, smiling. "Cal left instructions for you to sit upright once you woke."

Marjorie snapped her mouth closed and pressed her lips together to smother a protest. Dr. Johnson didn't actually expect her to move, did he? She couldn't—not yet. If breathing hurt this much, she could only imagine the agony that sitting up would cause. Great! Sam and his friend had grabbed her from the jaws of death, only to let her die a slow, torturous death from pain.

From the moment she'd met Dr. Sam, Marjorie had been looking for some imperfection. Anything. He was much too wonderful to be real. Now the flaw stood out like a fake diamond under a jeweler's eyepiece. Clearly, she decided in her still-drugged state, Sam Bretton enjoyed watching people suffer.

Again Sam proved her wrong. The nurse who came to her room came alone. Her name tag was pinned to her uniform: Bertha Powell, R.N.

"Dr. Sam sent me," Bertha announced.

Marjorie studied the older woman, who looked as though her previous profession had been mud wrestling. She was built as solid as a rock, and from the glinting light in her eyes, she was just waiting for Marjorie to start something.

"Where's Sam?"

"*Doctor* Sam asked me to tell you that he'll be back later this afternoon."

"Wonderful," Marjorie muttered, and wiggled her big toe as an experiment. The pain wasn't debilitating, but she wasn't exactly up to swinging from jungle vines, either.

Bertha pulled back the sheet. "Are you ready?"

Marjorie wondered what the other woman would do if she announced that she refused to move. Briefly she toyed with the idea, then decided against it. Her teeth gritted, she cautiously did what had been requested of her.

Exhausted afterward, Marjorie slept for six hours. Someone moving inside her room woke her. When she stirred and opened her eyes, she found Lydia standing at the foot of her bed with a small bouquet of flowers in her hand.

"Hi, Marjorie," Lydia said in a soft voice.

"I had my appendix out," Marjorie grumbled. "I stopped your friend in the nick of time from doing a lobotomy."

Lydia looked relieved and set the flowers on the bedside table. "Same ol' Marjorie."

"I didn't mean to snap at you."

"Hey, no problem. I'm used to it, remember?"

Marjorie tried to wipe the tiredness from her eyes. "I bet you're waiting for me to tell you how right you were."

"It'd feel good, but I can wait." Obviously she couldn't, because she added, "Didn't I tell you it had to be more than a queasy stomach? I figured it out long before you, didn't I?"

"Yup, you did," Marjorie returned, with more than a hint of amused sarcasm. "Where would I be without you?" That much wasn't in jest. She was sincerely grateful her friend had made the appointment when she did, especially after what Sam had told her.

Lydia pulled a chair close to the hospital bed and plunked herself down. Without so much as pausing to inhale, she started off with a long series of questions. "How do you like Dr. Sam? Isn't he wonderful? Didn't I tell you he was a marvel? Now that you've met him, you'll probably be like everyone else and fall madly in love with him."

"No doubt."

Lydia's face blossomed into a wide grin. "I knew you'd like him."

Just managing to avoid her friend's gaze, Marjorie asked, "What's his wife like?"

"His wife?" That stopped Lydia cold. She opened and closed her mouth twice. "I didn't know he was married."

"You mean he isn't?" Hope flared. Naw, he had to be married—and probably had a passel of kids to boot. All in diapers, no doubt. Knowing the type of doctor he was convinced Marjorie that Sam Bretton would be a devoted husband and father. She, on the other hand, was definitely not the mother type.

"I don't know anything about a wife," Lydia answered thoughtfully, chewing on the corner of her bottom lip. "I really don't think he's married. I can't remember seeing a wedding band, can you?"

"It doesn't matter," Marjorie muttered. He'd been wonderful...more than wonderful, but she had far more important matters to deal with that didn't involve risking her heart over a physician whose second job entailed throwing women's equilibriums off balance.

In order to change the subject Marjorie scooted her

gaze past Lydia to the bouquet of carnations and roses on the bedside table. "Thanks for the flowers."

"Hey, no problem. They're from all the salespeople at Dixon's."

"All?" Marjorie cocked one delicately shaped brow suspiciously. "Even Al Swanson?"

Lydia grinned sheepishly. "He tossed in a buck and suggested I buy a cactus."

That Marjorie could believe. Al had made it clear that he didn't approve of women in the car business. That was tough, she mused, since she was at Dixon Motors for the long haul, no matter what Al or anyone else thought. It wasn't that Al had taken a dislike to her and her alone. He had a problem with everyone. He had yet to learn that sales work was often a team effort. Marjorie's gut feeling was that Al Swanson wouldn't be around Dixon much longer.

"Oh!" Lydia exclaimed. "I nearly forgot. Dr. Sam phoned and told me to get the key to your apartment so I could pick up some personal items you're going to need."

Once again the man had amazed Marjorie with his thoughtfulness. "I hate to put you to all the trouble."

"It's no trouble. Honest. You'd do the same thing for me."

Marjorie smiled her thanks. Accepting anyone's assistance was difficult for her—more than it should have been, she realized. She'd practically raised Jody with little or no help from any state agencies. With a limited college education she'd forged her own way in the world, designed her career, and earned enough to support herself and pay for her sister's college tuition. Sam

Bretton had the wrong impression of her, and to Marjorie's utter embarrassment, she had to admit she'd been the one to give it to him.

"The key," Lydia reminded her.

"Oh, it's in my purse." Guessing where it would be stored, she nodded toward the closet door.

Lydia stood and moved in that direction. "Dr. Sam gave me a list, but you might want to read it over."

"I'm sure he thought of everything," Marjorie responded distractedly. She had to set Sam straight. She wasn't a helpless clinging vine, although he had good reason to believe she was. The memory of how she'd pleaded with him not to leave her was a keen source of her present chagrin.

Triumphantly Lydia held up Marjorie's key chain. "I'll run over to your place and get your things now."

Marjorie could do little more than nod. Her thoughts were light-years away, spinning out of control. She would talk to Sam the next time he stopped in to see her. She would explain everything. Yawning, she placed her hand over her mouth and determinedly tried to suppress the exhaustion that gripped her. How strange it felt to become so weary so easily. Of their own accord, her eyes drifted closed.

Sam was there when she woke. He smiled down on her before noting something on her chart. "How's the patient feeling?"

"I don't know yet. Give me a minute to sort through the various pains." To her surprise she noticed that her purple velvet housecoat was neatly folded across the bottom of her bed. Lydia must have returned with her things, and Marjorie realized she had somehow managed to sleep through her friend's second visit.

"Dr. Johnson wants you up and walking before dinner."

The protest that sprang automatically to her lips died a quick death. Sitting up in bed earlier had been difficult enough! Sam had to be out of his mind if he believed she was going to traipse around this room or down these halls, dragging an I.V. pole with her, and all because some man she barely knew had ordered her to. She, of all people, should know when she was ready to risk life and limb by walking again.

Sam glanced up from his notations, his eyes studying her. "What, no argument?"

"When can I get out of here?"

"Soon, but that's up to Cal," he answered noncommittally. "Listen, before you think about leaving the hospital, focus your energy on getting out of bed and moving."

He sounded so reasonable, so calm and confident, that the brick walls of her rebellion crumbled before she had them completely raised. Marjorie cautiously moved the sheet aside and struggled a little higher against her pillows.

"Careful, Marjorie. Don't try to move on your own." Sam closed her chart and hung it at the end of the bed.

"No," she said through gritted teeth. "I'll do it myself." One foot freed itself from the tangled sheet, and she raised herself up onto one elbow.

Disregarding her words, Sam placed his arm around her shoulders and helped her into an upright position. Flushed and embarrassed by how incredibly weak she was, Marjorie reached for her housecoat, astonished that the simple task of sitting could tire her so much that she was practically panting.

Sam draped her robe over her shoulders, then located her slippers and slipped them onto her feet. "Okay, let's take this nice and easy."

"Trust me, I'm not exactly ready to jump off this bed and race down the corridor." The spinning room gradually circled into place and came to a stop. "I think I'd feel better about this in the morning."

"Now, Marjorie."

She wanted to argue with him but hadn't the strength. "I'm not normally like this," she said, with as much force as she could muster. "I'm sorry I asked you to stay with me.... I realize now I shouldn't have...."

"Marjorie, I stayed because I wanted to, not out of any obligation." He stepped around the bed and stood directly in front of her, leaning down only slightly. Because the hospital bed was so high, their eyes met. His were warm and sincere, while hers flashed with frustration and regret.

Although his words had filled her with an absurd amount of pleasure, Marjorie still felt compelled to explain herself. "But I'm not like that...really."

"Like what?"

"Weak and sniveling."

"I never once thought that."

"Oh, you're impossible!"

Sam's thick brows shot upward. "I'm what?"

Marjorie lightly tossed her head. "Nothing."

"Do you doubt my word?"

"Not exactly. It's just that I feel I've given you the

wrong impression of me. I'm a capable, responsible adult. I even figured out my own taxes last year."

"I'm impressed." He pushed a small stool across the floor so she could use that as a step to climb off the bed.

"You're actually going to make me do this?" Marjorie couldn't seem to get her body to cooperate. One foot eased itself downward as she cautiously scooted to the edge of the mattress.

Sam placed a supporting arm under her elbow to help her down. She felt small and incredibly fragile in his embrace. Once again she reminded him of the rain-drenched kitten he'd discovered all those years ago. And like the half-drowned feline, Marjorie Majors required love and attention, too. Only Sam wasn't in any position to give those things to her. She was his patient, not a potential girlfriend. The two didn't mix. Couldn't mix.

With both feet firmly planted on the floor, Marjorie paused, half expecting to keel over. When she didn't, she felt a glowing sense of triumph. She'd made it, actually made it.

"Good job," Sam said, and reluctantly dropped his arm. "Now take a few steps."

"You don't really mean for me to walk, do you?" She was only hours from having been under the knife. Hours from the most frightening experience of her life.

"I certainly do want you to walk. You know, one foot in front of the other in a forward direction."

She flashed him a look of irritation.

"And soon, if you're good, I'll take you upstairs."

"Upstairs? Is there something up there that would interest me? Like food?"

"You're hungry?"

"Famished! I haven't eaten in two days." That was entirely true. Marjorie liked her food and seldom skipped a meal. Luckily, gaining weight had never been a problem. She guessed she was fortunate in that department, but it seemed she would quickly melt away if this hospital had anything to say about it. She hadn't been offered a single meal so far.

Sam knew her digestive system couldn't handle anything solid for a few days, but he decided against telling her so. He would leave as many unpleasant tasks as possible for Cal Johnson. After all, Cal was the physician of record.

While guiding the I.V. pole beside her, Sam manipulated them through the doorway and into the broad hallway.

"This afternoon, while you were sleeping, I delivered a set of twins," Sam boasted proudly. Birth, even after countless deliveries, had never ceased to humble him, and twins were always special. "They're upstairs," he continued. "I'll take you to see them later, if you want."

Marjorie looked at him and blinked. She didn't know how to explain that babies frightened her. All right, they terrified her. Some women took to motherhood and dirty diapers like hogs to mud. But, unfortunately, that would never be the case with her. The only times she'd ever been around babies, they'd cried. Within ten minutes she'd been ready to wail herself. After several embarrassing episodes in her youth, she had decided that anyone under two was allergic to her.

"I...I think I'd better wait until I've got more strength," she said.

"Of course," Sam agreed. "I wouldn't dream of dragging you upstairs your first time out. Tomorrow, maybe, or the next day."

"Sure. Anytime," Marjorie answered, but the words nearly stuck in her throat.

Three

Marjorie stared at the orange tray and grimaced in pure disgust. If she so much as looked at another bowl of plain gelatin, she was going to start screaming and say something unladylike that would shock the entire hospital staff. Everything they'd brought to her so far only vaguely resembled food.

"Good morning," the nurse's aide greeted her, as she strolled into the room. "And how was your breakfast?"

"You don't want to know."

The young girl glanced at the untouched tray. "You didn't eat a thing."

"I couldn't," Marjorie muttered. It wasn't this poor woman's fault that the hospital had chosen to starve her.

"Aren't you feeling better? Usually my patients are more than ready to eat by this time. Are you in a lot of pain? Perhaps I should notify Dr. Johnson."

"Contacting the doctor isn't going to convince me to eat…this. I'd rather die," Marjorie said dramatically. "I refuse to swallow anything that slithers down my throat."

The aide chuckled. "Let me see what I can do." She left, and Marjorie stared after her with visions of cheesy pizza, crisp fried chicken and a thick, juicy steak playing havoc with her imagination. Marjorie was convinced she smelled bacon frying in the distance, the odor wafting toward her and tormenting her with delicious dreams.

"Problems?" Sam sauntered into the room, looking sympathetic.

"Sam," Marjorie said, and brightened instantly. She hadn't seen him in nearly twenty hours and had rarely been more pleased to lay eyes on anyone. Sam Bretton could be trusted. She wasn't so sure about anyone else in this antiseptic place, but Sam would help straighten out this mealtime mess.

"You didn't eat your breakfast." His voice was only lightly accusing.

"I couldn't," she said, her eyes softly pleading with his. "The oatmeal had more lumps than a camel, and heaven only knows what flavor of gelatin they wanted me to eat…. Liver, I think, and even with whipped topping, it looked disgusting. As for the tea and toast, could they be any more boring? Why can't I have a mushroom omelet, with home fries on the side? Something…anything, but gelatin and oatmeal."

"Soon."

Marjorie's face mirrored her reaction. Obviously *soon* wasn't going to be this morning, and she needed nourishment *now*, if not earlier. Disappointment consumed her. She'd thought of Sam as her ally, her friend. The amazing part was that he seemed to look better to her every time he walked in the room. When he was with her, even the pain lessened. He filled her room with an assurance of well-being and safekeeping. He lent her confidence, stamina and the conviction that this, too, would pass, and when it did, he would be there for her.

Sam reached for her hand, and his eyes gentled. "Marjorie, listen." He did understand her position, but she had to realize that stronger foods had to be reintroduced gradually into her digestive system. "You're not being a very good patient."

"Oh, spare me," she snapped, quickly losing a grip on her fragile patience. Her temper was always quick to fire when she was hungry. "No one told me I had to pretend I was on the good ship Lollipop."

"All we're asking is that you do as we say."

"And die of starvation in the process."

"Don't be so dramatic. You're a long way from that. Most women look forward to dropping a few pounds during their hospital stay." The moment the words slipped from Sam's mouth, he recognized his terrible mistake. It was too late to retract his statement; his only hope was that she would let it slide. He tried smiling, praying the action would take any sting from his words. It didn't.

Marjorie's face grew as red as a California pepper, and her anger was just as hot. "Are you insinuating Tacoma General is a fat farm and that I'm overweight?"

"No, you misunderstood—"

"Your meaning was more than clear," she said coldly, and reached for the buzzer to call the nurse. Immediately the red light above her bed flashed on.

"Marjorie…I didn't mean to be so tactless. You're not the least bit plump…. I'm doing a poor job of this." Sam wiped a hand around the back of his neck and sighed. He regretted getting trapped in this no-win conversation. When it came to dealing with his patients, he usually had more finesse than this.

She ignored him and tossed aside the sheet, sticking her bare leg out in an ungraceful effort to climb down from the high hospital bed. "Nurse," she cried, but her voice was weak and wobbly.

"Marjorie, you have to stay where you are and eat your breakfast," Sam said.

Their eyes met and clashed. Marjorie was hurting and hungry, a lethal combination that resulted in the most embarrassing reaction. Tears. Embarrassed, she turned her face away from him and motioned toward the door, wordlessly asking him to leave.

Sam hesitated. Once again his heart went out to her, and he had to force himself to walk out of the room. In the few days since he'd met Marjorie, she'd touched him in ways few women ever had. He had been a silent witness to her courage and realized that she possessed a rare personal strength. Her laughter was a sweet melody, her movements innately graceful. Several times over the past twenty-four hours he'd found his thoughts drifting to her, and he smiled at the memory of her waking from the operation to ask if she was in the morgue. At each meeting he realized all the more how proud she was. Proud. Fiery. Straightforward. He found it utterly astonishing that she wasn't married. And he was grateful. He wanted to get to know her better—a whole lot better.

Sam knew he'd made a mess of this and was angry

with himself. He patted her shoulder and turned to leave the room.

The nurse's aide met him outside her door and raised questioning eyes to him. "Doctor?"

"I believe she'll eat her breakfast now," Sam answered, his thoughts distracted.

"Very good." The younger woman beamed him a warm smile—impressed, he imagined, with his ability to deal with a difficult situation.

Sam did his best to return the friendly gesture. He had a reputation for working well with unreasonable patients, but Marjorie wasn't that, only confused and miserable.

And he'd made a mess of things.

Marjorie heard Sam tell the nurse's aide that she would be eating her meal and glared after him, half tempted to toss the liver gelatin at his arrogant backside. She didn't, though, because he was right. Once again she'd made an idiot of herself in front of him and the hospital staff. She didn't like herself when she behaved this way, yet she seemed powerless to change.

The moisture on her cheeks felt like burning acid, and she brushed the tears aside, thoroughly embarrassed by their appearance. She wasn't a crybaby—at least she hadn't been until Sam Bretton walked into her life. Then everything had quickly fallen to pieces. Whatever it was about that insufferable, wonderful man that reduced her to this state should be outlawed.

The tea was only lukewarm, but at least it was strong enough to satisfy Marjorie's need for caffeine. The dry wheat toast was surprisingly filling, and the oatmeal passable as long as she dumped three sugar packets over the top. The gelatin she ignored.

In order to avoid the triumphant look on the nurse's aide's face, Marjorie pretended to be asleep when the woman returned for the tray. To her surprise, she actually did fall into a restful sleep and woke midmorning with a game show blaring from the TV positioned against the wall.

"I see you're awake." The mud-wrestling star was back. Bertha Powell, R.N., looked stiff in her starched white uniform. "Dr. Johnson wants you up and walking today. Ten laps."

"Laps?" Marjorie repeated, still caught in the last dregs of sleep. Did the hospital provide a running track for surgery patients?

"The corridor," the muscular woman informed her primly. "Ten times up and back. That's your goal for today. But don't do too much at once. Two or three round trips at a time. No more."

Marjorie resisted the urge to salute. Bertha Powell seemed to be looking for a few good men—or women— to gleefully whip into shape. Marjorie didn't doubt that the nurse would count every single lap.

To her credit, the nurse aided Marjorie into an upright position and helped her on with her robe. There was some confusion with the I.V., but Bertha figured it out, and after only a few minutes, Marjorie was on her way.

Steadier on her feet than she'd been before, she was pleased with her slow but sure progress. Although it was hours until noon, the hospital was a hive of activity. If she'd been in a grumbling mood, she would have pointed out that Dr. Johnson had suggested she get plenty of rest, but the hospital staff had awakened her before the sun was anywhere close to the horizon. The only people up at that time of the morning were mass murderers, teenagers and nurses' aides.

The woman who had brought in her breakfast tray grinned as Marjorie passed the nurses' station.

"Hey, you're doing great."

Marjorie smiled back. "Yes, I think I'll donate my body to science."

"Science fiction might appreciate it more," said a deep male voice from behind her.

"Sam?" Marjorie laughed and turned her head, pleased to see him again.

"To your room," he instructed.

Marjorie was more than happy to comply and glanced with wide-eyed curiosity toward the brown paper sack in his hand. "What's that?"

"You'll see."

"I thought you had appointments all day," she said once they were back in her room, not that she was disappointed to see him. Nothing could have been further from the truth; she was overjoyed.

"I just finished my rounds."

"Oh." Once again Marjorie couldn't take her eyes from his dazzling smile. "How are the twins?"

"As cute as a bug's ear. I'll take you to see them this evening, if you want."

It was all Marjorie could do to nod. She'd brought up the subject of the babies because she knew they were close to Sam's heart. She was interested, but not to the point of overcoming her instinctive apprehension. When the time came that she couldn't avoid it any longer, she would look through the glass and ooh and aah with appropriate enthusiasm, and Sam would never guess she was frightened to death.

"I brought you something to tide you over until lunch," he said, holding out the sack to her.

Marjorie took it and eagerly peeked inside. The chocolate-coated ice-cream bar produced a small squeal of delight. If they'd been anyplace but the middle of a hospital, she would have thrown her arms around his neck and smudged his face with kisses to thank him properly.

"Thank you, Sam. Really."

"It's my pleasure."

Those gorgeous eyes of his seemed to look straight into her heart. "I felt terrible about the scene I made earlier," Marjorie admitted, centering her greedy gaze on the melting Dove Bar. Her mouth started to water. This man was special. Really special.

"There's no need to apologize," he said. "I wasn't exactly helpful."

"But you tried." She didn't understand why he was so good to her, but she wasn't willing to question it. From the moment she'd walked into his office, he'd befriended her, then seen her through the most difficult days of her life, all the while hardly leaving her side. No wonder his patients were so willing to admit they fell in love with him.

Sam's heart throbbed painfully with desire. Marjorie's wide eyes regarded him with such sweet gratitude that it seemed the most natural thing in the world to lean forward and press his mouth to hers. He didn't, of course, but that didn't stop his imagination from running rampant. He could all but taste her honey-sweet lips. He could all but feel her mouth shaping and fitting to his own, and her ripe body pressing against him.

Inhaling deeply to discipline his thoughts, Sam took a step back. Marjorie Majors had caught him completely off guard. Over the years he'd been subjected to every female ploy imaginable, but the majority of women who were interested in him were mostly concerned with the money he was making and the social position that would go with becoming his wife. They hadn't soured him on marriage, but they *had* made him extra cautious. He didn't succumb easily to a woman's charms, and he wasn't about to start now. He was looking for a special woman to become his wife. A partner and a friend.

And now there was Marjorie. Her candor had caught him unaware. She was a natural beauty. Even without makeup and with her dark hair tied lifelessly away from her face, he couldn't help being attracted to her. From the moment she'd angrily jumped off his examining table, Sam had been enraptured with her. Everything about her acted as a powerful aphrodisiac, but nothing could come of this attraction until after she was released from the hospital.

Sam left abruptly, but Marjorie was too busy eating her ice-cream bar to pay much attention. She sucked on the wooden stick until the last bit of chocolate had long since melted on her tongue, then carefully set the stick aside.

Dragging the I.V. stand with her, she walked slowly and carefully down the corridor until she reached the nurses' station. There wasn't any way to be tactful about what she needed to know, but she was in dangerous territory here, feeling the way she did about Sam Bretton.

"Ms. Powell?" she said as sweetly as she could.

"Yes?" Bertha Powell glanced up from the chart she was updating, and her eyes narrowed with displeasure.

"I've done five laps."

"That leaves five more for this afternoon."

"Right."

The woman returned her attention to her work.

"Ms. Powell?"

"Yes." Once again the older woman's voice revealed her lack of patience. She gripped the pen tightly and glanced up at Marjorie before slowly exhaling one long breath.

"Dr. Bretton was in earlier. I was wondering if I could ask about…"

"His wife?" the older woman finished for her.

The room swayed, and the floor felt as if had buckled under Marjorie's unsteady feet. She gripped the edge of the counter until she regained her balance and the hospital had righted itself once more. But she had to ask, and surely the hospital staff would know for sure, while Lydia had only been guessing.

"That *is* what you wanted to know, isn't it?" the woman pressed.

It was all Marjorie could do to nod and say, "He's married, then?"

"Not as far as I know," Bertha answered almost kindly. "But I swear that man breaks more hearts than George Clooney. There isn't a woman on this floor who wouldn't give her eyeteeth to be married to him. He's the type we're all looking for."

"But…"

"Be smart, Ms. Majors. Listen to the voice of experience and learn from it. All Dr. Sam's patients fall in love with him. It's gratitude, I suppose. Heaven knows he's hunk enough to melt anyone's heart—even mine."

Marjorie clenched her jaw to hide her reaction.

"Now I don't want you to feel bad about this. It's common enough, believe me."

The heat that exploded into Marjorie's cheeks was hot enough to fry eggs. She hadn't realized her feelings were so obvious. Under normal conditions she didn't fluster easily, but when it came to Sam, she lost all her poise.

"He's a wonderful person," Marjorie managed to say with some semblance of calm.

"Honey, you don't know the half of it. I saw that man sit for hours with a young couple after their baby died. More than once I've been a witness to his tenderness— that's why I'm telling you what I am. Believe me, if I were twenty years younger, I'd be in love with the man myself. Truthfully, I *am* in love with him. We all are."

"Thank you." Already Marjorie was walking away, trying to disguise her embarrassment. She'd tried to be subtle, tried to find out what she could without making a total idiot of herself. And she'd failed.

After a few moments to think the nurse's words over, Marjorie relaxed. An odd reassurance replaced her chagrin. It was good to know she was merely one of the masses. Bertha Powell was right. Women tended to fall in love with their doctors. It was a common enough malady, and one she should have anticipated.

The sooner she was released from the hospital, the

better, Marjorie decided. With a determination that drove her to the brink of exhaustion, she did five more laps up and down the long corridor, then fell into a deep sleep the minute the dinner tray was removed from her room.

"Morning, doctor," Marjorie said casually when Cal Johnson paid his morning visit. He was a bald, grandfatherly type who certainly hadn't affected her the way Sam had.

"I see you've made considerable progress," he said, reading over her chart.

"I hope so."

"You're walking?"

"Every minute I can."

"Good." He nodded approvingly.

"When can I be discharged?" The question had been on her mind from the moment she talked to Bertha Powell. "I feel great—I want to go home."

"I'm pleased to hear that. However..."

"Doctor, please, I need to get home."

The grandfatherly brows molded into a tight frown. "I want to keep you until I'm sure you're a little stronger. A couple of days—maybe."

"Two days!" Marjorie would never last that long. For the sake of her sanity, she had to get out of this place. Heaven only knew what would happen when she saw Sam next. The way matters were progressing, she would profess her love for him the moment he walked in the door. That was just the kind of crazy, foolish thing she might do.

"We'll see how things progress today," Dr. Johnson said on his way out the door.

A half hour after Dr. Johnson had left her room, Sam appeared.

"How are you feeling?"

"Fine," Marjorie responded in a flat, emotionless tone. She did her utmost to pretend she was looking straight at him when in reality her gaze rested on the wall behind him. Even looking in Sam Bretton's direction was dangerous to her equilibrium. She should be reassured that she was like every one of his other patients, but she wasn't. Such strong emotions were strangers to her and best avoided.

"Marjorie, what's wrong?"

"I want out of here!"

"You aren't alone in that, you know. Everyone who ever stays in the hospital is eager to get home."

"But I feel terrific." That wasn't entirely true. "I'm as strong as an ox."

"Why don't you leave it in Dr. Johnson's hands?" he offered gently. "He knows what he's doing."

"But two days is an eternity," Marjorie insisted.

Sam's cajoling smile vanished. "Cal suggested you could leave then?"

"Yes."

"I'm sure he's mistaken."

"What do you mean?" Marjorie grumbled.

"Dr. Johnson's obviously forgotten that there isn't anyone at your apartment to watch over you when you're released."

"In case you hadn't noticed, I'm a big girl. I've been

taking care of myself for a long time now. I'm not going to keel over because someone isn't there to hold my hand and place wet washcloths over my forehead every ten minutes."

"That's not the issue, Marjorie."

"Then what exactly is?"

"You've gone through a life-threatening episode. Take advantage of this time to be waited on and pampered."

"Take advantage of it?" She laughed sharply. "You've got to be kidding. What's with you doctors? Do you get a kickback for every additional day a patient stays in the hospital?"

Marjorie's ability to attract him paled beside her capacity to anger him. He knotted his hands into tight fists, and clenched his jaw to keep from saying something he would regret. Her suggestion was so outrageous and so unfair that it offended him beyond anything he'd felt in years.

"I think it would be best if I left."

"By all means go, Doctor."

Sam retreated, shoving the door with such rage that it nearly slammed against the wall. A kickback? She couldn't actually believe that, could she?

Marjorie watched him go and swallowed down a mouthful of remorse, nearly choking on the aftertaste. She hadn't meant to suggest such a ridiculous thing, hadn't planned to say the words. But she was desperate to escape. How ironic it was that a man—a doctor who had dedicated his life to saving lives—could be responsible for breaking so many hearts.

All Marjorie wanted to do was to put this unfortunate episode behind her and get on with her life. Every day she spent in the hospital was another day without income. She hadn't been joking when she told Sam that if she didn't sell cars, she didn't eat. Most of her customers tended to glamorize her job, but it wasn't anything like they imagined. She was in a cutthroat business.

In her frustration, she walked the halls until she was convinced her feet had made imprints in the polished linoleum squares. When Lydia arrived at five-thirty, she was so pleased to see her friend that she nearly threw her arms around the other woman and wept for joy.

"You look great. I don't believe it! Your color's almost back." Lydia slid the lone chair closer to Marjorie's bed and took a seat. "Dixon's doesn't seem the same without you."

Despite her bad mood, Marjorie laughed, then sucked in a pain-filled breath and pressed her hand against her side. She hadn't healed as much as she thought.

"Are you resting enough?"

Just the mention of sleep produced a yawn that Marjorie hid with the back of her hand. "You wouldn't believe it. I haven't slept this much since I was a newborn."

"What about Dr. Sam? Have you seen much of him?"

"He's been in a few times," Marjorie said in a flat tone. The scene from that morning played back in her mind, along with the awful accusation she'd thrown at him. Once again, Marjorie was struck by her own foolishness.

Lydia paused and closely studied her friend. "What's the matter? You said that as though you don't want anything to do with the man."

"Oh, Sam Bretton is everything you said he was…

and more. But to be frank, he simply doesn't interest me."

The perfectly shaped eyebrows above Lydia's dark eyes drew together sharply. "He doesn't interest you?"

"Not really." Marjorie studied her fingernails with feigned interest.

"Do you have a raging fever, girl? Are you stupid? He's wonderful…. He's handsome enough to tempt any red-blooded American woman."

"Not me," Marjorie claimed, her voice gaining conviction. "Nice guy, but not my type."

"He's every woman's type!"

"Maybe." That was as much as Marjorie was willing to concede.

The way Lydia was regarding her, Marjorie had the feeling her friend was considering having her arrested for treason. If she didn't watch it, she would be dragged before a firing squad at dawn.

"I don't understand you," Lydia said in a low, curious tone. "The last time I came to visit, the scent of a good old-fashioned romance was so thick in this room that I walked away intoxicated. I was convinced you were hooked and would be head over heels in love with him within a week."

"I'm sorry to disappoint you."

"What went wrong?" Lydia crossed her arms and glared at Marjorie as though she'd let a million dollars' worth of gold slip through her fingers. "When Dr. Sam phoned before the surgery, he sounded… I don't know… interested, I guess. We must have talked for a half hour. He asked a hundred questions about you."

"He did?" Marjorie wasn't sure she wanted to hear that.

"I don't know what happened between then and now, but obviously something did."

"I'm his patient," Marjorie insisted, because to do anything else would be ludicrous. That relationship was not to be tampered with. All afternoon she'd forced herself to view it as something like the relationship between a woman and her priest. It was much safer that way.

"That's too bad," Lydia said with an exaggerated sigh. "I was really hoping things would work out between you two."

"Why?"

"Why?" Lydia repeated, astonished. "Because I think Dr. Sam is the most amazing man I know, and because you're my best friend. That's why. The two of you are perfect together."

"You've got to be kidding!" Marjorie cried. Her words resounded throughout the room; the echo taunted her for long hours afterward.

Four

Marjorie paused just inside the Mercedes showroom and drew a deep breath. It felt wonderful to be back. Wonderful and right. Three weeks recovery time was what Sam had told her she would need, and she had used every minute of those twenty-one days to recuperate. Even now she felt weak and a little shaky, but the thought of another day holed up in her tiny apartment was enough to make even the most sane person go stir-crazy.

With a sense of appreciation that never waned, Marjorie ran her hand over the trunk of an SLK roadster. Rarely had she been more eager to get to work. Bit by bit she had regained her strength, and now she would quietly resume her life.

"Welcome back," Lydia called eagerly from behind the customer-service counter. "How are you feeling?"

"Terrific, thanks." Marjorie realized her clothes were a little loose and her complexion a bit chalky, but all in all, she felt great.

"Has your sister gone back to Oregon?"

Marjorie nodded. Her sister had left a few days before, and it had not been a minute too soon. When Jody had learned about the surgery, there had been no stopping the twenty-year-old from coming to her sister's aid. Despite Marjorie's protests, Jody had dropped her studies and immediately driven to Tacoma to play the role of the indulgent nurse. Marjorie loved her sister, but after one entire week of Jody giving an Academy Award-level imitation of Clara Barton, Marjorie had been on the brink of madness.

Within the first hour of her return to Dixon Motors, two of the salesmen stopped by her desk to welcome her back. At ten Lydia delivered a cup of coffee, closed the door and pulled out a chair. "Well?" she asked, as she plunked herself down and leaned forward intently, propping her elbows on the corner of Marjorie's desk. Her eyes were both wide and curious.

Marjorie blinked back her surprise. "Well, what?"

"Did you hear from Dr. Sam?"

"Of course not." With jerky movements she tore off three weeks, a day at a time, from her desktop calendar.

"Dr. Sam didn't contact you?" Lydia's voice rose dramatically in disbelief.

"I just told you he didn't." Marjorie had seen Sam exactly twice since that heated episode when she'd accused him of getting a kickback from the hospital. Both times had been strained, as she battled her very strong and very real attraction toward him. Again and again she was forced to remind herself that women patients tend to fall in love with their doctors and that she wasn't any more immune to his charms than the rest. Keeping her perspective had been difficult, especially when

Sam returned the following day and behaved as though nothing had happened. He had chatted easily with her, but she noted regretfully that he stayed only a few minutes. His second visit had been even shorter.

"That depresses me," Lydia lamented, as she gracefully rose from her chair. "I was convinced he really liked you."

It depressed Marjorie, too, but it didn't surprise her. Overall, she was grateful to have met Sam Bretton. He'd taught her several surprising lessons about herself-mainly that she wasn't as invincible as she would like to think. And secondly, as much as she strove to avoid relationships that were more than casual, her heart was vulnerable. He'd proved beyond a doubt that plenty of red-hot blood flowed through her veins.

Painful experience had taught her that most men liked their women soft and clinging. A woman who could change her own oil, balance a checkbook and build a bookshelf seemed to intimidate them. That left the strong, independent types, like herself, out in the cold.

Sam Bretton sat in his office and chewed on the end of a pen. His thoughts were dark and heavy. He hadn't seen Marjorie in more than two weeks, but still she kept popping into his mind when he least expected it. He had seen her smile on a new patient's face as he entered the room to introduce himself. His coffee cup had made it halfway to his lips when he thought he heard Marjorie's laugh. Last week he'd been convinced he'd seen her in the parking lot. Even his dreams had been affected. A couple of times he'd caught himself staring into space, remembering something witty she'd said or the way her eyes narrowed when she was angry. Friends had begun to comment that he seemed preoccupied.

Preoccupied? That wasn't the half of it. Forcefully he opened his desk drawer and tossed the pen inside. He'd been thinking about her for days—all right, weeks—and still he wasn't convinced anything between them would work. She was so proud, so headstrong, and he wasn't entirely persuaded she was interested in him. Without being egotistical about it, Sam realized that there were plenty of women who found him attractive. Unfortunately, Marjorie didn't appear to be one of them.

Well, he was a big boy; he could deal with that. What was difficult to handle was the fact that he wasn't convinced that a future for them was out of the question. Her streak of independence was a mile wide; she didn't want or need anyone. At least that was what she wanted to think. He wasn't so sure, but so long as she stuck to her guns, he was stymied. He just wished he could put her out of his mind.

Marjorie looked at Lydia sitting across the table from her in the deli opposite Dixon Motors. She watched as her friend checked suspiciously between the thick slices of rye bread for the mustard she'd ordered with her pastrami sandwich. "I've been thinking," Lydia muttered under her breath.

"Careful," Marjorie warned, hiding a smile. "That could be dangerous."

"No, I'm serious." Her look gave credibility to her words.

"About what?" Marjorie continued to study her

friend while she wrapped the second half of her own turkey sandwich in a paper napkin to take back to the office for a snack later.

"Didn't you tell me Dr. Sam was interested in buying a Mercedes?"

"I… Yes, now that you mention it, he did say something along those lines."

The edges of Lydia's mouth lifted with unsuppressed delight. "Then get moving, girl! I've never known you to look a gift horse in the mouth."

"I…" Marjorie's tongue felt glued to the roof of her mouth.

"If you don't move on this, then you know Al Swanson will."

The arrow hit its mark. Al Swanson was her nemesis, and he wouldn't think twice about robbing his own mother of a sale. "I'll think about it," Marjorie said, and gave her friend a bright smile.

Lydia pushed her plate aside and stood, looking pleased with herself. Marjorie thought she looked determined to get her together with Sam even if she had to lock them in a room herself.

Marjorie checked her watch and was grateful to note that she was free to leave in fifteen minutes. After her second day back at work she was eager to get home and relax. Her afternoon hadn't gone well. She'd crossed swords with Al Swanson when he'd attempted to steal a sale. One of her clients had taken out a sedan for a test drive, and when he'd returned, Al had explained that Marjorie was out to lunch and had asked him to wrap up the deal. Luckily she had overheard him, and quickly inserted that she was back and would take over for him.

Incidents like this had happened in the past, and she refused to stand for it. She didn't like tattling to the manager, but she wasn't about to let Al cheat her out of her commission.

The bell chimed as the large double doors opened, indicating that a customer had entered the showroom. The salespeople took turns dealing with the influx of prospective buyers. She'd only recently finished helping a young executive, so she left the field open to Jim Preston, the senior salesman.

"Marjorie," Jim called, and stuck his head in the door. "Someone's here to see you."

Once again, she glanced at her watch. Staying late hadn't been a problem before, but she tired easily now and was eager to head back to her apartment. "Thanks, Jim," she muttered, and pushed herself away from her desk with both hands.

Out in the showroom, she paused in midstep and nearly faltered in an effort to disguise her surprise.

"Sam." His name came out in a rush of confusion and delight.

Sam turned away from the light blue convertible he'd been examining. He liked the sleek lines and the classic style of the SLK, but fifty-five thousand dollars for a car, any car, was more than he cared to spend.

"Hi." Some of Marjorie's composure had returned, and she greeted him with a careful smile. She didn't want to appear overjoyed to see him, although her heart felt as if it were doing somersaults inside her chest.

Sam couldn't take his eyes off her. She looked wonderful. If he'd found her attractive before, it was nothing compared to the way she appeared to him now. To think he'd once pictured this woman as a lost kitten trapped in a storm. This kitten wasn't an ordinary, run-of-the-mill stray. She was of the highest pedigree.

Without even realizing what he was doing, Sam gave a low wolf whistle. He couldn't stop looking at her and finally managed to say, "I see you've recovered."

"You promised I'd live and love again."

Sam grinned and, still a little bemused, rubbed the side of his jaw, unable to carry on the conversation.

Marjorie knew that men found her attractive, but what amused her was the shocked look on Sam's face. "I didn't think the brochure had time to reach you," she said, her gaze holding his.

"Brochure? What brochure?" He suspected he was beginning to sound like an echo.

"I mailed one off to you yesterday afternoon," she said, and casually crossed her arms over her double-breasted tweed jacket. "You'd mentioned something about wanting a Mercedes, and I extended an invitation for you to come in and take a test drive."

"I'd enjoy that," Sam murmured, glancing toward the sticker on the side window of the car he'd been inspecting.

"Perhaps it would be best if I explained the different models," Marjorie continued, her gaze following his. "Our cars start in the range of fifty thousand dollars," she said in an even, smooth voice, "depending, of course, on the options you decide on."

"Naturally."

Leading the way into her office, she turned back and asked, "Would you care for a cup of coffee?"

"Please."

Marjorie's thoughts were racing as she directed him toward a chair. From the corner of her eye she happened to catch a glimpse of Lydia, who flashed her a triumphant grin and the universal signal for okay.

Once Sam was comfortably seated, she poured him a mug of coffee. Although she remained outwardly poised, her heart was pumping so fast that she felt dizzy and a little shaky. She knew her face was flushed.

When Marjorie was dealing with a prospective buyer, she usually approached them with an angle. This involved asking a few subtle but pertinent questions and discovering their individual concerns. Some potential buyers were looking at a Mercedes for performance—the German-made automobile was built to cruise at twice the speed of U.S. freeways. Marjorie realized, though, that Sam wasn't interested in traveling over a hundred miles an hour. From what she knew about him, he wasn't the type who cared a great deal about prestige, either. The safety issue would evoke a response in him.

"The Mercedes-Benz is one of the safest cars in the world." She handed him a brochure from her desk drawer and took her seat.

As a saleswoman, she was as slick as frost on mossy rocks, Sam thought. Yes, she was a beautiful woman, but once she had a customer's attention, it was cars she was there to sell.

"I like to tell prospective buyers that purchasing a Mercedes-Benz is another form of life insurance," she continued. "As a physician, I'm sure you can appreciate our cars' many safety features."

Sam flipped through the pages of the glossy pamphlet and nodded. She knew her stuff, he had to give her credit for that. "You're very good."

Marjorie paused. "How do you mean?"

"As a salesman."

"Salesperson," she corrected with a smile.

"I don't think many men would be able to turn you down."

A couple of the salesmen had protested that very point when Marjorie was first hired, claiming she had an unfair advantage over the rest of them. They claimed that, sitting across the table from a good-looking female, a man would have a difficult time negotiating a price. The men might have convinced a few of the others they had a point, but Bud, the manager, was behind Marjorie. Her sales record spoke for itself. She sold cars, and that was the purpose of the dealership. If she possessed an unfair advantage, the manager didn't care as long as cars moved off the lot. But Marjorie knew that she didn't need to use her feminine wiles; the cars sold because she was a good salesperson.

"I get turned down plenty of times," she responded, her smile fading.

Sam turned the page of the brochure and read over the information on the E350. "I'll take this one."

"Pardon." Marjorie wasn't completely sure she had heard him right.

"This sedan—in a light blue, if you have it."

"You mean you want to buy one now?"

"Is that a problem?" He withdrew his checkbook from inside his coat pocket.

Marjorie had sold plenty of cars, but never any quite this way. "Don't you want to drive one? Negotiate the price?"

"Not particularly. I know you aren't going to cheat me."

"But…" Experience told her to shut up. She didn't need to kill a sale by arguing with him. She clamped her mouth closed and swallowed her questions. Sam was an adult; he knew what he wanted. Far be it from her to stand in his way.

"I trust you to be fair," he continued, adding the pertinent details to the blank check. "How much should I fill in for the amount?"

Hours later Marjorie was still completely bemused. She wandered around her apartment, moving from room to room, listless and bored and, at the same time, excited. She'd seen Sam again, and even if he had come into the showroom to buy a car and not just to see her, she was thrilled. At the same time, she regretted the encounter. Knowing that other patients fell in love with him had been reassuring, but to her dismay she'd learned that the attraction she'd experienced toward Sam hadn't lessened with time. It had been weeks since she'd last seen him, and he looked better to her than ever. All the emotions she'd struggled so valiantly to bury had surfaced the minute she'd walked into the showroom to discover him standing there. All the pleasure of seeing him again had returned to remind her how strongly Sam Bretton appealed to her.

* * *

When Sam walked back into Dixon Motors late the following morning, every word that Marjorie had rehearsed so carefully, every scenario she'd spent hours plotting, fell by the wayside. All she could see was the gentle man who had sat at her bedside and held her hand.

"Hello, Sam." It was amazing that she'd been able to utter those few words. She was trembling inside. No longer was she an inept hospital patient but a woman who knew what she liked—and Sam Bretton was it. The thought terrified her.

"Hello again."

"Everything's ready." She straightened the French cuffs of her sleeves, bemoaning the fact that virtually everything she owned was either blue, black or gray. It wasn't any wonder dates were few and far between. Marjorie swallowed her self-doubts and gestured toward the customer-service counter. "Lydia will need you to fill out a few forms."

Sam looked mildly surprised, but he followed Marjorie into the other office. Lydia greeted him with a wide smile, and Sam was left with the impression that he'd done something very right to have gained her undying gratitude.

Surely buying the Mercedes couldn't have been any more obvious, even to Marjorie. Against his better judgment, he'd decided he wanted to see her again. He'd planned on getting a luxury car someday, and now seemed as good a time as any. Besides, he wanted her to have this sale. He remembered her telling him once how she lived on commissions alone. This was his way of helping her through what was sure to be a difficult month, since the first three weeks had been spent recuperating from surgery. Because of that, he had even decided against negotiating the price.

While Sam was with Lydia, Marjorie stood on the showroom floor, pacing back and forth while she waited for him to finish. Her hands felt damp, her throat dry, and yet to all outward appearances she was as cool as a pumpkin on a frosty October morning.

When Sam was finished, she approached him with a grin and handed him the keys to his shiny new E350 sedan, which she'd arranged to have waiting for him in front of the dealership.

"That didn't take long," she said as if surprised, but it was just a means of starting a conversation. From experience, she knew the paperwork didn't take more than ten or fifteen minutes.

"Have you got time to take a spin with me?" Sam invited.

She nodded, hoping she didn't appear as eager as she felt. "Of course."

Like the true gentleman he was, Sam held open the passenger door for her, and she gracefully slipped inside. He joined her a moment later, inserted the key into the ignition, and paused to inhale the fresh scent of new leather and study the dials in front of him.

It was on the tip of Marjorie's tongue to give him another sales pitch and quote what *Car and Driver* had to say about the E350. She knew her stuff, but the sale had already been made, and he only had to drive the vehicle to be impressed.

Wordlessly Sam eased the sedan into the busy Ta-

coma traffic, quickly acquainting himself with the me-
chanics of the car. They rode past the digital signboard
above the Puget Sound Bank.

"Actually, you being able to pick up the car this
morning works rather well," Marjorie said.

"How's that?" Sam looked away from traffic long
enough to glance in her direction.

"I can treat you to lunch." As soon as the words
slipped from her lips, she was flabbergasted. She didn't
know where the invitation had come from.

"Marjorie…"

"That is unless you can't…I mean, if you're due back
at the office…. The reason I asked is that I always treat
new customers to lunch. It's my way of showing my appreciation for your business." She was convinced her
lies would someday return to haunt her.

"But *I* was thinking of taking *you* out."

"I owe you this one," she insisted. "For the car, yes,
and everything else."

"You're a difficult woman to refuse."

How Marjorie wished that were true. "How do you
like Mexican food?"

"Love it. But I really would prefer it if you allowed
me to buy lunch."

"You'd break tradition." She was convinced her nose
would start growing at any minute.

Sam grinned. The more he came to know this
woman, the more he learned about pride. "Are you always so stubborn?"

"Always," she answered evenly, and pointed to the
left-hand side of the street. "The restaurant is about a

block farther on. There's parking on the street and a small lot around back."

Sam parked easily. Once inside, they were forced to put their name on a list, but Marjorie assured him the food was well worth the wait. They were seated within ten minutes; the waitress seemed to know Marjorie.

"Do you come here often?"

She nodded and finished munching on a warm tortilla chip before answering. "At least once a week. I'm worthless in the kitchen, and it's easier for me to eat out."

Sam's insides tightened. He should have guessed that she would be a terrible cook, and he felt almost guilty because it bothered him. He'd always thought the woman he was looking to build his life with should possess at least the rudimentary culinary skills.

"The last time I experimented with a recipe," Marjorie continued, "I set off the fire alarm and cleared the entire apartment complex. Under direct orders of the building manager and the Tacoma Fire Department, I've been asked to refrain from any kitchen activities," she joked.

The sound of Sam's strained chuckle mingled with the chatter in the small restaurant.

"My sister swears that I'll make someone a wonderful husband." In many ways what Jody claimed was true; Marjorie could fix just about anything. But cooking and sewing were lost arts to her.

Sam found the food to be as good as Marjorie had claimed. He watched her eat with undisguised gusto and then pause, obviously embarrassed, to explain that she was only now regaining her appetite.

As she dabbed a drop of hot sauce from the corner of her mouth with a paper napkin, Marjorie's gaze fell to her empty plate. No doubt most women Sam dated were dainty things who ate like sparrows and wore a size two. She downed the remainder of her Mexican beer, equally sure she'd done the wrong thing by ordering it. Sam's women probably drank tea diluted with milk. For once in her life she wished she could be different. She wanted Sam to like her even with her healthy appetite and appreciation of good beer.

The waitress returned for their plates and served two cups of coffee. Sam noted the sudden lag in the conversation that followed and picked it up easily, entertaining Marjorie with anecdotes from his youth.

She was so engrossed in his stories that when she finally checked her watch, she saw that it was one-forty-five.

"Oh, Sam, I've got an appointment at two." A stockbroker was coming in to test-drive a S600 sedan, and she couldn't be late.

They hurried out of the restaurant, and Sam had her back at the dealership with minutes to spare. Even though her customer was due to arrive at any time, Marjorie was reluctant to get out of the car. She turned to face him, her hand on the door handle, wanting to tell him so many things and not knowing where to start.

"Thank you, Sam," she said softly. That seemed so inadequate. "It seems I'm always having to thank you for one reason or another. Have you noticed that?"

"No," he answered evenly. "Besides, I should be the one thanking you."

"It was only lunch." And she owed him so much

more than a simple meal. He'd given her another argument when the tab arrived, but she'd won. She realized now that it probably would have been better if she'd let him pay, male pride being what it is.

"Next time it's my turn."

Marjorie was outside the car before his words registered. "Right," she answered, and her smile broadened.

He waved. "Bye, Marjorie."

"Bye, Sam." She waited until he'd driven away and was out of sight before she entered the dealership.

No sooner had she stepped onto the showroom floor than Lydia appeared. "Where in heaven's name did the two of you take off to? You've been gone for hours! Where'd you go? Did he ask you out again? I told you he was interested. Remember what I said?"

"We went to lunch."

Lydia nodded approvingly. "I bet he took you to a fancy place on the waterfront for lobster."

Marjorie had a difficult time containing her amusement. "Actually, I treated him at The Lindo."

"That Mexican place you're always bragging about?"

"The food's wonderful."

"And you paid?"

"I...I told him I do that with all first-time car buyers."

Lydia's frown relaxed into a soft, encouraging smile. "Hey, not a bad idea."

"He said he'd treat next time." Marjorie cast her gaze longingly toward the street. "Do you think he'll phone?" She hated feeling so insecure, but more than anything else, she wanted to see Sam again.

"I bet you ten dollars he calls by tomorrow."

* * *

Lydia lost the bet.

Two days later Marjorie had chewed off two fingernails and was quickly becoming a nervous wreck. She'd never been a patient person, and waiting for Sam to contact her was slowly but surely driving her crazy.

"You aren't going to sit still for this, are you?" Lydia said over lunch.

"What other choice do I have?"

"Oh, come on, Marjorie!" Lydia declared, crumpling her napkin and tossing it atop her empty plate. "I've watched you chase after a sale when anyone else would have given it up. You have a reputation for putting deals together when others would have thrown their hands in the air."

"Yes, but selling cars and dealing with a man are two entirely different matters."

"No they're not," Lydia disagreed sharply.

"You think I should phone him?" The idea didn't appeal to her. Sam had left her with the impression that he'd contact her.

"No…" Lydia gazed thoughtfully at the ceiling fixture. "You need a more subtle approach."

"I suppose I could do what *he* did," Marjorie murmured thoughtfully.

Lydia's stare was blank. "What do you mean?"

"Meet him on his own ground. I could call for an appointment, claim I was having problems with the insurance company or something."

Lydia nearly tipped back the chair in her enthusiasm. "That's perfect, and there wouldn't be anything out of the ordinary in you showing up with the forms."

Even though it sounded easy, it took Marjorie nearly all afternoon to work up the courage to contact Sam's office. Since she feared the receptionist would probably handle any insurance work, she asked for an actual appointment and was given one later the following week. Now that she'd taken some positive action, she felt a hundred times better—until she saw Lydia's shocked face later that afternoon.

"What's the matter?"

"Dr. Sam's office just called."

"And?"

"And, well...apparently Dr. Sam looked over his schedule and saw your name."

"So?"

"Marjorie, I'm sure there's a logical explanation."

"Lydia, for heaven's sake, will you stop beating around the bush and tell me what's going on?"

"You know Mary and I are good friends, don't you?"

From what she remembered, Mary was Sam's receptionist. "Yes, what did she say?"

"Mary told me that when Dr. Sam saw your name, he got upset, swore under his breath, and asked Mary to call you and suggest you make an appointment with another doctor."

Five

Marjorie turned on the television, and plunked herself down on the overstuffed sofa, crossing her arms in a defiant gesture. Five minutes later she dug through the sofa cushions to find the remote and switched channels, not that it helped any. She was too furious for coherent thought, and the possibility of a mere television movie salving her injured ego was nil.

Men! Sam Bretton in particular! None of them were worth all this aggravation. She had behaved like a fool over Sam, and knowing it made her lack of savoir faire all the more difficult to swallow.

Hindsight nearly always proved to be twenty-twenty, but she should have known not to trust a man who preferred mild salsa on his enchiladas. If he couldn't eat a jalapeño straight from the jar, he wasn't her type. She liked her food *and* her men spicy and pungent. Sam was too…too wonderful. That was it, much too wonderful.

Depression settled over her shoulders like a dark mantle, and she rubbed her forearms to ward off a late-evening chill that had little to do with the mild Puget

Sound weather. Sam and she were simply too different. Sam no doubt liked moonlight walks and a glass of wine in front of the fireplace, and she liked…moonlight walks and a glass of wine in front of the fireplace. Well, going over every detail a hundred times wasn't going to settle anything. He didn't want to see her again, and that was that.

She was an adult; she should be able to handle disappointments. Obviously Sam was interested in meek, mild women who knew their place. She was neither, and it was far easier to face that truth now than later, when her heart was completely infected and the prognosis for recovery would be against her.

Once Marjorie had sorted through her myriad thoughts, she felt better, even good enough to put this unpleasantness behind her and think about fixing herself something to eat. She left the television on and wandered into the kitchen. The freezer contained a wide assortment of prepackaged meals, but none of them appealed to her. Popcorn suited her mood—something crunchy and salty would help to vent her frustration. Microwave popcorn, naturally. What she'd told Sam about her lack of expertise in the kitchen had been true. She could manage spreadsheets and calculators in her sleep, but recipes baffled her. Having her anywhere in the vicinity of hot grease was like putting a submachine gun in the hands of a raw recruit. In fact, she didn't even own a complete set of cookware. The less she involved herself with a stove top, the better.

Marjorie inserted the popcorn bag, set the timer and waited. Soon the sounds and smells of the butter-flavored kernels filled the small apartment.

She had just opened the bag and munched down the first handful when the doorbell chimed. A glance at the wall clock told her it was after nine. She certainly wasn't expecting anyone. The hope that it might be Sam caused her to hurry. It wouldn't be him, of course—she knew that—but she so wanted to see him again that her mind tormented her with the possibility.

With an eagerness that was difficult to explain, she opened her front door. Sam was standing on the other side. It was as though her wishful thinking had conjured him up.

"Hello, Sam." She greeted him as though she'd been expecting him all along, revealing no surprise.

He looked terrible. Exhausted, overworked and not himself. She would have thought he would never allow a strand of hair to fall out of place, but his hair wasn't the only thing rumpled; everything about him looked unkempt. His clothes hung on him, and the top two buttons of his shirt were unfastened. He hadn't shaved in a couple of days, or so it appeared.

"I have had the most exhausting day of my life," he announced, walking past her and into the apartment.

Bemused, Marjorie remained at the entrance, her hand on the doorknob. She'd expected contrition, guilt, grief, but not this out-and-out appeal for sympathy.

"It's been one thing after another," he continued undaunted. Without invitation, he picked up her remote and cued up the guide at the bottom of the screen.

"Would you like something to drink?" she offered, choosing to ignore his opening statement.

"Please." He sank onto her sofa and leaned forward to wipe the tiredness from his eyes. He'd planned on calling her hours earlier and inviting her to dinner. Before he could get to a phone, Nancy Brightfield had gone into labor, and he'd spent the next five hours at the hospital with her. The delivery had been difficult, and he hadn't been able to get away until now. The unexpected trip to the delivery room and the arrival of Baby Brightfield had been a climax to a long, tedious day.

Sam realized that arriving unannounced on Marjorie's doorstep probably hadn't been one of his most brilliant ideas, but he wanted to straighten out a few things between them, and delaying the discussion was potentially unwise. He was beginning to know Marjorie Majors, and the message she was bound to read into the canceled appointment would be all wrong.

Marjorie went into her kitchen to survey her meager supply of refreshments. All she could find was a two-liter bottle of flat cola in the back of her refrigerator, a can of tomato juice with a rusty crust over the aluminum top, and a carton of milk she'd been meaning to toss for the past week.

"Is instant coffee all right?"

"Fine, fine." He really didn't care. All he really wanted was the chance for a long talk with her. He leaned back and inhaled deeply, paused, then asked, "Do I smell popcorn?"

Grinning, Marjorie stuck her head around the corner of her kitchen. Nothing smelled better than freshly popped popcorn. "Want some?"

Sam shook his head. "No, thanks. I haven't had any dinner."

"This is my dinner."

His face twisted into a mock scowl that revealed his

amusement. She had to be joking with him. "You're kidding, right?"

"No."

Sam jumped up from the couch with a reserve of energy he hadn't realized he possessed. "You can't eat that for dinner...it's unhealthy."

"I disagree." Everything she'd read contradicted Sam. The kernels were reported to be a good source of fiber, and since she ate her main meal at noon, it made sense to have something light in the evenings.

"Don't you know you're not supposed to argue with a doctor?" Actually, Sam wasn't as concerned about the nutritional value of popcorn as he was that her choice for her evening meal gave him an excellent excuse to invite her out.

"Sam, it isn't any big deal...."

"Come on, I'll take you to dinner."

Marjorie hedged. "But you just said today's been the most exhausting day of your life. What you need is to put up your feet and enjoy a good home-cooked meal." Oh, heavens, why had she suggested that? Sam would assume she planned to do the cooking, and then there would be real trouble. She might be able to bluff her way through some things, but a complete meal was out of the question.

The idea of Marjorie preparing a meal for him appealed to Sam, but he studied her carefully. Maybe he'd misunderstood her earlier. "You told me you don't cook."

At that moment she would gladly have surrendered three commissions to Al Swanson in exchange for the ability to whip together a three-egg cheese-and-mushroom omelet, but she knew better than to offer. Still, the temptation was so strong. She opened her mouth and closed it again. "I make excellent microwave popcorn," she offered weakly, and gestured toward the open bag sitting on the counter behind her.

"Then popcorn it is," Sam said, lowering himself back onto the couch. While he waited, he glanced back at the television and recognized an old-fashioned romance from the late fifties. He wouldn't have thought Marjorie would appreciate anything so sentimental. But then, she'd surprised him before.

"Here's your coffee and dinner. It's the specialty of the house." She brought in a steaming cup and handed it to him, along with a breadbasket filled with hot popcorn. "I'll be back in a minute."

"I owe you a dinner, you know."

"As I recall, it's a lunch, and if you're counting that, you might as well add a movie and popcorn to the list." He didn't owe her anything. Not really. She was the one in debt to him. Sam had given her so much more than she could ever hope to repay.

He relaxed against the thick cushions and felt his body release a silent sigh of relief. He'd missed Marjorie over the past couple of days. Missed her wit. Missed her warmth. Missed her smile. He'd wanted to see her again despite his reservations. For two days he'd been trying to find the time to call her, but there were never more than those odd five minutes here or ten minutes there. Besides, what he had to say would be better said in person. There was too much room for misunderstanding over the phone. But letting another day pass without seeing her would only add to his mounting frustration, so he'd headed over here tonight despite the late hour.

She joined him a minute later, stretched her legs on top of the coffee table and crossed them at the ankles. Judging exactly where she should sit had been a problem. If she sat too close, he might read something into that. On the other hand, if she positioned herself as far away as possible, he might think she didn't want him around, and nothing could be further from the truth.

They sat quietly and watched the movie for a moment, then she ventured into conversation. "So. Tell me about your day."

"It was nonstop busy, and then, just as I was getting ready to leave, a woman came in, ready to have her first baby. And then, as sometimes happens, I had a difficult delivery."

Even as she tried not to, Marjorie started laughing. "*You* had a difficult delivery? How's the poor mother doing?"

"Better than me, I think. She got her girl."

"And what did you get?"

The same reward that came with every new life he brought into the world: pride and a deep sense of satisfaction.

"Plenty," he answered, in a gentle way that assured her that no matter what problems he faced, he was content with his life.

The unexpected vision of Marjorie with a baby, their baby, in her arms produced such an intense longing that his breath jammed in his lungs. He shook his head to dispel the image, but it remained, clearer than before. For years Sam had brought children into the world. He'd spent countless hours encouraging new mothers and an almost equal amount of time soothing soon-to-be fathers, but only rarely had he thought about the woman who would give *him* children one day.

Their eyes met, and Sam's smile embraced her. She didn't know what he was thinking, but if she'd been holding her coffee cup, it would have slipped from her fingers. Sam had the most sensuous smile of any man she'd ever known.

"So how have *you* been?"

"Good." She nodded once, then swallowed and headed for the deep end. "About that appointment…"

"Yes, I wanted to talk to you about that."

"I got the insurance papers straightened out—no problem."

"Insurance papers? You made the appointment to go over some papers?" Sam felt like a heel now. He'd thought she'd wanted a physical or something else equally impossible.

Her excuse to see him sounded so flimsy now that a deep flush crept up her neck and over her ears.

"It would be best if you got another physician," Sam said, and cleared his throat. "I'd be more than happy to recommend one if you want."

Marjorie couldn't believe what she was hearing. He said it so calmly, without so much as a hint of regret, as though they were discussing the weather or something equally trivial. With those few words he was telling her that he wanted her out of his life.

Unable to trust her voice, she nodded.

"It's important for everyone to have a regular physician," Sam insisted. "Cal Johnson will be doing the follow-up after your appendectomy, but he's a surgeon, and you need a general practitioner."

Marjorie's throat closed up on her, the tightness making it difficult to breathe evenly.

The wounded look in her eyes tore at Sam's heart. It was apparent that she still didn't understand. He would have to spell it out for her.

"I think you're wonderful, Marjorie."

Sure he did. Enough to dump her right when she needed him.

"I'd like to see a lot more of you," Sam continued, "and I can't do that if you continue to be my patient."

Marjorie jerked her head around. What had he said? He wanted to see her? As in date her? Spend time with her? Be with her? She blinked and pointed her index finger at her chest. "You want to see more of me?"

"Don't look so surprised."

"I'm not.... It's just that..."

"It shouldn't seem all that sudden. You must have known in the hospital I was interested. Believe me, I don't spend that much time with all my patients."

"I know, but...I don't know..." She was unsure, confused. Her gaze narrowed as she studied him. It would be best to clear away any misconceptions up front. "It's not gratitude, you know."

"It's not?" He didn't quite follow her meaning.

"Of course I'm grateful for everything you've done, but if we'd met on the street, I'd have felt the same things I do now."

"Which are?" he prompted, scooting closer to her. His dark eyes surveyed her with renewed interest.

"Never mind," she said with a small laugh. She could

see no reason to inflate his ego any higher than it was already.

With his eyes steadily holding hers, Sam tucked a finger beneath her chin and slowly raised her mouth to his. Marjorie's eyelids fluttered closed as she awaited the warm sensation of his lips settling over hers. He didn't keep her waiting long. His arms encircled her, drawing her gently against his hard chest.

Their lips met in an unrushed exploration, as though they had all the time in the world and there wasn't any reason to hurry anything. His mouth was moist and pliant against her own, moving with such gentleness, such care that a tiny shudder worked its way through Marjorie, and with it came a helpless moan.

After torturous seconds Sam's lips reluctantly left hers. He buried his face in the curve of her shoulder and inhaled a calming breath. He'd felt physically drained when he'd arrived. Now he was alive, more alive than he could ever remember being. Holding Marjorie, touching her, energized him, filled him with purpose, exhilarated him, eased the ache of loneliness that followed whenever he returned to an empty house after a delivery.

The wealth of sensation took Marjorie by surprise. A simple kiss—their first—had left her with a hunger as deep as the sea. Emotion clogged her throat, and she held him to her, her fingers weaving through the thick strands of his dark hair.

"Marjorie?"

"Hmm?"

"Do you always smell this good?"

Her eyes remained closed, and she grinned. "I think it's the popcorn."

"Not this. It's roses, I think."

"My perfume."

"And sunshine."

"I showered when I got home."

He shook his head, declining her explanation. "And something more, something I can't define."

"*That's* probably the popcorn."

Sam shook his head. "Not this," he countered softly. "Not this."

The reluctance with which he loosened his hold thrilled her. They straightened and went back to watching the movie. He tucked his arm around her, and she rested her head against his shoulder. The warmth of his nearness convinced her that the man beside her was indeed real and not the product of a fanciful imagination or some delayed anesthesia-induced illusion.

A multitude of unanswered questions ran through her mind. It was on the tip of her tongue to blurt out everything she felt for him, but she feared ruining this special evening.

"So you enjoy old movies," he said, the thought pleasing him.

"Especially the classics. They did romances so well in those days."

"You like romance?"

Marjorie nodded and hid a smile. "I'm liking it more all the time."

"I am, too," Sam agreed, and turned her toward him. He wanted to kiss her again, taste her sweetness and experience once again that special power she possessed that filled him with such energy.

It was a long time before Marjorie saw any more of the movie. Or cared.

Six

"You aren't going to let Al get away with it, are you?" Lydia cried in outrage, indignation flushing her cheeks.

Marjorie didn't need to be angry about Al Swanson's latest attempt to steal a customer from her; Lydia was furious enough for the both of them. "Bud will be the one to decide."

"But you know Al is lying."

"It's my word against his, and unfortunately Bud's only the manager, not Solomon."

"But it's so unfair."

"Tell me about it," Marjorie grumbled.

Once again Al had tried to horn in on her deal. Only this time he'd succeeded. Marjorie had spoken to a couple about a E63 AMG sedan, worked with them, called twice to keep them interested, and even rode with them as they went on four different test drives in order to answer their numerous questions. The last time, the couple had gone home to sleep on the decision and returned the following day with a deposit. Al had met them at the door, claimed Marjorie had stepped out of the office, and they had accepted his offer to write up the deal on her behalf. This was the same trick he'd used once before, only this time it worked. Once the paperwork was firmly clenched in his hand, Marjorie didn't have a leg to stand on. She had complained to the manager, insisted she had been at the dealership and not out, as Al had alleged. Since Bud had been gone and there wasn't anyone to verify her story, things didn't look good for her. But she knew the manager wasn't completely naive when it came to Al. She was certain he'd heard complaints from several of the other salespeople. Bud's fair assessment of the situation was Marjorie's only real hope. Unfortunately Al's name was on the paperwork.

The commission scale was based on how much profit the dealership made on the sale of each new car. Marjorie collected thirty percent of the capital gain. In this case she'd worked hard to give the couple the best deal possible. Her share was meager enough. If forced to split her commission with Al, she would have worked long, hard hours for practically nothing. Everything rested on Bud's decision.

"But Bud doesn't know Al the way we do," Lydia continued insistently.

Marjorie studied her friend and was hard-pressed to hold back her own indignation. Al might think he was getting away with something, but if she had anything to do with it, the cheating salesman would spend the next fifty years regretting his underhandedness. Given enough rope, Al Swanson was bound to hang himself sooner or later, and she intended to be around to see it happen.

"If he's tried those things with me, you know he's

done it with the others," she said thoughtfully after a while. Yes, she was furious, but losing her cool wouldn't solve anything.

"It's the meantime that I'm worried about," Lydia mumbled, crossing her arms and righteously over her chest. "When's Bud going to let you know?"

Marjorie glanced at her watch. "As soon as he gets in."

The low hum of the intercom caught their attention. "Marjorie, call on line three. Marjorie—line three."

"I better get that," Marjorie mumbled, and sighed. "It could mean another sale."

"Not if Al can get his greedy hands on it," Lydia responded sourly, and returned to her place behind the customer-service counter.

With her friend's words ringing in her ears, Marjorie walked over to her office and reached for the phone. "Marjorie Majors," she said in a cordial, businesslike tone.

"Dr. Sam Bretton here," Sam returned.

She sat down and propped her elbows on the desktop. A rush of pleasure washed over her, taking with it some of the bitter aftertaste of Al's trickery. "Hello."

"I was just thinking about you."

"Oh?" She knew that she sounded about as intelligent as mold, but he'd taken her by surprise.

"I just returned from the hospital, and my first appointment isn't scheduled for another five minutes, so I thought I'd give you a call. You don't mind, do you?"

"No…it's a pleasant surprise."

"How's your day going?"

"Fair." It would have been much better if things were

settled between her and Al, but none of this mess was Sam's problem. "How about your morning?"

"Hectic, as always." Actually, he'd been preoccupied, thinking about Marjorie and angry with himself for not setting a date for their next...well, date. He'd left her apartment feeling exhilarated and excited. They'd sat and talked long after the movie had finished, easily drifting from one subject to another. She was well-read and knowledgeable about current affairs. He'd found her opinions insightful and intelligent, and marveled that he'd found a woman who stirred his heart as well as his mind. So she didn't cook; he could deal with that. He enjoyed her company, relished their time together and longed to see her again soon. Unfortunately, his head had been in the clouds, and he hadn't thought to make plans. He'd tried calling her apartment, but she'd already left for work. He knew she worked long hours and decided his best chance of catching her was at Dixon's. He didn't want to wait another two days to see her again.

"I suppose I should apologize for last night," she said softly.

"Why?" Something was wrong. Sam could detect the subtle difference in her voice. Whatever it was, he hoped she would share it with him.

"I feel bad about not being able to offer you anything more appetizing than microwave popcorn."

"I can't remember when I've enjoyed a meal more."

Marjorie was sure that couldn't be true. No doubt there were a thousand nurses out there who longed to lure him into their arms with hot chocolate-chip cookies straight from the oven. Her microwave couldn't hope to compete with all the talented, domestically inclined women who wanted him.

"Are you free tonight?" he asked, thinking about taking her to the waterfront for a lobster dinner. He wanted to wine and dine her, and give her an evening she would remember the rest of her life. He thought about bringing her to his home and showing her his view of Commencement Bay. He wanted to sit by the fireplace with her and watch the flickering light dance over her face.

"Tonight?" she asked, confused by the unexpected invitation.

Sooner, if possible, Sam thought, but he knew his schedule wouldn't allow it.

"Actually, I'm working late, so maybe…"

"What time do you get off?"

She wished he wasn't so insistent. With Bud's decision hanging over her head, she needed some time alone to clear her thoughts. When she was with Sam, she wanted to look and feel her best. "Would it be all right if I called you next week sometime?"

Sam's breath caught at the implication. There wasn't a woman alive who threw him off course with as much ease as Marjorie. Just when he was prepared to overlook her flaws and lay his heart at her feet, she made it sound as though going to dinner with him was an inconvenience.

"Sure," he returned flippantly. "You call me. That won't be any problem."

But it was, and Marjorie recognized it from his stiff tone. She had just opened her mouth to explain when he spoke again.

"Listen, I've got to get back to my patients. We'll

talk soon." He was eager to get off the phone. The entire conversation had left a bad taste in his mouth. He'd read Marjorie wrong, read everything wrong. It wasn't the first time she'd led him astray. The stock market was more predictable than Marjorie Majors.

"Right." But her voice was barely audible. "Goodbye, Sam. Thanks for calling."

He didn't answer, and she bit her bottom lip to keep from shouting that she would love to see him any night, any time, if only she didn't have this mess with Al to settle first. The phone went dead, and Marjorie felt physically ill. She'd ruined everything.

The polite knock outside her office lifted her from the pit of despair.

"It's only me," Lydia said, opening the door and peeking inside. "Hey, you look like you just lost your best friend. What happened? Another deal fall through?"

The words congealed in Marjorie's throat, and it took a few moments for her to unscramble her thoughts. "That was Sam."

"Dr. Sam?"

It was all Marjorie could do to nod. "I blew it."

"Oh, good grief," Lydia said. "Not again."

Marjorie dropped her gaze to the floor. "I'm afraid so."

"What did you do?"

"He suggested we get together tonight, and I said I was busy and that it would be better if I contacted him next week."

A moment of stunned silence followed.

"You didn't! Tell me you didn't say that!" Lydia marched into the room and pressed both hands on top of Marjorie's desk, leaning forward so that their faces were scant inches apart. "If the two of you ever get together, I swear it will be a miracle. Good grief, what made you put him off that way?"

"I don't know. This thing with Al's really got me down, and I wanted Sam to see me at my best, not my worst."

Lydia closed her eyes and slowly shook her head. "I've got more bad news for you."

"What's that?"

"Bud's here," Lydia announced starkly. "And he's in one hell of a bad mood. He wants to see you right away."

Even before Marjorie left the dealership at a quarter after nine, she knew she wasn't heading home. Sam's Brown's Point address was tucked safely away in her purse, and she had every intention of talking to him before she did anything else. Maybe she could undo some of the damage.

She located the house without a problem, pulled into the wide driveway and turned off her engine. Sam's home was a magnificent sprawling ranch house made of used brick. Huge picture windows faced the street.

Her heart was pounding like a locomotive chugging uphill. Now she understood what courage it had taken for him to arrive unannounced at her apartment. She didn't often do this sort of thing, and the need to swallow her pride made it all the more difficult.

While her conviction held, she climbed out of the car and marched up to his front door like a soldier making his way to the front of a firing squad. Her hand faltered as she rang the bell.

She heard Sam's footsteps long before the door was opened.

"Marjorie." He blinked, certain she was a figment of his imagination.

"I know I should have called, but…"

"No," he said, and smiled that slow, sexy smile of his as he stepped aside. "Come in, please."

Relieved by his warm welcome, she entered his home. The first thing that she noticed when he led her into the huge, tiled entryway was the large, unobstructed view of Commencement Bay from the floor-to-ceiling living-room windows. The twinkling lights of barges and ferryboats lit up the inky black night and reflected off the water.

"Oh, Sam," she said, her voice low in wonder. "This is so beautiful…it's marvelous." Words failed her, and she simply stared into the night.

"I love it, too." He didn't know what had brought her here, and he didn't care. She'd been on his mind all day. He regretted the abrupt way in which he'd ended their telephone conversation, and all because his fragile ego had been pricked. Most of the evening had been spent trying to come up with a way to see her again and preserve both his pride as well as hers.

"Sam," she said, tearing her gaze from the water and turning to face him. Her features were strained with an expression of practiced poise. "I've come to apologize for this morning."

"No," he countered quickly, sensing her apprehension. "I should be the one to do that." The appeal in her gaze cut a path straight to his heart, but he kept his own features tightly controlled.

"You?" she said, and laughed shortly. "I was the one who was rude."

"Something was troubling you. I knew it the minute you spoke." He longed to ease whatever was bothering her and kicked himself more than once for having been such a fool.

Her eyes narrowed as she studied him. If Sam found her so readable, it would be difficult to hide anything from him.

"Come in and relax," he offered, leading her into the living room. The white leather couch was L-shaped, and decorated with several huge pillows in brilliant shades of blue to complement the plush carpet.

Marjorie sat, and her gaze drifted once more to the panoramic view of Commencement Bay. Just being here with Sam soothed her. All day she'd been battling her resentment toward Al and what the loss of this commission would mean to her already strained budget.

"Do you want to tell me about it?" Sam asked, taking a seat beside her.

Marjorie nodded. "I owe you that much, at least." For the next half hour she explained what had happened with Al—though she was careful not to name names—and how his devious methods had cheated her out of half the commission. By the time she'd finished, Sam was pacing in front of the coffee table with barely restrained anger. The corners of his mouth were pinched and white, his hands knotted in tight fists.

"What's being done about this?" he demanded.

"Nothing."

"Nothing?" Sam repeated incredulously.

"The decision's already been made."

"But he lied."

"I know that, and so does nearly everyone else, but it's his name on the contract, so he's entitled to a commission no matter how much time I spent with those people. At least my protest to the manager earned me half of it. That's the way things are done in sales."

It had been a long time since Sam had felt this angry. He wanted to find Marjorie's coworker in a dark alley some night and teach him a lesson. The intensity of his fury shocked him; he hated unnecessary violence.

"I'll take care of this for you," Sam said without any real plan in mind. He knew how hard Marjorie worked—the long hours with few free weekends. She'd climbed her way up the sales ladder and deserved to be a success. The last thing she needed was someone sabotaging her efforts. The burning desire to protect her seared through him like a surgical laser beam.

"Sam, please. I'm a big girl, I'll find a solution my own way."

"No." He shook his head once, hard. "I want to handle this."

"Sam." His reaction wasn't a joke, she realized. If she'd known this was the way he was going to be, then she wouldn't have told him about Al. As it was, she was glad she'd been careful not to mention Al's name. "Listen to me. I appreciate your concern, but I don't involve myself in your business, so I'm asking you not to interfere in mine. Things have a way of working themselves out."

"But this heel deserves—"

"Everything he's going to get." She stood and placed her hand on his forearm. "I don't need anyone to rescue me. I've been on my own for a long time now. This guy hasn't made many friends at Dixon's. He won't last long."

"You're sure?" At her nod, Sam relaxed a bit. "Have you eaten yet?"

"No," she answered with a smile, surprised to realize how hungry she was. "Are you offering to feed me?"

"Better than that," he answered with a slow, sensuous grin that edged his strong, well-shaped mouth upward. "I'm willing to cook for you."

Just looking at Sam made Marjorie feel light-headed. She could drown in those appealing eyes of his, dark, deep, penetrating.

"Follow me," he instructed, taking her hand and leading her into his kitchen. He was a good cook and thought he might be able to teach her a thing or two.

Sam's kitchen was huge and equipped with every modern convenience. An island with restaurant quality gas burners was set up in the middle of the expansive floor. A wide assortment of copper pots, pans and skillets was suspended from the ceiling above the island.

"Wow," Marjorie said, and released a slow, wondering breath. "You must be some chef."

"I try." He pulled out a stool for her to sit on. "First things first." With that he opened the wine refrigerator and, with little hesitation, drew out a bottle, then chose two tall wineglasses from a cabinet.

Expertly he removed the cork and poured them each a glass, pausing to taste his first. He gave his approval before handing the second glass to Marjorie.

While she sipped her Chablis, Sam set to work with

a huge wok, a large supply of fresh vegetables and a sharp cleaver.

It had been hours since she'd last eaten, and the first glass of wine went straight to her head. "Here, let me help," she offered, slipping off the stool.

"No, you don't. You're my guest," Sam insisted, noting the way her cheeks were reddening. She was already a little tipsy.

He refilled her glass, and she sat down again and took another sip. "So you don't want my help. Have you been talking to the fire department?"

"No." Sam chuckled and set about slicing the vegetables in neat, even sections. "This is a recipe a friend of mine from Hong Kong taught me several years back. It's authentic and delicious."

"Is there anything you can't do?" she asked, only a little intimidated.

"A few things."

She sighed, crossed her legs and sipped some more wine. "My grandmother used to do all the cooking."

"Your grandmother?" he prompted. She rarely talked about her childhood, he'd noticed.

"Jody and I went to live with her after Mom and Dad were killed in an automobile accident."

"How old were you?"

"Twelve going on twenty. Grandma loved us, don't get me wrong. She tried to make a decent home for the two of us, but she was old, and her health wasn't good. The main problem was money. Grandma took care of Jody and the house, and I found work to bring in extra income."

Sam reached for the wine bottle and replenished her glass. The Chablis was loosening her tongue.

"So your grandmother raised the two of you?"

She nodded, holding the stem of the glass with both hands. "Right. This room feels awfully warm?" she said, and fanned her face.

Suppressing a smile, he gazed at her, trying not to laugh outright. "I think I'd better feed you, and the sooner the better."

"I'd rather you kissed me," she told him, then blinked and covered her mouth with her hand. "Oops, I didn't mean to say that."

Sam pushed the vegetables aside. "Did you mean it?"

Sheepishly, she nodded. "I think the wine's gone to my head."

"I think so, too." He walked around to stand directly in front of her. His smile was filled with confident amusement.

Her dark eyes followed his movements and innocently pleaded with him for a kiss. Unable to resist her, he leaned forward and gently covered her mouth with his own. His intention had been to appease her until he'd finished stir-frying their dinner, but the instant his lips met hers, he was lost. He deepened the kiss, his lips playing over hers as though she were a rare musical instrument.

His kiss burned through Marjorie like fire raging through dry brush. When he reluctantly lifted his head from hers, she swayed, and his hands on her shoulders were all that kept her from tumbling to the floor.

"I think you're right," she admitted. "I need something to eat...quick."

Sam's eyes burned into hers, and his strong, steady voice shook slightly. "I was just thinking that we should forget about dinner and continue with the kissing."

She tilted her head up to look into his eyes, resisting the urge to reach out and cling to him. "You were?"

"But you're right."

"I am?" At the moment she didn't think so as she watched him turn back to the stove. After a while she stood on shaky feet, unfastened her jacket and removed it. By the time she'd finished loosening the top buttons of her shirt, Sam had their meal ready.

He handed her a plate and pulled another stool up beside hers. The tantalizing scent of hot oil and ginger wafted toward her, and her stomach reacted with a loud growl. She placed her hand over her abdomen and smiled sheepishly. "Sorry."

"When was the last time you had anything to eat?"

"Noon." Soup. She'd been too upset to down anything else, so now she was famished.

Sam used chopsticks, holding the plate with one hand while dexterously using the wooden sticks with the other. She tried the same thing and nearly dumped her dinner on her lap.

"You'd better use a fork," he advised, humor lurking in his eyes.

She nodded meekly. Once she had a fork in her hand, she discovered the food was both hot and spicy. Closing her eyes, she savored each mouthful as though she hadn't eaten in weeks instead of hours.

"Oh, Sam, this is really good."

"I do my best," he answered, but his interest wasn't in the dinner. Marjorie, the woman who had tormented his dreams for weeks, was sitting across from him. Part angel, part temptress. Complicated, vital and ripe, an opulent beauty. He'd dreamed of having her with him in his home, envisioned carrying her into his room and laying her across his king-size bed. He wanted to love her, ease the ache of loneliness he read in her eyes and make up to her for the childhood she'd lost.

Following the meal, Sam made a fresh pot of coffee. Marjorie, feeling sober and steady on her feet after the delicious dinner, poured them each a cup and carried them into the living room. They sat close to each other, and she tucked her feet up under her and placed her head on his sturdy shoulder.

"You're not going to drift off on me, are you?" he asked gently. His hand curved around her nape, and his fingers stroked the slope of her neck and shoulder.

"If you keep doing that, I will." She felt him smile against her hair. "I'm sorry to be such poor company," she said, uttering the words through a loud yawn.

"You're not."

She half lifted her head. "I don't know what it is, but every time I'm around you all I do is sleep."

"I often have that effect on women," Sam said, and chuckled. The rich sound of his amusement echoed around the room. He was thinking of going to bed, too, but not in the same sense she was. Holding her close was a tough temptation to handle.

She tried unsuccessfully to stifle another yawn. "Believe me, I know how women react to you."

"I'd better get you home, Kitten."

"Kitten?" No one had ever called her anything but her name, at least not to her face.

"You remind me of one," he explained softly. "You're all soft and cuddly."

"I have claws."

Again he smiled. "Now that's something I can personally attest to."

Marjorie was smiling when she unfolded her legs from beneath her and stood. She collected her jacket and purse, and paused in the entryway. "It seems I'm always in your debt."

Sam's brow furrowed as he rose. "How's that?"

"First you rescue me from the jaws of death…"

"That's a slight exaggeration."

"Then you buy a car from me…"

"One I intended to purchase anyway."

"Next you feed me."

There was a lot more Sam was interested in doing for her, and if she didn't hurry up and leave, he was going to have more problems refusing her.

"Thank you, Sam, once again."

"Thank *you*."

They paused in front of the door, and Sam turned her in his arms. His hands locked at the small of her back, pulling her closer against the solid wall of his chest. His hips and thighs pressed against hers, and still they weren't close enough.

Marjorie had no intention of refusing his kiss, not when she craved it herself. His mouth closed possessively over hers, searing his name onto her heart. Again and again he kissed her with a fierce tenderness, shaping and fitting her lips with his own.

Sam's arms circled her protectively while his tongue explored the soft recesses of her mouth until she shook with a sensation she had never known.

"Sam..."

"Kitten," he murmured.

Wildly consuming kisses followed, and Marjorie felt as though she were on fire. Never had she felt so willing, so sensuous. There'd been little time for puppy love when she was young. Later, the men she'd dated had resented her streak of independence. When it came to lovemaking and men, she was shockingly innocent. The sensations Sam had awakened in her had been dormant far too long. Now that she'd discovered love, she wasn't going to let go lightly.

An insistent beeping surrounded them, and Sam's impatient groan told her the noise wasn't the bells on the hill tolling their love.

"What is it?" she whispered, hardly able to find her voice.

"Not what, but who."

She blinked, not understanding.

"That's my pager. I'm needed at the hospital."

Seven

The phone pealed loudly in the darkened bedroom. At first Marjorie incorporated the irritating sound into her dream. By the third ear-shattering ring she realized it was her telephone.

Without lifting her head from the pillow, she stretched out her arm and groped for the receiver, locating it in time to cut off the fourth ring.

"Yes," she mumbled, and brushed the wild confusion of hair from her face.

"Kitten?"

Her eyes flew open, and she struggled into a sitting position and reached for the small clock on her nightstand. "Sam?"

"I'm sorry to wake you, but I wanted to be sure you got home safely."

She blinked and focused her gaze on the illuminated clock dial. It was a few minutes after four. "I didn't have any problems. How did things go at the hospital?"

"Great. Wonderful, in fact."

She relaxed and leaned against the thick goose-down pillow, savoring the warmth that never failed to infuse her whenever Sam called. "Did you deliver another baby?"

"Two, actually, or I would have been back hours ago."

"Girls? Boys?"

"One of each." He felt like a fool, calling her at this ungodly hour, but he'd walked into his empty house, and everywhere he looked, he thought of Marjorie. The memory of her presence swirled around him like the soft scent of summer. Often the stark loneliness of his lifestyle had hit him after a nighttime delivery, but never more than it had this time. He would have given anything in the world to have found her curled up and sleeping in his bed, waiting for him. Hearing her voice was a poor substitute, but one he couldn't deny himself.

"I realized when I got back to the house," he continued, "that I hadn't asked to see you again." Even to his own ears, the explanation sounded lame.

"No, we both had other things on our minds."

"Dinner tonight, then?" he asked.

Marjorie wasn't thinking clearly; her mind was clouded with the last dregs of sleep. "What day is this?"

"Friday."

Her disappointment was potent enough to produce a bout of aching frustration. "I can't," she moaned. "My sister is driving up from Portland, and I'm working late both days this weekend."

"I'll take both you and your sister to dinner, then." That was an easy enough solution.

"But, Sam…"

"No arguing. Your sister, and anyone else you want,

is welcome to join us." He didn't care if he had to buy dinner for every employee at Dixon Motors as long as he could spend time with Marjorie.

"You're sure?"

"Absolutely. And while we're on the subject of dinners and dates, I know it's next week and you might be busy, but do you have plans for July Fourth?"

"No."

"You don't have to work?"

"No," she murmured, and smiled. "That would be un-American. What makes you ask…about the Fourth, I mean?"

"Another doctor and his wife, Bernie and Betty Miller, have a cabin on Hood Canal, and they invited me up. Would you spend the day with me?"

Marjorie closed her eyes to hold back the tears of joy. "I'd be thrilled."

"I'll let the Millers know, then."

They must have talked for another half hour before Marjorie realized that Sam's slow responses revealed his exhaustion.

"Oh, Sam, I'm sorry. You must be dead on your feet, and I'm talking your head off."

His grin was both lazy and content. "No. Listening to you relaxes me. Normally when I get back from the hospital, especially this late, I'm too tense to sleep— too keyed up. Now I feel like I could easily drift off."

"Good night, then," she murmured softly, regretfully. She was falling head over heels for Sam Bretton. She knew the pitfalls and still wanted to love him.

"A doctor?" Jody squealed with unrestrained delight. At twenty she was a younger version of Marjorie, the only difference being her hair, which was cut fashionably short, and her sportier and more colorful clothes.

"You behave yourself," Marjorie warned. Now that her health was back and she didn't have to submit to Jody's orders, she could more fully appreciate her sibling.

Jody looked her sister full in the eye. "You mean I can't tell Sam about the time you snuck out of the house to kiss Freddy Fletcher behind the toolshed?"

"You do, and I'll smack you upside the head."

The light, musical sound of Jody's laughter filled the cozy apartment. "I have to admit, though, you look a hundred times better than the last time I was here. I wonder if your doctor friend has anything to do with that?"

"I look better because I haven't been forced to eat your cooking, which is even worse than my own."

Jody pretended the remark had greatly offended her, but neither of them had been blessed with talent in the kitchen, and they enjoyed teasing each other about that fact.

"So Sam was your doctor," Jody said, as she slumped on the couch and crossed her legs Indian style beneath her. "How come you didn't mention him before now?"

"I… He… Well, what really happened is…"

"Oh honestly, Marjie, look at your face. You're actually blushing. I can't believe it. My big sister is in love. Well, good grief, it took you long enough."

Marjorie's hands flew to her cheeks in embarrassment. They did feel hot and were no doubt as flushed as her sister claimed.

"You're in love with him, aren't you?" Jody asked,

pretending to study her nails, but actually aiming her gaze toward her older sister.

"Yes," Marjorie answered honestly.

"Have you gone to bed with him yet?"

"Jody!"

"Well, have you?"

The heat in Marjorie's face intensified a hundred-fold. "Of course not! What kind of question is that?"

Jody's eyebrows rose suggestively. "But you'd like to, wouldn't you."

"I can't believe we're having this conversation." With as much composure as she could muster, which wasn't much, Marjorie reached for her glass of iced tea and took a large swallow.

Amused, Jody pinched her lips together in mock disapproval. "Come on, Marjie, would you stop being my mother long enough to talk to me like a big sister? Tell me everything. I want to know the most intimate desires of your heart."

Despite the subject matter, Marjorie relaxed. "My desires? That's easy."

"Sam?" Jody coaxed.

"Sam," Marjorie repeated. "I can't believe this is happening to me after all these years of being so sensible about men. With Sam, everything's different." She paused and then continued, telling her sister how Sam Bretton had stayed with her in the hours following her surgery. "I didn't know any man so wonderful existed. I feel giddy every time I'm with him."

Jody nodded knowingly and smiled through a haze of tears.

"Honey, what's wrong?" Marjorie asked quickly.

Jody wiped the moisture off the high arch of her cheekbones. "This is the first time I can remember when you've talked to me like a...sister. You never shared anything with me before—at least not like this. I'm happy for you, really happy."

Marjorie blinked back her surprise, ready to argue the point. Then she thought about how right her sister was. She had never felt she could share with Jody; her sister was so much younger that it hadn't seemed right to burden Jody with her problems. Jody had to be protected, and because of that their relationship had to be part parent, part sibling. She'd had to be Jody's mother and sister both.

"You know something," Jody said, her voice unsteady. "I love Sam already."

"Wait until you meet him," Marjorie answered, her own voice wavering. "He's been so good to me."

"You deserve him, and he deserves you."

They wrapped their arms around each other and squeezed tightly, neither willing to let the other go. They had reached a deeper understanding of what it meant to be sisters, and for that Marjorie would always be grateful.

Sam arrived about fifteen minutes later, amazed at Jody's warm welcome. He liked her immediately but wished he could have had time alone with Marjorie. It seemed a hundred years since he'd last talked to her, and a thousand since he'd held her sweet warmth against him and relished the special feel of her in his arms.

The evening proved to be a fun one. He treated the two women to a delicious seafood dinner in a four-star restaurant that overlooked Commencement Bay. Following the meal, the three of them walked along the dock outside the Lobster Shop and gazed at the bright lights that sparkled like shiny stars from the opposite shore.

"I can't remember the last time I ate this well," Jody said, holding her stomach and exhaling a deep, contented sigh. "I'm stuffed."

Marjorie's worried gaze instantly flew to her younger sister. "I knew it! You're not eating right."

"I'm in perfect health."

Sam's arm around Marjorie's waist tightened, and she managed to hold back any further argument.

Jody looked at the two of them, and with a smile lifting the corners of her full mouth, she feigned a loud yawn. "I can't believe how tired I am all of a sudden. That drive from Portland can really wear a person out."

Sam and Marjorie shared a secret look and struggled to hide their amusement. Jody couldn't have been any less subtle had she tried.

"I think she's offering us some time alone," Sam whispered close to Marjorie's ear. He was hard-pressed not to flick his tongue over her lobe, knowing her instant response. "Are we going to accept?"

Marjorie's nod was eager.

"Just drop me off at the apartment, and you two can escape," Jody announced, looking pleased with herself. "Far be it from me to block the path of true love."

"Far be it from me to let you," Sam joked, as they headed toward the restaurant parking lot.

Sam drove directly back to Marjorie's apartment, and Jody hurriedly scooted out of the car, winked and reached for Marjorie's keys. "Don't hurry back on my account."

"We won't," Sam assured her. He appreciated what Jody was doing, but he wouldn't keep Marjorie out long. It was obvious the two sisters were close. He'd seen for himself the various roles Marjorie played in Jody's life, slipping from one to the other with hardly a breath in between.

Marjorie remained in Sam's car while Jody let herself into the apartment. Then he reached for her hand, squeezing gently. "I like your sister."

"She's impressed with you, too." That was a gross understatement, Marjorie thought to herself. Jody had been giving her signals all night that showed her wholehearted approval of Sam. In the ladies' room she had gone so far as to suggest that if Marjorie didn't want Sam, she'd take him.

But Marjorie wanted Sam Bretton even more than before. She couldn't look in his direction without her eyes revealing everything that was stored in her heart. She couldn't hide her love for him any longer.

"I have to stop off at the hospital for a minute," he said, as he pulled out of the parking lot of the apartment complex. "Is that a problem?"

"No, of course not. If you want, I'll stay in the car."

"There's no need for you to do that," Sam came back quickly. "I want to introduce you to a couple of my friends. And this will give you a chance to see the two babies I delivered the other night."

Marjorie's heart shot to her throat. Babies. Sam was as comfortable with them as she was with interest rates and electromechanically fuel-injected engines. Anyone under the age of two terrorized her; babies made her nervous and served to remind her of how inadequate she was in the traditional female role. Her biggest fear was that Sam would bring her into the hospital and expect her to go inside the nursery. He might even expect her to hold an infant, and then he would learn that not only were babies allergic to her, she was allergic to them.

"How does that sound?" Sam asked, cutting into her troubled thoughts.

"About the babies?" she hedged.

"Yes, they're—"

"Sam, listen," she said, rushing her words. "Maybe it would be better if I went back to the apartment with Jody."

He shot her a puzzled frown. The disappointment that welled up in him was strong. He couldn't understand her sudden objection. Sure, she hadn't especially enjoyed her hospital stay, and he could understand why. But her hesitation now puzzled him. "Go back to the apartment? Whatever for?"

Marjorie made the pretense of glancing at her watch. "It's late and…"

"It's barely after nine," he countered, studying her. She was growing paler by the minute.

Marjorie couldn't look into Sam's eyes and refuse him anything. "You're right," she said, determination squaring her shoulders. "I'm being silly. Of course I'll go with you and meet your friends and see the babies. Everything will be wonderful."

She knew her tone was falsely cheerful, but she decided it was far better for her to confront her fears than leave them unconquered. He would be with her—nothing would go wrong.

He helped her out of the car, and led her through a side entrance and to the elevator beyond. When the door shut, he punched the floor number and pulled her into his arms for a brief, ardent kiss.

She tried to respond, but her heart was beating as hard and loud as a drum, and her insides were quivering with apprehension. She wanted to do everything right with Sam, and her fear of babies was sure to ruin her chances.

He pulled her close to his side and stared at the closed doors. Marjorie was perfect, with her soft skin, her wide, soulful eyes, and a heart he longed to fill with his love.

The elevator doors smoothly glided open, and Marjorie braced herself for the inevitable. Sam meant so much to her, and it was vital that she be the kind of woman he needed. Without meaning to, she pressed her flattened palms together and rubbed them back and forth several times. When he looked her way, he frowned, so she smiled tightly and freed her hands, letting her arms drop lifelessly to her sides.

With his hand at the base of her spine, Sam directed Marjorie over to the nurses' station and introduced her to three of the staff members he worked with regularly. The purpose of this visit was more social than anything else. He'd partially fabricated the need to stop in, in an effort to casually introduce her to his peers. It seemed as though she'd been a natural part of his life forever.

"Is Bernie around?" Sam asked the oldest of the

nurses, who reminded Marjorie of Bertha Powell. The two could have been sisters.

"Dr. Miller's in the lounge."

Sam reached for Marjorie's hand, lacing his fingers through his as he led her down the wide hallway.

"Nice to have met you," Marjorie said brightly over her shoulder.

"A pleasure," the oldest nurse returned. The other two said nothing. Their wide-eyed stares told her that both of them were convinced she wasn't good enough for their beloved Dr. Sam. The feeling of being watched persisted long after the staff members were out of sight.

Bernie Miller was sitting at the round table in the middle of the doctors' lounge, holding a cup of coffee. He was leaning over the table and holding his head up with one hand. When Sam and Marjorie entered the room, he raised his head, his gaze brightening. His fatigued features relaxed into a slow grin.

"Bernie, I'd like you to meet Marjorie Majors."

Slowly Dr. Miller rose to his feet, but his gaze didn't waver from Marjorie's. "Hello there."

"Hi." She stepped forward and offered him her hand.

"So this is her?" Bernie's gaze shot from Marjorie back to Sam as they ended the brief handshake.

"In the flesh." Sam draped his arm across Marjorie's shoulder as he smiled down on her, his gaze filled with warmth. He hadn't told many of his friends about Marjorie, but hiding the news of how he felt from his best buddy had been impossible. Bernie had known he'd met someone important the minute Sam casually mentioned her a few days earlier. Bernie had wanted to know all about her, but Sam had hesitated. He hadn't been sure of his own feelings then. Marjorie appealed to him more than anyone in a long time, but she wasn't exactly the happy homemaker, and that realization had pulled him up short. Until he'd met Marjorie, the woman he'd pictured in his life had been able to both seduce him in the bedroom and whip up a five-course dinner.

"I understand that you're joining us for our picnic on Wednesday."

"Yes," Marjorie said, and nodded for emphasis. "Thank you for including me."

Sam poured two more cups of coffee while she sat down and talked to Bernie, then joined them at the table. Marjorie mused to herself that things were going well. If only they could stop here. She had no trouble relating to adults; it was infants and children who caused her to break out in hives.

"I'm going to take Marjorie to the nursery," Sam was saying.

Doing her utmost not to choke on her coffee, she pushed her cup aside and stood. If she thought her heart had been pounding in the elevator, now it was crashing like a Chinese gong as she followed Sam out of the doctors' lounge. No doubt the three nurses she'd met earlier never had this problem. Most likely any one of them would gladly surrender her eyeteeth to have Dr. Sam Bretton.

He led her down the wide corridor and into the nursery. Rows of bassinets were lined up in uniform fashion. Some of the infants were blanketed in pink, others in blue. Their surnames were written in bold letters in front of their mock cribs. Two of the nurses that Marjorie had just met now sat in rocking chairs, soothing crying infants.

Sam donned a surgical robe and handed Marjorie one.

"Sam," she whispered, barely able to speak. "There's something you should know."

"Just a minute," he murmured, grinning boyishly. With a gentleness she'd witnessed several times in the last month, Sam lifted a small pink bundle from a crib and looked up at Marjorie, beaming proudly.

"What do you think?" he asked, scooting sideways so she could more easily view the squirming infant in his wide embrace.

Her eyes dropped to the scrunched-up face and minute fists as the baby struggled to get free of her bindings. She forced a smile, unable to think of anything to say.

"Would you care to hold her?"

Her dark eyes widened with alarm, and she forcefully shook her head. "No...thanks." By the time she'd finished speaking, she'd backed herself out the door.

"Marjorie, are you feeling all right?"

"I'm a little... I'm fine," she managed somehow. "Really."

As carefully as he'd lifted the infant, Sam replaced her in her bassinet. By the time he'd finished, Marjorie was leaning against the wall in the corridor outside the nursery.

"What's wrong?" he asked softly, coming to stand beside her.

"I...it's no big thing."

"You look like you're about to faint."

"Don't worry, I'm not the type," she said. "I'm not the kind of woman who goes all mushy at the sight of a baby, either. In case you hadn't noticed, not all of us are alike. There are some of us who cook and crochet and get pregnant at the drop of a hat. And then there are others, like me, who are allergic to baby powder and dirty diapers, and content to eat TV dinners the rest of our miserable lives."

Sam's eyes were incredulous. "Are you trying to tell me you don't like babies?"

"Sure, I do," she said. "In somebody else's arms."

Sam blinked, hardly able to believe his ears. He felt as if the world were crashing in around him. He'd decided not to worry about Marjorie's lack of culinary skills, deciding that her strength and independence were more important than any domestic qualities. But when it came to having children, he wouldn't—couldn't—compromise.

"Babies are fine for the right kind of woman," she said. Her voice had gained in volume with the strength of her convictions. "Unfortunately I'm not one of them."

"You don't mean that." His words were sharp.

By now their heated exchange had attracted the attention of the hospital staff. If Sam's nursing friends had disapproved of her earlier, it was nothing to the censure she felt being aimed at her now. They thought Sam deserved someone far better than she would ever be, and every accusing glare said as much.

Without thought for the wisdom of her actions, she turned and half ran, half walked, down the polished corridor to the elevator, fighting back tears all the way.

"Marjorie, wait!" Sam cried.

Since the elevator wasn't there yet anyway, she didn't have much choice if she wanted to maintain her dignity. They descended in tense silence. Even when they left the hospital building and headed toward Sam's car, neither of them spoke. By that time her throat was so clogged that it felt as though someone had a stranglehold on her. With everything that was in her, she yearned to be all Sam wanted in a woman, yet she'd failed miserably.

Sam opened her door for her. His feet felt heavy as he walked around the car and let himself in. He didn't know what to say or how to say it. He wanted a family, longed for children, and he yearned for Marjorie to give them to him.

She watched him with despair. The tears that had been so close to the surface ran down her cheeks like water over a dam after an early spring thaw, and she turned her head away so he couldn't see. At that moment she would have sold her soul to be different. She took a deep, shuddering breath. "You want children, don't you?"

Her heart cracked when he was silent, and she realized he couldn't deny it. Sam Bretton would make a wonderful father; he was a natural.

"Yes," he answered finally. He couldn't deny his desire for a family. Almost from the beginning, he'd pictured Marjorie with a child in her arms—their child. For years he'd been seeking a woman who was strong enough to stand on her own, and tender enough to need and love him. These last weeks with Marjorie had led him to believe he'd found that special woman…until tonight.

"I'm no good with babies, and I'm even worse with children," she whispered in a choked voice. "That's not going to change."

Eight

For the second time that morning, Marjorie checked the picnic basket. Her nerves were shot. She hadn't heard from Sam, nor had she contacted him. For three days she'd done nothing but think about him and how wrong they were for each other. The realization didn't do any good, though; she still loved him, still wanted him, still yearned for them to build a life together. She would give anything to be the right person for him, but she couldn't change what she was, couldn't become someone different.

Now it was the Fourth of July, and she wasn't even sure he would show up to take her to the picnic and wouldn't blame him if he didn't.

She paused to take a calming breath and rubbed her hands down the thighs of her new jeans. They had been Jody's idea. Marjorie hadn't told her sister what happened between her and Sam, but Jody had guessed something was drastically wrong. The following morning she had insisted they go shopping, claiming there wasn't any ailment a department store couldn't cure. The jeans, Jody claimed, did great things for Marjorie's legs. For all Marjorie cared, they could have been made from sackcloth.

The weather outside wasn't promising; thick gray clouds had formed overhead. As an afterthought, she tucked a thick sweater inside the basket.

The doorbell chimed, and her heart lurched. She swallowed and opened the door. Sam, dressed in jeans and a T-shirt, stood on the other side. He didn't look any better than she felt. Although he was outwardly composed, turmoil and regret were evident in his eyes and the hard set of his mouth.

He stepped inside her living room and hesitated, then smiled. The movement transformed his face.

"What's wrong?" she asked, convinced she should have worn anything but jeans. Denim might help her legs, but it didn't do a thing for her hips.

"The jeans," Sam managed.

"They're all wrong, aren't they?" Silently she blamed her sister. Marjorie knew better than to listen to the advice of a college student who was toying with the idea of tinting her hair blue.

"No," he murmured.

"I can change, don't worry," she went on brightly. "It'll only take a minute."

"Don't," he said, and smiled briefly. "You look fantastic." His gaze was warm and sincere.

Marjorie thought she would cry. She'd been as taut as a violin bow, as well as nervous and worried. Until the minute he spoke, she'd had no idea what he was thinking. Apparently he'd decided to put the incident in the hospital behind them—at least for today. She knew that they should talk and try to settle this problem, but in three days she hadn't been able to come up with a solution, and from his haggard look, she suspected that Sam hadn't, either. Today they would put their troubles aside and enjoy the holiday. She was grateful.

"Every woman should look so good in Levi's," he said.

A smile curved her mouth. "You honestly like them?"

"Yes, Kitten, I do."

Sam longed to take her in his arms and hold her, but he didn't dare. These last days without her had been a self-imposed nightmare. After years of searching for a woman he could love, respect and admire, he'd been convinced he'd found her in Marjorie. No, she wasn't exactly the woman he'd pictured, but he'd discovered he could accept her quirks, loved her all the more because of them. They were part and parcel of who she was. But children... He'd dedicated his life to reproduction and childbirth. To him, children were as essential as food and water. He needed a woman who wanted to give him a family. He could find no way to compromise on an issue so basic to his happiness.

After that night at the hospital, Sam had decided to make a clean break from her. There didn't seem to be any purpose in prolonging the agony. But he'd learned it wasn't that simple. He thought about her constantly, longed to talk to her. After two torturous days he'd known that forgetting about her would be impossible. He would have to think of something to help him solve this problem.

"I've missed you," he murmured, as his eyes held hers.

"I've missed you, too," she answered, and her voice

was filled with regret. "Sam," she whispered, "I'm so sorry."

"I am, too, Kitten." He drew a deep breath, then exhaled slowly. She couldn't change what she was, and he couldn't help loving her. He prayed they could find a solution to this, because now that he had found Marjorie, he couldn't let her go.

"Betty," Sam said, his arm loosely draped over Marjorie's shoulder. "This is Marjorie Majors. Marjorie, Betty."

"Hi," Betty Miller said cordially, her blue eyes twinkling. She was bouncing a toddler on her hip, and the shy little boy hid his face against his mother's shoulder. "I'm so pleased you could make it. Can you believe this weather? Only on Puget Sound would we have a fireplace going on the Fourth of July."

"Thank you for inviting me."

Betty was slender and pretty, exactly the type Marjorie had always pictured as a doctor's wife. Her deep blue eyes were warm and gentle, and Marjorie doubted that Betty Miller had an enemy in this world.

"The ruffian on my hip is Kevin. He's three," Betty added, and encouraged her son to look up long enough to greet their company. Kevin, however, held his fists over his eyes and refused to acknowledge Marjorie *or* Sam.

"Hi, Kevin," Marjorie offered stiffly but to no avail.

The little boy buried his face deeper into his mother's shoulder. "He's a little bit shy," Betty explained, her face flushed with embarrassment.

"That's all right," Marjorie said, in an effort to reassure her. She understood far better than Betty could realize. Kids instinctively knew she was rotten mother material. She didn't know how they knew, but they did.

"Kevin, do you want to show Uncle Sam where your daddy is?" Betty asked, and there was a hopeful note in her voice.

To everyone's surprise, Kevin nodded eagerly and climbed off his mother's hip. Without looking in Marjorie's direction, the three-year-old held out his hand in order to lead Sam away.

Sam must have noted the distress in Marjorie's eyes, because he murmured something about being right back.

"Take your time," Betty returned. Once Sam and Kevin were out of sight, she let out a soft sigh and changed the topic as she led the way toward the cabin, which was located on the fertile bank of Hood Canal and was surprisingly modern. She gestured expansively. "You'd think Bernie had constructed the Empire State Building for the amount of time and effort that's gone into this infamous deck."

"Bernie built the deck himself?" Marjorie had to admit she was impressed with the wraparound structure, as she followed her hostess into the kitchen. A series of stairs led down onto the sandy, smooth beach below.

"Don't encourage him," Betty warned with a short laugh. "In his former life Bernie claims to have been a carpenter. He thinks he missed his calling." Still grinning, she poured them each a tall glass of iced tea and led Marjorie into the living room. A small fire gave the room a cozy feeling.

Marjorie sat in the overstuffed chair opposite her hostess.

Betty's chest rose with a deep breath, and she smiled at Marjorie. "You don't know how relieved I am to finally meet you."

"Me?"

"Sam's hardly talked about anything else from the day you went in for surgery."

"He told you about me?" Amazed, Marjorie flattened her hand over her heart.

"In elaborate detail. Does that surprise you?"

"It shocks me." And pleased her. And excited her. Then she remembered there could be no future for them.

"Bernie and I have been waiting years for Sam to finally meet the right woman. We'd almost given up hope. He's so dedicated to his patients. The one thing that's suffered most over the last few years has been his personal life."

"He *is* a wonderful doctor."

"You won't get any arguments out of me. I should know—Sam delivered both Kevin and Shelley."

"Shelley?" She was going to have to deal with more than one child?

"Shelley's sleeping, like all good four-month-olds. You'll see her later."

Marjorie only nodded. She liked Betty and didn't want to disillusion her with her own lack of anything approaching the maternal instinct.

"You know, I knew Sam before I even met Bernie," Betty explained, gazing into her iced tea. Her face took on a solemn look.

"Are you a nurse?"

Betty nodded. "I know that sounds old hat, but the path of romance was anything but smooth for Bernie and me. It isn't like we saw each other from across a crowded room and instantly heard fate calling."

"No?"

Betty crossed her legs and grinned sheepishly. "Well, to be honest, I was dating Sam when I met Bernie. Later Bernie was assigned to the ward where I was working."

"So it was being in close proximity that ignited the fires between you?"

Laughing, Betty shook her head. "Hardly. If there were any fires ignited, they were from the arguments we had. Bernie and I couldn't agree on anything, and I found him impossible to work with. Once he even went so far as to warn Sam that I was a meddling busybody and he'd do well not to see me again."

Marjorie found all this a little difficult to believe. She'd met Bernie and seen for herself the way his gaze softened when he mentioned his wife's name.

"I know it sounds unbelievable now, but we had serious problems." Betty paused and ran the tips of her fingers over the chair's armrest, caught up in her memories. "It seemed that no matter what I did or how careful I was, I couldn't please the demanding Dr. Miller. Every time he and I were together, we ended up in a shouting match. There wasn't a staff member on the entire floor who would come within twenty feet of us when we got going."

"What happened to change all that?"

Betty shrugged, then a lazy smile began to grow until it practically lit up her round face. "Bernie came to my apartment one night after work. I'll admit he looked terrible, but we'd had another one of our confrontations that day, and I wasn't in any mood to be friendly."

"What did he say?" Marjorie couldn't help being curious.

"He wanted to talk." Betty paused and grinned. "I told him to take a flying leap into the nearest cow pasture."

Marjorie laughed outright. The idea of tiny Betty standing up to a stern-faced Bernie made for a comical picture. "I don't imagine he was any too pleased with that suggestion."

"No. I could tell he was struggling not to tell me where I should fly. But he didn't. Instead he asked me how serious I was about Sam."

Marjorie suspected that Bernie had been attracted to Betty from the first, but he was decent enough not to get involved with his best friend's girlfriend.

"Sam was a friend," Betty continued. "A good one. We'd dated off and on for years, but there was never anything serious between us. Fun stuff. You know—a baseball game, hikes now and again, that sort of thing. Neither one of us ever thought it was a romance for the ages."

"But you let Bernie think otherwise."

"Why not? He'd been a pill from the first. Besides, what was happening between Sam and me wasn't any of his business. I told him that, too."

"I suppose he left then."

"Yeah, how'd you know?"

"Lucky guess," Marjorie said, holding in a knowing smile.

"We didn't argue after that. Not once. Bernie treated

me like every other nurse on the ward, and within a week I was so bored I wanted to cry. Until that moment I didn't realize how much I looked forward to sparring with him." She smiled as she remembered. "That was when Sam invited me to have coffee with him in the cafeteria after work one day. When I sat down, the first thing he did was ask about Bernie. I said I didn't have any idea what he was talking about. Sam looked surprised at that. He claimed Bernie had gotten drunk one night and stormed at him to hurry up and marry me before he—Bernie—did something stupid."

"I can imagine Sam's reaction to that."

Betty grinned and continued. "Sam told him he liked me fine, but he couldn't see the two of us ever getting married."

"What did Bernie say to that?"

Betty rolled her eyes toward the ceiling. "Apparently he tried to swing on Sam. You have to understand how out of character that is for Bernie to fully appreciate him doing something like that."

"I think I can understand," Marjorie said. Any person who would dedicate his life to the care and well-being of his fellow man would naturally deplore violence. "How did the two of you ever manage to get together?"

"It was easy once I sorted through my feelings. I figured that since he'd come to me once, I'd have to be the one to approach him. Not right away, mind you. It took some thinking on my part. The most difficult part was realizing I was in love with Bernie Miller and had been for weeks. The hardest thing I've ever done was invite him over for dinner. Funny thing, though, once we stopped arguing, we discovered how much we had in common. Within a month of our first dinner date we were engaged, and you can guess the rest of the story."

Marjorie took a sip of her tea. "The two of you are perfect together. It's obvious talking to either one of you that you and Bernie are in love."

"We work on it." Betty slapped the armrest. "Enough about me. I want to know about you."

"There really isn't much to tell." A bit uneasy, Marjorie spoke in general terms about her job and her sister. The whole time she was talking, she was aware that there was nothing that made her any different than the other women Sam had dated in the past ten years.

"He's crazy about you," Betty commented. "You know that, don't you?"

Marjorie could feel the other woman studying her. Sam might have been crazy for her at one time, but she had ruined that.

"To be honest, I wondered what made you different. But ten minutes with you and I can understand it. You're exactly the type of woman Sam needs."

Marjorie's look must have revealed her disbelief.

"A doctor needs a woman in his life who has a strong and independent nature. So many other people are constantly making demands on his time and his energy that sometimes there's not much left for anyone else. Above anything else, Sam needs a respite from the demands of work. For men like Sam and Bernie, death is the enemy, and they'll fight for a life with little or no thought to the physical or emotional cost to themselves."

Marjorie nibbled on her lower lip. "I hadn't thought about it like that." Betty had far more insight into Sam and Bernie's needs than she'd considered. All she herself knew was that she loved Sam Bretton and that she would consider herself the most fortunate woman in the world to be his wife.

"I know Bernie so well that I recognize the signs now. He doesn't need to say a word," Betty went on. "There's a look about him, a tiredness in his eyes and in the way he walks. All of those things tell me the kind of day he's had. He'll snap at me every now and again, but I forgive him because I know that he's probably had to tell someone's son or daughter that their mother won't be coming home from the hospital, or he's had to tell someone that their test results show they have cancer."

The thought of having to give someone such bad news tightened a knot of compassion in Marjorie's stomach.

"The last thing Bernie needs when he gets home is a list of demands from me. I wouldn't do that to him, and you wouldn't do that to Sam. He knows that, just the way I did as soon as we met."

A cool sip of her drink helped alleviate the tightness in Marjorie's throat. "I'm not the right woman for him. I don't deserve him."

Betty settled back in her chair and grinned. "He said almost exactly those same words to Bernie about you."

Marjorie blinked back her surprise and lowered her gaze. Her heart was filled with such misery that it was impossible to hold it all inside. She felt as though she would burst into tears in another minute.

"In fact, Bernie got so sick of hearing about you that he threatened to cancel their poker night if Sam didn't bring you around and introduce you."

"He must have taken him seriously, because we made a trip to the hospital Friday night."

"Bernie mentioned that, too. He told me that one look at the two of you together and he knew Sam had finally found the right woman. By the way, what is it about Sundays with you?"

"Sundays?"

"Yes. Sam phoned the other day and said the only time he can play poker from now on is Sunday afternoons."

Marjorie set the tall glass aside. "I work weekends. Hopefully someday I'll have Sundays free, but unfortunately, that probably won't be for some time yet."

Slowly Betty shook her head. "Believe me, when a man puts a woman before a long-standing poker game, he's serious about her."

Marjorie dropped her gaze and felt obliged to add, "We aren't serious. There are…problems."

"Wait and see, you'll settle them," Betty returned with unshakable confidence. "Sam's never been more ready for a wife than he is now."

Betty looked as if there were more she wanted to say, but before she could speak the sliding-glass door opened, and the two men, plus Kevin, walked into the house.

"Have you shown Marjorie my deck yet?" Bernie asked, beaming proudly.

Betty tried not to smile and failed. "It was the first thing I mentioned."

"I've been thinking that since this project went so well, I might try my hand at something a little more complicated."

Betty eyed her husband speculatively. "Like what?"

"An addition to the house," he said enthusiastically. "I could add on to the master bedroom. You've told me more than once that we need more closet space."

"Men," Betty groaned under her breath to Marjorie.

Sam walked over to Marjorie and sat beside her on the cushioned arm of the chair. He slipped his arm around her and cupped her shoulder.

A warm sensation filled her, and when she glanced up, she discovered Sam studying her. The love that filled her eyes was as unexpected as it was embarrassing.

His fingers bit into her shoulder as his gaze held hers. "I love you," he whispered. "We'll work this out."

"But, Sam…"

He bent down and kissed the top of her head. "Listen, we'll adopt kids. Older kids. Okay?"

Biting her bottom lip, Marjorie nodded.

Sam reached for her hand, lacing their fingers together, as though bonding them. She loved this man more than she ever thought it was possible to care about another human being. Whatever problems they faced in the future could be conquered with Sam at her side. She was sure of it.

"When are we going to eat?" Kevin demanded, placing his hands on his hips. "I'm hungry." The little boy still wouldn't look directly at Marjorie, but that was an improvement from hiding his face in his mother's shoulder.

"The barbecue's already hot," Bernie told his wife. "I'll put the steaks on now, if everything else is ready."

"I want a hamburger," Kevin insisted.

"And you will get one," his father promised. "Come along, big boy, and you can help your dear ol' dad and Uncle Sam with the cooking."

"I'll start setting the table out on the deck," Betty said.

"Is there anything I can do?" Marjorie volunteered, quickly rising to her feet. "I brought some chips and dip, and some potato salad and sliced pickles." Sam caught her eye and revealed his surprise. "Deli made," she whispered, and he grinned back.

"Why don't you unpack those while I set the picnic table?" Betty suggested.

The others left to take care of things, and Marjorie found herself alone in the kitchen. She went over to the wicker basket and lifted the top. The potato salad was nestled between the pickle jar and the dip. As she was drawing it out, she heard a faint cry coming from the back of the house. She paused, then remembered Betty mentioning that the baby was napping. Marjorie went to the cabinet and proceeded to take out a couple of bowls and fill them with the potato salad and dip. To her chagrin, the infant's crying grew louder.

A quick check outside told her that Kevin had managed to distract his mother from the job of setting the table. The two of them were down on the beach. Betty was bent over, examining something Kevin was pointing to in the sand. The men were across the yard, busy chatting while Bernie stuck T-bone steaks onto the hot grill.

Before Marjorie could call out to anyone, the baby's cry split the air.

Alarmed, she ran into the back bedroom. The infant's cries died to a soft gurgle once she arrived.

"Hi," she said stiffly, standing a good three feet from the crib. "Your mother's on the beach. Would you like me to do something before she gets here?"

The baby's fists flailed in the air.

"Don't cry, okay? I'm sure she'll be back any minute."

The infant whimpered softly, and that alone was enough to cause Marjorie to take two steps in retreat. Once four-month-old Shelley realized she was losing her audience, she let go with another loud, earnest cry. She paused then, and inserted her fist into her mouth, sucking on it greedily.

"Oh, I get it," Marjorie murmured, retracing her steps. "You're hungry." She dropped her gaze to her own full breasts. "Sorry, I can't help you in that department." She smiled at her own joke.

The baby gurgled again, seemingly amused by Marjorie's attempt at humor.

"I suppose you've got a wet diaper, as well."

Shelley made a chuckling sound that cut straight through Marjorie's heart. "I don't think I'm going to be much help in that area, either. You see, babies and I don't get along."

Shelley giggled at that. Two arms and legs punched the air as she smiled up at Marjorie, who found she had somehow ended up leaning over the crib.

Sam came into the house and took a Pepsi from the refrigerator. He looked around for Marjorie, and when he didn't find her, he opened the front door, thinking she might have forgotten something in the car. She wasn't there, either. Concerned now, he started for the deck to find Betty.

A faint noise stopped him. It was almost indiscernible at first, so faint that he didn't recognize it until he paused and listened intently. It was a baby cooing happily. He turned into the narrow hallway that led to Shelley Miller's bedroom and found Marjorie at last.

She was sitting in a rocking chair, cuddling Shelley in her arms as though she never intended to let the baby go. Tear tracks streaked her face, creating a bright sheen on her flushed cheeks. She sniffled loudly and wasn't able to keep her chin from trembling.

"Marjorie," he murmured, falling to his knees in front of her, hardly able to believe his eyes.

Nine

"Sam," Marjorie whimpered softly. "I'm holding a baby."

"I see that, Kitten."

"She's so beautiful." A teardrop rolled down her face and landed ingloriously on Shelley's cotton jumpsuit. Cooing, the baby reached out to catch the next drop.

With the gentleness she had come to expect from him, Sam tenderly brushed his hand over her face, wiping away the tears. "I've never seen a woman as beautiful as you are right this minute."

"Sam, I didn't think I could get close to a baby. I didn't dare dream I'd feel this way—ever."

"I suspected as much," he countered, resisting the urge to wrap her and the baby in his arms and hold them both for eternity. "I prayed it would only be a matter of time until you recognized the mothering instincts were there. They have been all along."

"They're here, all right," she whispered, smiling and crying at once. "I feel so tender inside—I don't know how to describe it. Sam," she said, raising her eyes to meet his, "if I feel this strongly about a baby I barely know, I can't imagine how much love I'd have for one of my own."

"We'll discover that together, Kitten."

The tightness that jammed her throat made it impossible to speak. He was talking about them having children together, and although the thought frightened her, it thrilled her far more. She yearned to ask him if he meant it and to tell him she was willing, but every time she opened her mouth, all that came out were soft, strangled sounds. She managed to free one hand from beneath Shelley to caress the rugged line of Sam's jaw. Closing her eyes, she pressed her cheek against the side of his head.

He edged away from her, and their gazes met and held. The promise between them was more potent than anything she had ever known. She didn't need words to recognize what was in his heart; his feelings were all there for her to read in his eyes.

Sam bent toward her, and her dark eyes shimmered with an aching need for his love, a need that was echoed in his own heart. Her parted lips offered him an invitation he couldn't ignore.

This was the man she loved, the man who had filled her life with purpose and realized her dreams. He'd helped her to conquer her fears, laying the groundwork to destroy one after another with unlimited patience. He had gently proved to her that there wasn't anything they couldn't face together, nothing the force of their love couldn't overcome.

"Oh, Sam," she murmured, not wanting him to stop but knowing he had to. "The baby…"

He nodded and straightened, although his hands continued to grip her shoulders. The sight of Marjorie holding Shelley, knowing that someday she would be cradling their own baby, burned through him with the effectiveness of a hot knife. He felt weak with desire, weak and yet so powerful.

"Was that Shelley I heard?" Betty asked as she came into the small bedroom. If she noticed Marjorie's tears, or the fact that Sam was on the floor beside her and the baby, she didn't comment. "Thanks for getting her up for me," she said smoothly, and reached for her daughter.

With some reluctance, Marjorie surrendered the infant. "She's a wonderful baby."

"I'm convinced she gets that easygoing disposition from her mother," Betty said with a cheerful smile.

Bernie coughed in the background. "What about her old man?"

"*And* her father," Betty amended, and shared a secret smile, a wordless disclaimer, with Marjorie.

Marjorie managed to smother a laugh. When she stood, Sam slipped his arm around her waist and gently hugged her. "Do you think it'd be considered impolite to eat and run?" he whispered, so she alone could hear.

"Not if we're not too obvious," she said after a moment. As much as she liked Bernie and Betty, there were so many things she wanted to tell Sam, so much she yearned to share.

"It's selfish, I know, but I want to be alone with you," he added, after their hosts had taken the baby and headed into the other room.

Marjorie wanted it, too, and her gaze told him so.

"Soon," he promised.

"Soon," she agreed.

By the time they returned to the living room, Bernie had finished barbecuing the steaks. They all worked together, and within a few minutes the picnic table on the Millers' newly finished deck was set. The salads, potato chips and other dishes were brought out.

Sam sat beside Marjorie, and the four of them talked and joked throughout the meal. When they'd finished, Marjorie sat on the lounge chair and cradled Shelley as though she'd been handling babies all her life. Every now and again she felt Sam's loving gaze, and they shared a special look that said more than mere words.

"I can't get over the way Shelley's taken to you," Betty commented, joining her. The weather had cleared as the lazy afternoon sun burned off the clouds.

"Marjorie's a natural with children," Sam said proudly. "I don't suppose she told you, but she nearly raised her sister."

"Sam!" she cried, embarrassed. "I'm not a natural at all."

A sharp shake of his head discounted that notion. "She's been around children most of her life," he added. Studying her, his mouth curved into a faint smile. He had prayed that, given time, she would recognize most of her fears as unfounded. The mothering instinct was as strong in her as it was in any woman, only Marjorie had failed to recognize it.

She held out her hand to him, and he gripped it firmly. In many ways he understood her better than she did herself. Sometime, somewhere, she'd done something very good in her life to deserve this man.

* * *

Late Saturday afternoon Marjorie had changed her outfit twice, unable to decide what to wear. Sam wanted her to meet his parents. Although she had readily agreed to dinner with his family, she was a nervous wreck. She'd been in and out of clothes faster than a quick-change artist. Worse, she was convinced that his mother was bound to disapprove of her lack of domestic skills, though Sam himself had dismissed that fear.

Five minutes before he was due to arrive, she chose a soft knit dress Jody had suggested when she made a frantic call to Portland. It was more casual than anything she wore to work, and she was doubtful. This meeting was so important, and she longed to make a good impression so as not to embarrass Sam.

She needn't have worried. His parents stepped onto the front porch when he pulled into the driveway, and they looked as anxious as she felt.

"Don't be so nervous," Sam said, reaching over to squeeze her clenched fist. "They're going to love you."

"Oh, Sam, I hope so." She forced herself to relax, uncoiling her fingers and flexing them a couple of times to restore the blood flow. Normally she was able to disguise any uneasiness, but the prospect of meeting his family had completely unnerved her.

"Mom and Dad have been waiting years to meet you."

"I only hope I'm not a disappointment."

"You won't be, Kitten, I promise."

Sam's mother came down the front steps and walked toward the car. Marjorie studied the streaks of silver in the older woman's dark hair, then shifted her gaze to the classic profile. None of the other woman's features resembled Sam's. Not the faint gleam in her dark eyes, not the warm, friendly glow in her complexion. Yet if Marjorie had met her in a crowded room, she would have known instantly that this woman was his mother.

Sam helped Marjorie out of the car and slipped his arm over her shoulders.

"Mom and Dad," he said proudly, "this is Marjorie Majors. Marjorie, my parents, Roy and Irene Bretton."

"I hope you don't mind us coming out to greet you like this, but Roy and I couldn't wait another minute." Irene took both of Marjorie's hands in her own and nodded approvingly. "I can't tell you how very pleased we are to meet you—at last."

"Thank you. The pleasure is all mine." Marjorie felt stiff and awkward. The inside of her mouth was dry, yet her hands were moist. Sam's warmth was the only thing that kept the chill of anxiety from seeping all the way through her bones. She had so little to impress this family with—no real background or prestigious relatives. She could offer them nothing but her love for their son.

"Please come inside. Dinner's almost ready," Irene invited, leading the way. "I fixed your favorite, Sam— fried chicken, potatoes and gravy, with my homemade biscuits."

"Mom's a wonderful cook," Sam explained, grinning down at her. He hoped Marjorie knew that he wasn't concerned about her ability to burn water.

Marjorie's return smile was feeble at best.

"I'll give you all his favorite recipes if you want them," Irene offered Marjorie.

She nodded her thanks, knowing it would be a complete waste of time, but she hated to disillusion Sam's mother so quickly. Later she would explain that her presence in the kitchen invariably resulted in a fiasco, that when she turned on the stove, the entire Tacoma Fire Department went on standby.

"I better go check on the chicken," Sam's mother said, as soon as they entered the house.

The luscious smells that greeted them could have rivaled a four-star restaurant. It was obvious that Sam had underplayed his mother's culinary abilities.

"Let me help," Marjorie offered hurriedly.

"Nonsense, you're our guest." Irene gestured toward the sofa. "Sit down and make yourself at home. I insist."

Marjorie smiled and tried to relax. Sam's parents were exactly as she'd expected: warm and sincere.

She lowered herself onto the wide sofa. An afghan, crocheted in fall colors of gold, orange and brown, was spread across the back.

Sam claimed the seat next to her and reached for her hand. His father saw the gesture and grinned proudly, as though he were personally responsible for bringing the two of them together.

A moment later Irene Bretton returned. "Dinner will be ready in another fifteen minutes," she announced, and took the chair beside Sam's father.

Roy Bretton looked all the more pleased. "Good. We have enough time for a glass of wine first." He eyed his son intently, as though he expected Sam to make some momentous proclamation.

"Dad patronizes several local vineyards," Sam explained, ignoring his father's look.

"There are a dozen or so excellent wines bottled

right here in Washington state," Roy added, filling in the conversation. "I found another superior winery recently, near Bonney Lake."

Marjorie nodded and started to relax against the back of the sofa. There wasn't anything to be nervous about, especially since Sam's parents appeared to be even more anxious to make a good impression than she was.

"Give me a hand, son," Roy said, standing.

"Sure."

The two men left the room, leaving Marjorie and Irene alone.

"Sam has spoken fondly of you on several occasions," his mother said, clearly seeking a way to start the conversation. "His father and I are very proud of him."

"You have every right to be."

"It will take a special woman to share his life."

Marjorie dropped her lashes, fearing that Sam's mother was suggesting that she wasn't the right one for their only son. Her heart pounded wildly, filled with doubts.

"I knew from the moment he mentioned your name that you were special to him." Irene smiled and smoothed her hand across her skirt in a nervous gesture. "A mother knows these things about her children. For instance, I knew long before Sam—or even his father—did that he would be a physician. Roy was sure Sam's career would involve animals. He had pets from the time he was little and was forever collecting more."

"He's the kindest, most generous man I've ever known."

"He always was," Irene said. "I swear, that boy brought home more stray dogs than the city pound ever collected. His heart would melt over things that you and I would hardly notice." She warmed to her subject and scooted forward in the chair, her face bright with love for her son. "I remember one time—he must have been around ten or twelve—anyway, he found an orphaned kitten in a rainstorm, a sickly, weak, half-drowned little thing. By the time he got her home, she was more dead than alive."

Marjorie's smile went weak. Sam called her Kitten, had for weeks now, and like the stray cat he'd found in his youth, she, too, was an orphan. Little things played back in her mind. Minor incidents came into focus. Puzzle pieces fell into place, painting a clear picture. Sam was a rescuer, always had been and always would be. He'd seen it as his duty to take care of her the night she went into surgery.

When they'd first started dating, he had tried several times to rescue her. He'd wanted to step in when Al had cheated her out of her commission. He'd bought the Mercedes more for her benefit than his own. Now that she was seeing him regularly, she knew that he had a perfectly serviceable car and had no reason to purchase another.

"What happened with the kitten?" She was almost afraid to ask.

"He nursed her back to health. You should have seen that silly cat. She was the most prickly, bad-tempered thing—wouldn't let anyone near her. You'd think she would have been more appreciative of everything he had done for her."

The knot in Marjorie's stomach tightened to a punishing level of discomfort. After her surgery she'd lashed out at Sam at every turn. She'd even accused him of getting a kickback from the hospital for every patient he forced to stay. At least she'd felt guilty later and had apologized.

"He... Sam kept the cat, though, right?" she asked, sure she already knew the answer.

"Named her Kitten and ignored her bad moods."

"Didn't he get tired of her moods and lose interest after a while?" Once again, she was certain of the answer, and her stomach sank.

Irene nodded. "It was bound to happen. Summer came, and Sam had his friends. But he kept her, and she became a regular member of the family. I remember the funniest thing about that cat. The first time Kitten became a mother, she wouldn't let anyone close to her except Sam. He was with her when she gave birth. Years later, when she died, Sam was in his first year of high school, and he was real broken up for a long time afterward. But he got over her, and he's owned several cats since."

Marjorie struggled to disguise her distress. All his talk about accepting her as she was, loving her and needing her, was a lie. Sam hadn't accepted her. He never had. To him, she was a pitiful, lost soul, helpless and in need of being rescued. From what his mother had told her and from what she'd seen herself, she was forced to admit that Sam had yet to accept how truly independent she was. And like the kitten from his youth, Sam would eventually replace her, too. His interest would wander, and his feelings for her would change.

A numb, tingling sensation spread to her arms and

legs. She felt physically ill along with being emotionally distraught.

How she made it through dinner was a mystery to her, but somehow she managed to say and do what was expected of her as though nothing were wrong. She answered his parents' questions and responded appropriately to what was going on around her. Yet all the while the world was crashing down around her feet.

At one point Sam's father commented that she didn't eat enough to keep a bird alive, and Sam responded that he planned on taking care of her from now on. It had taken every ounce of composure she possessed not to inform him that she was perfectly capable of taking care of herself. She didn't need him to see to her meals or ensure that she made enough money to pay the rent or anything else.

By the time they left, she had never been so grateful to get away from anywhere in her life. The sun had set, and dusk had settled over the landscape. Grateful for the cover of impending night, she hoped that Sam wouldn't notice how pale she was or how sick to her stomach she felt.

Neither spoke as they rode back to her apartment, and when they arrived, he climbed out of the car and walked her to her door.

"Invite me inside," he said.

She felt so unsure, so unsettled. Still, she couldn't resist him, so she nodded and unlocked the front door. "I'll make coffee," she murmured, heading toward the kitchen.

Sam followed her. She'd been unusually quiet on the ride back, but then again, so had he. All evening he'd been mentally rehearsing everything he wanted to say to her. It wasn't every day a man asked a woman to be his wife, and he wanted to make this moment special.

Briefly he toyed with the idea of pulling the diamond out of his pocket and just handing it to her. But that seemed so abrupt, especially when there was so much he longed to tell her. First he planned on saying how loving her had changed his life. Since he'd met her, he felt totally alive. He loved her—that much was obvious and had been for weeks—but simply telling her that he loved her was too inadequate, especially since there was so much more to the way he felt than mere words could express.

Marjorie's hands shook as she turned on the faucet to fill the teakettle. Her back was to him as she spoke. "I like your parents."

"They like you, too, Kitten. I knew they would."

She flinched. "Why do you call me that?"

"Kitten?"

Nodding, she set the kettle on the stove.

"I'm not exactly sure," Sam responded. "I had a cat named that once."

"The one you found in a rainstorm?"

He glanced up, surprised. "Yes. How'd you know?"

"Your mother mentioned it." She swallowed tightly, still unable to turn and face him. "She told me what a prickly, ungrateful cat she was."

Sam chuckled. "She came around in time."

"Like I did," Marjorie said in a wobbly but controlled voice.

"You?" Sam asked, surprised. "I thought we were talking about Kitten."

"We are!" She whirled around to face him, her hands braced against the counter behind her. "Me. *I'm* Kitten."

Sam looked stunned. "That's ridiculous!"

"Tell me, Sam, why did you buy the Mercedes? You didn't need another car."

He shifted uncomfortably. "No, but my other one's a couple of years old now and…"

"And you wanted me to collect the commission from the sale."

"All right," he said, struggling not to respond to the anger in her voice. "That's true, but I was looking for a way to see you again, and buying the car seemed a perfect solution."

"It was an expensive one, too, don't you think?"

"I didn't care."

"This may surprise you, Sam Bretton, but *I* care. In fact, I care a great deal. I don't want your charity. The next time you want to throw money away, give it to cancer research."

"It wasn't charity!" he shouted.

Marjorie ignored him, clenching her hands into tight fists at her sides. "What was it about me that attracted you in the first place?" She didn't give him a chance to respond as she hurried on. "There's nothing that makes me any different than a thousand other women who parade through your office."

Drawing a calming breath, Sam waited a moment before answering. "This conversation isn't getting us anywhere. I suggest—"

"You can't answer me, can you, Sam?"

"I think it would be best if I left and gave you a chance to calm down."

"I don't need any time!" she shouted, and to her horror, her voice cracked.

Unable to see her cry and not do something to ease the pain, Sam took a step toward her and held out his arms. "Kitten, listen…"

"Don't call me that!" she cried, pointing at him and retreating several steps. "Or I'll…I'll…" She couldn't think of anything to threaten him with. "Or I'll scream," she said finally.

"Or worse yet, you might cook for me."

Marjorie's eyes widened with the pain his words inflicted. "Just leave, Sam. The next time I need someone to rescue me, I'll give you a call. But don't wait around for me to phone. It might astonish you to learn that I'm a capable human being."

His frustration was nearly overwhelming, and Sam paused to rub his hand along the back of his neck. "I didn't mean that wisecrack about your cooking."

Her back stiffened with resolve. "No? Well, I meant every word *I* said," she responded coolly, struggling to maintain her crumbling composure.

"No, you don't. You love me. You need me."

He was so confident, so sure of himself, that Marjorie wanted to kick herself for being so gullible. The signs had been there from the beginning, and she'd refused to see them, refused to believe. Her love for Sam had blinded her to the truth. She was a charity case to him in the same way that kitten had been all those years ago. He might believe he felt something for her now, but time would prove him wrong. He honestly believed she couldn't get by without him.

"Marjorie, I'm not exactly sure what's going on in

that wonderfully crazy mind of yours, but if you want me to tell you that I associated you with that lost kitten, then I'll admit as much—but only in the beginning."

The room swayed, and she reached out a hand in an effort to maintain her balance. Briefly she closed her eyes. "You admit it?"

"Yes. But only in the beginning," he repeated softly. "You were so fragile, so afraid, and there was no one there for you when you were ill."

"Do I hear violin music in the background?" she taunted. It dented her considerable pride to hear Sam refer to her in those terms, though, to be fair, she remembered how she'd clung to him, begging him to stay with her. That had been a low point in her life, and now he was using it against her. Worse, he hadn't an inkling of why she was so offended, and she'd thought he knew her so well.

"Later I was attracted to your courage," he added, ignoring her gibe. "And your pride and your candor. I discovered that I spent half my time thinking about you. When you were discharged, I racked my brain for days trying to think of a way to see you again. I wanted to help you—and I finally came up with the idea of buying the car. By then I knew you were special."

"As I explained before, I don't need your charity."

"It wasn't charity, not in the way you think!" Sam shouted, losing his patience. "The only thing I did was help you, and you make it sound as if I've committed some terrible crime."

As far as Marjorie was concerned, he had.

"I was in love with you then—only I didn't know it. And now I know I love you. More than I thought it was possible to love another human being. If you don't want me to call you *kitten* again, then fine, I won't."

A tense silence wrapped itself around them. She couldn't believe that she was having the most important discussion of her life while standing in her kitchen waiting for the kettle to boil.

Sam's level gaze trapped hers from across the room. His anger had vanished as quickly as it had come, leaving his face an impassive mask of pride. Abruptly, he spun away, his impatient strides carrying him to the door. He paused and turned toward her.

"There's a diamond ring in my pocket, Marjorie. I'd planned to ask you to be my wife."

Calmly she met his gaze. She wanted Sam. The temptation to swallow her doubts and dismiss her pride nearly overwhelmed her. She would have, too, if she hadn't remembered what his mother had said about him losing interest in the kitten after a while. He had his friends, his mother had said. There was nothing to guarantee that anything would be different when it came to *her*, that within a few months he wouldn't regret having married her.

"I think you already know my answer to that," she said, looking everywhere but at the huge diamond he now held in his hand.

"You're right—I do know." With that, he slipped the ring back inside his pocket. Then he turned and walked away from her in lightning-quick strides.

The door slammed. Feeling incredibly weak, Marjorie cupped her hands over her face and sagged against the counter.

Ten

Confounded, Marjorie stepped out of her manager's office and paused, her hand lingering on the doorknob. Her mind was racing with the details of her conversation with Bud.

"Well, what happened?" Lydia wanted to know. She walked around the customer-service counter and stood expectantly in front of her friend. When Marjorie didn't immediately respond, Lydia waved her hand in front of her bemused face.

The action captured Marjorie's attention. "I got a promotion," she said, shaking her head, still befuddled. Starting the first of the month, her Sundays would be free. For weeks her schedule had conflicted with Sam's. Now, when it didn't matter if she had the day off, her Sundays were open. Life was filled with such ironies.

"A promotion!" Lydia cried. "Cool!"

"I can't believe it myself," Marjorie returned, and shook her head in an attempt to dispel her pensive mood. She'd been numb for days; nothing seemed to penetrate the dull ache that had ruled her thoughts and actions since she'd last seen Sam. Not even this promotion, which would have given her plenty of reason to celebrate a week earlier, could penetrate the fog of her sadness.

"What did Bud say to Al Swanson?" Lydia asked next, her eyes wide with curiosity.

"I'm not sure...he's still in there." Marjorie had noted how disgruntled he'd looked when Bud announced her promotion. That alone had been worth the apprehension she'd suffered all morning before the meeting.

"And you thought you were going to get fired." Lydia flashed her a triumphant smile and shook her head knowingly. "What did I tell you?"

"Not to worry," Marjorie quoted back to her friend in a monotone, and rolled her eyes toward the ceiling.

Lydia was obviously pleased that her words had proven to be prophetic. "Now all I have to do is straighten out this mess between you and Dr. Sam."

Marjorie stiffened at the mention of his name. "Don't even try," she said forcefully. "As far as I'm concerned, the subject of Sam Bretton is off-limits."

"What did he do, for heaven's sake?"

"Lydia, I already told you, I refuse to discuss the matter!" Purposeful strides carried her across the showroom floor. Once again she was running away, doing anything she could to escape the emotional pain that blossomed when anyone asked her about Sam. Before she'd met him, she had prided herself on her ability to confront unpleasantness. Since her last evening with him, she found it easier to hide than deal with her feelings.

Undeterred, Lydia followed her friend. "Hey, we're

talking about the man who had you waltzing around here with your head in the clouds not more than a week ago. Something happened, and I want to know what it was."

"Lydia, please, just drop it." The pain was so fresh that even hearing someone casually mention him produced an ache that came all the way from her soul.

She walked into her office and braced her hands against the side of her desk, inhaling deeply, praying the action would alleviate the surge of emotional pain. She'd done a great deal of thinking since the last time she'd seen Sam. As much as she hated to admit it, she needed him. The realization that she depended on him hadn't been easy to swallow. She loved him, but she hated to think she was nothing but the subject of his charity.

Following close on Marjorie's heels, Lydia came into the office and shut the door. "Listen, I've tried to be a good friend and—"

"I know," Marjorie said, cutting her off. "And I appreciate that, but there are some things that are better left alone." She couldn't deal with Lydia's questions *and* answer her own. She whirled around to confront her friend. "And this is one of them."

Lydia hesitated, then. "If you'd just tell me what he did that was so terrible, then I could hate him, too."

Marjorie could deal with any multitude of problems—irate customers, unreasonable loan officers, cheating salesmen—but her friend's persistent inquisitiveness had finally worn her down.

She crossed her arms over her chest and exhaled a slow, laborious breath. "He called me *kitten*."

Before she could go on, Lydia's mouth fell open in astonished disbelief. "That was it?"

"No. He asked me to marry him, too."

A pregnant pause followed as Lydia's eyes narrowed in speculative scorn. "You're right," she finally said in mock disgust. "The man should be sent before a firing squad. He wanted to marry you. Well, of all the nerve!"

All Marjorie could manage was a sharp nod.

Lydia ran her fingertips over the top of the desk, avoiding eye contact. "Marjorie…when was the last time you had a decent vacation?"

"About ten years ago. Listen, I can see what you're getting at. You think I've gone off the deep end, and maybe I have. I don't know anymore. I…turned Sam down, but my reasons are my own. Just accept that I know what I'm doing, and it's for the best, and kindly leave it at that."

"I can't believe you turned Dr. Sam down." Lydia glared at her as though Marjorie should be psychoanalyzed that very minute. "The most marvelous man I've ever known, and he wanted to marry you and…"

"And I refused him," Marjorie said flatly.

"You're not going to see him again?"

"No…I don't think so."

"And that's the way you want it?" The incredulousness was back in Lydia's voice, raising it half an octave.

Marjorie couldn't answer. Lying by saying "yes" to Lydia was one thing, but trying to fool herself was another. She was slowly shriveling up without Sam. Her days felt like empty, wasted years. The hours dragged, especially when she was home alone. The walls seemed to close in around her, suffocating her. Normally she

enjoyed her own company, but since she'd been without Sam, even the everyday routines seemed useless.
The happy expectancy was missing from her life, as
was the excitement. Without him, her future looked
astonishingly bleak.

It would have been far better, she decided, if she'd
never met the man. Again and again she'd gone over the
events of that last evening with his family, seeking a
solution that would salvage both his pride and her own,
some misunderstanding about the way he saw her. But
he had made that impossible. He'd admitted openly that
he pitied her, and she was scared to death of the fact that
she needed him. What a mess this had turned out to be.

Lydia's steady gaze lacked any sign of sympathy.
"It's your decision."

Marjorie's gaze held her friend's. "I know."

Lydia headed out of the office. "Be miserable, then.
See if I care."

With Lydia gone, the emptiness inside the small
office was oppressive. Dejected, Marjorie sat at her
desk and read over some paperwork she'd been putting
off. However, nothing held her attention for long, and
within moments she was silently staring at the walls,
her thoughts focused on Sam.

Suddenly Lydia burst into her office and excitedly
clapped her hands. She marched around Marjorie's desk
to confront her face to face.

"Lydia! What's going on?"

"You're going to love this. I certainly do."

Sam. Marjorie's heart rocketed into space. He'd
come for her. He'd decided that his life would be an

empty wasteland without her. He'd realized he honestly needed her.

"Sam?" Marjorie asked expectantly, half rising from her chair. "He's here?" Oh, please, God, she prayed, let him be here.

"Sam? Heavens no." Lydia gave her an odd look and shook her head. "It's Al Swanson. Bud just gave him the ax."

"Bud fired Al Swanson? You mean…he's leaving?"

"From the way he's packing up his things, I'd say he can't wait to get out of here. He'll be gone in five minutes."

"Oh." Marjorie was surprised by how little elation she felt at the news. A week ago, her behavior would have rivaled her friend's. Now all she felt was a cloying sense of disappointment that Sam hadn't come for her. Discouraged, she reclaimed her seat.

"Apparently," Lydia went on to explain, "one of Al's schemes backfired on him. Bud found out about it, and Al's out of here."

Marjorie had known from the first that Al was his own worst enemy, and that, given enough rope, he would do himself in without any help from anyone else.

Crossing her arms, a subdued Lydia paused to study her friend. "You thought Sam had come to talk to you?"

Marjorie's fingers tightened around the pencil she was holding; it was a miracle it didn't snap in two. "It wouldn't have done any good."

"Hey, he could have withdrawn his marriage proposal. That might have settled things, don't you think?"

Marjorie shook her head. "Lydia, please. I don't want to talk about him."

"Hurt too much?" her friend asked, lowering her voice into a soft, coaxing tone.

The answer was so obvious that the question didn't require a response. Marjorie was lost without Sam, but she would get over him in time. The only question that remained was how long it would take. A lifetime, her heart told her, but she refused to listen.

Two days later, a cocky smile curving her lips, Lydia sauntered into Marjorie's office, her hands clasped behind her back.

Pretending she'd been interrupted, Marjorie glanced up from the report she'd been trying to read. "You look like the cat that just swallowed the canary."

"Really?" Lydia swayed back and forth on the balls of her feet. "I have a tasty tidbit of information, if you're interested."

"About Al Swanson?" The details of what had happened between the salesman and the manager had been the favorite topic of conversation with the other staff members ever since his firing. The rumors had been flying around the dealership like combat planes, dropping bombs of speculation.

Lydia shook her head. "What I have to tell you involves a certain doctor, but according to you, I'm not supposed to mention his name."

"Sam?" Marjorie's heart stopped, then pounded frantically against her ribs.

"The one and only."

The temptation to strangle Lydia was powerful. Marjorie returned her gaze to the report. "I refuse to play your games."

"Okay," Lydia announced with typical nonchalance. "If you don't care, then far be it from me to announce that the very doctor in question happens to be in this building at this precise minute."

Marjorie's gaze froze. "Here?"

"Not more than twenty yards from this office door, if you must know."

The papers Marjorie had been holding slipped from her fingers and fell to the top of her desk. Uncaring, she left the scattered sheets there.

"But you are apparently over Dr. Sam," Lydia commented, studying the ends of her polished nails, "so it would be best if you stayed holed up in here and did your best to pretend he isn't anywhere around."

Without realizing what she was doing, Marjorie stood, her knees barely strong enough to keep her upright.

"I don't mind telling you," Lydia said, grinning, "I'm having a difficult time not giving Dr. Sam a piece of my mind. The man is obviously a pervert."

Marjorie blinked, sure she'd misunderstood her friend. "Sam's nothing of the sort."

"Imagine Dr. Sam wanting to get married," Lydia continued with a sigh. "Doesn't he realize how old-fashioned that is? A woman should live with a man fifty, maybe sixty, years before making that kind of commitment. Dr. Sam expects too much."

As best she could, Marjorie ignored her friend's sarcasm. "Sam's here?"

Smiling unabashedly, Lydia nodded. "You'll see him the minute you walk out of this office."

Nothing could have kept Marjorie where she was.

As Lydia had claimed, Sam was in the dealership, standing at the service counter. For a solid minute Marjorie was unable to breathe. He looked tired, overworked, hassled. He wasn't taking care of himself, and he looked as though he'd lost weight. As if drawn by a magnet, she walked to his side.

"Sam." His name came from her lips without her even being aware she'd spoken out loud.

He tossed a look over his shoulder and froze when his eyes met hers.

"Hello," she said in an effort to avoid calling attention to herself. "How are you?"

"Fine," he answered stiffly. "And you?"

"Okay...wonderful, actually."

"Yeah, me too."

A tense silence followed while she struggled for something more to say. Her gaze fell to the service desk. "Is something wrong with the car?"

He shook his head. "It's time for an oil change."

The tense quiet returned.

"...babies?"

"...work?"

They spoke simultaneously.

Sam gestured with his hand. "You first."

"I got a promotion." She didn't mention that her Sundays would be free from now on; she couldn't see the point.

"Congratulations."

She attempted a smile. "Thank you." In the ensuing silence, she nodded at him, indicating it was his turn. "You look like you've been busy."

He nodded. "I delivered another set of twins last week."

"Girls?"

"No, both boys. Identical."

"Oh." For the life of her, Marjorie couldn't think of another thing to say. Small talk had always been her forte, and there were a thousand things she wanted to tell him but couldn't.

Seeing him like this made her feel so unsure, so uncertain. Her mind stumbled over her thoughts. "Kitten" wasn't such a terrible name, she realized. So she'd reminded him of a pathetic cat; no doubt that was the way she'd looked when she visited his office that first time. She loved the way his pet name for her sounded on his lips, almost as though the word were a gentle caress. So she needed him. That wasn't such a terrible thing. It was time—more than time—that she faced the fact that needing someone was normal and right. It was on the tip of her tongue to tell him so when Bud strolled past.

"There's a customer here to see you."

Feeling guilty, although she didn't know why, she nodded and glanced over her shoulder. "I guess I'd better get back to work," she said, getting back to Sam.

He didn't respond. "I suppose you should."

"Goodbye, Sam."

"Goodbye, Kitten." The instant the word slipped out of his mouth, he wanted to take it back. "I apologize. I didn't mean to say that."

"Don't worry. It's not such a bad name."

"Only it's not right for you," he said, his gaze unwavering.

Marjorie wasn't in any position to argue with him;

holding back tears required all the energy she could muster. "Right," she answered weakly, giving up the fight.

Without looking back, she headed outside, where the insurance salesman she'd talked to earlier in the week was waiting for her. As she walked out the door, she heard Sam ask what time he could expect his car to be finished. By the time she returned, he was gone.

Lydia seemed to be waiting for her when she got back inside, though. Her friend came over to meet her. "Well, what did he have to say?"

"The insurance salesman?" Marjorie asked, playing stupid.

"Of course not. Sam!"

"Nothing."

"But he must have said something! You two talked for three minutes. I timed you. You must have gotten something settled in that amount of time."

"Unfortunately, we didn't."

"Marjorie, this craziness had got to stop. I talked to Mary, Dr. Sam's receptionist, and she told me he hasn't been the same from the moment you two split up. He's melancholy and moody, and everyone knows that's not the least bit like him."

"He'll get over it," Marjorie said flippantly.

"Maybe," Lydia returned with barely controlled skepticism. "But will you?"

Her friend's words echoed in her mind for the remainder of the afternoon. Lydia was right. Her world was crumbling at her feet, and she was too proud, too stubborn, to do anything about it. Just seeing Sam again had proven that. She was ruining her life over something incredibly silly. She'd overreacted and behaved stupidly, and the time had come to own up to that.

Filled with determination, she marched over to the service department.

"What time did you tell Dr. Bretton his car would be ready?"

Pete, the head mechanic, who had been with Dixon Motors for ten years, flipped the pages of the service book. "After three. As I recall, he told me he wouldn't be in to pick it up until six."

Marjorie nodded, pleased. "Have you finished with it?"

"Yeah. It seemed pointless to change the oil on a vehicle that doesn't even have a thousand miles on it. But we did it—couldn't see the point in arguing with him."

That small bit of information sent Marjorie's spirits soaring. Sam must have used the Mercedes as an excuse to see her. Her relief felt like a thirst-quenching rain after a long August drought. "Could I have his keys, please?"

The mechanic gave her an odd look. "You want Dr. Bretton's car keys?"

"Right. When he comes in, send him to my office."

The barrel-chested mechanic scratched the side of his head. "If that's the way you want it, Ms. Majors."

"I do. Thanks, Pete."

The remainder of the afternoon crept by. At precisely six, Marjorie was waiting in her office. Sam didn't keep her in suspense long.

He knocked once and stepped inside. "What's this about you having my car keys?" he demanded, his temper showing. He'd been a fool to think that coming to the car dealership would solve anything between them. She wanted blood, and he wasn't about to give it to her. The more he reviewed their earlier conversation, the angrier he became. That wounded, hurt look in her eyes had accused him of greatly wronging her. All he'd ever wanted was to marry her and make her happy, and she'd reacted as though he'd insulted her.

Marjorie blinked. "Yes, I have your keys."

He held out his open palm. "I'd like them back."

"Of course." She remained outwardly calm, but adrenaline was racing through her system as though she were running the Boston Marathon. "I have a couple of questions first, if you don't mind answering them."

He made a show of glancing at his watch. "Make it quick—I have an appointment."

"Oh, Sam, you always were such a poor liar."

He snapped his jaw closed and pulled out a chair. "As it happens, I do have to be someplace in less than an hour. But obviously my word isn't to be trusted."

"This will only take a minute."

He crossed his legs, hoping to give the impression of indifference. Nothing could be further from the truth, but anger was his only defense against Marjorie. It was either yell at her or yank her into his arms and kiss some sense into her.

Her fingers closed around the cold metal keys. "It's about that ring you offered me."

Sam shot to his feet. "Listen, Marjorie, we're talking about our lives here, not a car deal. There are no counteroffers."

"Yes, I know."

"The offer stands as it was."

"All right," she said, her voice strong and sure.

"All right, what?"

"I'll marry you."

If Sam had been flustered before, it was nothing compared to the confusion he felt now. "You will?"

"That is…if you still want me for your wife."

He ran his fingers through his hair. "What happened? Did you check around and discover that you couldn't make a better deal than me?"

"No…that's not it at all." This was going so much worse than she'd hoped.

He eyed her speculatively. "I'll call you *kitten* any time I please!"

She nodded, because speaking would have been impossible.

"We won't have a long engagement, either. I want us married before the end of the summer."

She met his fiery gaze with feigned calm, then answered him with a quick nod of her head.

He mellowed somewhat and lowered his voice. "Do you have to check this out with your manager?"

"No."

His gaze moved to the shimmering moistness of her lips. He was dying to hold her, starved for a taste of her, and just looking at her disturbed his concentration. His control was slipping fast. Walking around to her side of the desk, he reached for her. Hungrily his mouth devoured hers as he pulled her hard against the solid length of his body so she would know how desperate he'd been without her. His hand roamed possessively over her, molding her to him, uncaring that anyone outside the office might be watching.

Only partially satisfied, Sam dragged his mouth from her, his hunger sated for the moment.

The iron band of his arms held her a willing prisoner. "Sam, I love you… I'm sorry to be so insecure. I don't know what made me say those things. It's just that I've been on my own so long that it hurt my pride to think you pitied me, and I…"

"It doesn't matter, Kitten," he said, his voice husky and thick against her hair.

Overcome by a searing happiness, she laughed breathlessly. The sound was short and sweet. "I can't imagine why I objected so strongly when I love the name *kitten*."

"Good, because I meant what I said about calling you that."

Her arms circled his waist, and her heart swelled. She was home, truly home, for the first time since she'd lost her parents.

"We're getting married as soon as I can arrange it."

She grinned, more than agreeable to any terms he wanted. "Any Sunday."

He paused and looked deep into her misty, diamond-bright eyes, letting her words sink in. "You got a promotion?"

She nodded and started to say more when Lydia burst into her office.

Her friend's mouth dropped open as she stopped abruptly. "Oh…hi."

"Hi," Marjorie answered for them.

"Have you two patched things up?" Lydia asked casually.

"It's either that or we have a peculiar way of arguing," Sam answered, and chuckled softly.

"So are you two getting married or what?"

"We're getting married," Marjorie said, beaming.

It looked for a moment as though Lydia doubted them. "When?" she asked speculatively.

Sam and Marjorie shared a lingering look. "Any Sunday," they answered in unison.

* * * * *

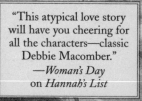

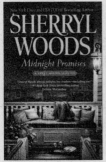  

REQUEST YOUR
FREE BOOKS!

2 FREE NOVELS
FROM THE ROMANCE COLLECTION
PLUS 2 FREE GIFTS!

YES! Please send me 2 FREE novels from the Romance Collection and my 2 FREE gifts (gifts are worth about $10). After receiving them, if I don't wish to receive any more books, I can return the shipping statement marked "cancel." If I don't cancel, I will receive 4 brand-new novels every month and be billed just $5.99 per book in the U.S. or $6.49 per book in Canada. That's a saving of at least 25% off the cover price. It's quite a bargain! Shipping and handling is just 50¢ per book in the U.S. and 75¢ per book in Canada.* I understand that accepting the 2 free books and gifts places me under no obligation to buy anything. I can always return a shipment and cancel at any time. Even if I never buy another book, the two free books and gifts are mine to keep forever.

194/394 MDN FELQ

Name _____ (PLEASE PRINT) _____

Address _____ Apt. #

City _____ State/Prov. _____ Zip/Postal Code

Signature (if under 18, a parent or guardian must sign)

Mail to the **Reader Service:**
IN U.S.A.: P.O. Box 1867, Buffalo, NY 14240-1867
IN CANADA: P.O. Box 609, Fort Erie, Ontario L2A 5X3

Not valid for current subscribers to the Romance Collection
or the Romance/Suspense Collection.

Want to try two free books from another line?
Call 1-800-873-8635 or visit www.ReaderService.com.

* Terms and prices subject to change without notice. Prices do not include applicable taxes. Sales tax applicable in N.Y. Canadian residents will be charged applicable taxes. Offer not valid in Quebec. This offer is limited to one order per household. All orders subject to credit approval. Credit or debit balances in a customer's account(s) may be offset by any other outstanding balance owed by or to the customer. Please allow 4 to 6 weeks for delivery. Offer available while quantities last.

Your Privacy—The Reader Service is committed to protecting your privacy. Our Privacy Policy is available online at www.ReaderService.com or upon request from the Reader Service.

We make a portion of our mailing list available to reputable third parties that offer products we believe may interest you. If you prefer that we not exchange your name with third parties, or if you wish to clarify or modify your communication preferences, please visit us at www.ReaderService.com/consumerchoice or write to us at Reader Service Preference Service, P.O. Box 9062, Buffalo, NY 14269. Include your complete name and address.

Two stories about love, marriage and trying again from

#1 *NEW YORK TIMES* & *USA TODAY* BESTSELLING AUTHOR

DEBBIE MACOMBER

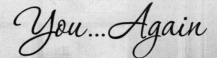

You...Again

"Macomber has a gift for evoking the emotions
that are at the heart of the genre's popularity."
—*Publishers Weekly*

Available now wherever books are sold!

DEBBIE MACOMBER

32988	OUT OF THE RAIN	___ $7.99 U.S.	___ $9.99 CAN.
32971	92 PACIFIC BOULEVARD	___ $7.99 U.S.	___ $9.99 CAN.
32970	8 SANDPIPER WAY	___ $7.99 U.S.	___ $9.99 CAN.
32969	74 SEASIDE AVENUE	___ $7.99 U.S.	___ $9.99 CAN.
32968	6 RAINIER DRIVE	___ $7.99 U.S.	___ $9.99 CAN.
32967	44 CRANBERRY POINT	___ $7.99 U.S.	___ $9.99 CAN.
32929	HANNAH'S LIST	___ $7.99 U.S.	___ $9.99 CAN.
32918	AN ENGAGEMENT IN SEATTLE	___ $7.99 U.S.	___ $9.99 CAN.
32911	THE MANNING SISTERS	___ $7.99 U.S.	___ $9.99 CAN.
32884	SUSANNAH'S GARDEN	___ $7.99 U.S.	___ $9.99 CAN.
32861	204 ROSEWOOD LANE	___ $7.99 U.S.	___ $9.99 CAN.
32860	16 LIGHTHOUSE ROAD	___ $7.99 U.S.	___ $9.99 CAN.
32858	HOME FOR THE HOLIDAYS	___ $7.99 U.S.	___ $9.99 CAN.
32828	ORCHARD VALLEY BRIDES	___ $7.99 U.S.	___ $9.99 CAN.
32822	CHRISTMAS IN CEDAR COVE	___ $7.99 U.S.	___ $9.99 CAN.
32806	1022 EVERGREEN PLACE	___ $7.99 U.S.	___ $9.99 CAN.
32798	ORCHARD VALLEY GROOMS	___ $7.99 U.S.	___ $9.99 CAN.
32783	THE MAN YOU'LL MARRY	___ $7.99 U.S.	___ $9.99 CAN.
32743	THE SOONER THE BETTER	___ $7.99 U.S.	___ $9.99 CAN.
32702	FAIRY TALE WEDDINGS	___ $7.99 U.S.	___ $9.99 CAN.
32701	WYOMING BRIDES	___ $7.99 U.S.	___ $8.99 CAN.
32602	THE MANNING GROOMS	___ $7.99 U.S.	___ $7.99 CAN.
32569	ALWAYS DAKOTA	___ $7.99 U.S.	___ $7.99 CAN.
32506	CHRISTMAS WISHES	___ $7.99 U.S.	___ $9.50 CAN.
32474	THE MANNING BRIDES	___ $7.99 U.S.	___ $7.99 CAN.
32362	COUNTRY BRIDES	___ $7.99 U.S.	___ $9.50 CAN.
31325	A TURN IN THE ROAD	___ $7.99 U.S.	___ $9.99 CAN.
31299	YOU...AGAIN	___ $7.99 U.S.	___ $9.99 CAN.
31298	LEARNING TO LOVE	___ $7.99 U.S.	___ $9.99 CAN.
31251	1105 YAKIMA STREET	___ $7.99 U.S.	___ $9.99 CAN.

(limited quantities available)

TOTAL AMOUNT	$	_____
POSTAGE & HANDLING	$	_____
($1.00 for 1 book, 50¢ for each additional)		
APPLICABLE TAXES*	$	_____
TOTAL PAYABLE	$	_____

(check or money order—please do not send cash)

To order, complete this form and send it, along with a check or money order for the total above, payable to MIRA Books, to: **In the U.S.:** 3010 Walden Avenue, P.O. Box 9077, Buffalo, NY 14269-9077; **In Canada:** P.O. Box 636, Fort Erie, Ontario, L2A 5X3.

Name: _____
Address: _____ City: _____
State/Prov.: _____ Zip/Postal Code: _____
Account Number (if applicable): _____
075 CSAS

*New York residents remit applicable sales taxes.
*Canadian residents remit applicable GST and provincial taxes.

MIRA   ◆ HARLEQUIN®
www.Harlequin.com

MDM0612BL